THE GRIEF OF GODLESS GAMES

Book One of The Godless Saga

by

J. T. Audsley

Published by Earth Island Books
Pickforde Lodge
Pickforde Lane
Ticehurst
East Sussex
TN5 7BN

www.earthislandbooks.com

© Earth Island Books

First published by Earth Island Books 2023

ISBN 9781739443849

Printed and bound by Solopress

Edokand – Post-Cataclysm

Skaldgard
(Utajima)

Skaldgard Port

Sui Bay
Sekando City
Sekando
Koseki

Tsul

Takakawa
Halju

Yongtown

Chuton

Trim

Wu Wei

N
W   E
S

Table of Contents

THE GRIEF OF GODLESS GAMES

Book One of The Godless Saga

by

J. T. Audsley

[CHAPTER 1] — WU WEI

The palace sat proudly in the caldera, and the city cascaded down the dormant volcano like magma. Farms and pastures hugged the great wall that encircled the metropolis, and the vibrant greens crawled into the city, blending with the jade and turquoise of the lower quarter. The buildings further up were more significant, changing to reds and golds as flags waved from the bamboo and tile rooftops. The streets crossed each other in rattan patterns, and the vast span of homes, shops, and temples was a giant collage of astounding architecture.

His blue eyes, sharp as stilettos and campfire-bright, floated back and forth, taking in as much as possible. The size, the architecture, and the clearly defined districts fell rigidly down the mountain. He had sailed across the world, but then Akkael knew; he'd never seen a city until he saw *Wu Wei*.

Akkael squatted, rolling a blade of dark green grass between his dirt-clad fingers as he gazed at the City of Disciplines, peering from a forest he didn't know the name of. The horse he arrived on whinnied impatiently as it tugged against the tether connecting it to a tree. Akkael reached over to settle it, still not taking his eyes off the city. None of his kin had seen it, and he rushed ahead of his company to be the first. Akkael had sojourned in Edokand for many years, but only as far as Tsul. The central island of Trim seemed a distant dream. But now he was there, on invitation from the Emperor himself.

"Akkael!" someone bellowed behind him. He turned to see two men on horseback leading a divided contingent. Half were people dressed in furs, padded leather, or nothing to hide their scarred torsos, which recorded the battles they'd fought. The other half were men wearing the heavy red armour of the Edokand'i.

The two at the front, wearing their leather and furs, were Akkael's brothers. The largest was Magar, who shared little more than eye colour and dirty blond hair with Akkael. A broad sword strapped across his back, contrasting the hand axe in his brothers' belts. Doran, the other rider, was the spit of Akkael, right down to the

1

clothes they wore and weapons they chose. The only differences were the crow's feet drawing trenches through Doran's pale skin and the crown on top of his head.

"Brothers!" he yelled back at them, gesturing to the city. "I present Wu Wei! The prize of the east."

Doran fiddled with the necklace around his neck. It was a thin chain with a silver pendant. His fingers glided across the triangular spiral, leaving smudges across the symbol like streaks on a desert dune. It was strange seeing someone wear such a necklace. If Akkael didn't know better, he'd think Doran was religious. Of course, that was nonsense.

Everyone knew the truth all over the world. Religion had died, and gods didn't exist.

King Doran glared down at Akkael from atop his horse. "Not a prize, Akkael. We don't want to take it. We want to settle here peacefully," he said. "And you shouldn't have ridden ahead like that."

"Seeing it for myself was the prize," grinned Akkael. "Seeing it first was a little extra just for me."

Magar rolled his eyes. "You're a shit, 'Kael."

Akkael held out his thumb, smiling wider. Magar responded with a different finger.

"It really is beautiful." Doran rode closer to Akkael as he took in the view of Wu Wei. He slowly inhaled. The atmosphere seemed fresher on this island than on the others in Edokand. The size of Trim and the distance from the small vents off the coast that released toxic, volcanic ash made breathing refreshing. It was like a glass of cool water after a night of heavy drinking.

"Shame these *goutuizi* get to live there and not us."

The armoured soldiers shuffled in the saddles at the use of the insult. Akkael turned around and smirked at their scowls. He knew many slurs for the Edokand'i army, but goutuizi seemed to strike hardest and used it often in their presence.

For the first time, Akkael saw how the Edokand'i horse riders saw him. The three brothers, the enemy, looked upon their capital with hunger in their eyes and jest on their lips. It was a nightmare many of them had. Akkael kept grinning like a wolf.

"Four years," he said. Walking up to the closest mounted soldier, who was trying hard to stay silent and disciplined, the tenants of the Edokand'i army. He tapped the mounted man on the armoured leg before continuing. "Four years of war and bloodshed. All water under the bridge, I'm sure."

He turned back towards his brothers, still marvelling at the city below them. Akkael wondered if the temples or the wall had caught their gaze. Or was it the tip of the palace pagoda peaking over the caldera's ridge? Were they trying to make out landmarks they'd only heard of in passing or in books?

"Well," started Doran, "now we're here; let's finish this." The King didn't smile, but Akkael could still tell when his brother was happy. The slow blink, the deep exhale, the tightening of his hands around the reins. He was a man who had achieved his ambition, and it was nice to see.

"Let's finish this," Akkael repeated before freeing his horse and lining up with his brothers.

Hooves drummed at the earth as the horses galloped towards the city, all twenty-four riders kicking up clods of dirt and grass. As they declined the hill, it was as if the wall began to hug the city tighter, rising to conceal more as Wu Wei sunk below the crenellated battlements. On the straight road to the lone mountain, Akkael could barely see any of the city but the red building peaking over the ramparts.

They rode up to the giant wooden gates of Wu Wei and waited as a second party rode to greet them. Three riders also headed a company of goutuizi soldiers, their red armour stark against the grey of their city's walls. Akkael recognised the centre rider by his gold-trimmed pauldrons and ornate katana strapped to his belt. Lord Hideo's hair was ivory white and tied back in a wolf tail. The hanafuda earring that hung from his left ear was so long it brushed his shoulder. He was a thin man. But the brothers never let that deceive them. A stern expression suppressed the derelict laugh lines and kindness, like an old civilisation buried under the sands of deserts.

To his right was his herald. A black-haired, porky lordling with a pompous pout dressing his face. To his left was a female monk in purple robes.

The herald was the first to speak, his appearance excited by the sound of his own voice. "Lord Doran. Magar. Akkael. The famous brothers Torne, we welcome you to our esteemed capital. You are in the presence of Lord Hideo Kazar of Sekando, general of the Sentinel Guard." – goutuizi – "The iron hand of Wu Wei and the Second Pillar of Edokand."

"I know who he is." Doran understood the lengths Hideo was prepared to go to mock his people. He would have sent the herald alone if he could still see the ridicule unfold. He turned to Hideo. "We were invited here by the Emperor himself. Surely that's enough for you to talk to my brothers and me directly?"

After staring coldly at Hideo, waiting for him to reply, Akkael smirked and began to address the herald himself. "It was nice of you to accompany him, however. Did you want to see us yourself, or did Hideo need a hand?" He looked back at Hideo but not at his face. He was looking at the prosthetic iron hand across his lap.

"Lord Hideo has the authority to demand my presence on any outing he sees fit," the herald retorted rapidly.

"So, he needed a hand." Doran tried to stifle a grin at Akkael's mocking.

"His lordship saw it as a polite formality to address you with the pomp befitting a fellow Lord." Doran was a king, but he stayed silent at this hidden insult. The herald flicked between Magar and Akkael. "Speaking of politeness, it is customary for those of lower rank to bow to their betters."

Akkael just raised his brow and smiled. "It's customary for a lord to fight alongside his men. I saw a lot of dead goutuizi at Takakawa. Where was your lordship then?"

Hideo twisted his reins and kept them taut. He stayed silent, but his horse's confused half-step proved the defeat was still a fresh wound.

The herald sputtered. "The Sentinel Guard of Edokand allows for a distribution of power that you would not understand. I'll have you know Lord Hideo's cousin was at Takakawa on his behalf as he conducted the defence of the capital. He has mourned his loss since he heard the news."

"And I'm sure the dead care." Magar rarely spoke in parleys, so the comment seemed particularly cutting.

"To be fair, I'm sure his men were relieved he wasn't present," added Akkael. "After what happened at Skaldgard, I doubt they'd be comfortable following him into a bakery."

"There is no such place as Skaldgard!" The herald raised his voice suddenly. "Lord Hideo acknowledges his defeat in Utajima and treats it as a lesson in dealing with savages like you."

"I'm sorry, herald, what's your name?" asked Doran, raising his voice.

"Ponzu. And I'm a steward."

"Well, I don't know the difference. But, anyway, Ponzu, we renamed Utajima to Skaldgard after we won it," declared Doran. "The fact we are here proves you have not learned to deal with us."

Hideo's right fist clenched so tightly the tips of his fingers might have pierced through the back. "That's enough, Doran."

"So, he does speak." Akkael became deflated, almost bored by Hideo's surrender.

"Where's the Emperor?"

"Waiting for you in the palace, King Doran," said Hideo, spitting the name. "You think we'd allow our Emperor to meet you in an open field surrounded by Northmen?"

Akkael looked behind. "We hardly surround you. There are only a dozen of us, and we're outnumbered three to one."

Doran sighed. "But very well, I'll go meet your Emperor."

Akkael rose in his saddle and spoke in Solstic, the language of his people. "Brother, you can't! You're the King. Have me go instead."

Doran hissed before Hideo spoke. "We agreed our meeting was to be conducted in Edokand'i!"

"We also agreed on a dozen men each," Akkael responded.

"What did he say?" Hideo asked Doran, ignoring Akkael's remark.

"My brother has voiced fair concerns." Doran shrugged. "If I enter the city, how do I know I'll be safe? We need reassurance."

Hideo nodded. "And you'll have it." He indicated left. Monks in purple robes often escorted dignitaries, so Akkael had barely noticed the female sage riding beside Hideo. "This is Rigpa, the Grand Sage and Third Pillar of Edokand. She has volunteered to be part of a hostage exchange as you negotiate peace terms with the Emperor."

She was an older woman with grey hair held in a bun by two sticks. However, she wasn't ancient. Her brown eyes still had a youthfulness to them, and her wrinkles were the kind that would add character to a sculpture. The lines around her mouth made her look like she was smiling, even if she wasn't.

"Grand Sage?" Akkael was grinning like an excited child. "I've always wanted to meet the queen of the wizards."

The trivialisation of Rigpa's station affronted Hideo. "The Grand Sage is the holiest example of human life!" yelled Hideo. "Their attachment to the spiritual links them to the cosmic energy in the universe. Rigpa is the incarnation of the Seraphim himself."

"Oh, right, of course," said Akkael sarcastically.

"She is our country's third most important person!" yelled the herald.

"Well, that's very specific," said Akkael, widening his eyes as if he was impressed that they kept a record. "It just so happens my brother is the most important person in mine. We are not going to –"

"I accept the swap."

Akkael hissed at Doran. He spoke in Solstic again. "You are not thinking straight."

6

Hideo ignored the words he couldn't understand from Akkael with a thin-lipped grin. "So, it's done. Have your entourage bring the Grand Sage back in two days, and we will turn you over to them unharmed."

Doran nodded with no emotion on his face. "Well, let's not waste any more daylight." He removed the crown from atop his head and thrust it into Akkael's reluctant arms. Then, he rode slowly towards Hideo. After Lord Hideo's signal, the sage rode towards Akkael, crossing the Northerner King in the centre of the gap between the two groups. The air stood still as they rode, only allowing the breeze to continue east once Rigpa and the King had settled.

The groups said their farewells. Akkael's eyes locked on his brother before turning to ride back the way they came. Akkael looked behind, more at the stone walls than his brother's back, and sighed.

He rode in tandem with the Grand Sage. Akkael was so close that he could feel Rigpa's horse brush against his leg in the stirrup. Once they entered the forest, Akkael leant in and whispered in the older woman's ear. "If anything happens to my brother, I'll kill you myself. I don't make empty promises."

Rigpa just kept her eyes on the path ahead.

[CHAPTER 2] — ALANI

Rigpa arrived with the Northmen at their beached ship and bid the goutuizi escorts farewell, leaving them the horses they supplied. The Grand Sage had heard about the Northmen's longships. The simplistic shape was designed to travel oceans and rivers and was light enough to draw onto the shore.

Large sails of woven wool dyed orange were lowered onto the clinker-built oak hull resembling waves overlapping themselves. The sheen of the resin that kept the wood from rotting glistened with the sinking sun, bouncing off the sheep's wool stuffed between the gaps in the planks to prevent leaks. A steering oar was the only thing differentiating the front from the back. Carved figureheads of dragons roared on the stern and the bough, with forked tongues pointing inland and out to sea.

Akkael threw Doran's crown onto one of the oar benches before jumping into the ship. The crown was nothing ornate. Sharp, iron prongs jutted out of the large band. No jewels, enamel, or carvings decorated the crown, and it looked highly uncomfortable to wear.

As soon as it was out of Akkael's hands, he paid it no mind, stroking the ship's side like a pet.

Magar assessed the wind with his finger. "The breeze is blowing our way, so we'll row to the island," he said, looking at the grey silhouette to the north and trying desperately to remember the island's name.

Akkael saw Magar's eyes roll up as he thought. "Tsul."

"Tsul!" Magar nodded, scrunching his face as if it were on the tip of his tongue.

Akkael beckoned Rigpa into the ship to sit with him as the other Northmen prepared the boat. He then looked backwards.

"What about our people in the forest?" He spoke in his native language and tried to use an impersonal tone.

Akkael tried to reassure him. "They are probably at the camp already. Those goutuizi ride like a snail crawls." The rest of the Northmen were securing the lowered sail and fixing their shields to the racks that stretched from gunwale to stern.

Akkael just sat, looking at Rigpa with his head tilted. "Oh, and Magar, try not to divulge anything, even in Solstic. This one understands everything we say. Am I right?"

The Grand Sage smiled. "That is true."

Magar's face defaulted to rage instead of knowing how to feel. No one in Edokand spoke Solstic, offended by the prospect of its barbarity. Also, a Solstic teacher would be hard to come by, considering the only Northmen in Edokand were at war. "How do you know it?" he asked.

Akkael answered before Rigpa could open her mouth. "It's one of her gifts as a sage to comprehend every language."

"I did not mean to deceive you," she said, bowing her head. "I will not tell Lord Hideo of the archers you positioned in the forest."

Magar leaned against the ship, his bright blue eyes darting between Rigpa's. "Why would we trust you?"

If the sage was intimidated by the giant figure of Magar Torne looming over the conversation or the quiet intensity Akkael could turn on at a moment's notice, she didn't show it. She stayed the calm expected of a sage and looked at them kindly. "I could have told him during the parley, but I didn't."

Magar squinted and looked at Akkael, who just shrugged. "Another thing she can do; is sense changes in the land around her. Dozens of feet pressing against the grass must have been like smelling manure; easy if you're close enough."

Rigpa tilted her head. "You seem to know a lot about my gifts."

Akkael nodded, happy to take in the praise. "I have done my research. Some books. Word of mouth. My brother employed a sage on his council in Skaldgard, so I asked him a few things. It's important to know the place you're invading. Most of us learned your language and memorised the map, and I took it a bit further."

Suddenly he lunged towards the sage. Rigpa did her best not to jump out of her skin, but the sharp intake of breath was enough for Akkael to notice and grin. He pinched the sleeve of the sage's robe and rubbed it between his fingers.

"What I don't understand," continued Akkael, "is how, despite having forgotten your religions like everywhere else in the world, Edokand still has a cult of monks lingering."

Rigpa kept a smile on her face. "Religions died because people were disillusioned by the lack of evidence of their gods' existence. But my abilities are proven; my history is a fact. You can't stop believing in something right before your eyes."

Akkael folded his bottom lip and nodded. "Well said. You're lucky. All that stuff about gods would have set Doran off on one, and you'd be hearing about it all night."

Rigpa tilted her head. "What does he say?"

"Oh, I don't know," said Akkael, throwing his head back. "He finds it strange that every culture stopped believing in gods simultaneously. Honestly, it's best to let Doran talk until he tires himself out, right, Magar?"

Magar grunted his confirmation.

A Northman approached, wearing furs that covered half of the eagle tattoo across his chest. "Akkael, the ship is prepared."

Akkael looked at the Northman and nodded. "Let's head off then."

He nodded and beckoned for the rest of the Solstic to push the boat into the water. Rigpa and Akkael still sat in the ship as Magar walked beside them, shaking his head. "Lazy arse."

Akkael held up his thumb and smiled.

The strait took less than an hour to cross. As a sage, Rigpa prided herself on viewing people by their character rather than stereotypes and prejudices. However, even she was shocked by what she saw as the camp on the shore of Tsul burst into view. Children ran along the shoreline, screaming and yelling at those in the boat. The Northmen who rowed laughed and shouted back. A fire was roaring in the centre of a compact group of tents, with a pen for goats and storage for grain set up along the side. The Northmen may be invaders, but they looked at home and at peace. Their brutish, war-hungry image faded with the camp, and Rigpa saw the Northmen for what they were; people looking for a better life.

The ship hit the sand next to a collection of other beached boats, and they jumped out to drag it in line with the rest. Akkael and Magar helped Rigpa out and escorted her to the camp. A crowd gathered, and raucous applause filled the air. Northmen cheered and yelled their praises as they made their way through the throng.

One woman approached the two brothers with dirt caked on her face and a shield tied to her back. Her blonde, braided hair rested on her broad shoulders, and her leather tunic hugged her figure. She brushed her hand against Akkael's bicep as she walked past.

"Good to have you back, Akkael," she whispered. "I missed you."

Akkael smiled at the woman, his face moving closer to hers until their noses nearly touched. "Thank you, Bodil," said Akkael. He leaned in more, but she backed away, smiling from ear to ear. She stepped backwards before spinning around and going to the shore, letting Akkael watch her walk away.

Magar glanced at his brother from the corner of his eye, which took Akkael a while to notice.

"What?" said Akkael defensively when he noticed his brother's look. "Not everyone can be as happy in marriage as you."

As they reached the grass where they had pitched the tents, a man as big as Magar, in his heavy set of steel armour, approached with a smile. His chin was sharp, and his nose was crooked as if he had broken it a few times. Hair clung to his forehead from the sweat, and his strong jawline looked as if it had been forged along with his breastplate.

Magar approached the stranger and hugged him before they pulled away to kiss.

Akkael was staring at the Grand Sage, smiling as he shrugged. "Secret to being a pillow-biter," Akkael joked, "be large enough to crush the skull of anyone who frowns on it."

"Or anyone who pisses me off." Stern expressions and a tense silence filled the air between the stranger and Akkael. But it didn't last long, a smirk cracking onto the large man's face.

"Good to see you, Skane," said Akkael, bringing his arm to clasp his countryman's. "How was the forest?"

"Got back almost an hour ago," Skane answered. "Those goutuizi ride like children scared to fall off their horse."

As the Grand Sage had heard him called in Wu Wei court, Skane Brick-Chest was less intimidating than she's heard from fear-mongered rumours. His face was more suited to a smile than a scowl, his demeanour more kindness than scorn. His eyes were a dull blue, and his hair was brown and braided.

Skane's brow furrowed as he looked at the Northmen leaving the ship. "Where is Doran?"

"In Wu Wei having tea with the Emperor." Akkael gestured to Rigpa. "This is our hostage exchange."

Skane left Magar's side, standing only a few inches from the sage. He may be less suited to it, but his scowl still looked intimidating. "Well, just know, if anything happens to him, we'll let you choose how you want to die."

Before she could think of anything in response, a gleeful yell exploded from deeper in the campsite and took all her focus.

"Dada!" Akkael, beaming at the little voice, crouched, arms outstretched and letting the young girl run into his embrace.

"Ahh, my little shield maiden," said Akkael, lifting the girl.

Skane smiled as Akkael spun his daughter in the air, making her scream between fits of laughter. "Alani has been learning about pottery," he said.

Akkael squinted as he spoke. "Pottery?"

"Yes!" said Alani indignantly as her feet planted back on the ground. She marched back to the line of tents and retrieved a pot. It was undecorated, painted a deep red, the colour of Edokand. It was only when she returned did Akkael notice the glistening veins that ran across its surface. Alani held it up to Akkael and grinned from ear to ear.

"What's so important about the pot?" Akkael asked, confused.

Alani rolled her eyes at her father, making Magar and Skane snicker. "Well, it broke. See the cracks," Alani began sharply. She took her father's hand and ran his finger along one of the veins, the grooves of it catching along his calluses. "They fixed it with gold."

Akkael beamed at the wide eyes of his daughter. "And why did they do that?" he asked, sitting on the ground before her so they were closer to eye level.

"It's an art." She looked down at the pot as if she were reading from it. "The Edokand'i believe that the cracks are a part of the pot's history and everything, even the broken bits, can be turned into something beautiful."

Alani gave her father the pot, and, with his spare hand, he lifted her into the air. "This is the third most beautiful thing in Edokand."

"Am I the first?" she asked, smiling.

"No, you're second. First is reserved for your mother, I'm afraid."

She didn't look disappointed, instead conceding and nodding. Then she sighed. "I miss Mama."

"So do I, little shield maiden. So do I." Akkael kissed Alani's cheek, which did little to lift her spirits. "As soon as Uncle Doran is done with the Emperor, we'll return to Skaldgard."

"Okay," said Alani with a sigh.

Akkael looked at the face of his deflated daughter and thought hard for something to cheer her up. "Now I've got something to show you." He put her back down and handed her back the pot before walking over to Rigpa, placing his hands on the old woman's shoulders. "This is the Grand Sage."

Alani's green eyes lit up as she looked down at the purple robes. "The queen of the wizards!"

"Apparently not." Akkael shrugged. "But she has special powers."

"I know!" she cheered. "I know a lot about sages. I heard you can tell what people will do before they do it, and you can read minds."

"Well, that's not entirely true," Rigpa said, smirking, "But it's close enough."

"Can you talk to animals?" Alani was jumping on the spot, eyes wider than plates. "I heard you can talk to animals."

"You're an inquisitive one, aren't you?" Rigpa knelt to be at eye level with her.

"Maybe," she nodded, clearly not knowing what inquisitive meant.

"Why don't we let Rigpa settle in, Alani," said Akkael, stepping in front of the Grand Sage and scooping his daughter up.

Rigpa watched Alani strop as her father trundled her away. She smiled. Having only heard the fear-mongered stories of the Northmen, more beast than human, it was nice to see them in a different light. A kinder light.

As she thought, Rigpa felt a large hand land on her shoulder. She looked up and saw Skane standing over her.

"Come with me, sage," he said, gently nudging her forward. "Let's find you a place to sleep."

Having no choice, Rigpa complied, going in the direction the large man pushed her and delving deeper into the Northmen's camp.

[CHAPTER 3] — THE ISLANDS OF EDOKAND

Seagulls cawed overhead as the Northmen camp relaxed in the afternoon sun. Once they unloaded the ship, there was a lull, and those who had travelled to Wu Wei had settled. Akkael suspected that feeling would persist until Doran returned. It was as if time stood still, everyone waiting for the end of the negotiations, wondering how Doran was faring, contemplating the war's conclusion while the sun hovered above them.

Skane was chugging what remained of a bowl of the previous night's stew, which he had left to cool in his tent, while Magar sat beside him, washing the large blade of his sword. Akkael sat in the grass a little further away, waiting with the Grand Sage in awkward silence for Alani to return with whatever she'd excitedly run off to retrieve.

He didn't know why he suddenly felt nervous as he sat beside Rigpa. The initial rush of adrenaline that came from watching his brother ride alone into the enemy city faded away. Having to create an acceptably safe environment for the Third Pillar of Edokand was an outcome he didn't expect on the ride to Wu Wei.

Akkael and Rigpa shared a brief look before simultaneously turning away. The worst part about the awkward exchange was that Rigpa could use her sage gifts to know every feeling in Akkael's head. That awoke a frustration which he knew the sage could also sense, which exasperated it. After a little more silence, Akkael decides to break it.

"So," he started. Rigpa turned to face him with a broad smile and eyes that were hopefully optimistic for Akkael's attempt at conversation. "How's being a hostage? You must feel like you drew the short straw."

"I volunteered." Akkael squinted at the Grand Sage, allowing her to elaborate. "I know the Emperor very well, and he has spoken often about allowing your people to settle here as a way of ending the war and bloodshed. I wanted to see for myself if peace was possible. To do that, I needed to be amongst you."

"And what do you think?" asked Akkael, gesturing to the camp around him.

Rigpa gave him a look from the side of her eye, the smile struggling to cling to her face. "That's yet to be seen."

Akkael folded his bottom lip and nodded. "Fair enough. So, this Emperor, is he honest about peace? This isn't some trap?"

"The Emperor is sincere," she answered. "You can trust him."

"Can I trust you?"

"Can you?"

"That has yet to be seen."

Suddenly, Alani appeared from deeper inside the camp. She had a piece of parchment clutched in her fist, her hair was slightly more unkempt, and she was out of breath. Akkael backed away somewhat as Alani knelt in the grass opposite the sage.

She unfurled the parchment and slammed it on the ground. It was a map with a string of five distinct islands sketched across it. "This is my map of Edokand," she told the sage. "It doesn't show all the islands, just the five big ones. The rest are too small to draw on here."

Rigpa nodded as she considered the sketches. "It's very well drawn."

Alani beamed. "Thank you." She pointed at the topmost island on the map with such force that she made a dent in the dirt underneath. "This island is Skaldgard, right at the top of the moon. I call it a moon because the whole country looks like a crescent. Or, if I turn it this way, it looks like a boat. See?"

Akkael leant in to prompt her. "What was the island originally called, Alani?"

The look she gave her father could have crushed the self-esteem of a wild boar. "Utajima. Everyone knows that."

"All right," said Akkael, slightly exasperated. "Name the other four, then."

She rolled her eyes and turned back to Rigpa and the map. Akkael retreated to the log where Skane was sitting. If he had a tail, it would be tucked between his legs.

"Next is the island we are on," continued Alani. "It's called Tsul. I remember it because the shape reminds me of a big shoe. Shoes have soles and, if you say it fast, 'sole' sounds like 'Tsul'."

Rigpa scoffed. "I've never thought of it like that."

"Do you want me to tell you how I remember the next one?" asked Alani excitedly.

"Of course," replied the Grand Sage.

"Well, it's called Trim," Alani began, pointing at the third island on the map; the home of the capital city, Wu Wei; the heart of Edokand. A dream the Solstic had kept in their minds and now had at their backs. "The shape is kind of like messy hair, and if I had hair that looked like that, I'd say, 'I need a Trim.'"

Alani seemed oblivious to the smirks of those in earshot as they tried to hide their amusement. Akkael covered his mouth so she wouldn't notice his silent laugh. Rigpa was the only one who kept a straight face, which was impressive.

Alani continued. "I don't have ways of remembering the other two, so I always forget them."

"I forget about them too." Magar was still washing his giant sword, and it surprised Akkael that he spoke. "They're just for easy raids when we run out of money. Wars are expensive."

Akkael noticed Rigpa's brief solemness at his brother's comments. Trivialising the deaths of her countrymen in that way would have caused any Edokand'i to abandon their composure. The old woman did a commendable job of retaining it.

"I know one of them is called Kiibi," continued Alani, oblivious to the emotional tightrope the Grand Sage was balancing on. "But I can't remember which one."

"The fourth one," said Akkael.

Rigpa shot a wide-eyed look at Akkael before turning back.

Alani folded the map and placed it under her knee so it wouldn't blow away. "Anyway, enough of that. Do you want to hear what else I've learned about Edokand?"

Rigpa gave a warm smile. "I would love to."

"Okay. So, Edokand'i birds are fascinating..." She began listing all the unique birds she knew about, as well as describing them by how beautiful their colours were.

Akkael grinned as she spoke. Some people liked the sounds of waves or the wind rustling leaves; they were the sort of calming sounds that made sense of the world and eased the soul. For Akkael, it was his daughter's higher-pitched, formal voice when she talked about things she liked.

He leant to his right and whispered to Skane. "Alani seems to be getting on with the sage."

"Yeah," he said, briefly looking up from his bowl of cold soup. "I still don't know why you brought her."

Akkael folded his arms behind his head and shut his eyes. "She seems happy enough."

"She'd be safer in Skaldgard," said Skane, shovelling another spoon of stew into his mouth.

Skane and Akkael had known each other for over a decade. As young sell swords, they met on a job in Urkanza. They bonded instantaneously after copious near-death experiences and long, back-breaking marches. They had an inseparable partnership for years. Akkael believed their friendship came from a complimentary battle tact and a charm that even Skane couldn't resist. But he knew the real reason.

Their first job together was a land dispute between Urkanzan chieftains. After the first couple of weeks, Akkael received the news that his wife had given birth to a baby girl. Akkael struggled to admit it, even a decade on, but he was too scared to raise his axe during the next incursion of the enemy chieftain. Panic led to cowardice, and if it weren't for Skane, Akkael would probably have died in that fight. He didn't know why, but after that, Skane never left his side, and a few months later, Akkael met Alani for the first time.

Over time, Akkael introduced his brother-in-arms to his brother-by-blood, and he and Skane became brothers-in-law.

Skane was one of the only people who could criticise Akkael's parenting without physical consequences. Akkael inhaled and spoke calmly. "We're perfectly safe. Wu Wei has never sent an army to Tsul, and we own this half of the island."

He looked to his right just in time to catch the tail-end of Skane's side-eye stare before he returned to his bowl.

"Come on," Akkael groaned. "If I left her with Astrid, all she would be learning is combat. And that's great; there is no better teacher than my wife. But, look at her..."

Alani was discussing all the volcanoes she'd read about, which ones were the biggest, and when they last erupted. Mostly the Grand Sage nodded along, but every so often, she'd look as if Alani had taught her something.

Akkael nodded to himself. "She may be a shield maiden, but she's also a Torne. The mind needs just as much training as the sword arm."

After a moment of listening to her list all the dormant volcanoes in Edokand, Skane sighed. "I suppose you're right," he conceded. "As the sage said, she's a very inquisitive kid."

"Rigpa, who's older, you or da?" inquired Alani out of nowhere.

Skane nearly spilt his soup all over himself as he burst into intense laughter. Magar also donned a satisfied grin, taking his eyes off his sword for the first time.

"What!" Akkael gripped the log under him as he bellowed at his daughter. "Is that a serious question?"

Alani spoke as soon as Akkael finished, as if she had prepared her reply. "You said I should never be afraid to ask a question I don't know the answer to."

"Alani," groaned Akkael, as if he was too busy nursing his wounds to speak at an average volume. "I'm twenty-eight."

The silence that lingered complimented Alani's vacant expression. Akkael raised his brow, an action Alani imitated. Skane wiped tears from his eyes as he bobbed with stifled enjoyment. Eventually, Rigpa spoke, breaking the tension.

"I'm older," the Grand Sage clarified.

"Thanks, Rigpa," said Alani, stressing the sage's name. The exasperation in her voice suggested her father's insecurity was an inconvenience.

Unlike Akkael, Alani seemed to completely forget the previous exchange, returning her focus to the sage. "Can you tell me more about your magic powers?" she asked.

Rigpa snickered. "It's not magic, but sure," she said before thinking of the perfect demonstration. "Say something."

"Say what? WHOA!" Alani's voice was the volume of a thunderstorm. Skane dropped his bowl, and Akkael looked up as if the source of his daughter's voice were coming from the sky.

"That is amazing. Do it again!" the Grand Sage obliged again, amplifying Alani's voice. "Hello."

Startled murmurs erupted from the camp as Alani spoke with her enhanced voice; some mingled with curiosity, others with genuine fright.

Akkael looked around to see his brother's reaction. However, Magar wasn't sitting next to Skane anymore. Instead, he strapped his giant sword to his back and looked out over the ocean towards Trim. Akkael squinted to see what he was looking at but eventually turned back to Alani.

"That is awesome!" she yelled, no longer amplified by the sage's gifts but loud enough. "What else can you do?"

The Grand Sage raised her index finger and looked up in concentration. "There are... ninety-six men, fifty-four women, nine goats and four sheep in the camp."

Alani looked at her father for confirmation. He just shrugged. "I know about the goats."

"Umm, Akkael." Magar was still looking to the sea, but Akkael didn't hear him.

Alani continued unimpeded. "What else?"

"Well," Rigpa thought momentarily, "I can also sense the ants in the grass, the birds nesting in the trees, and a hedgehog sleeping in that bush."

"Oh, I saw her last night!"

"Him," Rigpa corrected.

"No, she was too brave to be a boy."

The sage laughed.

"Akkael," Magar repeated, his voice too meek.

"Show me something else!" Alani's eyes somehow got more prominent as she clasped her hands together.

"Well, I, umm." Rigpa froze like a deer noticing a hunter. "Something is changing."

"Akkael!"

Magar finally got his brother's attention. "What is it?"

"It's Trim."

Akkael stood up and walked to his brother's side. In the following pause, he wanted nothing more than to realise he was hallucinating like everyone else facing the central island.

Magar squinted, trying to focus on the land opposite, hoping what he was about to say wasn't true. "It looks like it's getting closer."

Akkael took a few more steps forward, staring at the sliver of land across the strait. He could see more colour, less dull greys and more greens and browns. The sea was shorter, and the island eclipsed more of the sky.

He wasn't sure what it meant, but his confusion was concerning. "I think we need to go," said Akkael. "I think we need to move more inland."

Skane nodded in confirmation before ordering everyone to pack up and get ready to leave. Akkael picked up the closest rucksack before leading his daughter by the hand away from the beach. Rigpa followed him, looking behind now and again, gazing at the sea.

[CHAPTER 4] — THE GROANING EARTH

Rigpa stood with Akkael on the incline overlooking the encampment, watching the islands move closer together. Alani hugged her father tightly while Magar and Skane directed the fleeing Solstic inland. Some were still packing below, oblivious to the urgency the Grand Sage felt under her feet. The land was shifting rapidly, reforming and remaking itself. But more terrifying was what was under the earth's crust, babbling like an over-boiled pot.

Akkael must have noticed the sweat beading on her forehead as Rigpa's eyes darted back and forth, sifting through the chaos she sensed under her. Akkael turned to speak but quickly turned away, taking a deep sigh as his daughter whimpered at his side.

Then, the quaking started. The ground below snored and groaned as the islands pushed against each other. A lifetime in Edokand meant Rigpa was used to earthquakes, but she'd never felt one of this magnitude.

The sea was as thin as a river, and the tides frantically beat against the sand as if to cling to the shore they knew so well. The ground began to crack, and the sand fell into the new gaps like falling through an hourglass. The veins spread past those still loading their belongings and towards the fleeing Northmen.

Akkael felt his daughter shake as she clutched tighter to his leg. He looked around and beaconed to the shield maiden who had spoken with him on the beach as she followed the line out of the camp.

"Bodil, take Alani to safety. Alani go with Bodil. I'll follow behind."

Alani's eyes betrayed her desire to object, but she was too petrified to speak.

Bodil held out her hand. "Come, Alani." She walked slightly out of line toward her. That was the last thing Bodil did before the ground swallowed her with a mouth that spread from the sea, pouring into the crevice. Alani's eyes squeezed tight, turning away from where Bodil used to be.

Those in the line broke formation to keep from falling in the forming canyon, but those nearer the shore weren't so lucky. Screams erupted from the camp as people fell through the fissures, and the rest abandoned their belongings. The ships splintered, smashing against the faults' walls as they fell into the earth's bowels.

Rigpa and Akkael stood in place as people rushed past, watching the land rip apart, unable to believe their eyes. Alani clutched even tighter to her father's leg as the cracks grew in number and size, and the final drops of the strait had depleted.

There was a lull. A quiet where everyone stood still and listened to the uneasy calm. The rumbling was still there but was fainter, coming from deeper below. Akkael looked into his daughter's eyes and smiled, trying to calm her nerves.

Rigpa knew it would happen before it did, her gaze darting to where the shore used to be just in time to see magma explode from the fractures. Panic turned to a frenzy as the Northmen ran for their lives from the liquid fire and black gas erupting from the old beach. In the shock, many were engulfed by the molten rivers. Akkael grabbed his daughter's hand as he fled, with Rigpa following behind.

That was when the land started to rise behind them, jagged rock sprouting up like trees. Lava flowed from the schisms they left. Alani's weeping could occasionally be heard over the eruptions, but it was rare. Akkael ran as the rest of his people slowly overtook him. He pulled Alani along, using his free hand to keep the smoke out of his eyes.

Rigpa looked behind for a brief second. The land, red as tempered steel, had risen to eye level and continued to expand towards them. Akkael was struggling to keep up while holding Alani. The smoke pouring into his lungs made it hard to breathe or see anything before him.

Rigpa had an advantage. The smoke blocking her vision didn't take away her gifts. She could sense the soldering grass. The Northmen sprinting ahead were just faint silhouettes, but she could feel every step they took. She even saw the rock Akkael tripped over before it caught his foot. Rigpa tried to warn him but was too late, and Akkael tumbled into the mud, rolling down a decline and losing grip of his daughter's hand.

Alani fell to her knees as Akkael stopped a few feet away. She cried for her father, but the smoke made it difficult for him to see her in the dense grey.

"Da!" She yelled.

"Alani!" he yelled, clambering to his feet and coughing hot soot.

She shouted for him again just before the solid black smoke turned orange in an explosion close enough to burn. It shook Akkael to his core.

"Alani!" There was no answer. "Alani!"

The Grand Sage knew Akkael would never leave that spot. He'd run into the lava if he got the chance. And Rigpa knew Alani was gone.

Soot fell, and cracks started to spread like deltas, moving too close for comfort. No words Rigpa could say would stop Akkael from yelling his daughter's name into the plume that had engulfed her. The sage had to use a gift she kept inside herself, and she held out her hand towards Akkael and overwhelmed his mind. Using her gift, Rigpa made Akkael forget his mourning, fear, and rage. Rigpa took away every emotion Akkael had, and he sagged like a sail without wind.

The sage put her arm around Akkael's shoulders. "Come with me." And he did, having no reason not to anymore. Akkael dawdled vacantly in the direction Rigpa pointed him in, pockets of fumes bursting up from the ground. He started to remember his urgency a little and picked up the pace. He ran with Rigpa, and the sage's influence over his emotions wore off with each step. A tear rolled down Akkael's cheek.

It was a while before they made it to a clearing, where Magar stood at the head of the Northmen, searching for his brother. When Akkael saw Magar, Rigpa's gifts faded, and he began to weep, staggering into his large brother's arms before his knees gave way and hit the floor. All the surviving Northmen watched in harrowing silence at the fit of anguish at their feet.

Then the shooting started. Dust rose from the ground in clouds. Leaves floated eight feet in the air, as did worms who only desired the solace of the damp soil. It was almost unnoticeable initially, but the smoke got denser until it was blacker than the volcanic ash they'd left behind.

Skane noticed it first. The smoke was in three places: to the left, the right and behind the surviving Northmen. "Look out!" he screeched, removing the shield from his back and holding it towards the closest whirl of smoke.

Archers dressed in crimson emerged from the three tornadoes, wielding crossbows already aimed into the crowd. A woman turned to her left and received a bolt through the eye, and another Northman was shot in the neck. The third bolt hit Skane's shield, deep into the thick spruce. The archers vanished as quickly as they appeared, and all was quiet, in brutal suspense.

Magar looked between his husband as his brother still clutched him, weeping, oblivious to the shadow archers surrounding them. "We have to go, Akkael!" he shouted over another explosion from the south.

"Shield wall!" Skane yelled, and those whose shields weren't left at the ruined camp formed a tight circle around those defenceless, trying to protect from all angles like a turtle's shell.

Rigpa helped Magar lift Akkael to his feet, and they moved to the rest of the Northmen. They made a gap in the shield wall so the brothers and the sage could enter before rapidly closing it again.

It was a few more seconds before the archers reappeared, all three bolts hitting shields. Magar couldn't get the leverage to remove his large sword from his back in the packed crowd. He went to take the hand axe from Akkael's hip, and Akkael grabbed his brother's wrist and removed his axe himself. Magar noticed how bloodshot Akkael's eyes were and the brightness of his irises.

"Again!" Rigpa yelled, sensing the archers just before they appeared. The Edokand'i shadow archers burst into view, this time elevated to get a better angle at the crowd. Two Northmen were killed, and their bodies were dropped out of the shield wall in the interim between attacks.

Rigpa tried to sense the archers sooner but was distracted by the frantic heartbeats of everyone around her. The allegro of fast breath and pumping blood, mingled with the metronomic beat of tears hitting the grass below. None added to this small orchestra more than Akkael, with his metred breathing and tensing muscles.

"We need to get out of here," said Skane, whispering to Magar. "We're in no fit state to take shadow archers on in a fight."

"I agree," said Magar.

Skane lowered his shield to get a better view of the surroundings. He scanned the landscape just before a whirlwind appeared in his line of sight. He raised his shield in time to catch the bolt aimed at him.

One more body collapsed from the cluster of Northmen, and Magar pilfered the shield, placing it in the gap the dead man left.

"There's a forest to the east. The trees and the smoke from the eruptions might give us enough cover. We can crawl to it."

"It'll take too long. If we go in the shield wall, they'll pick us off like fish in a barrel," said Magar, and two more Northmen were shot as if to punctuate his point. "Our best chance is to run."

Skane thought for a moment and nodded. "Okay!" Skane bellowed to the scared contingent, "get ready to drop your shields and retreat east. Right after the next attack."

The seconds before the archers remerged were an exhausting wait, but once all three bolts landed in round shields, Skane gave his signal. "RUN!"

The Northmen and the Grand Sage sprinted for the forest, ignoring the advancing volcanic ash and the impeding archers. Magar and Rigpa were the only ones to look back, noticing Akkael was not with those running toward the tree cover.

"Akkael!" Magar's cries were ignored as Akkael stood with his head pointed towards the ground, twirling his axe in his hand.

"Archers!" Rigpa alerted the Northmen as she sensed them return. Some Northmen turned, pointing their shields toward the billow. A bolt hit Magar's shield, which was the only one aimed at the fleeing crowd. Magar lowered his defence to look back at his brother, standing still on the field.

Akkael timed the first strike perfectly. Just before the archer arrived, he swung his axe into the torrent, launching it into the shadow archer's skull and killing him instantly. The archer collapsed to the ground and Akkael drove his axe back down repeatedly, reducing his face to pulp. Then the second missing archer saw his opportunity, teleporting behind Akkael while he was striking the first archer's corpse in a fit of rage.

Magar yelled to his brother, but Akkael couldn't hear him over the sound of metal crushing bone and his furious roar. It would have been too late anyway. The archer was already aimed at the back of Akkael's head, and the bolt was already loose.

[CHAPTER 5] — THE AFTERLIFE

When Akkael woke, he noticed the stench first. Rotten flesh perfumed his surroundings, mingling with the dehydrated urine and ordure. He focused on the smell because all he could see was darkness. Darkness was everything: damp, cold, hard, and dry.

"Hello!" A choir of screams and maddening shrieks answered Akkael through the black. Their songs could curdle the blood, percussed by the banging on the bars, like a violent idiophone.

Akkael tried to remember what had happened, seeing if he could work out how he ended up there. But remembering proved too painful. He saw the ash turn orange as the flames engulfed his daughter. The moment his world shattered. No other memories surfaced. Suddenly, his hand began to ache. It was his left hand, the same one Alani held. The dull pain made it seem like she was still there, clutching him out of fear.

Most of the noises in the dungeon could be ignored. The ramblings of the mad became atmospheric, like the whistling of the wind and the rain tapping. But, eventually, Akkael noticed the sound of something shuffling towards him, stopping right in front of him, still veiled by the pitch-black room.

"I've always found the idea of namesakes an odd tradition," said the stranger with a whisper that ground at the back of their throat. "Being a famous warrior or poet with the same name as an even more famous warrior or poet can only harm your own renown. But I suppose the Northmen of Solstr understand it more than me. It is the basis of your culture."

"Who are you?" Akkael asked, still kneeling on the unlit ground.

"You were named after your uncle, correct?" This time Akkael didn't respond, allowing the stranger to continue. "Akkael the Giant, the famous scourge of Urkanza. Quite a reputation to live up to."

His uncle's face flashed through Akkael's mind like lightning at the top of the sky. He recounted every story about his uncle: his ventures, impacts, and conquests. He felt the texture of his name. It was the only thing he shared with his uncle, but even that felt like a connection he didn't deserve. For Akkael, his name was just a word; but with his uncle, it was a story.

Akkael shook away the thought of his uncle. His head flooded with more important things. "I never cared much for fame," said Akkael.

"Right, of course." The stranger's voice was how the wind would speak if it could. "You see yourself as a traveller and want to see more of the world than any other man. Well, death isn't the best for those opportunities, and it gets lonely in the dark. You are not being able to walk the land and sail the seas. Do you wonder what's happening out there? What has the world turned into?"

The sound of the eruptions replayed in Akkael's ears, along with the smell of volcanic gas and the heat and the dull ache in his hand. "Who are you?" Akkael's voice broke.

"Ahh, I understand," the stranger said, ignoring Akkael's question for the second time. "Your kind does attach a lot to the process of death. Sentimentality for those you lose, sorrow for their lack, vengeance towards those responsible."

Akkael's head tilted up toward where he thought the voice was coming from but remained silent.

"Fame doesn't interest you. Discovery doesn't persuade you." Akkael could hear the smile. "But vengeance; that gets your attention."

"Who are you?" Akkael repeated, more indignantly this time.

Signalled by the sound of snapping fingers, green light illuminated everything around Akkael. It wasn't bright. However, sitting in the dark made Akkael's eyes sensitive. What was once just darkness was now a prison. Cells holding gaunt captives were situated along the thin corridor where Akkael was kneeling. Each filthy cell contained a litany of chains and a wooden shelf for a bed.

But what disturbed Akkael most was the stranger. It wasn't a man or any creature Akkael had seen or imagined. The green light came from an amorphous cloud of smoke the stranger was floating inside. Disembodied tentacles and black eyes of varied sizes appeared and disappeared inside the void, and a fanged, lipless mouth grinned just below.

Akkael couldn't blink or take his eyes off the wretched fiend, no matter how much he wanted to. "What do you want?"

The creature's grin widened, ending at a tentacle on either side where cheeks would've been. "To give you everything you want. Shadow archers don't work of their own volition. Someone ordered them to attack. Which means someone knew what was going to happen. Don't you want to find them? Don't you want to wring their neck?" He snarled through the last word.

Akkael took a moment before he spoke. "How do you plan to give me that? I'm dead, aren't I?" Akkael sounded unsure. He started to remember the moment he died, the crossbow bolt crunching through the back of his skull. But, despite the dead religion of his people and all the other religions he had read about worldwide, he never imagined anything resembling an afterlife. He always thought there'd be nothing. He looked at the monster and wondered what else he could be wrong about. No one believed in gods anymore, but could that be a mistake too? Was this a god?

"Don't do it!" A yell burst from the closest cell to Akkael, and a weeping Urkanzan sat whimpering in the dim green light, dried blood crusting on his dark skin. "Don't take what it offers you! Save your-"

The prisoner was silenced as the creature raised a tentacle, lunging it through the bars of his cell and impaling him. A voiceless cry emanated from the Urkanzan as the creature lifted him from the grimy floor. After a few seconds of torture, the beast removed his tentacle from the Urkanzan's chest, and he collapsed in a shivering heap. He didn't have a hole in his chest like Akkael would have thought, but the man's brown complexion paled, and his eyes were haunting.

"As I was saying," said the creature, "all I want is to give you what you want, an ample chance at revenge. Trust me when I say I can give you that. So, what say you, Akkael?"

Akkael tried to look it in the eye, but he couldn't focus long enough on one before it slid away or vanished. So, he stared at its mouth instead. Its snarl was the

31

only constant in its being. Akkael didn't know exactly what he was offering, but, looking at the Urkanzan, the price was easy to guess. Common sense told him to refuse his offer. But then he felt the throb in his hand from where Alani had held on to him. He saw Magar, Skane, and the rest of their camp running for their lives and knowing how slim their chances were. He saw Doran riding into Wu Wei, and his imagination did the rest. With each image, rage coursed as readily as blood through a vein.

His gaze returned to the restless collection of eyes, and his fists clenched. Akkael gave his answer.

[CHAPTER 6] — SHADOW ARCHER

Akkael must have blinked. He was in the monster's dungeon one minute, and the next, he watched the sunset. The smoke from the south made the sky glow red, and the dusk air was so cold he could see his breath.

Lying on his side, disorientated, he faced the direction of the destruction. He could still feel rumbling under him, and although he was further away than before, he could see the ash had encroached, engulfing the forest and rising higher into the clouds. As the disorientation faded, he got a clearer bearing of his surroundings. He could hear metal rubbing against metal, the huffs and whinnies of horses, and some murmuring.

"And I was like, you know what I was like. I was like, you know," someone said, speaking Edokand'i.

Adrenaline gave Akkael the strength to sit up, and his heart raced faster as he looked at the army of goutuizi surrounding him. He must have been captured, he thought, but when he looked down at his wrists, they weren't bound as he expected. He was also in different clothing. Crimson gloves and a studded leather outfit. They were more protective than the furs, tunic, and slacks he was wearing previously, and he couldn't understand why the goutuizi had dressed him.

He moved his hands to his side and knocked something to his left. He saw a crossbow in the grass; three bolts clipped to the underside. Why they left him unbound with a weapon, Akkael was sure he didn't know, but he wanted to make the Edokand'i regret that choice. Then he paused, realising three bolts weren't enough to take out all the voices he heard behind him. Maybe that was what the Edokand'i wanted, he thought. For him to attack so they had an excuse to kill him.

But why would they need an excuse?

"I'm sorry to hear about your brother." Two goutuizi soldiers appeared from behind Akkael and sat in front of him. One had wide sympathetic eyes, and even Akkael felt the man was placing too much pity on someone who had killed too many of his countrymen to count. The other goutuizi just folded his arms, looking bored.

The sympathetic one spoke again. "I can only imagine what you're going through."

Akkael's mind started racing. His fears had been confirmed. His brother was dead. But the goutuizi only said brother, so he assumed Magar was still alive. He didn't want to consider any other alternative and had already lost so much.

Akkael tried to swear, attempted to spit the vitriol he felt at those responsible. Why did he bother learning Edokand'i if not for that? But when he tried to speak, all that came out was an incoherent mumble.

The other goutuizi snickered. "I don't know why you're bothering. You know it can't talk back."

"Quiet, Shu!" said the first soldier. "He's in mourning."

Akkael tried to speak again, searching for the problem. He found it. It was strange that he hadn't noticed it before. His mouth felt so empty with the absence of his tongue. Akkael grimaced, knowing exactly where the first two bolts of that crossbow would go. He didn't know if they were the ones who cut out his tongue, but that didn't matter.

But then, some rational part of his brain spoke again. If he had just had his tongue cut out, shouldn't it still hurt?

Shu rolled his eyes and laughed at Akkael's attempts to speak before the other goutuizi continued. "Ignore my friend. It's been a long day. Sorry again. I was shocked when I found out what happened. Those Northmen are savages."

Akkael squinted in confusion.

"But hey, I heard you avenged him." The soldier tapped Akkael on the shoulder. "Driving that bolt right through the back of Akkael Torne's skull. The Emperor will give you a medal for that."

"The Emperor doesn't give medals to shadow archers," said Shu.

"He'll make an exception," spat the other.

"What the fuck?" said Akkael. Or he would have said if the sick, twisted culture of the Edokand'i didn't have a tongue-removing ritual for their shadow archers. Akkael's heart was racing at a gallop. He looked down at his gloves again. He hadn't noticed before, but they were shadow archer colours, and the crossbow at his side was the weapon they used. He was one of them.

More of the goutuizi's words made sense in Akkael's mind. He wasn't just any shadow archer. He was the one that had shot him in the back of the head. The tentacled beast had said he would get ample opportunity to seek revenge, though he never gave any specifics. But, Akkael had worked out this part at least. He had taken over the body of the man who had killed him.

Akkael's head was spinning. All the puzzle pieces fit into place, but he had no idea how or why. There were so many thoughts in his head that he tried to pick one to focus on. Existential panic mingled with a strange self-mourning as he considered how he would never be the man he once was. He knew his eyes were no longer blue, his hair no longer dirty blond. Only his thoughts were his own.

But as he calmed down, he noticed something that transferred from his old self. He may have the sullied body of an Edokand'i shadow archer, but his mind was his, and so was the dull feeling in his left hand from where Alani had clutched onto him.

The phantom ache gave him focus, and he got a handle on himself again. All that mattered was making the most of whatever second chance the monster had given him after he had died. There would be moments to think about his situation but now wasn't it.

Akkael raised his head and smiled at the sympathetic goutuizi playing the part. The man in red armour smiled back, and the second soldier rolled his eyes.

"Men, get in positions!" A male voice Akkael recognised boomed from behind him. When the voice beckoned, the warriors stood from their kneel, and Akkael followed their eye line.

Now, Akkael understood that the shadow archer he had somehow become must have, in his mourning, picked a spot looking out to solitude. However, that

35

didn't prepare him for what was happening behind him. Horses and goutuizi littered the hillside like stains. There must have been thousands, a force that could take a city.

Akkael picked up the crossbow and looked wide-eyed at the forming battalion. The army wasn't just made up of goutuizi. The archers behind the cavalry were all women, wearing the cerulean plate mail of Sekando. Each woman wore a quiver and a geom blade on opposite sides of their hip to make room for a sashimono; banners on their backs supported by flagpoles running down the spine. The eight goutuizi cavalry captains also wore sashimono, spreading evenly across the line. A captain typically led two hundred men, so sixteen-hundred men were in the cavalry alone. Their flags were solidly red, but the women had the blue circle of Sekando at the centre of their standards.

The rest of the army was infantry. They still wore the goutuizi red, but the armour was less decadent. They were the bulk of the force, with at least double the number of the cavalry, three-thousand katanas ready to spill the blood of barely a dozen Northmen.

Two figures stood at the head of the army, both of whom Akkael knew.

The first was the Queen of Sekando, Kya. They sat straight-backed on their horse, chin up with no discernible expression. The Queen's outfit didn't look fit for war on the surface, but the sapphire silk costume concealed plate mail that was so well hidden Akkael wouldn't have noticed if he hadn't already known it was there. They held the reins with both hands and wore silk gloves, the same colour silver as the circlet on their head.

So far, the women of Sekando had stayed out of the war as best they could, sometimes even cooperating with the Northmen and supplying them with food and farming equipment. To see Queen Kya here sent a shiver down Akkael's new spine.

Their nephew, Koji, was to their left, but Akkael knew him more as the son of the Second Pillar of Edokand, Lord Hideo. After ordering his men into formation, Koji wore his goutuizi armour and held himself much like his auntie. He looked at the spitting image of his father, with the only difference being youth and the fact that

Koji had both his hands. He wore a helmet with a large peacock feather erupting from the top, a fashion decision he'd no doubt regret once he had a few more years behind him.

Akkael was so fixated on the amassing army that he didn't notice the cloud of black smoke building beside him until the shadow archer spawned next to him. "Maaaaaaa!" he screamed with a tongueless mouth, immediately gratefully no one could understand his involuntary reaction.

The shadow archer looked concerned, signing something in a hand language Akkael couldn't understand. He wanted to keep up his charade but had no idea how to interpret those hand signals. After a moment, Akkael smiled. The archer furrowed his brow, but Akkael's clumsy grin seemed to abate him.

The shadow archer walked over to the two heading the army, making Akkael wonder why he didn't just teleport straight there. Then Akkael remembered he was probably in the body of the shadow archer's friend, the body of someone who had just lost their brother or brother-in-arms. Akkael wasn't sure, but he needed to remember all the details if he didn't want to look suspicious.

The Queen and Koji whispered to themselves as Akkael followed the second shadow archer to their side. The archer signed something, and Akkael thought rapidly for an appropriate response. He held his hand up and pretended to hold back tears. The shadow archer accepted the answer, nodding and turning to face the forest and cloud of ash in front of them.

Akkael mimicked the archer's stance, gripping the crossbow and letting it hang unnotched. His fake brother-in-arms had two more bolts than Akkael, and he wasn't sure how he could replenish his stock since shadow archers carried no quivers.

Koji broke from his army before turning to face them. The backdrop of the volcanic ash and his height atop his Edokand'i steed made him look intimidating, even though Akkael knew him as anything but. Koji grinned and slowly rode down the line of his militia.

"This is a good day, men!" An eruption punctuated his statement as a section of the smoke burst into an orange hue. "This is the day the tide turns in this endless war against the peril of the Northmen." The army cheered, which seemed to catch Koji off-guard. "Today, we sever the strength of the infamous Tornes. My father, Lord Hideo, is making light work of the head of their family, Doran Torne. And earlier on this glorious day in Edokand'i history, our esteemed shades took down the villain, Akkael Torne!"

Akkael couldn't help clearing his throat as the rest of the army yelled in joy. It was a strange mixture of pride and affront listening to people gleefully cheer his death. It was a more profound insult when he thought about the consequences killing him brought. All his people and his daughter were just collateral damage in the endeavour to kill him and his brothers. Akkael's hand hurt so much that he winced.

"Now, in that forest," said Koji, pointing behind him, ash slowly engulfing the woods, "is the last of that villainous family. Any second now, Magar Torne will come out with Skane Brick-Chest, and the miserable dregs of their encampment." The army cheered once again. "After we make short work of them, we will march on Takakawa. We will reclaim our land across Tsul and Utajima. We will kill Astrid Torne, Trygve and whatever northern bastard stands in our way. This is the day to mark the end of the Northmen's tyranny! This is the day the ground spat fire, and we looked beyond despair and found our hope! This is the day we win!"

Akkael looked around him. The army contrasted Queen Kya's still expression with a harrowing orchestra of chants, calling for the blood of those in the woods. He had seen the sorry state the Solstic were in and knew they had no chance of besting a force this strong. Akkael couldn't save Doran or those swallowed by the earth. He couldn't even hold his daughter safe. Maybe he had a shot at saving Magar.

But, if he blew his cover, he would surely die again, maybe permanently this time. Even if he knew how to teleport, as his shadow archer form would suggest, he couldn't take out a whole army by himself. Whatever that horrifying creature was, it gave him a chance to seek complete revenge for his daughter's death, and it was revenge he intended to see through.

Akkael deliberated on the choice ahead of him. Either stay and watch his brother die or give away his only shot at his revenge. He twirled the crossbow in his hands, cursing the part of his mind that even suggested there might be a choice in letting Magar fail.

Akkael prayed but didn't know why. He knew there were no gods. Maybe that tentacled abomination could do something. Anything to stop Magar from making him choose between abandoning his revenge, or letting his brother die.

[CHAPTER 7] — INSURRECTION

Names were important, and Hideo knew it. In the past, Emperors had renamed the City of Disciplines to illustrate the country's governing philosophy. When Trim wanted to close its borders, the city was named *Guli Zhuyi*. When the island set on expanding its influence across the entirety of Edokand, it held the name *Kuo Zhang*. When peace was seen as more appealing than conflict, it was changed to *Wu Wei*.

Before, Hideo saw this tradition as little more than a way to simplify the job of historians, separating eras succinctly. But as the day progressed and events mounted upon themselves like a glutton's plate, he understood it as a way of making change a little more palatable.

The people of Wu Wei could hear the rumbling earth miles away and even see the ash if they were high enough up the volcano on which the city was built. They witnessed the Sentinel Guard leave their post and lay siege to the palace they had sworn to protect. The people gathered in awed silence as Hideo stood on the Emperor's balcony in full red plate, which did well to hide the blood of the officials that stood in opposition.

The metal of his false hand rang as he dropped it, harder than he expected, to the balcony bannister. With his good hand, he removed his helmet, placing it under his arm. The palace was in the volcano's caldera, so the walls built onto the rim made the complex's gate higher than the balcony. He couldn't see the faces of those peering through, nor those of the magistrates below him, but he knew they were scared. The rich inside the gates and the poor outside were alike in that way, neither knowing more than the other.

Hideo turned and nodded to a sage behind him, distracted by the splotches that stained his purple robe. When he noticed Hideo's gaze, he nodded back, clenching his eyes. The Second Pillar of Edokand then turned to face the shaking populous.

"This is a historic day." The sage used his gifts to amplify Hideo's speech across the city, which meant everyone could hear his voice waver. He tried to steel himself before continuing.

"We have made changes." An eruption sounded in the north. "Some changes are more significant than others. I hope soon you'll see this as a comfort. These are the extent your sages and your military are willing to go to keep you safe from invaders.

"The Northmen have slept too long on our shores. Gorged themselves from our fields. Annexed too much of our land." He didn't know why, but the nationalist motifs Hideo had relied on to revitalise his cause were falling flat even for him. "We need to be rid of them. We have to be. We *have* to be!"

He rubbed the sweat from his forehead before noticing the blood coated his sleeve. He continued. "Right now, my son is heading an army, along with the support of my sister, the Queen of Sekando. Together they will liberate Tsul. I have no doubt. Moving a Trim army into Tsul will be anathema to some more traditional amongst you. The principle of Wu Wei has been one of inaction; inexertion. That's one of the things that will change."

Hideo took a deep breath, which sounded like a tornado due to the sage's powers. "From now on, the City of Disciplines will be known as *Jin Bu* and built on a single mission; reclaiming the lands we have lost."

Hideo moved his helmet under his other arm and turned. A sentinel, advisor, and friend of Hideo's, Ieyasu Nobu, stood behind him. He was wearing a mask of a demon under his helmet and held a scroll, which Hideo reached out to take.

"This is a document with the Emperor's seal," Hideo continued, "ratifying the changes I have just mentioned."

"Where is the Emperor?" yelled a noble from below the balcony.

Hideo sucked his teeth. "That is all I have to say right now. I will present the rest of the changes to you over the coming days, and I look forward to ending this war."

"You heard me, Hideo!" screamed the same noble. "Where is the Emperor?"

A burst of smoke appeared behind the questioner, and an assassin all in crimson emerged from it, slitting the noble's throat quickly before vanishing. Hideo clasped his eyes shut, taking another torrential deep breath. All heads turned to the dying man as he collapsed, drowning in his blood. No one made a sound.

Hideo turned away from the scene, clenching his jaw. He noticed a tear rolling down the sage's cheek and looked down at his feet. As he walked past Ieyasu, Hideo lent towards him. "Bury the body."

Ieyasu gave a slow nod, and Hideo retreated into the palace. He was weary, but he knew he wouldn't sleep.

[CHAPTER 8] — DEATHLESS

It had been an hour, and, despite the crucial decision he had to make and the Edokand'i potentially wiping out his people, Akkael was getting bored. Twirling his crossbow in his hand, he stood shoulder to shoulder with the other shadow archer, who had tried to make conversation in sign language numerous times. Akkael, not understanding any of it, attempted to avoid his line of sight.

Every muscle in his body was aching to strike at Koji as his horse casually paced back and forth along the vanguard. However, he fought the urge, knowing how little it would accomplish and how much he'd have to lose. The monster who'd given him this second life in the body of his killer did so under the pretence of a chance at revenge. Although he didn't feel he owed it anything, retribution for Alani's death was everything to him. His hand ached just at the thought of it.

There was no guarantee that killing Koji would save his countrymen that fled into the woods. They were as good as dead the moment the earth erupted, and that's what he kept telling himself.

The army hadn't broken rank, but the rattling of steel with every fidget and deep sigh suggested they were just as bored as Akkael. The only one who looked unphased by the wait was Queen Kya, their blue dress cascading down the cloud-white horse was still bright despite the deepening twilight.

The Queen was joined by their First Blade, Ichika, whom Akkael knew only by reputation. Stories of a small woman besting dozens of Solstic warriors in battle had graced songs and poems by this point in the war, and adoration for her spread through Akkael's people and her own. On foot, she wielded a spear with a large blade at the end, which looked long enough for a sword. She tied her black hair in a wolf's tail, a style typically adopted by men. She was the only one on the field not wearing armour, going instead for a blue coat and hakama trousers.

Her brow furrowed as she looked at the ash still engulfing the skyline to the south, and Akkael could guess from context her conversation with the Queen. It was the same thing that plagued his mind. The soot and smoke still sat thick on the

43

skyline. But, against the purpling sky, a new, strange outline peered over the smoulder, which looked like the silhouette of mountain peaks.

When Akkael first noticed it, his curiosity was a welcome distraction from letting his brother die. But, after a while, even that lost its solace. Contemplating something powerful enough to lift mountains from the sea made his revenge mission seem just as futile as taking out a whole army himself. He relegated it to just a trick of the light and went back to thinking about his brother's quick and inevitable murder.

He wondered what Astrid was doing. His wife had stayed back at Skaldgard to train shield maidens. The last words she had said to him before he left were, *"Going to Wu Wei just to talk sounds boring as shit. I'd rather slice the hay out of this dummy for a few days and watch the grass grow."*

"Look after Alani. I love you."

Does she have any idea what happened? Once this army finished with the stragglers in the woods, it would take the fight to Takakawa and Skaldgard, burning Solstic villages as they went. Astrid would meet this army, and vengeance would be on her mind just as much as his, and, despite her ferocity, she would lose.

Akkael sighed and shook his head. He habitually talked himself into doing reckless things with good intentions. He thought about all his ill-advised decisions since he'd woken up that morning. He counted four in the time it took him to unclip a bolt from the bottom of his crossbow and notch it. Akkael took another deep breath, knowing his window to act would be brief.

He was never much of an archer. Swords, axes, and spears were in his wheelhouse, even if Astrid always mocked how he held a polearm. He could even throw an axe and a knife with surprising accuracy. But once a string is added, it all goes to shit.

Koji rode along the line of his army while Akkael tracked him with his eyes. It was a while before he was confident enough to aim.

He raised the crossbow and wrapped his finger around the trigger. But he was too slow. Almost as soon as he lifted the bow, Akkael saw, in the corner of his vision, the shadow archer summoning a kunai dagger from a black cloud that formed around his hand. It was half a second later before the weapon plunged into Akkael's neck. The bolt loosed, launching way too high. The last thing Akkael saw was Koji, unscathed, turning in confusion.

As he drowned in his own blood, Akkael laughed. The tentacle creature would probably roll all its shifting eyes at once when Akkael told it how he'd wasted his second chance. He looked up at the shadow archer. Confusion and sorrow tore across his face as he watched the light in his friend's eyes go out. Akkael felt a pang of guilt, having made this man end the life of who he thought was his brother-in-arms. But that went almost as soon as it came, and Alani flashed into his mind. He closed his eyes, his consciousness fading for a second time.

Akkael gasped so hard he burned the back of his throat. Going from drowning in blood to suddenly breathing without issue was shocking, and he started tearing up. He reached to his neck, grasping it as air filled him with ease. He thought he'd be slick with blood, but all he felt was the leather of shadow archer armour. The only blood on him was trickling down his cheek from where he moved his hands too fast and cut himself with the knife he was holding.

The first question he had when the shock had abated was where he'd gotten the knife from, but a hundred other questions quickly engulfed that. When the tears started clearing up from his eyes and his vision returned, he saw a shadow archer lying at his feet. The corpse clutched a crossbow and had a knife wound in his neck.

He looked at the kunai blade in his hand, which had more blood than the scratch on his face would suggest. All the faces of the Edokand'i army were on him. Akkael looked around until the murmuring and uncertainty led him to Koji's stunned expression.

Koji spoke briefly, looking at Akkael. "Thank you, shade. You just saved my life."

Akkael had put two and two together by now, but the answer wasn't as simple as just saying four. Somehow, he'd once again taken over the body of his killer, and the corpse in front of him was the shadow archer he used to be, who'd killed him the first time. He knew this, but he couldn't believe it. There was something in the improbability, the impossibility of it all, that Akkael couldn't fathom. Is this what the monster meant when he said, "Ample opportunity"?

He had to test it to know if what he thought was happening was really happening. Luckily, he had a whole army of test subjects.

"Let this shade be an example to you all," said Koji atop his horse. "The heroism of Edokand can overcome any threat, any obstacle, any-"

Akkael didn't waste time and was much better at throwing knives than shooting a bow. Akkael flung the dagger, striking right between Koji's eyes with a crunch that resonated across the field. It was a few seconds before Koji fell dead from his horse and an even stiller moment later.

It was Queen Kya who broke the silence. "Kill him," they said with a strange calmness.

Before Akkael could turn to look at the regent who made the order, an infantryman decapitated Akkael with one swift motion from his broadsword.

Akkael went from a spinning head to a stationary goutuizi soldier, and the motion sickness made him throw up almost as soon as he took over the body. However, now with a new tongue in his mouth, he could voice his discomfort.

"Fuck me!" he said.

"What did you just say?" At first, Akkael thought the man beside him was against cursing. However, when he noticed the soldier's language, Akkael realised he'd just sworn in Solstic.

Akkael killed him almost as soon as he realised his mistake, managing to slice the throat of a second man with a parabolic arch before a spear lunged straight into his heart.

Since the spearman had thrown his weapon, the next person Akkael took over was unarmed, with only a tiny knife stuck to his belt. He unsheathed it and turned, launching it at one of the cavalrymen, which caused a domino effect, crushing four more under the weight of their horses. While a spear lunged into his gut, Akkael considered the almost five thousand goutuizi and two thousand Sekandans he still had left to fight, and, as he pulled the spear out of the belly he used to have, he wondered how long he could keep this up.

Luckily, after a few more corpses littered the ground, confusion spread across the whole army, and no one knew who was fighting whom. Akkael could back away, and they'd still be killing each other for a few minutes before they realised. The Sekandan Queen called for their women to retreat. They tried to do this subtly as possible, so none of the goutuizi followed, riding to the back line where they had not yet joined the confused conflict.

Akkael watched Kya ride away with Ichika, who led the rest of the Sekandans away on foot. A katana crushed his skull, and Kya's flowing blue dress was the last thing he saw with those eyes.

The next pair were already looking towards a soldier in red armour. Maybe they were friends, and he sought comfort just before Akkael became him. From there, it was easy for Akkael to switch stance and lunge straight for the goutuizi. He didn't see it coming, and his eyes widened with shock.

He killed three more men before a dismounted captain sliced his neck. The sashimono banner the captain wore gave Akkael much influence. The Edokand'i assumed whomever he was killing deserved it, and he managed to slay over a dozen before someone put him down.

After that, Akkael spent the rest of the fight trying desperately to find another captain to kill him. He went through waves of lives where he was so focused on finding a sashimono in the crowd that he didn't manage to kill anyone before he moved on to inhabit the next man.

People started fleeing, knowing the plot to wipe out the Northmen for good was lost. With the retreating Sekandans and the amassing pile of dead, they had already lost half their force, along with their commander, Koji. Akkael didn't blame their cowardice.

He didn't understand what had happened to him, but in the heat of the fight, it didn't matter. Each goutuizi he killed was one step closer to retribution. The pain of each death was punishment for losing his daughter. At that moment, it was everything he needed. To die and cause death. He would think of the implications later.

He had ample opportunity for that.

[CHAPTER 9] — IN THE FOREST

"The fighting seems to be dying down," said Rigpa, clutching a tree trunk as she scried what was happening in the field beyond.

It had been hours since the goutuizi had started killing each other, and the solstic survivors huddled and listened to the monk's updates like she were a town crier announcing the day's news. No one had slept, not even the children. Five had survived, but unfortunately, none of their parents had. The surviving fourteen adults - eight women, six men - had taken to looking after them, keeping them warm with whatever clothes and cloaks they had spare or even with just an arm around the shoulder.

Magar stood, looking away from the stragglers of the encampment. Skane, two surviving men, and one shield maiden were on alert, ensuring none of the goutuizi found them. The solstic had already lost three people to scared soldiers fleeing whatever happened.

"Two sentinels just entered the forest," Rigpa whispered in the dark. "But they look like they'll miss us if we stay quiet."

A deep sigh came from behind Magar as he looked at Rigpa, eyes bloodshot and teeth clenched under his scowl. "Call them goutuizi."

The sage glanced at Magar. He'd spoken little since they'd entered the woods, not that Rigpa wanted him to say anything more. She thought goutuizi was clever as slurs go. It meant 'ones who fight for the villain'. No bigotry is rooted in intelligence, but using the Edokand'i language to call their warriors little more than thugs got the insult across. To Rigpa, those men fighting each other out there for no apparent reason were still the sentinels of Edokand. She appalled the aspersion like blasphemy.

But to those warriors, the Solstic were the vaguely named Northmen, brutish killers from a foreign land with no place on their soil. She'd heard the same bile in her countrymen's spit as in Magar's. The Grand Sage kept her mouth shut and turned back to the ground.

49

Rigpa didn't know why she helped the Solstic. She had many excuses. Rigpa knew the Emperor too well to suspect the amassed army was his doing, especially after what had ensued. She also liked the justification that she was looking out for herself. She couldn't outrun the Northmen, so she was just doing whatever kept her alive. Or, she defended her actions with the forlorn expressions of the children behind her.

Over the hours, excuses cycled in her head like spokes on a wheel. She was thankful she had stayed once the army began slaughtering each other. But she was in no real danger of leaving the desperate Solstic anyway. She didn't know why she was helping them, but nothing could stop her, and all the rationalizations just helped her soften her own inbred sense of treason.

Rigpa could feel less than a tenth of the original force still on the field. A few had fled like the Sekandans, but the corpses piled up on each other were substantial. The fighting seemed to have started near the front. A shadow archer killed the commander, a sentinel killed them, and then... Chaos. There was a domino effect to it that Rigpa couldn't understand. Why had they started killing each other? Rigpa had watched volcanoes erupt before, so she could understand what happened on the beach. But a whole army imploding was something she'd never witnessed, and it chilled her spine.

Over the next few hours, the warring slowed to an end while Rigpa pondered theories. Sages had the power to subdue emotions like she'd done to Akkael after Alani was engulfed by the lava. It can make a subject more pliable and open to suggestions. But it doesn't last as long as the battle had, and not even she could affect that many people at once. Also, it's not mind control, just mind suppression. You can't make someone do something that involves inertia, and the effort is undesirable to a suppressed mind.

It could be a similar power. A darker power. A gross abuse of control that could entirely alter a mind and pull mountains from the sea. Rigpa looked up through a hole in the tree cover. The dawn perfectly lit the peaks that had formed in the calamity.

Whatever had started the battle, it had run its course. Rigpa felt the field as a dozen survivors timidly waited on a floor of corpses. One of the soldiers broke the lull, charging and killing two before someone put him down. Rigpa thought it would be over, but then the man who had just slain the defector threw his spear at one of the soldiers, still frozen in place. Had sides been drawn that Rigpa didn't understand?

"What's happening?" asked Skane as a sentinel charged and killed the spear thrower. He was wiping Edokand'i blood off his axe from those who'd found the Solstic while trying to escape. Why had she helped them?

"It's almost over. Seven left," Rigpa said. "Wait, five. Two more just ran off towards the east."

Rigpa then felt a sudden whiplash as Magar grabbed her by the throat and pinned her against a tree.

"Magar!" said Skane, dropping his axe and grabbing his husband by the shoulder. The two prominent men shared a glance before Magar returned his ice-cold eyes to the Grand Sage.

"This is your fault," he said, tightening his grip on Rigpa's neck.

"She's done nothing but help us," Skane pleaded. "She saved our lives against the shadow archers, and if it weren't for her, we would have walked right out into that horde of goutuizi."

Magar just shook his head. "My brother is dead."

"Akkael chose his fate," said Skane. "Nothing to do with her."

"And Doran?" he said, almost as if he was hoping for an answer.

"We don't know what's happened to Doran."

Magar shook his head again, squeezing tighter and making Rigpa's eyes water.

"But if he is dead, your actions here mean more. If Doran and Akkael are dead, that means..." Skane paused, knowing what he was about to say would break Magar's heart. "That means you're king. And a king killing the Grand Sage of Edokand is an act of war, not just on Wu Wei, but on every island in Edokand."

Magar snorted. "They declared war first."

51

"And now their army is gone," said Skane, searching deep for anything that would get Magar to drop Rigpa. "We might be able to use the monk as some form of leverage. At least wait until we have more information before you kill her."

Magar growled before throwing Rigpa into the mud and rotting leaves. Then he pulled the great sword off his back and walked towards the thinning tree cover.

Skane helped Rigpa up. Then, once she was on her feet, the large man tightened his grip on Rigpa's hand. His face was still as stone. "We're even now, sage. If I find out you knew about anything that happened, I'll kill you. Slowly."

With that, he let go of Rigpa's hand, tapping her on the shoulder with a fondness oblivious to the threat he'd just given. Skane followed Magar, beckoning the rest of the Solstic to do the same.

When they reached the battlefield, no one was there. The last man had fled by horse just a few moments before. Rigpa knew this but didn't dare speak, fearing any word would quickly become her last.

The sky was red like the stained grass, the armour of the fallen, and the steel of their weapons. Thousands of corpses littered the slight incline. Walking out to the army standing in rows upon the hill would have been a fierce sight. The Northmen would have been the exact level of forlorn the Edokand'i hoped for. Fear in their last moments.

Rigpa supposed they got what was coming to them. The world was harsh, and people rarely got that kind of justice. Even a sage could appreciate that. But looking out at such a disposal of sacred life brought a tear to her eye. She quickly wiped it away so Magar couldn't see.

Magar wasn't looking at the sage anyway. He repeatedly slammed his sword into one of the corpses, growling like a bear with each plunge. Rigpa could feel the corpse lifting off the ground each time Magar pulled back, and she recoiled at the gore.

Rigpa surveyed the deceased, looking at each for signifiers of rank. A few had sashimono, which meant they were captains. She assumed they were part of the cavalry from the number of dead horses surrounding them. Some of the mounts were still alive, having run off to eat grass in peace. They could get to Takakawa in half a day's ride, the first good fortune they'd had.

Skane's eyes then fell on an ornate suit of armour, gold trimming around the red and a helmet with a peacock's feather sticking from the top. He pointed at the body. "I know him. Isn't that Koji Kazar?"

Magar shot past Rigpa to see who Skane was pointing at. He then looked south, almost as if looking through the new mountains, still curtained by a layer of smoke.

"Hideo." Magar's lips turned like a wolf, and he began stomping towards the mountains.

"Magar!" Skane yelled. "Magar! What's your plan here? You're just gonna walk to Wu Wei, knock on the door, and kill whoever you think is to blame?"

"Yes." He continued walking.

"No! Stop!" Magar reluctantly listened to Skane, still not turning to face him. "We're going to get these people to Takakawa. Our priority is food and rest."

Magar took a moment before turning back around, barging past everyone in the general direction of Takakawa.

Skane took it as a sign to rally the rest of the Solstic to do the same. "Come on. Sage, help me calm some of these horses with your magic. The journey won't be too long."

Rigpa was still looking over the dead, unable to peel her gaze away. "What about them?"

Magar stopped but remained silent.

Rigpa spoke on. "They deserve a burial. They-"

"If I could string every rotten shit to a horse, I would," said Magar. "Then I'd put every head on spikes outside Takakawa."

He turned to face the sage, tensing every muscle almost in apoplexy. "Fuck them. Fuck them all!"

The giant continued walking, growling with each breath. Skane put his hand on Rigpa's back in a comforting gesture as Rigpa tried not to flinch.

They all left, abandoning a banquet that waited for any maggot or crow who wanted a taste. The children clutched onto women who weren't their mothers as they tried to suppress their whimpering. The horses were military trained with a gentle demeanour, so it was relatively easy to get the mounts needed. Then they rode towards Takakawa in silence.

Rigpa took one last look at the mountains. Everyone did.

[CHAPTER 10] — ASTRID

Doran was unmarried. This meant that when he was away for battle or business, the duty of ruling would fall to his heir, Akkael. His flippant politics and sarcastic jibes gave Doran more work when he returned than if he'd left his settlement ungoverned. When Akkael was also away, Magar would govern. He was better than Akkael, but only marginally. Whenever there was a debate between diplomacy and war, he always chose war. But, since all three brothers had gone to broker peace with the Emperor, the job fell to Astrid.

Usually, it wasn't so bad. Doran had a string of skalds to handle much of the minutia. There was a skald for trade, for finance, for war. An Edokand'i sage was appointed as skald of education, which was not a position in any of the other Solstic settlements. Most of the responsibilities were handled without Astrid's input, so on the rare occasion she was temporarily in charge, it didn't conflict too much with her usual schedule of training and drinking.

However, Doran happened to organise peace talks during the monthly assembly, and, in Astrid's mind, there was no way that wasn't planned.

The main hall was more extensive than any three rooms in Skaldgard's pagoda and was decorated to look like a great hall on Solstr. Long tables bordered with thick benches lay in regimented lines around a firepit at the centre of the room. Smoke from the fire clouded the ceiling as it tried desperately to escape through the paper windows. The entrance was parallel to the large, engraved throne where Astrid sat.

Astrid had blonde hair tied in plaits and green eyes that were rare in Solstr. She was also very imposing. Her biceps were more prominent than most thighs, and she had a strong jaw. She lent lazily across the armrests. Her cithara, a beautiful hand harp with ornate carvings, was held in her lap as she strummed what she could remember from a song played at a mead hall the night before.

She hissed when she plucked the wrong note, baring her scarred teeth. It was a custom she picked up from her time in Urkanza. The Urkanzans would mark

55

their teeth to denote rank. Hers bore diagonal lines crossing on both front teeth, and a horizontal line cut straight through the middle. The mark of a royal.

Of all the places the Solstic had expanded, Urkanza, with its hot weather, open landscape, and gorgeous dark-skinned men, was the place she felt most comfortable. She carried an Urkanzan dagger next to the hand axe on her weapon's belt as a memento of the home she missed.

It was the place she'd like to raise Alani once Doran's war was over.

When Astrid was on Doran's chair, the spaces between seconds increased, and hours lasted a millennium. Even the room seemed to drag. The long tables stretched for miles as subjects dawdled past them to discuss their issues. The fur rug at the entrance was the length of a country, and the steps to the throne were like climbing to a mountain's summit. Every floorboard became an acre of hill land, and expeditions into the room seemed to take a lifetime.

Astrid strummed as she blatantly ignored Two farmers, Elmer, and Bernard, bickering in front of the throne. Elmer accused Bernard of stealing his cow, Gretel, and Astrid had to arbitrate. She hated the assembly.

She was barely listening when, suddenly, Elmer said something to make Astrid pause her song and listen.

"I know it was him! Never trust an Orison; that's what my grandpa always said. 'Course, I never took him seriously. Just a bit of banter; that's what I thought of it. Then this. I've seen him eyeing my cows, I have. He's been jealous of Gretel since she won first place at the cheese festival."

"Sorry, what?" Having grown up a jarl's daughter, Astrid found country life absurd. She didn't fear it, like the gentry of Edokand, who believed countryfolk ate each other, married their cousins, and lay with livestock. Nor did she have a problem getting her hands dirty. But it constantly made her question the value humans place on their lives. "You have a festival dedicated to cheese?"

"Well, that's not the only thing we do there," Elmer said defensively. "There's a sheep shearing stage and some dancing. Also, there was a livestock competition, and Gretel was the best bovine, so Bernard stole her."

"How do they judge the cows?" Astrid asked, sitting up for the first time in hours.

"Sorry?"

"How do you know a cow is the best without eating it or tanning its leather?"

"Well." Elmer was getting visibly irate at Astrid but reluctantly indulged her. "There are different ways to judge: the size of the udder in relation to the hock, the size of the chest, the blend of their skin." He sniffled. "Gretel had it all."

"Right." Astrid raised her brow and blinked in quick succession. "What a great use of your time." She turned to Bernard. "Do you have anything to say in your defence?"

"I didn't do it," he said.

Astrid nodded. "Convincing." She went back to strumming her cithara and staring at the ceiling. "Okay, to be honest with you, I don't give a shit about any of this. So, here's what I'm going to do. If Elmer's cow isn't returned by sunset, I will permit him to take any two of your cows he chooses."

Astrid could sense Bernard's exasperation without looking. "But I didn't steal it!"

She shrugged. "Well, bad luck. Now please leave."

Astrid knew she was by far the worst at governing in Doran's stead but was content regardless.

The farmers left, and as the door closed behind them, she lapped up the moment's reprieve. She set the cithara down momentarily and tilted her head to the ceiling. Just as a long, slow breath had depleted the capacity of her lungs, the door swung open again. Astrid's eyes shot open when she realised she had been nodding off.

The two to enter the hall were some of Doran's skalds. The sage, Jiro, wore his purple robes, while Frode, the skald for finance, donned a cloth tunic tied at the neckline. The two had a history of opposing each other. When Jiro pushed to end slavery, Frode was against it. When the sage proposed making unapproved raiding

57

illegal, Astrid's fellow countryman was up in arms. Doran typically fell on Jiro's side in these arguments, and Frode accused the king of going native. However, Astrid could see why those were pretty cut-and-dry issues.

The fact that both men awaited the king's absence before approaching the throne sank Astrid's heart. She rolled her eyes and braced herself.

"My lady, Astrid," said Jiro.

"What is it?" she said curtly.

Jiro was caught off guard by her abruptness. He was a sage, trained in proper Edokand'i etiquette and was a stickler for manners.

Unfortunately for Jiro, Frode was not. The Northman snatched the opportunity to speak in the sage's wake. "While I was reviewing the resources log, I found a surplus in building materials and money that would allow for one of the many construction projects we've discussed in our council meetings. The King has long talked about making Skaldgard a thriving city of abundance, and by finishing these projects, we will be one step closer to achieving that goal."

"Okay," she said. "And I'm guessing you two want the resources to go towards different projects?"

"That's right, princess," said Jiro.

"Don't call me that." Astrid may have been noble born, but she prided herself on nothing she hadn't earned. Being Akkael's wife was not enough to warrant a title. However, she felt bad for snapping at the sage, so she directed her attention towards him. "Jiro, what do you want to spend the money on?"

The sage took a deep breath, regaining his composure. "King Doran and I have always discussed the idea of a crèche. I have been impressed by the Solstic people's proficiency in learning languages and adapting to the culture. Since your empire has colonies in multiple countries, all unique, it is important to teach children how to speak and acclimate to different people from an early age. Also, basic things like arithmetic, agriculture, and art. It's a crucial step in giving the next generation in Skaldgard a better life than the last."

Astrid tried to wrap her head around it. A whole building designed to teach things that may or may not be necessary. Astrid had picked things up as she went about her life. She knew four languages. But that had been because she lived where those languages were spoken. She didn't see much point in studying something without it being immediately applicable. However, that did seem like something on which Doran would waste money.

She turned to Frode. "What about you?" she asked, hoping she didn't have to hear a speech about the monetary value of a state-funded brothel.

"An orphanage." Astrid was pleasantly surprised, letting Frode continue. "You and I have fought together in the shield wall, and we both fought at Takakawa and lost great friends during this war. I can't be the only person who's noticed an increase in street urchins who've lost mothers and fathers to the goutuizi." Frode left a deliberately long pause, turning to Jiro before correcting himself. "Edokand'i."

Astrid stopped him. "Okay, I've heard both of your pitches. Give me a moment to think."

"The longer we wait, the longer these children go without a home," said Frode.

"Yes, thanks, Frode; I know how time works."

"I think it's important to tell you," Jiro interjected, "that Frode intends to put in place a fee for adopting these children and a tax to fund the orphanage."

Astrid shot a glance at Frode. "Really? So, it's less philanthrope, more a child shop?"

"When these children are under the state's care, they are bedded, clothed, and fed from our own treasury," said Frode. "The payment is to mitigate the damage they cause. It's goodwill with a few negligible benefits."

"Goodwill with benefits? It's an orphanage, not a sex partner." Astrid sighed deeply, running her fingers down the strings of her cithara. "Just leave. I'll have an answer for you by morning."

Reluctantly they both bowed and left. The door slammed behind them, and Astrid could soak in the silence again. She returned her focus to her instrument, still trying to remember the bard song from the night before. She had the music roughly in her mind, but the lyrics had escaped her.

Akkael was always better at remembering words to songs. Whenever they drank together, he would stand on their table and belt whatever old Solstic ballad came into his head. Astrid smiled when she recalled when Akkael had fallen off the table, knocking all the drinks onto Magar's lap. He'd left in such a huff.

It was easy to remember those moments and easier still to omit the incessant arguing that would take place when they would return home drunk. They would both say things they didn't mean and were too stubborn to regret it in the morning. Astrid strummed through those thoughts. The fighting happened more often than singing in taverns, but the good memories were like a song she couldn't stop replaying.

The next person to enter the hall was a housecarl named Lindsay. She didn't come from the main entrance like everyone else, instead entering through one of the doors behind Astrid's chair.

"Oh! You startled me," said Astrid, expelled from her reveries of drunken nights and glee.

"I'm sorry, princess." Lindsay bowed just in time to miss Astrid's reactionary scowl. "My lady, I have-"

There was something in the housecarl's face that took Astrid by surprise. Lindsay's lower lip quivered, and her chin creased as if she were suppressing tears. Her bloodshot eyes were like sapphires in a fire. "... I have..."

"Spit it out." Astrid wished her voice sounded stronger.

The housecarl took a deep breath. "Jarl Trygve requests your urgent presence at Takakawa."

Astrid squinted, treading carefully with each word. "Tell Trygve I can't. He knows I'm covering for Doran while he's brokering peace."

"Princess Astrid," said the housecarl, trying to steel herself. She didn't open her mouth again until her eyes met Astrid's, loosely clinging to her courage. "Something happened in Tsul..."

[CHAPTER 11] — DANGER ON THE ROAD

Wisteria petals descended, but the silver grass and clods of mud caught them before they reached the pool forming under Akkael as he bled out on the road. He raised the bottle of sake to his lips and felt it warm him as he shivered towards his death.

A lot had happened since he left the battlefield.

He rode away on a stolen horse through the steady rain and exhaustion. He had died a thousand times throughout the night, and each was unique. The slower ones were bad. He would lay on the ground for minutes that stretched like hours, trying to pull out his intestines while the whirl of battle raged around him, and no one had any idea why they were fighting. In those moments, his main fear was that his killer would die before he did. What would happen then? Those were the questions he had to ask himself. What were the rules to his strange new life?

Luckily, each new life followed smoothly from the last, and he left the field unscathed in his new body for at least a few hours.

The faster deaths, though less painful, were what haunted him most. Sometimes the transfer from life to life happened in such quick succession that he hadn't recovered from the whiplash of the last change before being thrust into the next. Inertia would blur his vision, and vertigo expelled the contents of his stomach. A lot of the time, he would regain his mind forty feet from the last place he remembered dying.

But it wasn't so much the physical turmoil that stayed with him. The sheer number of people he'd replaced, deleted, or moved aside to make room for just a few seconds of extra life. Akkael had washed away whole personalities. Then he'd just discard their empty shell and move on to the next person he'd erase. No one should have that power, least of all him. He had already given up his own life for a small satisfaction. Akkael knew he shouldn't have been entrusted with his life, let alone anyone else's.

"Keep Alani safe. I love you."

That thought got stronger the quicker the deaths came.

The silver grass brushed against his heels as his horse walked on the trodden mud that acted as an excuse for a road. The violet wisteria trees Akkael approached hung low like a curtain, and the wind danced across the puddles in front of him. At the same time, birds he couldn't name flew overhead.

Alani would have known what they were. She loved birds. When she was younger, Akkael would tell her a story before bed, and Alani always tried to direct the narrative. She'd put herself in the story, and eventually, the only role Akkael had was asking her what she wanted to do next.

"Once upon a time, Alani went on an adventure. What did she find?"

"Birds."

"What did she do?"

"Chase them!"

Akkael rode in a direction and that was as specific as he could be. The new mountains were as small as fish teeth behind him, so he saw that as a good sign. But, as for what to do next, he had yet to figure out.

He knew at least part of the blame for what had happened fell to Hideo Kazar, safely tucked away in Wu Wei, and even with his new powers, he couldn't exactly storm the capital and assassinate him. Akkael had been lucky on the battlefield thanks to the chaos, but if he were maimed instead of killed and thrown into a cell to rot, what would happen then? No one is to blame for his death if he dies of dysentery in prison.

He had a power he didn't understand, and until he knew more, he needed to be careful.

Also, Hideo didn't habitually pull mountains out of the sea in an explosion of magma and ash. He may have known what would happen, and that was enough to earn a place on Akkael's list, but someone else was involved. Or something else like the tentacle creature Akkael saw.

Question after question entered his head, and each of them was unanswerable. How was he meant to get revenge on whoever was capable of this? What was he? What was that creature that gave him this strange new life? Akkael realised he was spurring the horse into a gallop and tried to bring it to a steady trot just as faces filled his head. His brother, Doran. Everyone said they looked alike back when Akkael was himself. He remembered Bodil falling through the fissure and blamed himself, just as he blamed himself for all their deaths. Then Alani shot like a bolt through his mind, and he realised he could still feel her hand in his. He saw the magma, the ground cracking, and the land rising.

He heard a rumbling in the distance, and his mind erupted.

Akkael tried to dismount while his horse was still moving, but his foot got caught in the stirrups, and he hit the ground hard, the goutuizi armour breaking most of the fall. He clambered to his feet and collapsed again in front of a puddle. He splashed the rainwater on his face to cool himself down, hoping it would steady his heartbeat.

He froze, bobbing to the ferocity of his breathing. After a time, he screamed at the damp mud and slapped into the puddle. Akkael wasn't sure what was rain and what were tears as water streamed down his face. He crumpled in the grass, flattening the silver blades with his armoured back.

He always expected his life to flash before his eyes before he died. He never thought that, after his death, he would have plenty of time to summon every moment he'd lived in a slow, intricate slog. The previous day played in his mind again. He considered the kills, tasted the blood, and smelled the open guts. However, if he was honest with himself, he had no problem with that.

There was only one thing he would change. He would have refused to make that deal with the tendril creature. At that moment, he accepted his death; he wanted it. Everything he had done told him he deserved it, and every part of him knew it should have happened.

But that wasn't his fate now. He was going to live too long. After accepting death and accepting life with the same nihilistic melancholy, he took the next best thing. He fell asleep, lying on the muddy path.

That, he'd learn, was a mistake.

When he woke, the first thing he saw was his horse standing diligently over him. He admired how obedient the Edokand'i horses were. Akkael must have slept all night, judging by the dawn-coloured sky. The horse waited there for him to wake. It stayed through the rain and the chilly night. It even stood still as three men pilfered the bags on its saddle.

Akkael coughed up blood, remembering the bandits' stunned expressions when they noticed he'd woken up. They probably saw him and thought he was a corpse like all the other goutuizi from where he'd come. Each highwayman had a bird's head embroidered on their rucksacks and coats and carried daggers on their hips.

Akkael wasn't used to wearing armour, and the highwayman got to him before he could draw his katana. Two of them pinned his arms down while the third knelt on his chest.

"What is the meaning of this?" said Akkael, remembering to speak in Edokand'i and talk with an entitlement that came with his status.

"Sorry, sentinel," said the man on his chest. Akkael considered him the leader since he was the only one who spoke. "Usually, we wouldn't think about robbing a man in that armour."

"Damn right," said Akkael. He raised his pitch with his chin, thinking that was how high-ranking sentinels should speak. "Unhand me, and we will forget this transgression."

The leader gave Akkael a look that almost seemed like pity. "These aren't normal times, sentinel. We saw what happened to your friends back there and the mountains, so I know you understand that." The leader sighed deeply before continuing. "You're probably better trained than all of us here, so we're going to have to kill you now you've woken up. I'm sorry about that."

A wave of fear washed over Akkael until he realised that nothing mattered. He wasn't really going to die.

"Here's what's going to happen; I'm going to stab you in the gut right through here," he said, pointing to a gap between Akkael's breastplate and his grieves. "It'll be a long death, but I'm gonna leave you a bottle of sake from my rucksack and this drawing I found in yours."

The bandit unfolded a piece of paper that looked like a child's drawing. There was a castle under a volcano and three disproportionately sized people standing beside it. One was a woman with the Edokand'i word for 'mum' written above her head. There was a man with 'dad' written above his head and, between them was a more petite figure with long hair and a skirt, labelled 'me.'

He placed the drawing beside Akkael. "I'm sorry you'll never see your little girl again."

The goutuizi whose daughter drew it lay dead. Maybe Akkael had been him briefly. Perhaps he was him now. It made no difference. But after the thief spoke, Akkael looked down at the drawing, and his eyes began to water. He felt someone hold his hand tight.

The bandit said something else, but Akkael didn't hear it. He barely even felt the knife go in or the sake bottle placed tight between his thighs, so it didn't blow over. The thieves decided to take the horse since Akkael wouldn't need it anymore. The beast went with them obediently.

Akkael had drunk half the bottle of sake since then. He had dragged himself to a nice spot to die; the trees above cast a cool shade, and the mossy rock acted as a backrest. There were worse ways to die.

The pain was terrible, but he was used to it, or at least he had ways to ignore it. He kept his mind busy, looking at the drawing and thinking about the highwayman who thrust the knife into his belly. The top half of his face was covered by a mask, but Akkael noticed his murderer's defined cheekbones and chiselled jawline. He was handsome as killers go and even had all his hair despite being in his forties. Highwaymen tended not to have the most outstanding quality of life, but if he was going to have to be one, at least this one was good-looking.

Part of him had been excited to be a goutuizi for a while, but that life was over. All that was left to do was drink until he faded away, only to wake up in some cave around a campfire, hopefully with more sake.

He took a large swig, the rice wine burning his wound as it dripped down his armour. He tried hard to recall how many lives there had been for him now. Too many to count. He drank to his curse, the embodiment of retribution and corporal punishment. An immortal hermit-crab.

He slid down the rock slightly to look up at the sky. He assumed death was imminent since he couldn't lift the bottle to his mouth anymore. He let it fall into the grass. Birds sang as they sat in the trees, and the wind rustled the wisteria. He hung on to those sounds as he closed his eyes.

Then he heard a new sound.

It was like a whetstone running along an axe, but deeper. It echoed across the landscape as the wind picked up speed each time the noise repeated. Akkael struggled to reopen his eyes, and a shadow shot across the sky as he did. Giant wings the size of boats beat at the ground, the force snapping branches and crushing grass into the dirt. Its body was like a snake, wriggling unnaturally in flight. Black scales shimmered as it flew overhead, the dawn sun at its left.

Akkael tracked it until his vision started to fade. The last thing he saw before he died was the massive creature, barely as perceptible as the mountains it was approaching.

Akkael stood up, looking at the soup pot boiling over a fire. He took a deep breath from his new lungs.

"You okay, Rui?" said one of the bandits that had pinned Akkael down earlier.

Akkael surveyed the cave he'd woken up in, part of him taking a moment to appreciate that he'd guessed right before he bolted for the opening. At the mouth of the cave, he stared up at the empty blue sky. He looked south and saw nothing but the faint, grey mountains.

He thought he must have hallucinated from the pain. Dragons were like gods; imaginary and fit only for stories. There was no way he had just seen one. He looked to his left and saw his horse tied up outside, visibly uneasy for the first time since Akkael had taken him. His head shook violently with every bray, and its hoof clawed at the stones below him. Akkael turned back to the mountains.

"Rui, what are you doing?" said the second bandit.

Rui, the man Akkael had turned into, hadn't cleaned his knife, blood still smeared on the blade from its last use. He cleaned it properly after he'd dispatched the two other thieves and threw their corpses outside to make himself at home. After further investigating the cave, Akkael found he was right about another thing: Plenty of sake.

[CHAPTER 12] — TAKAKAWA

Takakawa was a coastal city and a significant contributor to Edokand's food stores. Fish from Takakawa filled banquet halls in Wu Wei and Sekando, and the rice paddies outside its walls comprised a substantial portion of the island's reserves.

That was until the war. Even before the Solstic took the city, the blockades in the western sea made it difficult to export anything, and constant fear of imminent invasion caused a significant portion of the workforce to flee. It may have taken years to capture the city, but the damage was done long before Doran set foot in its pagoda.

Ironically, what made the city so important was what made it an easy target. The dock was half a mile wide, and most of the defences faced inland in case the Sekandans laid siege. The streets were narrow, flanked by food stalls and apartments, so it made quite a capable defensive position. But once the Northmen broke through to the centre, the city widened with gardens and ponds, making the battle easier. Since then, Takakawa has been rebuilt, the architecture shifting drastically Solstic. Long halls and longships replaced fishing hauliers and flats.

Over a hundred men and women rowed with Astrid in her longboat, the sail tied down as many sat on oar benches and paddled towards the harbour. They had been rowing long before it was necessary, but that was what Astrid wanted. The ache in her arms, the smell of the sea, and the metronomic yelling that kept everyone in unison; were all distractions.

But eventually, it came to an end, and the longship glided into port. Astrid jumped out first, mooring the ship and helping to remove luggage and supplies. She didn't blink until she realised how dry her eyes were.

"Astrid," called Lindsay, the housecarl who'd told her about what had happened after Wu Wei.

Astrid ignored her.

"Princess, we have to keep going," said Lindsay. "Magar and Skane will be waiting for us at the pagoda."

Again, she was ignored as Astrid kept removing things from the boat.

"Astrid." Lindsay touched her shoulder, and Astrid pounced on her like a wolf. Before Lindsay knew it, her feet were swept from under her, and she was flat on her back. Astrid had her hand on the housecarl's throat, baring her marked teeth as Lindsay's braid brushed the water below the dock.

One of the bags from the ship was knocked into the sea, and the splash woke Astrid from her rage. She immediately got to her feet, and her green eyes moved frantically to each gawking bystander. Lindsay gasped for air to fill her lungs.

Before anyone noticed her eyes filling, Astrid barged through the crowd towards the city's centre. Lindsay kept her distance, but the occasional coughs let Astrid know she was following.

Takakawa was a city of thin cobbled alleys and felt almost unkempt. Winding streets were permeated with the smell of grilled fish and cooked salt wafting from the open stalls. Edokand'i lanterns and stone sculptures stood from before the Solstic invaded and before their religions died. Red bunting crossed from building to building.

Magar had wanted to take down all the traces of the Edokand'i, but Doran and Akkael had disagreed.

"We have more important things to deal with than taking down cool-looking shit," Akkael had said. She always thought her husband had a way with words.

Doran was more concerned about alienating the Edokand'i living in the city. Despite the fighting, graffiti, and assassination attempts, he was determined to make a city for both peoples. Astrid never understood why but kept quiet. Everyone knew Doran had a plan, but no one understood it, not even Akkael.

She guessed she'd never know what his plan was after everything.

Astrid walked past an Edokand'i beggar sitting against a wall marked with the words, 'Row back home.' Astrid assumed whoever wrote it thought they were being clever, but she walked on unamused. The beggar didn't even bother to ask her for money, just staring daggers as she passed.

69

As she left the poorer quarter of the city, the street immediately opened, and the harsh greys and browns became painted tiles and natural vibrance. Astrid tried to take in as much as she could from her walk, consuming the new floral smells and gorgeous architecture instead of thinking about...

The pagoda poked its layered red roofs into the sky, and candlelight pierced through paper windows on all five floors. The red flag of Edokand had been replaced with the white banner. Three black snowflakes were sent vertically down each flag, which was Doran's sigil. He chose it when he took the mantle of King; each snowflake represents the three Torne brothers and signifies their snowy homeland. Doran wanted to embroider more of these emblems when the war was over. He planned to make a flag for every settlement, a sail for every ship to replace the orange of his father's clan, and maybe even have three snowflakes embossed on armour.

Another one of Doran's ideas that would not come to fruition.

She stopped at the gates to the pagoda square, watching them open as Lindsay caught up to her. Standing six feet apart, they waited silently, the metal grinding arcs in the cobblestone. Eventually, Astrid spoke softly, barely loud enough to hear.

"I'm sorry." She didn't look at Lindsay.

"I know." Lindsay didn't look either.

When the gates had opened enough, Astrid squeezed through, Lindsay keeping her tail. The garden was kept beautifully. Bonsai trees floated on small barges in the ponds, breaking paths in the pink blossom that disturbed their surfaces. The ground floor of the pagoda was made of sliding wooden doors all the way around, with paper windows and porches splitting off like the harbour. Benches, pillows, and blanket tables were dotted about for decadence. She could still picture Edokand'i lords painting and writing poetry in the sun.

Astrid approached one of the doors and slid it open. Housecarls and servants, who were clearly not expecting her to barge in, quickly jumped to attention.

"Princess Astrid." Astrid sighed deeply as the servant bowed. He continued. "We are honoured to welcome you to Takakawa."

"King Skane is waiting for you in the war room," said another servant who looked almost identical to the first.

"Would you like a chicken leg?" Astrid squinted as a third servant held a plate in front of her.

"Where is Magar?" asked Astrid.

"King Magar is... in town." Astrid inferred what that meant, and, taking the plate of chicken legs, she stepped out of the foyer, shoes still on, and left for the war room.

Skane was hunched over a map of Edokand and a pile of reports from all over the Solstic territories in Tsul. When Astrid walked in, he looked up, and she could almost see the pulse beating in his neck. She took another bite of chicken and waited for him to speak.

Skane sighed and gestured to the map. "We have cartographers all along the border, trying to draw how the land has been sutured together. Where the mountains start. What the coasts look like. Of course, our research is useless without Sekando and Trim." He sighed again. "We found Akkael's body. In case you want to plan for a funeral."

Astrid's mind immediately started preparing. He'd want to be buried in a barrow, like his father. But sending him to Solstr just to be put in some hole in the ground seemed a waste of time. Maybe he could be the first in a royal cairn in Skaldgard. She thought about congregation number, confectionery, and decor. It was all so clinical in her mind, like something to keep her hands busy.

She started to get appalled by her eagerness and began eating again. "What's the next step?"

"We're working on something," said Skane. "But we don't have anything concrete. Now you're here, we can start setting things in stone. We didn't want to decide anything without you."

Astrid nodded, looking around the room. She saw a painting she didn't recognise and wondered if it was new. Then she turned back to Skane. "So, what do I call you? Does this make you King now?"

"Come on," Skane smiled, "I care less than you do about all of Doran's pomp and titles. Magar is King; that's all anyone needs."

"That's not what I need," said Astrid.

Skane looked up. "Astrid, if you-"

"I'm fine," she snapped. She realised her plate was finished, a dozen bones crossing over each other like vines. "Are we done?"

Before waiting for an answer, she made her way to a staircase on the other side of the room. The war room was connected to the kitchen so generals could have serfs bring snacks while they plotted wars. The Solstic didn't invade Edokand for their lack of great ideas.

"Astrid!" Skane yelled, following her to the kitchen.

When Astrid and Skane entered, the staff were already boiling soapy water to clean up after lunch. "Astrid, look, you're not taking this as well as you're trying to show. Just talk to me."

"I'm fine," said Astrid. She poured the chicken bones into a bucket ready to be taken to the kennels and pushed aside the kitchen staff so she could wash the plate.

"Astrid, you're not," said Skane.

"Well, I'm coping," she barked. After cleaning her plate, she moved to another from a pile to her left.

"Astrid, look."

"Say my name one more time!" Skane and the staff recoiled as the plate she held flew across the kitchen. She froze after her outburst and took a breath like the stammering wind.

"What do you want from me, Skane?" she said, eyes red as she spat his name back at him. "You want me to talk about how I'll never hug my daughter again? Do you want me to say that I'm so angry at my husband for taking her to that fucking place that part of me, a significant part of me, is glad that he's dead? Do you want me to discuss my guilt, my rage? Do you want me to cry? Is that it, Skane?

"Well, I don't give a shit what you want, okay?" she continued. "All I want to do is not have a brain to think with. I don't want to talk about it; I just want to do anything else. Yes, that's unhealthy, and it's probably better to talk about it, but I don't care."

She started tasting salt water and quickly returned to the washing bowl. "Everyone, get out!"

There was a stunned silence until Skane finally spoke. "Come on. Everyone out."

Astrid waited until the door closed and the kitchen was empty before she wept. However, she didn't give herself long before she took another plate from the dirty pile and cleaned it. She thought about the dishes, the shards of porcelain scattered across the floor, and the bones that needed to be taken to the kennels.

And nothing else.

[CHAPTER 13] — LAID PLANS

Papers were strewn across the war table. Sketches from cartographers, accounts of conflicts across Tsul, reports of casualties from both sides, letters from Solstic thanes demanding war, and unsolicited guesses about what happened to Koji's army. Skane rubbed his forehead as he stared, alone and in silence, at the pages too many to count.

When the Solstic discovered new lands, there was a sense that the world had changed. The voyagers would return home, and the country would erupt in celebration and stunned pride. No matter how many lands were discovered, that feeling never changed. Divinity may not exist, but the shape of the world was something sacred. The more accurately a map could be drawn, the closer they were to perfect knowledge.

Part of that belief came from the idea that the world was static. They could move across it and learn as much as they could, with the fundamental truth that, in a thousand years, those maps would still be important.

Two islands collided, and mountains rose from the sea. The world changed, but there was no celebration.

Skane waited for Astrid, Magar, and Jarl Trygve to join him in the war room to decide their fate. Skane had arrived an hour early, sitting quietly, overwhelmed in the calm before the storm.

Astrid was the first to join him, who looked almost disappointed that Skane had beaten her there. In the days since she had arrived at Takakawa, she had spent every waking hour, which was practically all of them, working. She would clean, build, or moor ships as vassals arrived in the city, anticipating battle. If there were no chores to do, she would be training, throwing axes, and beating dummies until straw littered the ground and she couldn't stand. Those were the only moments where she'd opt to rest.

She didn't greet Skane. She just sat and began perusing through the documents he'd kept in a messy pile on the table.

Next to arrive was Jarl Trygve. He was a skinny man with a forked beard who never went anywhere without the two knives strapped to his belt.

"Who died?" he said as soon as he walked in, smiling through a thick accent. His eyes were always strained wide and were so blue they looked white. "Ha!" He bellowed when neither Skane nor Astrid responded to him. Then he perched on the chair opposite Skane, knees up to his chin.

Skane couldn't understand why Doran had appointed Trygve as Jarl of Takakawa. He was the antithesis of the calm that Doran had, for the most part, surrounded himself. His sharp smile stayed on his face as he looked excitedly at the sheets Astrid was still working through, hoping they all suggested war.

Skane waited in silence for another ten minutes. Astrid was preoccupied, reading a list of notable names that lay dead in the goutuizi army. After trying to start a conversation half a dozen times, Trygve remained quiet, too, twirling one of his knives against the tabletop.

Eventually, Skane sighed. "I think we should start without King Magar, and we can fill him in when he arrives."

Trygve saluted with his blade, and Skane continued.

"So, I wanted to start with the influx of refugees from our settlements in Tsul." Skane organised some of the papers before him and began to read. "The survivors of whatever happened to the goutuizi have banded as a marauder force, burning farmsteads like Bansthorpe and Hildby.

"In retaliation, the displaced Solstic have burned major temples and towns on their way here. We're not sure who's worse off from these attacks, but both sides have made one thing painfully clear; war is inevitable."

"Woo!" Trygve placed his knife between his teeth and clapped loudly. Astrid didn't look at him, instead keeping her eyes locked on Skane.

"Edokand killed our King," she spat. "War has been inevitable for days, and you're a fool if you thought otherwise."

"I didn't think otherwise," said Skane, looking down at the tabletop. "I just hoped-"

Magar burst through the war room door, blood from his nose dripping onto the floorboards. Everyone turned to look at their new king's bruised and beaten face as he limped to an empty seat around the table.

Skane fluctuated from fear to embarrassment and eventually landed on rage. "You were late to our meeting, so you could brawl in some tavern?"

He knew what Magar was doing. Of course, he knew. Magar fought when he was sad. He fought when frustrated, bored, or needed time to think. He even fought when he was happy. But this was different. He spent most of his time in the ring, brawling with the most brutal men and women. He never lost, but even victory could be lethal. Skane couldn't look at him for too long without holding back tears.

"When are we executing the monk?" asked Magar, ignoring Skane.

"What?"

"I can schedule it for this afternoon," suggested Jarl Trygve, shrugging.

"Can I organise it?" asked Astrid. "So many of our people will want to witness it."

"No," Skane said, a bit too loudly. "Since when did this become about killing Rigpa?"

"It was always about that," spat Magar.

"No, it wasn't." Skane sighed, pinching the bridge of his nose for a moment before continuing. "This is about retribution for Akkael and Doran. The sage has shown she's willing to work with us, and we would have been killed by those shadow archers without her. Rigpa is coming with me to Skaldgard while I raise the rest of our army."

The room went quiet. Skane almost moved on, shuffling through documents for the next meeting point.

"No," Magar said before Skane could continue. "She dies."

Skane slowly stood away from his chair as Magar began to square up to him. "No, she doesn't."

"Okay, then, let's duel for it. The winner gets his way." Skane noticed Magar's fists were clenched. When he didn't respond, Magar was unrelenting. "Come on, you've always wondered who would win if we fought."

Skane paused. "No, my love, I can't say I have."

The two men stood an inch from each other as their dispute consumed the room, neither backing down. Eventually, Magar's eyes widened as if suddenly realising what he was doing. He backed away. Skane tried to force himself to calm down but knew it wouldn't work. He turned back to the table, heart racing.

"So," said Astrid, her voice making Skane jump slightly, "if you and the sage are going to Skaldgard, what are the rest of us doing?"

Skane couldn't sit down; he just stared at his shaking hand, using every strength he had to speak. "The goutuizi and the Sekandans fought side by side, which has never happened before in this war." His voice sounded higher, wavering slightly. "Wu Wei must have offered them something they couldn't refuse, or we must have pushed them somehow. You will go to Sekando and see if we can't make a similar deal."

"We're just going to allow Sekando to live as well?" bellowed Magar. "Why don't we just turn back to Solstr with our tails tucked in our arses?"

Skane didn't look at him as he answered. "We need a large force to take Wu Wei, and Sekando has just as much reason to turn their swords towards Trim as they do towards us." Skane looked at Astrid, keeping interactions with Magar to a minimum. "Since men can't enter Sekando city, Astrid must go. You will be protected by Magar, Trygve and every warrior we have in Takakawa and the surrounding areas. They will wait for you outside the city."

Skane felt his heartbeat in his ears, and tears were welling in his eyes. He looked down at the tabletop to hide his face. "You will meet me at Sui Bay on the next full moon. Hopefully, Astrid would have made a deal with Queen Kya by that time, and we would have a large enough army to take Wu Wei. Any questions?"

"A lot of your plan relies on ifs and buts," said Astrid. Skane had hoped the meeting would be over, and Astrid's statement brought a scowl to his lips. "What happens if I can't make a deal with Kya? What if she kills me and wipes out Magar and Trygve's siege?"

"You're right; it's not a great plan." His neck snapped towards Astrid more violently than he'd expected. "Got a better one?"

A tear hit the papers below him like a gong. It was the only one that had left his eyes, but the wet spot on the parchment drew everyone's gaze as it stretched across the page. The room stared at Skane in silence as he tried to look stoic.

"Didn't think so," said Skane when no one answered. "I'll set off in a few days; I suggest the rest of you do the same." He said no more, instead barging past Magar and leaving.

He calmed down the moment he left the room, his hand barely shaking when he got to his chambers. For as long as they've been together, his husband has never threatened him. Magar had always been a brute but with calmness and self-awareness. Skane worried he'd never get the Magar he knew back again.

He tried to push that away. When he thought about Magar, insurmountable hopelessness deflated him and drove him closer to a resigned despair. Instead, Skane focused on the one thing he had some control over: the unavoidable war. He lay on his bed thinking about Skaldgard, Sekando, and what to do after. He thought about bloodshed and death until he drifted off to sleep.

[CHAPTER 14] — THE CAVE

Akkael was sitting on the floor of a dank cave with a bottle in his fist. He was drunk.

He had spent the last four days drinking in the bandit's cave. However, between the last two bottles, he decided to leave in the morning. Not because he wanted to or had any concrete idea of what to do next, but because he ran out of the bandit's food and, most importantly, sake.

Spending every day inebriated, picking millipedes off his clothes that had crawled from the cracks in the seeping stone walls had slowed the planning progress. Yet one thought repeated in his head. It was less a strategy, more a simple truth.

He was a lost cause on his own.

Even though no one could kill him, there was no evidence that he couldn't die. What if he was injured or captured and left to starve? He couldn't take over the body of thirst or disease. Akkael knew he had lucked out on the battlefield. But going to Wu Wei alone would be too risky.

Also, Akkael didn't know if what he'd become was common in Edokand. He suspected it wasn't since none of the books Akkael had read mentioned shifting from body to body, except in the context of the Grand Sage's reincarnations. But still, in a country of disappearing archers and wizards, it wouldn't be a surprise. In any event, the longer he took, the more time people would have to determine what he could do.

So, he'd need an army before he even set foot in Trim. To do that, he'd need the person in charge of a large force to kill him. Akkael was getting good at being killed. The only question was, 'Who?' Tsul had three large armies occupying it.

First, his own people, but to get control of the Solstic, he'd have to take over his brother, practically killing him. Not ideal. Also, his kin was probably already on their way to Wu Wei, making it redundant. Better to point another force at the capital to have more of a shot at the revenge he craved.

The second army was what remained of the goutuizi that fled outside the forest. However, they remained loyal to their country. Even if Akkael became their general, they'd execute him for treason as soon as the words "march on Wu Wei" left his new Edokand'i lips. Also, he had no idea what their general even looked like. With Koji Kazar already dead, Akkael was clueless about who would succeed him.

That left the Sekandans. It was still a shock to see the women of Sekando fighting alongside the goutuizi. There were a few battles here and there towards the beginning of the war, but, for the most part, Sekando had no problem with the Solstic. So long as Doran didn't stray into their borders, they had an amicable relationship. Akkael couldn't work out what had antagonised Queen Kya.

The Sekandans were quite different to the rest of Edokand. They viewed themselves as wholly autonomous and saw Wu Wei as the symbol of an oppressive foreign power. No one would blink twice if Kya Kazar raised a force against the Emperor.

Kazar Kya, Akkael corrected himself, remembering that, in Sekando, the family name came first. That was the main issue. All the research Akkael did about Edokand'i culture was about Edokand, not Sekando. They had unique traditions and customs, and if he were going to move into Queen Kya's body, it would be a finite number of blunders before people realised something was wrong.

But Sekando was the only way to make this work. Getting to the Queen wouldn't be too hard either. One Sekandan tradition Akkael had learned about was that men were forbidden in their city. Boys are expelled from Sekando City at sixteen. If a man enters the city illegally, it's a crime punishable by death.

Even Hideo was sent to Wu Wei at sixteen after his exile from the city. Akkael spat through a scowl at the mere thought of his name.

The last bottle was coming to dregs. Akkael thought hard enough about plans and revenge, so he decided it was time to enjoy his last night as he sat on the cave's rocky floor. A stagecoach's trunk acted as a table, on which he'd already played five games of chess against himself on a beautifully carved, probably stolen, board while serenading his horse with every song in his roster.

After the last verse of *'The Homesick Voyager,'* Akkael realised he'd never named his horse. He'd started using possessive pronouns when referring to him, so it's only fair he gave him a name.

"What shall we name her?" asked Astrid, looking down at the bald head of the most beautiful thing Akkael had ever seen.

"I thought you were in charge of the name if it was a girl?" said Akkael.

"I know, but none of my ideas seems good enough." The baby stirred in Astrid's arms, and Akkael watched her smile. "You've always been better at this sort of thing."

His wife looked up with the same green eyes as his new-born daughter. "Okay." He thought for a second about the names of influential women in his life. Akkael was his uncle's namesake; continuing the tradition with his daughter made sense.

"How about –"

As the memory faded, Akkael inhaled so sharply that he startled the nameless horse. When he regained control, he noticed the sake puddling against his thigh from where the bottle had smashed against the stone ground. A tear dropped off his chin before he saw it was even there.

Akkael lay down on the cave floor. He tried to distract himself, running through his plan again, or the sorry excuse of one he had concocted, while ignoring the faint stinging in his left hand.

He clenched it tightly as he fell asleep.

[CHAPTER 15] — LAID TO REST

Akkael's corpse looked almost grand. However, after an hour, Skane started to see the putrid signs the servants tried to hide. Akkael died over a week ago, a light veil covering his green-tinted, ash-ridden face. His fingernails, hidden by gloves, had turned black and begun to peel. A stench lingered around the coffin, so someone had fetched roses and other plants with a natural fragrance to hide it.

Skane looked from Astrid's expressionless face to Magar, who was bruised and cut from bar fights. It was hard for Skane to see him like that. His appearance was a portrait of his sadness and pain. But what scared Skane most was Astrid. Her eyes looked down at the man she had married without a single emotion in them. Skane couldn't remember if he'd even seen her blink.

"I've arranged for his funeral after we return," said Astrid, monotone. "Unless you want to finish it quickly before we set off for Sekando."

"Up to you," said Skane.

Astrid nodded slowly, still not taking her eyes off Akkael's corpse. "After, then."

A few more silent moments went by before Magar turned away from his brother's body and went to leave.

"Where are you going?" asked Skane, standing in his way.

With Magar's lazy drawl, Skane couldn't determine whether he said, "Got *a* fight" or "Got *to* fight." He hoped it was the first one; something about the latter made Skane's stomach sink.

"Shouldn't you stay?" He tried not to sound desperate. "The cartographers brought some more maps and drawings of the mountains. Plus, you've got to prepare for Sekando."

"I'll do it when I get back."

Skane knew Magar was lying even if he didn't realise it himself. Regardless he let Magar leave.

He stood with Astrid in silence for another ten minutes, unable to imagine her feelings. Skane and Magar usually fought side by side, but on the rare occasions they didn't, Skane would be stricken with fear. It was a concern in anticipation of the sorrow Astrid felt. The shield maiden tried to look sturdy, but, as with Akkael's corpse, Skane was starting to recognise what was under the surface.

"Does the sage know what's been decided?" asked Astrid, still not meeting Skane's eye.

"I was going to tell her after this," he said.

Astrid sucked her scarred teeth. "Best not delay. We'll need the army as soon as possible, so you must leave before we do."

There was so much Skane wanted to say. However, when he tried to speak, he couldn't. He saw the signs of someone straining against breaking. She was like a bowstring over-taut, jaw tensed, and lips thinned.

Skane just nodded and left Astrid alone with her husband's body. It was strange, but on the way out, a memory came to Skane like a leaf blowing into view. Astrid had mispronounced a word in her wedding vows, and she swore through happy tears and made everyone laugh. Skane didn't know why that memory suddenly appeared, but it brought a small smile to his face.

Takakawa's dungeons were a short walk outside the gates of the pagoda and were kept well. The cells were much more spacious than those in Solstr, with thick spruce wood for bars. Only one cell was occupied, and the occupant wasn't suited for gaol.

Rigpa sat with her legs folded and her eyes closed. Her purple robes, still covered in soot, now mingled with the dirt and grease, and her grey hair hung in clumps over her face.

When Skane approached, Rigpa's eyes flung open as if she knew he was coming.

"Hello," Skane said, transitioning to Edokand'i.

"I understand, Solstic," Rigpa said reassuringly.

"Oh, right. How are you doing?" Skane asked.

Rigpa smiled in a way that seemed impossible for her situation. "I've slept in better places. When are we going to Utajima?"

Skane's eyebrows raised. "You know already?"

"The guards have been taunting me." Her smile faded. "I'm to be executed in front of ten thousand Northmen, apparently."

Skane shook his head. "You're not going to be executed. You'll be with me the entire time."

Rigpa looked surprised more than relieved. "And your husband? What does he think about that?"

"I know him enough to know he'll kill you the first excuse you give him," said Skane. "He'll be nowhere near you."

"I understand," Rigpa said, nodding before she looked to her left. Skane couldn't see, but he knew Rigpa was facing the pagoda, using her gifts to sense everything happening there. "I've never been in a place with so much pain."

Something got caught in Skane's throat. "Can you really feel that? The pain?"

"I can," answered Rigpa.

"Must be a curse," Skane said.

Rigpa shook her head. "I don't really see it like that. It's much easier to help people if I know how they feel."

Skane snickered to himself, sitting down against the wall. "I can't seem to help people even when I know."

"You don't know what your problem is; that's your problem," stated Rigpa.

"I know exactly what my problem is," said Skane.

"You do?" She raised her eyebrows as if she were amused by Skane's indignation. "What is your problem then?"

"My problem is I've heard the word problem so much it doesn't sound like a word anymore."

Rigpa laughed. "Your issue then."

Skane smiled before sitting in silence as he thought. "I feel guilty."

"Why?" asked Rigpa.

Skane just shrugged. "Magar lost his brothers; Astrid lost her husband and her daughter. I had great affection for the people who died, but I didn't lose anyone I couldn't live without."

"So, survivor's guilt." Rigpa shook her head. "That's not it."

"What are you talking about?" Skane had more venom in his words than intended. But Rigpa didn't seem phased.

"You feel guilty because you think you don't deserve to mourn as much as everyone else," the sage told him. "How do you hope to help those around you if you need help?"

"I don't need help," Skane interjected too quickly.

Rigpa stared at Skane for a moment before speaking. "When was the last time you heard Magar say exactly that?"

The lump in Skane's throat had returned, and he started to notice the tears blurring his vision. He took a deep breath. "Magic in this country really is pointless. I was expecting fireballs, not a lengthy discussion about my feelings."

"It's not magic," corrected Rigpa. "It's just a way of communicating with the world."

"How do you even learn this magic anyway?" Skane continued.

"I was born with it," said the Grand Sage.

"Are all sages?" asked Skane.

"No," she answered, shaking her head. "Anyone can unlock these gifts within themselves once they rise closer to divinity."

Skane scoffed so hard he snorted. "Divinity? Everyone from the decrepit to the juvenile knows there is no such thing. Gods don't exist."

Rigpa rolled her eyes. "I'm not talking about gods. Whatever you want to call it, then. Anyone can climb within themselves and reach the Seraphim's power."

He wanted to mock the sage again, but something about what she said caught Skane's interest. "And how does one do that?"

Skane shuffled closer to the bars to hear the sage's words. "To master the Seraphim's gifts, you must rid yourself of the turmoil within yourself." She paused for a second, thinking about how to continue. "Have you heard of the chakras?"

"No," said Skane. Rigpa gave him a look that told Skane he'd just added a tonne of work to her explanation.

"Chakras are sources of energy within our bodies that can be blocked by the external experiences of our world," said Rigpa. "They deal with different aspects of humanity, but once all seven are open, the Seraphim's energy can channel through our bodies, and we can access a sliver of his power."

"So, how come you get the easy route?"

"Through a process called reincarnation." Rigpa paused as Skane broke the word down in his head. "The Seraphim's last act in this world was gifting his spirit to humanity. My soul is intertwined with his. When I die, my spirit will fade away. Yet his will carry on, passing from person to person for eternity."

"Sounds like more nonsense about gods and religion." Skane folded his arms as he spoke.

"The Seraphim wasn't a god," said Rigpa. "He was a man like you and me."

"Then how did he get these powers he's so freely handing out?" asked Skane.

Rigpa thought for a moment before lifting her shoulders. "That's not for me to know. But, if it wasn't him, how do you explain what I can do?"

Skane thought about that, imagining an eternal life jumping from body to body. This Seraphim, this pseudo-god, gives his power repeatedly to help humanity. Something was strange about that to him, and it took him a few seconds to realise why.

"But, why here?"

"What do you mean?" asked Rigpa.

"Well, humanity is all over the world," said Skane. "The Seraphim has never reincarnated in Solstr. Or Urkanza. Only here. Why?"

Rigpa squinted, eyes rolling up in thought before she began shaking her head. "I don't have that answer, either."

After a moment of silence, Skane moved the conversation along. "So, these chakras. How do I open them?"

"You can't," Rigpa said, with a look that almost seemed like pity.

"Why?" asked Skane.

Rigpa shrugged. "You only want to open the chakras for the power they offer. You'll never gain the Seraphim's gifts if you go into it with the wrong motives."

Skane also shrugged. "No harm in trying."

The sage stared blankly at him for a moment but, after a while, broke a smile. "Okay. Sit like me."

Skane folded his legs and straightened his back to imitate the imprisoned sage. Rigpa closed her eyes, and Skane did the same.

"You must open each Chakra individually," she continued. "Each one is located at a different point in your body. The root chakra is first and is at the base of the spine. This one deals with self-preservation, stability, and strength. The enemy of all three comes in the form of fear. The first chakra will open once you face your fears and learn to overcome them."

Skane opened his eyes. "Is that it?"

"It's harder than it sounds," said Rigpa. "Think about it. Think about what truly scares you. Then we'll talk about this again."

Skane rolled his eyes and stood up. "Well, this has been enlightening," he said sarcastically. "We'll be leaving for Skaldgard in a few days." He went to turn around but stopped and looked sternly at Rigpa. "Make sure you don't call it Utajima around anyone else. My people won't take kindly to that."

"Force of habit." Rigpa smiled and nodded. "Take care, friend."

Skane didn't know how to respond, so he just gave a thin-lipped smile before leaving the dungeon.

On the way back to the pagoda, he let a childish rendition of himself with sage powers play out in his mind. He could feel the world under his feet, sense the life around him, and help people in pain. He wondered how good it would feel to look at Magar and know precisely how to fix him. He could protect his loved ones like Rigpa had protected them against the shadow archers. He could do his bit and finally feel helpful.

That fantasy faded as soon as he walked past the room where Akkael's corpse had been. Astrid was still there. He couldn't see her, but the linen tablecloth Akkael was lying on was pulled taut by the source of quiet weeping. He stood in the doorway, listening to Astrid's muted pleas and sharp breathing.

Skane knew at that moment that no magic in the world would help. He thought about going in, comforting her. But eventually, he moved out of the doorframe, bowed his head, and continued to his chambers.

[CHAPTER 16] — SERADOK AND HIDEO

The Wu Wei policy was a natural progression for an island empire. Since the capital faced south, it was much easier to communicate with the southern islands than it was with Tsul and Utajima. Inaction meant the northern territories had to be self-reliant. Border disputes between Sekando and the other Tsul territories were handled without Wu Wei's input. As were trade agreements, fishing policies, and, consequently, the Northman invasion.

That communication problem was made worse by the mountains. Trim was more isolated from the north than it had ever been. Hideo spent the best part of two weeks sitting around the palace in his red kimono, waiting for a glimpse of good news from his son. His white hair was down, covering his eyes, and he hadn't moved from his sofa for hours. He hadn't even bothered to strap on his iron hand since he only needed one to raise the sake to his lips.

Hideo imagined the siege that must be taking place at Takakawa. He thought about the other Torne brothers, if not dead now, then soon, as they huddled behind Takakawa's walls with their spouses. That image filled Hideo with relief. But even that was bittersweet.

He finished the rest of his fourth cup of sake and rang a bell. The large double doors to his chambers opened, and a petite girl answered his call, stopping in front of Hideo with a timid stance.

"Another glass," said Hideo.

"Yes, sir." She almost turned but stopped midway, and Hideo watched her try to summon confidence enough to speak.

"Yes, girl?" said Hideo, making her jump.

She took a second to calm herself before she spoke. "Sir, the kitchen staff were wondering what to do about the Emperor's lunch."

Usually, Hideo's steward, Ponzu, would be an intermediary between him and the help. However, since Hideo was acting as Emperor in place of His Majesty, he had many more instances in which Ponzu had to assist. Hideo was irritated by his

89

grating voice and cocky demeanour, so he sent Ponzu as an envoy to Chuton, a garrison town near the capital. That way, he didn't have to look at him.

However, this created other problems. Over the last few days, that question and others much like it had come out of almost every serf's mouth. The kitchen staff ask when they should give his highness meals, and the cleaning staff ask to clean his rooms. Hideo had stationed sentinels outside the Emperor's chambers to make sure none of that happened.

"The sentinels know what to do," said Hideo, swigging the dregs of his sake and rubbing his forehead. "Leave the food with Ieyasu."

The girl delayed. But eventually, she did what all the servants who asked these questions had. She resigned, bowed, and walked to the door.

She knocked, and the guards on the other side opened the door. The girl stopped in the frame as four sentinels passed, causing her breathing to waver slightly. She waited a few seconds for them to pass before she left, the double doors closing behind her.

The palace had become akin to a kingdom under occupation. Soldiers patrolled the halls and performed searches on diplomats and politicians that Hideo feared were harbouring loyalist ideals. The elite would either comply or be thrown in Wu Wei's - Jin Bu's - already brimming dungeons.

Those were the most common occurrences, but there was a third option. On five occasions, the sentinels performed impromptu searches on some lord's quarters, walking in to see an already cold body, a short sword protruding from their gut.

Seppuku could be used politically to tarnish a new leader's position. It's an extreme, final act of protest, but it could be effective. Which is why Hideo had done his best to conceal their deaths. Rumours about the political suicides had spread, but no one had concrete evidence.

None of it mattered to Hideo, anyway. He knew that he'd accept any judgment the Emperor would give him when the war was over. But he would not risk anything getting in his way until the Northmen were driven out of Edokand.

For some reason, his thoughts turned to home. He didn't know whether it was the sentinels reminding him of the women that patrolled Sekando's streets or thinking of his sister, Queen Kya, fighting alongside his son. Or maybe it was just fear and overwhelming pressure making him yearn for a home he hadn't been welcome to since he turned sixteen. Whatever it was, images of Sekando, the academy, the great fountain, and the bazaar flashed in his mind. He smiled.

The servant returned with his sake, giving him a whole bottle. She left without saying a word, nearly forgetting to bow in haste.

Hideo struggled to pour the sake with one hand, so he just drank from the bottle. He downed a quarter of it in one gulp before wiping the bitter taste from his lips.

"Well, aren't you a sight?" The voice sent a shiver down Hideo's spine. He turned to see the green, pulsing abyss, undulating tendrils and countless eyes hanging in the incorporeal mist.

"Seradok?" said Hideo, trying to keep his voice steady as he looked at the living nightmare.

"I'm disappointed in you, Hideo," said Seradok, leering in the corner. "I gave you a gift. The likes of which the world has never seen. And you've barely used it. Why?"

Opening his mouth was as strenuous as lifting an anchor. "I was waiting for news from the North."

"Why?" repeated Seradok. "You could wipe out the Solstic with what I've given you."

"I want to do it the right way." Hideo found it hard to believe his words were anything more than empty platitudes.

"The right way? How Edokand'i," Seradok snickered. "But engulfing a campsite in magma doesn't seem right."

"That was different." Hideo tried to sound convincing. "We need to finish this properly. If a sentinel army defeats the Northmen, history will remember our strength. It's a better story than an act of -" Hideo stopped himself, and Seradok's eyes widened.

"You can say it," it said. "Go on, I like when people say it."

Hideo didn't speak. Eventually, Seradok changed the subject, dismissively waving a tendril.

"So, if, hypothetically, things didn't go to plan in Tsul, what then?" A hint of amusement in Seradok's tone sunk Hideo's stomach. "Would you abandon your 'better story' in the name of revenge?"

"Things will go as planned," was all Hideo could say.

Seradok paused before speaking. "Where is my gift?"

Hideo delayed but eventually gestured to a triple-locked chest against the wall. "In there."

"When I came to you, you were helpless," said Seradok after a deep and disappointed sigh. "Your Emperor would have sold your land to a pack of foreign barbarians. I came to you as the tip of your short sword drew a dot of blood from your belly, do you remember? All those other victims of seppuku that have arisen since your coup, I didn't bother with. You were special. You showed promise. And what have you done with it? Made a nice little hiking spot, and barely a dent."

"That's not all I did," said Hideo a little too quickly.

"Oh, I know," said Seradok. "Twelve guards outside the Emperor's door gave that away. I doubt you'll even get the chance to use my gift again. You know, before you get assassinated."

"I will use it, if necessary," said Hideo, steeling himself. "But communication has been hindered by the mountains going up, and I can no longer send reinforcements as fast as I would like."

"You know as well as I do you can make communication faster," said Seradok. "You know what I think? I think you don't want to use it again. I think you're scared, and that fear is making you ungrateful."

"I'm not scared," spat Hideo.

"Oh, of course not." Seradok floated in a circle around Hideo, who was trying not to show any emotion. "You're Lord Hideo Kazar, the Second Pillar of the Edokand'i triumvirate. Brother to the Queen, and exile of, Sekando."

"I wasn't exiled." Hideo's voice cracked.

"What would you call it then?" said the monster, darting into Hideo's eye line. "You can't go back. You'll be executed if you go back. What is that if not exile?"

Hideo had nothing to say, and Seradok continued trying to get a rise from him.

"Excluded? Expelled?" It moved closer to Hideo. "I like the 'X' sound. It sounds like breaking bones."

Suddenly the beast shot back to where it had appeared. It let the silence sit for a moment as Hideo tried to remain stoic. "Do you have what it takes to do what is necessary even if it's not the 'right way'?"

Hideo actually thought about the answer. After the chaos he'd already caused, could he do it again, or something worse, for his country? Was he prepared to defend to the hilt the only home he'd ever been truly accepted? What would he do to hold on to the security he had spent his adolescence being denied? He thought of Sekando and knew the answer to Seradok's question.

"Yes."

"That's all I wanted to hear," said Seradok, relieved. "I'll be back in six days."

Hideo squinted. "What will happen in-"

In a burst of repulsive light, Seradok vanished. Hideo recoiled, and the room returned to the dimness of candlelight. Hideo stared at the shadow where Seradok had been before turning back to the table. He sat down, clasped the sake bottle in his hand, and tried to ignore the doubt he'd let settle in his mind.

[CHAPTER 17] — SEKANDO

Akkael spent the night at a shanty border town outside Sekando City. Tents and caravans expanded across the dunes, occupied by men from around the world. Akkael's brother, Doran, had always desired to create a place where diverse people and cultures existed together. He probably imagined stone buildings instead of fabric propped by sticks. Still, these small campsites proved his brother's dream wasn't too far-fetched with the right motivation.

Dark-skinned Urkanzan sell-swords mingled with olive-toned Rhaynese merchants and drank with native Edokand'i men, all with the same drive. To spend the night with the women behind Sekando's walls.

It was a lucrative venture. Since no men over sixteen could enter the city, the women often made their way to the shanty towns for a fun night before returning home behind the walls. Sekandans rarely took husbands, and marriages were held and spent exclusively in the region's rural areas. City women were typically polyamorous.

This town was the most extensive of its type. A large, heart-shaped pond sat in the centre of a tight group of caravans. Some of these wagons opened at the side. They acted as kiosks, selling alcohol, trinkets from foreign countries, or even effects left behind by the city's women, like garnets, weaponry, or clothing.

Akkael found it appalling that these men would spend days of their finite lives obsessing over these women due to their elusive culture. But part of him knew it was inevitable. People were their basest when it came to war and lust.

Akkael took as much as he could carry from the bandit cave. The coat with the vulture's head embroidered on the sleeve was wrapped around his waist, keeping a stolen katana tight against his thigh. He pilfered enough coin to keep his horse at the stable, a night at the large pavilion that acted as an inn, and a hot meal before venturing into the city.

"You want more bread for your stew, sir?" Akkael didn't know why, but the vulture sigil on his jacket incited fearful deference in those he met in the shanty town. The bandit he had taken over had a reputation he didn't understand but was fully prepared to take advantage.

"I think I'll have two more rolls and keep the soju coming," he said, shaking his small cup.

"On the house, sir." When the server left, Akkael felt the weight of his wallet and smiled. Even though he probably wouldn't have the chance to spend it, it was still a good feeling not having to.

When he left the pavilion, Akkael's view was immediately dominated by the walls of Sekando City. The tight pattern of sandstone bricks was striking from half a mile away and concealed the metropolis behind them.

Akkael stared briefly, allowing himself to be the wide-eyed adventurer. For a second, he was the eight-year-old boy who cried seeing Urkanza for the first time, the twenty-four-year-old who watched Edokand's grey outline approach on the horizon, the twenty-eight-year-old who rode ahead for the first sight of Wu Wei. But then his left hand pulsed with phantom pain, and he started towards the city.

On the way out of the shanty town, Akkael walked past the stable that held Knarr. Knarr was the name of his father's ship, so Akkael saw it as a fitting name for his horse. He stopped before he passed and turned back.

The stable hand was a girl of about fourteen. Her raven hair and dark eyes clashed with the bright blue of her Sekandan tunic. Akkael approached as she happened to be cleaning out Knarr's stall.

"Hey, girl," said Akkael. She looked up, eyes widening as she saw him approach. "I need your help with something."

"Yes, sir, anything for the brotherhood." She bowed her head, holding her left hand up like a claw.

Akkael desperately tried not to look too surprised by the stable hand's reaction, instead untying his coin purse.

"This horse," he said, tilting his head towards Knarr, "will need food and shelter until I return."

The girl nodded, taking the coin purse and remaining silent out of respect.

Before Akkael left the stall, he remembered he wouldn't return looking like he did and turned around again. "Actually, I won't be the one retrieving the horse. I know this will sound strange, but he'll be picked up by the Queen of Sekando or someone working for her."

The stable hand looked at Akkael in confusion. She opened her mouth to speak before closing it again. After repeating that a few more times, eyes darting across the straw-strewn floor, she finally said. "Forgive me. Why is the brotherhood gifting the Queen with a horse? Is there something I don't understand?"

Akkael had no idea what the brotherhood was and didn't have the patience to find out. He knew the bandit he had become was involved and was content with viewing the free food and drink as a happy coincidence. Akkael put on a face that implied the girl was as ignorant as he was. "Yes. Of course, there is something you don't understand."

The stable hand gave a sigh of relief. "Of course, silly me. The brotherhood would never give something to the Queen without a plan. It must be marked by an assassin, or the satchels must be lined with flammables. Anything to unite Edokand, right?"

Akkael couldn't help the shocked expression. "Mmmhmm," he said, nodding slowly.

The stable hand grinned and bowed. "For the Empire."

Not wanting to get too deep into Sekandan politics, Akkael just waved and left, making his way towards the city, which was sure to confuse the loyalist stable hand even more.

There was only one gate into the city, and it was guarded by two women with large halberds. For his plan to work, he'd have to get detained inside. It was illegal for men to enter Sekando City, so the actual arrest would be easy enough. But entering was going to be difficult.

The large bricks of Sekando's wall fitted together like a jigsaw and were smooth to the touch. Akkael ran his hand across the sandstone as he circumnavigated the city. Twelve watchtowers, evenly spread along the wall, looked like prongs on a crown. He counted four before he found a way over the wall.

Sand butted against Sekando City, leaving only five metres of wall unburied. Akkael remembers an ancient tower back on Solstr. It was so old and deep in the permafrost that the snow had shifted, burying six floors. It looked like the building had been thrust into the ground like a sword.

The sand made it impossible to run at the wall, so Akkael unsheathed his katana and drove it into the mortar between the sandstone bricks. Choosing not to stand on the blade too long, he placed one foot on it and launched off, both hands gripping the crenellated wall above. The upper body strength of the bandit he had become was impressive, and he could pull himself onto the rampart.

He rolled onto his back and stared at the cloudless sky momentarily. When he sat up, looking to his left, he saw Sekando open over the parapet. The yellowed clump of apartments and stalls closest to him resembled the city's more open, affluent districts. No building was higher than the outer walls except the palace pagoda, making Sekando City almost look foetal or like a field that had barely sprouted its first yield.

With a birds-eye view of the city, he could see the other side of the wall like spotting a ship on the horizon. Most of the architecture took a lot of work to distinguish. Still, he had an unobstructed view of the open acres of the palace grounds, ornate with blue banners that cracked holes in the beige canvas of Sekando.

Just below him was a stall propped against the wall that sold ramen, which Akkael could smell before he peeked over the parapet. He was close enough to both watchtowers to be spotted by any guards inside them, so he had to act quickly. After one more glance at the view, he prepared himself to jump the thirty-foot drop onto the roof of the ramen stall.

However, before he leapt, Akkael glanced at the watchtower to his right and saw a staircase in the gap between it and him. Stepping back onto the rampart, Akkael sighed in relief, wiped a bead of sweat from his forehead, and sauntered over to the stairs.

The ramen vendor was oblivious to how close her stall was to being crushed under the weight of Akkael's bandit body. In fact, she looked blasé about an illegal male strolling down the city walls. He supposed he wasn't the first man to use the sandbank outside, and she must have set up shop here to make some money from the doomed intruders.

The ramen did smell good, but Akkael had given all his money to the teenage extremist, so he moved on through a narrow alleyway and into the dense lower quarter of the city.

The city was a cacophony of smells from various food stalls. Yells from women promoting their wares mingled with the quieter haggling and mumbling from the crowd Akkael tried to blend into. Smoke from grills wafted into the street, adding to the claustrophobic feeling of the narrow pavements and endless lines of overhanging buildings. Tarps and bunting hung above Akkael, crossing the road like a spider's web, dancing in shadows on the cobbled sandstone path beneath his feet.

He was drawing the eyes of the saleswomen. However, with the same mentality as the ramen vendor, they still tried to make money off him, beckoning him to every other stall he passed. He could probably make it into the middle of the city before anyone cared enough to turn him in.

However, he didn't mind. He was one of the first men in history to explore Sekando City, let alone the first of his people.

Ukbul, the capital city of Urkanza, was the first foreign city Akkael had ever visited. It was small but so different to anything he had ever seen before. For a moment, Akkael allowed himself to feel how he did as a child. Wide-eyed, he absorbed the Sekandan structures around him, the trinkets in the stalls, the unique food on grills facing out to the street.

This was who Akkael was. He may have had a thousand different faces by now, but the wonder and excitement that stretched across them were more him than the sky-blue eyes with which he was born.

"STOP! INTRUDER!" The exclamation came from behind him. He turned to see two women in blue armour, carrying polearms with large blades. The childlike wonder drained away, and he began to run through the dense crowd. The vendors, who were quite content to let him browse moments ago, quickly turned, yelled slurs and throwing things they couldn't sell, like brown apples and broken items.

Akkael had left his katana lodged in the wall outside, so he was unarmed, running through waves of women for no apparent reason. His objective was to get arrested and executed, so fleeing seemed counter-productive. He held to the excuse that giving chase made the charade look natural instead of admitting to himself that he just wanted to see more of the city before he was thrown in a cell.

He found his way to a more open part of the city. Instead of stalls, there were shops. He sprinted past a bank and a bookshop before nearly crashing into a boy. At first, seeing him was a shock, but he looked younger than sixteen. The longer he ran, the more boys he found. He realised he must have found his way to the male quarter, where young men are educated and accommodated before being cast out.

After that, he came to a large opening. Eight streets going in each cardinal direction. In the centre of the space was a three-tiered fountain, the sun casting rainbows from it as the gushing water spat droplets onto the yellow tile ground. Unlit lanterns floated in the pool, and lamp posts surrounded it at every angle. There was a plaque Akkael desperately wanted to stop and read. But instead, he kept running, taking the third left away from the fountain.

The women were gaining on Akkael fast, and he had no idea where he was going. He almost made another left turn before he realised it was a dead-end and corrected himself, turning right instead. Akkael was no longer taking in any of the city and was beginning to wonder why he was still running. He started to slow down and thought about how to make his surrender look believable. He opted to take a controlled fall, tripping over nothing and knocking over a barrel on his way down. The two guards caught up to him quickly, flanking him on either side with their polearms pointed down at him. Akkael slowly raised his hands.

Whenever he imagined getting arrested, he always had an excellent one-liner to throw back at his captors before he was trundled away. He considered it briefly before opening his mouth.

"I guess I –"

One of the women clocked him with the bottom of her spear, instantly knocking him unconscious.

[CHAPTER 18] — SKALDGARD

Waves lapped at the side of the longship, and the breeze rippled in the orange sailcloth as Skane sat looking off towards the dot on the horizon that would soon take the shape of Skaldgard. The wind hit the sails perfectly, the first thing that had gone right for the Northmen since Wu Wei. However, it didn't seem like a blessing. It was almost ominous like a nefarious god propelled them to the next catastrophe.

Rigpa, sat at the stern with Skane. Her hands were bound, and a gag hung loose around her neck in case she spoke out of turn. She looked over the ship's side as water flicked at her cheek, wrinkles making way for her smile. "I can see why Northmen choose this life."

Skane stayed quiet, tightening the fur wrappings that covered him from the cold.

Rigpa turned back towards the water, watching foam dance on the surface. Driftwood chased the ship but was cast about by the current of its wake. The water was so blue, sometimes Rigpa couldn't tell where the sea ended and the sky began.

None of the Northmen seemed to appreciate what Rigpa saw over the prow, instead staring blankly into the middle distance, unflinching in the chilly sea air.

She turned back to Skane. "So, how long will we be in Uta-... Skaldgard?" she asked, correcting herself just before Skane's sharp glance.

He took a deep breath before speaking. "Hopefully, we'll set sail before the week's end. I think Skaldgard has five-thousand fighting men with enough ships to carry them. If Astrid secures a deal with Sekando, that should be enough." There was sadness in the way Skane spoke. Forlorn and resigned as he huddled tight in his furs.

Rigpa looked the giant man up and down before speaking. "You don't sound happy about that," she said quietly.

"Well, war wouldn't be my first choice," he said, the muscles in his neck tensing as he spoke.

The sage squinted at that. "Really?"

Skane's blue eyes found Rigpa's in a blink, and his voice had grown deeper. "What do you mean by that?"

"Well, forgive me, Skane. I know you're a good man. But didn't the Northmen start this war?" Rigpa spoke carefully, but something told her this was an important conversation.

"Doesn't mean it was my first choice."

"But-"

"What do you know of it?" Skane snapped, causing the whole ship to jump in shock.

"Want me to gag her, Skane?" asked someone further down the longship.

He tried to calm himself with another sigh, shaking his head at the one man who spoke. He clutched his eyes shut, controlling his breathing to the tempo of a gentle tide. After a moment, he opened his eyes again. "Sorry for yelling," he said to Rigpa.

"It's okay," she said back.

"What do you know of Solstr?" he asked, this time with genuine curiosity.

All Rigpa could do was shake her head. "Almost nothing."

Skane paused momentarily, smiling to himself, eyes dancing across his memories. "It's beautiful. The sunlight would bounce off the snow, and the mountains glowed. Some trees keep their leaves all year round, with crystal blue fjords you could walk across on deep winter nights. The whole country smelled of smoke from log fires and grilled fish. It could be a paradise if life there were easier.

"Crop yields are weak. Some years we would have to get by with eating bark and praying that the next season would be more fruitful. It makes you realise why people from the past relied on their fake gods so much. Most starved young. If starvation didn't get you, the cold would. Or the beasts. Wolves the size of bears, bears the size of trees; all just as hungry as us."

Skane looked back down at the bottom of his ship. "Rigpa, you said that Northmen choose this life. It isn't much of a choice. For most, it's essential. We can't survive in our own country, and most people aren't willing to give up land to hungry foreigners. Yes, some – the Tornes, Astrid – don't understand why most of us set sail. For them, there is a small part that does this for conquest. But they grew up rich. That's not their fault. It's just the way they are. But war was never my first choice, and I don't want it to be the last choice either."

Rigpa let the silence hang there until she finally spoke softly. "What do you mean by 'the last choice'?"

Skane snickered briefly before his face turned to stone again. "Back in Takakawa, you asked me what my biggest fear was. I've been thinking about it, and I think that's it. We came to Edokand to have a better life for our people. To give them space to farm and prosper. But that's also why we went to Rhayne and Urkanza. I don't know when it'll be enough, and I'm scared it never will be. Once we win in Wu Wei, how long before I end up chasing my husband to some other far-off land to start a war there?

"My biggest fear is that this will be all I do. Kill until I'm killed, or worse, I lose everything I love first."

Skane wiped a tear from his eye. After a few seconds, he spoke again. "So, you said to open my root chakra, I must overcome my fears. How do I get over that?"

Rigpa thought for a moment before opening her mouth. "It's not about getting over our fears. When a man who was afraid of the dark as a child looks down a dark hallway, do you think some part of him isn't still afraid? It's about managing those fears. Making them bearable. For you, I don't have the answers. Your fears are unique to you. All I can say is that your decisions are your own as well. Maybe some faith in the control of your own life, the positive influence you give to those you love, and the sway you possess will be enough to pave the path you need. The worst-case scenario is rarely the one that comes to fruition. After all, it's only one possibility out of limitless outcomes."

The muttering sea spat salt water into the ship, spraying against the lonely tears on Skane's face until he couldn't tell which was which. He looked up to see some colour in the silhouette of Skaldgard. He wiped his face and stood up, stumbling down the ship's length as it rocked back and forth. "Lower the sails. Start rowing."

The Northmen discarded their furs, stretched, and yawned before performing Skane's tasks. The sail was clasped down, and fifty Northmen rowed in unison, Skane beckoning instructions to keep them in time.

Skaldgard was yet another volcanic island that Edokand had in abundance. However, the architecture was much older than that of Tsul and Trim. The island's principal port, where the Northman had made their main settlement, was a collage of stilted homes and appropriated ruins. Two cliff sides flanked the dock. Derelict temples made for faiths that no longer existed perched atop them like birds of prey, as wooden houses clung to the cliffs as if painted to the rocks. Stairs and scaffolding connect them all like ivy. The village, tight against the bluffs, gave way to an ample open space in the centre, where a market led all the way to a five-story pagoda, red roofs streaking from it like a pine tree.

The Solstic additions to the village were stark against the original Edokand'i homestead. A boat builder's workshop was constructed on the beach, and grain reserves were erected next to the pagoda. Taverns and inns were scattered between the cliffs, built in the long hall fashion of Solstr, and the smoke of a blacksmith billowed above them.

More construction was being done further from the water and on top of the cliffs, alluding to the future of the Solstic that Doran had curated. As the ship entered the port, white banners with three black snowflakes welcomed them to the docks. Rigpa had never seen the flag that Doran had designed but thought its simplicity was beautiful.

Two men were waiting at the beach's edge for Skane to moor. One was a Northman with a large beard and a potbelly. The second was a young sage, hands tucked in the sleeves of his purple robes.

Once the ship was unpacked and tied up, Skane approached the two onlookers, leading Rigpa along with him so she didn't spend time alone with his crew. "Frode. Jiro."

"Skane," said the man who Rigpa assumed was Frode, as the name sounded Solstic. "We've sent word to every jarl on the island, and we'll have our army in a matter of days."

"Good," nodded Skane. "I want to return to Magar and Astrid as soon as possible."

"If I may," said Jiro, who had looked up from his feet for the first time since they had approached. "It is a pleasure to see you again, Skane, and trust me when I say I'm grateful you have arrived in one piece. It is also a privilege to be in the presence of the Grand Sage. But, if I may speak my mind, I think it's unwise to keep the Third Pillar of the Edokand'i triumvirate tied up. Many Edokand'i still live here, and although the Sekandans don't identify with Edokand, they still recognise Sage Rigpa's station."

"That, Jiro," answered Skane, "is exactly why she's still alive. If Magar had his way, her head would be on a spike outside Takakawa."

Jiro flinched, which made Frode snicker.

Skane looked at Jiro and took a deep breath. "I'm sorry. I hear what you're saying, and if I had my way, she'd be free. But having her bound appeases most of my countrymen. If they see she's been freed, they'll demand blood."

The young monk considered that momentarily, looking at the Grand Sage. Rigpa gave Jiro a reassuring smile and nodded. Jiro clasped his eyes shut and imitated the gesture.

"So," said Skane, steering the conversation differently. "Surely you both didn't come to the sea to greet me. What do you want?"

Frode cleared his throat, making it clear he wanted to talk next. "Well, we have one pressing matter we're both eager to put to bed. Shall we walk and talk?"

Skane nodded, and the four of them went to the pagoda. It was a few moments before Frode continued. "For a while now, Jiro and I have been debating where to place a surplus in resources to improve the future of Skaldgard. Before Astrid left, we approached her with two separate plans. I wanted to build an orphanage which, at a reasonable tax, would house many of our children who lost their parents to the war. Jiro wanted to build a school, which I didn't see much point in doing."

Skane saw Jiro roll his eyes, a strange gesture for a sage. "Why not save this money and spend it on the war effort?" said Skane. "Our soldiers need provisions, and the resources could be used to build boats and weapons."

"We did have that conversation," said Frode, nodding. "However, we've got more than enough ships and weapons from before the peace attempt. Also, with an influx of children coming from the settlements in Tsul without homes or parents, Jiro and I have both agreed that an orphanage is paramount."

"Okay," shrugged Skane. "So, if you both agree, what's the problem?"

"The problem," said Jiro, interrupting Frode before he had a chance to speak again, "is that we have different ideas on how it would be run. Homeless children aren't a problem exclusive to the Solstic. Edokand'i orphans are also struggling all over this island and in Tsul. I would have this orphanage house, not just your children, but ours."

Skane stopped in his tracks, and the rest followed suit. "So, you want to make an orphanage for both, Solstic and Edokand'i children?"

"Of course, I want the orphanage for ours and ours alone," said Frode. "Why waste money feeding and clothing the children of our enemy, the very people who killed your brothers-in-law during peace talks? We should be looking after our own, not them."

Jiro stepped in front of Frode, meeting Skane's line of sight. "Skane, the way we conduct ourselves in these moments is crucial. I'm loyal to this island, meaning that while you occupy it and name it Skaldgard, I am devoted to you, just as I was with Doran. So, believe me when I say this is the best course of action.

"The Edokand'i will be grateful for your mercy. They'll see that the propaganda Wu Wei proliferates about your people is wrong, just as I have in the years I've spent in your company. We can gear towards war because you deserve justice. But we don't have to hurt everyone while we go about it. If we don't do what's right here, we'll further alienate the people of Edokand, and the war, the strife, the conflict; it'll never end."

Rigpa could feel Skane's heartbeat reverberate through his whole body like a gong as Jiro breathed for the first time since he started talking. For a moment, Skane froze in place, feeling all the processes of his body; his blood pumping, his muscles tensing, his lungs expelling air.

Then he looked at Rigpa, her reassuring smile and kind, elderly eyes locked on him.

"You're in charge of Skaldgard while King Magar is away," said Jiro, his voice hitting Skane's ears as slowly as a leaf floating along the surface of a lake. "It's your choice."

Rigpa sometimes viewed her gifts as a curse. She could feel people's emotions, which often gave her a dose of anguish and sorrow she didn't want to feel. However, it also allowed her to view internal moments that would otherwise go undescribed or missed entirely. She smiled as she used her powers on Skane.

For the first time since Wu Wei, Skane suddenly felt calm. The fear he let choreograph his movements and rule his every thought seemed almost surmountable, and, for one small instance, he kept it at bay. This was his chance to sway the future away from the worst-case scenario he had invented. It wouldn't be hard. It was only one possible outcome, after all.

Instead of worrying how his people would react or how others would perceive his decision, he let himself do the right thing, like allowing sunlight through a window. "The orphanage will be for both peoples," decreed Skane, smiling. "I want construction to start as soon as possible."

"The foundations have already been built," said Jiro, smiling too.

Frode's face was so red he looked sunburnt, barely avoiding apoplexy. "Is this really what you want, Skane? Doran would've done what his people needed. Not helping the enemy feed their urchins."

"Doran wanted peace and prosperity," said Skane, not even looking at Frode as he turned to face Rigpa. "He would agree with me, and you know that too, Frode."

Skane locked eyes with the Grand Sage, removed the hand axe from his belt, and, with one swift motion, cut the rope that bound Rigpa's hands. He looked at the old woman's face. Sea water had run trenches through the dirt that coated her skin. She hadn't washed since Wu Wei and had been kept in a filthy prison cell for a week. She smiled warmly at Skane, rubbing the rope burns on her wrists.

"If this is all I need to do to beat the first chakra," said Skane, "then I'm ready for the second."

Rigpa laughed louder than she anticipated. "You don't beat chakras. You open them, and you are still a long way off from opening the root chakra." She shrugged coyly. "But I don't see the harm in teaching you more of our ways."

Skane smiled before turning back around. He didn't bother to see how Jiro or Frode reacted to him cutting the binds. He just started to walk toward the pagoda, a tranquillity washing over him with each step.

[CHAPTER 19] — ICHIKA

Three thousand Solstic warriors had spent half a day conducting the siege of Sekando. They had co-opted a shanty town outside the city walls as their encampment. A sizeable heart-shaped pond supplied them with fresh water, and plundered resources from the town bolstered their own supply train.

They had decided not to kill anyone in the town to avoid inciting conflict with the Sekandans. The displaced refugees from the shanty town were primarily men, so the added pressure on Sekando to protect them from the Northmen would hopefully expedite a parley. Magar could understand the principle of the plan, but rage still burned deep in his heart. So, by the first hour of their sojourn, he had set up a fighting ring with other pent-up warriors who needed to release their bridled fury while others toiled.

Astrid was still working on the construction of their camp. Pavilions were being added to the collection of caravans and tents already erected in the border town. Logs carved into spikes were being unloaded from carts and plunged deep into the sand around their perimeter while trenches were being dug. Lindsay had joined Astrid in erecting the fence. She'd been by Astrid's side every day since Skaldgard. Sometimes she found it irritating. But only sometimes.

She'd done a lot with her hands over the last few weeks, and blisters formed on her already calloused palms. Her back muscles began to burn from lifting the spiked logs, and her legs ached from trudging in the sand. Breathing turned to panting, and she could feel her heartbeat in her neck. There was a slight tremor in her arms, sweat was falling from her hair like leaves in autumn, and her mind was completely empty. She didn't have the energy to work and think and chose what hurt the least.

Trygve was also working on construction further from the camp. A few feet from the trenches, he had ordered people to dig deeper holes and cover them with sand-laden tarps. In the gap of the fence they used for access, he'd hidden a gate of sharp logs that the Solstic could pull into place if they were charged. A ring of flammables doused with oil was set up around their perimeter.

As the sun rose behind Sekando, twelve women on horseback left the city gates. Astrid was finishing the back of the fence, in case the Sekandans attacked them from the rear, when she saw their blue armour contrasting the beige city and the pink sky. As the riders got closer, Astrid recognised the head of the company as Ichika, the First Blade of Sekando. Trygve noticed her, too, spitting on the ground as she approached.

Ichika stopped a quarter of a kilometre from the spiked boundary, raising her fist for the other women to do the same. They then dismounted, taking careful steps to avoid Trygve's ditches.

He cursed, rolling his eyes. "That would have been funny."

Astrid was the first to reach the front of the amassing crowd, Lindsay just behind her. Trygve, twirling a knife between his fingers, had lined up with Astrid. Magar joined them as Ichika felt the lowered gate submerged in the sand under her heavy riding boots. Magar wiped dried blood from below his nose and repeatedly clenched his fist, staring down at his crimson knuckles and smiling. Someone from the crowd brought him his giant sword, and he fastened it to his back. The leather straps dug into his bare torso and tightened hastily before the Sekandans reached them.

Astrid considered the sword for a moment. She never understood why Magar used his sword over an axe or something smaller he could wear on his hip. The claymore was too large to draw from its scabbard, so a slit in the leather along the top side helped him clumsily remove the blade. A clasp kept the weapon from slipping out when it wasn't on his back, which had to be undone before the sheath was worn. It looked imposing when he donned it, but anyone who knows battle could see how impractical it was.

The dozen Sekandans looked imposing as the sky brightened. The light blue steel was still stark in the approaching dawn, and the women of Sekando, standing a foot above Astrid with muscles like over-stuffed sacks, gazed over the Solstic army in front of them, clasping the geom blades at their sides. Ichika's hazel eyes were brighter than even Magar's sapphire glare, her hair was held in a wolf's tail knot, and her sharp, strict features looked more dangerous than her blade.

After a few moments of silence, Ichika shrugged. "What is this?" she said, speaking in Edokand'i.

"That's your question?" said Astrid, squinting. She tried to look as nonchalant as Ichika but couldn't quite capture her disinterest. "You know what this is."

"It looks like a cute little siege." She folded her bottom lip and spoke slowly. "The kind a child might orchestrate. It's nice, but don't big-girl sieges usually go all the way around a city?"

"Well, there are a lot of ridiculous campsites around your city," Astrid spoke in monotone, trying not to let Ichika under her skin. In truth, Doran and Akkael were the strategists of their military. Trygve had his moments but lost as many battles as he'd won. Astrid tried to sound confident, folding her arms across her chest. "We've opted to take one for the moment and spread outwards as the days go. But our intentions aren't to cause conflict. At least they don't have to be."

"How mature," said Ichika, still sounding patronising.

"Get a new joke, Ichika," Trygve spat, probably speaking louder than he intended.

"Ahh, Trygve," said, Ichika, smiling. "Surprised you're here. Things didn't turn out great for you the last time you strayed into Sekandan territory. In fact, every time you've come to Sekando, things haven't gone well for you."

Trygve's grin was thin and crooked, like a tear in a shirt. "Trust me, if things turn violent, they won't go the same as before."

"You sound confident," snickered Ichika.

In the early days of the war, before Doran understood the nuance between Edokand and Sekando, Trygve attempted three invasions of the Queen's land. He was chewed out each time by Ichika and her forces. Trygve's smile got broader and thinner. "I've been thinking of our rematch for some time."

111

"Weird," Ichika shrugged, "I don't think about you at all."

Trygve ran his foot through the sand like a bull ready to charge, but Astrid spoke before he could do anything. "You've caused a lot of commotion for someone who doesn't give us any thought."

"If you're referring to what happened after your 'peace talks', that was purely business." Ichika's voice was flat like what occurred at the new mountains was as mundane as an assembly. "Queen Kya owed some of their relatives a favour, and having one viper in your bed is better than two."

Astrid's lips turned up like a wolf's snarl. "Is that it?"

"What can I say?" she shrugged again. "Anyway, you got out of that situation unscathed. I don't know what happened to Koji's army, but it worked out for you."

Magar removed the large sword on his back with a scrape of metal across the leather that could drown out a thunderclap. When Astrid looked back to Ichika, all twelve women held their geoms, silently drawing them from their belts quicker than the wind.

Magar rarely spoke during parleys; when he did, it always shocked those on his side of the ranks. "Unscathed?"

The tension hung between the groups like a taut bowstring. Trygve twirled his knives in his fingers, quietly laughing as the rest of the nearby Northmen apprehensively drew their weapons. Astrid left her axe in her belt ring but kept her hands at her side just in case.

Eventually, Ichika sent her eyes towards the sand and exhaled. "Look," she started, sheathing her blade and indicating for the rest of the Sekandans to do the same. "I've got a busy day today. I have training, council meetings, trade agreements to organise. I have to execute some male unionist who entered the city yesterday. Could we forgo the banter for now and just move this along?"

Astrid looked at Magar. He was breathing heavily, eyebrows darting towards the bridge of his nose. After a few moments, he locked eyes with Astrid and threw his sword down into the sand and submerged into the crowd of Solstic behind him. Those with their weapons drawn returned them to their belts, and Trygve gave a deflated sigh.

Astrid turned back to Ichika. "Why are you here, then?"

"Queen Kya has granted you an audience in their tea house," said Ichika. She had more tone to her words now, adrenaline making her voice higher and louder. "I don't have to remind you that men can't enter the city, do I?"

"You just did," said Trygve.

Ichika shot a look at him, accompanied by a scowl.

"I'll be going in King Magar's stead," said Astrid, "accompanied by my shield maidens."

Ichika nodded. "Good, I didn't want to add any more executions to the docket," she said, glancing at Trygve again before returning to Astrid. "We can allow five women to join you."

Astrid shook her head and folded her arms. "We will be twelve to match the company you came here with."

Ichika rolled her eyes. "Fine."

Astrid turned back to the crowd. She pointed at Lindsay and ten other women, shields strapped to each of their backs and axes hanging from their hips. The twelve Solstic women followed the twelve Sekandans slowly back to their horses. They mounted and led them to the city.

Astrid knew she had an essential job in Sekando, but she began feeling excited as the sandstone walls approached. Guards in blue cuirasses lined the wall and stood outside the large wooden gate of Edokand's second city. She thought for a moment how unique her situation was. A natural curiosity and adventurer's high comes with being Solstic that Astrid couldn't deny, and being the first of her people to enter Sekando sent a tingle down her back.

Ichika's group dismounted, and some of the women outside the gates grabbed the reigns of the gentle horses, leading them behind. The guards stared unflinchingly at the Solstic women, but Astrid didn't care. Some leaned over the parapet to look at the barbarous foreigners they'd heard stories about.

One gate woman approached Astrid and held out her hand. "Weapons," she demanded.

Astrid looked blankly at the woman in blue. "No," she said.

The guardswoman looked over to Ichika, who just sighed and nodded. She then slowly stepped backwards out of Astrid's way and called up to those on the wall. "Open the gates!"

The grinding of chains and the clicking and creaking of hinges filled the sand dunes as the gates of Sekando slowly opened. After a few moments, Ichika waved her hand for them to follow. The Solstic walked behind Ichika's soldiers, and the women with the horses followed them, keeping their distance as they led the mares through the walls.

As Astrid entered the arched gateway and looked through the tunnel at the city itself, only one thought entered her mind: Akkael would have been jealous.

[CHAPTER 20] — WHAT HAPPENED BEYOND THE MOUNTAINS?

Seradok had told Hideo he would return six days from its last visit. Hideo didn't know how long he had to wallow by himself at the news of what happened beyond the mountains. A message had arrived from Koseki, a mining town in Sekando. Two-hundred miles away from Takakawa, where Hideo had expected his army to be.

The message was long but could be summed up by the first line: *Lord Hideo, our mission has failed.*

Hideo's bottom lip quivered as more tears poured down his cheek. His son's birth was the worst day of his life. He remembered trying to smile down at his newborn, clutching the baby in his arms while sitting on a bed covered in his wife's blood. He named his son Koji, meaning to cultivate, to pursue healing. His son's name was a promise he made to himself.

Being a father was demanding. Hideo tried not to blame Koji for his wife's death or show animosity towards him. He knew how hard missing a parent was and how it felt when the only one left kept their distance. Hideo's mother always regretted having a boy first, and he never wanted Koji to feel like he'd failed by being born. Hideo dwelled on every small failure, and it punctured his heart, knowing he could never hold his son again.

The letter tried desperately to cling to the small victories. Akkael Torne was killed, and the Solstic at the beach were eradicated. Anger overwhelmed him when he read these trivial compensations. Akkael and a hundred Northmen were nothing compared to five-thousand sentinels: nothing compared to his son.

Doran Torne was with the Emperor. But that still left Magar, Skane Brick-Chest, Astrid Scarred-tooth, and Trygve. He needed all six to end the war. With four still in play, there was no telling the carnage they would cause.

A rag-tag force of about a thousand had survived what happened to Koji's army and had taken shelter in Koseki. The report couldn't tell Hideo how the military had fallen apart. Still, he speculated those loyal to the Emperor were within his son's army and caught wind of Hideo's actions in Wu Wei.

Jin Bu! Even for Hideo, the man who invented the name, it was hard to take the retitling seriously, especially now that his hopes of securing Tsul were broken.

There were three places where Hideo had cast blame for the failure. The first was his army torn apart by turncoats loyal to a dithering Emperor and his court of sycophants who happily let half their empire fall to a group of barbarous invaders. Hideo's message from Koseki begged for reinforcements, but that aid would never come. Hideo would feel nothing when Magar's Northmen ripped the flesh from their traitorous bones.

The second was with the shadow archers, a cult of mute cowards who killed Hideo's son when his guard was down. He didn't know how long their order had conspired against him, but now the facts were laid bare; he would devote however long it took until the rest of the shades rotted in the ground.

Shadow archer was more of a nickname, referring to their weapon of choice and strange gifts. A bloody, violent ritual left those in the Order of Shades mutilated and shrouded in darkness. No one knew why, but only thirteen men could simultaneously possess these powers, despite every generation attempting to bypass this arbitrary rule. Their temple was at the bottom of the volcano on which the capital was built and not viewable from the city's gates. Black spires made it look as if it was cast like a shadow.

Just as Hideo fed more vitriol into the thoughts of shadow archers, a knock at the door woke him from his hate, and a malicious grin sliced across his face. He moved from the bed, hiding the soju he was drinking for breakfast, and went to the red silk sofa facing the door to his chambers. He cleared his throat before beckoning those on the other side to enter.

Ieyasu Nobu, the man who helped Hideo secure the palace what already seemed like a lifetime ago, entered Hideo's room. The gold gilding was the only indication of how much blood had been splattered across his plate mail, with most of it camouflaged by the red of the sentinel's armour. He held his helmet under his arm as the demon mask shook on his belt. He bowed to Hideo before stepping aside.

Seven more sentinels entered the room, each holding a red silk pillow. The soldiers balanced the pads with one hand, keeping the other free to remove the veils from whatever was concealed, like small hills, atop the cushions.

Hideo looked at Ieyasu, grinning like a wolf. He tilted his head towards the men carrying the pillows. "Is it done?"

"Yes, my lord," Ieyasu said, nodding like a child proud of his schoolwork. "And with only six of ours dead for every one of them. Much less than we expected."

Once Ieyasu saw Hideo's unamused expression, he indicated to the first sentinel in the line. "Han, show the Iron Hand of Wu Wei-"

Hideo coughed, and Ieyasu corrected himself.

"I mean, show the Iron Hand of Jin Bu what you got for him."

Han, a stocky man shorter than the other sentinels in the line, stepped forward, holding his pillow in front of him. He pinched the veil and lifted it to reveal a severed head resting atop the silk cushion. Its eyes were vacant, and its lips were agape, showing the inside of its tongueless mouth. The skin was already turning grey, and all the muscles had relaxed, making it look eerily calm as if it had been carved or scrapped from clay.

"This is Kage," said Ieyasu, gesturing to the head. "He carried out many political assassinations for the previous Emperor, securing his power and lineage would last long enough for his son to succeed him. He was the first shade to fall, killed before he could teleport away."

Han stepped back, and the second sentinel, skinnier and taller, moved forward to reveal the head of another shadow archer, its gaunt cheekbones making it look like a ghost.

"This was Heurin," declared Ieyasu, listing the past accomplishments and prestige of the head atop the pillow before stating how he had died. Hideo sat in silence as each shadow archer was presented. All seven freshly severed heads, tongueless and vacant, were shown in sequence as Ieyasu spoke of their activities in life and their last moments before their death.

When the last was presented, and the sentinel holding it had retreated back into line, Hideo turned to a bemused Ieyasu. "Where are the rest?" he asked, waving his hand to any empty space in the room.

Ieyasu was caught off guard. "Excuse me?"

"There are always thirteen," Hideo said, speaking softly as if to a child. "Three died in Tsul; there are seven here. Where are the other three?"

"Well," Ieyasu said, clearing his throat. "Not all archers were at the Temple of Shades, sir. We have reason to suspect the other three have left for Sekando."

Hideo's eyes widened. "Get out."

"Sir, trust me, we will work tirelessly until all these abominations-"

"GET OUT!" Hideo screamed.

Ieyasu froze for a moment, petrified like a statue. Eventually, he pulled in a lungful, bowed with his free arm at his side, and left the room. The seven cushion-bearers also bowed, foreheads touching the grey scalps of the men they had killed, and followed Ieyasu, the door closing behind them with the weight of a coffin lid.

"Sekando," Hideo whispered, the word stuttering along the breath that carried it. Sekando was the third muse of his vengeful ire. Hideo knew how his sister, Queen Kya, and the rest of their forces had fled and let his army fall to the traitors amongst them. His lip twitched as he imagined how his sister relished his humiliation. Sekando's hatred of the rest of Edokand was known, but he thought he could trust his sister.

But now he knew that he could trust no one. The Sekandans couldn't carry out his orders, Koji couldn't keep his army together, and Ieyasu couldn't even kill ten people. The only person Hideo could trust to win this war was himself.

As the room grew quiet and the thumping of his heart was draining from his ears, Hideo could hear a ticking sound behind him. He looked over to the chest, triple-locked and kept in the far corner of his bedroom. He hadn't opened it since the mountains had risen. The object inside scared him, just like the pulsating abyss of tentacles and eyes that had given it to him.

Hideo stared at the chest, listening to the steady tick of what lay inside. After a moment, he stood from the sofa and walked over to a bookcase. On the third shelf lay a ring of a dozen keys. He retrieved it with his good hand and walked over to the chest. The box was made of polished spruce, lined with iron ridging. Hideo knelt in front of it.

The first lock was a chain coiled vertically around the trunk like a snake. Hideo unlocked it, fumbling the lock up with his iron hand so he could fit the key in. The following two locks held down latches on either side of the box's lid. As each lock fell, the ticking from inside seemed to get louder until the last lock was unhooked and hit the floorboards.

Hideo delayed momentarily before opening it, trying to calm his shaking hand. However, the pulse of the box, though slower and less sporadic than his own, unnerved him even more. He put his iron hand under the lip of the lid and lifted it open. Inside, covered in dust and drowned by shadows, was a small, black metronome.

It was no bigger than a book, its hand waving back and forth as it cast each beat to echo inside the hollow chest. Patterns like barbs or waves were carved into its slate-like surface, running along it in spirals. Hideo lifted the metronome out of the trunk, careful not to disturb the rod's consistent pacing, before walking over to his writing desk, placing it down gently. Then he lowered into his chair.

Staring at the metronome, its hypnotic pendulum swinging from one side to the other, Hideo tried to build his courage. It was still strange to him; so much chaos was caused by an instrument used to teach children to play music. But he didn't allow himself to be deceived; he knew how dangerous it was. He also learned how to use the weapon that Seradok had given him. All he had to was stop the hammer's path. But, despite only having to lift a finger, his arm hung limp at his side.

He tried to flood his brain with thoughts of Sekando. He had no love for the home that had abandoned him. His own people had cast him aside, his mother made it clear she never wanted him, and he'd be executed if he ever tried to return to the streets he played in as a boy. He thought of his mother, a cold woman whose position was the only reason he could thrive once he left the Second City.

Then there was his sister. Kya was four when Hideo was made to leave. Hideo couldn't attend their mother's funeral, not that he'd want to, nor could he attend Kya's coronation. His mother was so happy when Kya was born, and it was the first time Hideo had seen her smile. They hadn't seen much of each other, but from what he had heard, they were less callous and malicious than the woman who bore them. But, after hearing how they abandoned his army to be slaughtered, Hideo could see that not only had the apple not fallen far from the tree, but it was propped up by the trunk.

Hideo's heart began to beat as ferociously as before. His blood boiled like magma as his nostrils wrestled air into his lungs. He'd leave the dregs of his traitorous coward army to die in Tsul; he'd hunt the shadow archers until they were vanquished. But Sekando? He'd bleed them slowly until they drowned. Hideo's arm darted for the metronome, ready to pinch the rod of the instrument.

However, his arm froze a few inches away; his fingers could feel the feint waft of air as the metronome continued its course. His whole body tensed as he got closer to Seradok's gift. Eventually, his hand rolled into a fist, and he pulled it away. He closed his eyes, squeezing a tear out as his whole body shook. He screamed down at nothing, blood so hot he worried he would combust. After a moment, he fell back into his chair, the only sound being the ticking of the instrument on his desk.

"Poor Hideo." A voice, rough and grating, like hail rapping at a windowpane, caused Hideo to jump from his seat. Hideo turned to see the green hue and vile form of Seradok, tendrils wriggling like worms, eyes floating like rotten apples in a barrel.

Hideo didn't speak, watching the darkness Seradok brought shroud the room.

"Oh, don't get cold feet now," Seradok said, gliding closer to Hideo. "We're just getting started."

"Getting started?" Hideo tried to smother the fear in his voice.

"Of course." Seradok's jagged maw contorted into a grin. "You see it, don't you. Your army is gone, and your allies have abandoned you. Your son is dead. How do you hope to win this war without my metronome?"

Hideo turned to the device, ticking as if unconcerned by Seradok's presence. Hideo had almost forgotten his war in the moments consumed by revenge. The Northmen had to be stopped. The scourge who invaded their land. The rhetoric that had once emboldened him now sat in his head like prose from a book he was too tired to read.

"Hideo, I'm your only friend now. Trust me like you once did." A tentacle touched Hideo's cheek, turning his head to look at the gross light. "I have a plan. Trust me, it's going to be exquisite. If you come with me, I promise I will make you a legend."

Hideo stared at the mouth of the beast for a moment, expressionless, before looking up to the slowest moving eye and holding its gaze. "Where are we going?"

Seradok just grinned and, like a farmer who had no choice but to sow the seeds he'd bought, Hideo felt a calming resignation as he accepted the fate Seradok was orchestrating. He had no other course now. He'd gone too far to stop. The only chance to win the war was to follow the abyss.

[CHAPTER 21] — QUEEN KYA

Ichika led Astrid and Lindsay through the long expanse of the palace grounds. Open spaces lined with trees from around the world, cultivated carefully to survive in the sand dunes, comprised most of the gardens. Paths like veins cut through the gravel, grass, and grains of sand. Halls, gazebos, pagodas, and dais were scattered messily and, in the centre next to a lake filled with ducks and lanterns, was the tea house.

Queen Kya's tea house was a small gazebo resting on thick stone stilts. Steps rolled down like a tongue, black streaks running through the pure white marble. Blue pillars stretched from the dark, plank flooring, carved with old characters Astrid couldn't read. The columns kept the jade-coloured roof from collapsing. However, the winged corners and feathered patterns made it look like the pillars were tethers, preventing it from floating away.

A large tree sat outside the tea house, guarded by imperial-style fencing. Astrid noticed the tree had begun to blossom, signalling the start of spring.

"Take off your shoes," said Ichika, facing Astrid and Lindsay as she removed her sandals at the bottom of the steps.

The Solstic women looked at each other before kneeling to untie their boots. The rest of Astrid's shield maidens were escorted to the palace. Astrid looked behind her towards the large villa where they were being boarded and couldn't help but think about Doran. Was this how he felt right before they killed him, isolated in an unfamiliar place?

"Her Majesty really picked a nice, secluded place for us to meet," said Astrid, shimmying her left boot off her foot.

"Not *her*. You must address Their Majesty as they or them at all times," said Ichika.

Astrid and Lindsay stood up barefoot.

Ichika continued. "You must bow after I introduce you. You must speak only after Their Majesty has spoken. You must sit only when instructed. Clear?"

"Uhm, yeah," shrugged Astrid. Lindsay also approved, and Ichika turned to lead them on.

As the three women climbed the stairs, Astrid could see Queen Kya. They were well made-up and looked almost a decade younger than they were. Their lips were as pink as the burgeoning cherry blossoms, with skin made to look as white as snow. Black hair, held back by a tiara, flowed down their back to the end of a cyan jeogori, meeting the darker chima that covered them from the diaphragm to ankles.

They were already kneeling at the low table before them, shins digging into a cyan pillow with gold trims around its cylindrical edge. There wasn't much in the way of furniture. The teapot sat in the centre of the table, and three ceramic cups and saucers had already been laid out, one in front of the Queen and two to their right. Four guardswomen stood at each corner of the platform holding spears, and behind Kya was an easel and half-painted canvas of the palace grounds, as vibrant as it looked peeking through the pillars.

Astrid and Lindsay were told to stand at the top of the steps as Ichika made her way to Queen Kya's left. When she got into position, hands firmly planted behind her, she spoke. "You are in the presence of Their Royal Majesty, Queen Kazar Kya, ruler of Sekando, from the northern sea to the –" Ichika stopped herself, realising the southern strait she was about to speak of no longer existed and was now mountains. She took a second to regain composure before continuing. "The city's protector and the lone pillar of these lands."

A silence lingered before Astrid and Lindsay remembered to bow, arms at their sides. The Queen raised their right hand like a feather blown up by the wind, indicating to the pillow that ran along the floor to each corner of the table. "Please sit."

Astrid and Lindsay walked over and sat with their knees up to their chins. The Queen, their legs folded neatly under them, tried not to look for too long at the way they sat, gesturing for Ichika to fill all three cups.

Once she returned to her position, Kya smiled softly and spoke. "Our guests, you must be tired after such a long journey from Takakawa. This tea is made from the ginseng we grow in our garden. We also added a bit of honey to sweeten it. Please try some; it is our favourite tea."

After a few seconds of watching the Queen's gaze dart back and forth between her and the cup, Astrid rolled her eyes, grabbing her cup like an eagle grips its prey. However, she didn't drink it, instead reaching for the cup in front of Kya and replacing it with her mug. Astrid then sipped the Queen's tea. Astrid winced at the sharp taste before setting the cup on her saucer.

The Queen blinked rapidly before they understood Astrid's reaction. "Princess Astrid, we know that, given recent events, you would naturally distrust hospitality on these islands. We promise you; you are in no danger of being poisoned under our protection." The Queen drank out of the cup before them to punctuate their point.

"Yeah, well, that all depends on how long you decide that protection should last," said Astrid, shrugging.

"We've let you in here with your weapon belts," said Kya, gesturing to the gleaming iron at Astrid's hip. "And we are sitting an arm's stroke away from you. You'd have done away with us before the guards could swarm you."

Astrid looked around her before returning to the Queen, giving a resigned nod.

Kya looked back down at the weapon's belt around Astrid's hip. "Is that an Urkanzan knife around your waist?"

Astrid looked at her belt and nodded.

"Can we see it?" asked the Queen.

Astrid noticed that Kya referred to themself as if they were multiple people. Some parts of the world call this the *Royal We*, some call it a personality disorder. Astrid assumed it was linked to why the Queen made others use 'they' or 'them'. Regardless, she was content to ignore it. Those kinds of social quirks were easy to disregard when the person on the other side of the conversation was little more than a means to an end.

Astrid squinted before unsheathing the knife, the sound of shifting steel causing the guards to silently tense up, which brought a grin to her face. She handed the dagger to Kya, who inspected it with wide, childlike eyes.

"This is incredible," they said, running their fingers down the carved bone handle. "The craftsmen who made this have incredible artistry. And your teeth, that's also an Urkanzan tradition, correct?"

Astrid nodded. "It shows a warrior's rank. This symbol means royalty. I was working with a tribe in the western peninsula, and the chieftain permitted me to mark my teeth like this. It's considered a huge dishonour to take a marking you've not earned."

Astrid moved her legs under her, leaned over the table, and moved her tea to the side.

"Extraordinary," said Kya, still analysing the knife. "How long did you live in Urkanza?"

"Four years," said Astrid. "I wanted to return once this war ended, and Doran secured our settlements here. My daughter has never seen it, and I want to take her to all the places I fought. There is a mountain in the middle of this plateau in the northern region, and I've imagined taking her there so often. The view is beautiful when the summer sun sets."

Queen Kya was polite enough not to mention the tear rolling down the Northwoman's face. Astrid hadn't noticed it until it became a cold streak on her cheek and a dark dot on her slacks.

"We're such a blind world," said Kya. "We disagree with the methods your people invoke. However, the interest and credence you allow to cultures unlike your own are envious. You're quick to learn language and traditions and seem genuinely interested. Our brother could go a thousand years only seeing Edokand'i faces and be content. The Solstic could never live in such a bland world."

Astrid nodded at that and sighed. "Our intrigue and our methods come from the same need. The land we were born to is hard. Winters are cruel, beasts are crueller, and people are the cruellest. We turn to other lands out of necessity. When you start associating your culture with the gruelling and the bitter, you turn to other stories and traditions for comfort and escape."

"We've never thought of it like that," said Queen Kya.

"Of course, you haven't," scoffed Astrid, pointing to the easel behind Kya. "You have the luxury of landscape painting and tea making."

Queen Kya laughed at that. "Now, Astrid, it is our impression that you had a rather affluent life yourself."

"I don't know," shrugged Astrid.

"You don't know if you've lived an affluent life?"

"I don't know what affluent means."

Kya chortled. "You are the daughter of a lord, are you not?"

"A jarl," Astrid corrected.

"And we're sure you have some artistic hobbies, do you not?"

Astrid thought for a second. "I play the cithara."

"The cithara?" Kya raised their eyebrows. "That's quite a difficult instrument to learn and must have taken much time and practice."

"Alright," said Astrid, smiling. "I see what you're getting at, but it's a bad example. Even people with hard lives can play instruments. It doesn't show off how *affluent* I am."

"That is our point." Kya turned to look at their painting. "When you say painting is a hobby denoting our status, we concede maybe there is some truth to that. Our life hasn't been particularly tumultuous. But we choose to see it differently. Those lucky enough to have easier lives will always turn to art as a natural recourse. Even those who live difficult lives express themselves through art or song. Imagine the creations that would come from a world free of hardship. Think of the beautiful things we are losing out on as we continue to sow strife and conflict."

Astrid folded her lip and nodded. "That seems optimistic, but I understand what you're saying. However, maybe that strife is what people need. Laziness, hedonism, debauchery, complacency. Those are symptoms of prosperity, just as much as art." Astrid took a sip of her tea, which had started to grow on her, and spoke as she refilled her cup. "Regardless, I'm sure you didn't invite me here to talk about how rich people live their lives. Surely you have scholars for that shit."

Like a child hearing a swear word for the first time, Queen Kya raised their hand to their mouth and giggled. They sipped their tea before shifting the conversation to the dower topic that had hung in the air like the roof above their heads. They put their cup down as their expression turned sullen. "There has been so much we have learned in the days since the mountains rose," said Kya, voice soft, eyes brushing over the tabletop. "We had no idea your King was in peace talks with the Emperor. Our brother, Hideo, made it seem you were advancing into Trim. He asked us to 'save him.' The desperation in his words made us concerned he was close to doing something extreme. He played our emotions, and, for that, we are ashamed."

Kya raised their head and stared at Astrid. Her jaw tensed. "We also had no idea what was going to happen. Our spies in the capital have been investigating how he achieved such devastation and came up short. All we know is that our brother has overthrown the Emperor and arrested many officials loyal to the throne."

Astrid squinted and exhaled sharply. "Why are you telling me this?"

"Because we want you to have the same information we have, however little that may be." Astrid couldn't tell if Kya was being sincere but couldn't find any tell to think otherwise. "We have realised that this war has committed irreparable calamities. Our only goal is to stop those horrors from hitting Sekando more than they already have. Some on our council, including Lady Ichika, have expressed that the best way for Sekando to remain untouched is to avoid more contact with the war itself. Others say we should support Wu Wei and fight with the rest of Edokand."

"Sounds like a spirited debate," said Astrid, sucking her marked teeth. "Has a decision been made?"

"Sort of." Kya looked to Ichika and tilted their head towards the steps. Ichika then reached the top of the marble staircase and gestured to someone below. Eight footsteps later, a large woman in a leather vest entered the gazebo. Her arms were the size of the pillars of the tea house, and a well-suited scowl tore across her face when her amber eyes locked on the Solstic woman.

The stranger put her arms to her side and bowed to Kya, remaining where she stood as Ichika walked back to the Queen's side.

"This is Yuri," said Kya, gesturing to the imposing woman. "She is the champion chosen by the delegation that aligns with Edokand."

Astrid looked at Yuri before rapidly turning her head towards the Queen, cricking her neck. "Champion?" she asked.

"Ichika has been chosen as a champion for the party that voted for passivism." Ichika kept her eyes front, but a grin broke onto her face as the realisation sank Astrid's stomach.

"And you, Astrid, will be the champion chosen for those, like ourself, who believe that we should side with your people in ending this war."

Astrid looked at each of the three Sekandans and then at Lindsay, who Astrid had entirely forgotten was present. She turned back to the Queen. "Wait a minute, why do you want to side with us? You were ready to kill us all two weeks ago."

"We have our reasons," the Queen shrugged. "We want this war to end and believe our intervention is the best way to achieve that. In the four years you have occupied this island, Doran has mostly respected Sekando's borders. Much more than Edokand ever did. Furthermore, how Doran and Hideo have conducted themselves have been diametrically opposed. Your King's ambition for peace matches our own. Also, after what happened to Koji's army, we believe your people have the better shot of winning this war, so by siding with you, the better our chances are of securing peace with those with whom we share borders."

Astrid nodded, folding her lip as she comprehended the Queen's reasoning.

"However," the Queen continued. "Other opinions are just as valid as our own in this matter. Ichika and Yuri approached the council with a *duel of sway*. It's a longstanding tradition for ending debates in such political matters."

Astrid couldn't stop her eyes from dancing between her two potential opponents. Ichika exuded confidence, and the stories Astrid had heard about how she fought gave credence to her bravado. Also, Yuri's appearance and stature were enough for concern. "When will this duel take place?"

"At dusk," said Kya. "And we will need assurance that, whatever the outcome, you will respect the terms. The same goes for the Solstic outside the walls. It is not a duel to the death, but accidents happen. If you do end up dying, we need to know your allies will not seek retribution."

"What if Yuri wins?" asked Astrid.

"The Solstic outside our walls will be given a grace period to retreat peacefully; you have our word." After a moment of pause, Kya continued. "Do you accept these terms?"

Astrid thought for a moment before turning to Lindsay. They both nodded to each other before Astrid turned back to Queen Kya, grinning to match Ichika's confidence. "I'm in."

[CHAPTER 22] — EXECUTION

Akkael woke up suspended in the air with the same jeering as when he had fallen asleep. His back ached from hours of hunching inside the cold metal birdcage, and his head still pulsed from the beating he'd received after he got caught infiltrating Sekando.

He couldn't remember exactly how long it had been, but the day had turned to freezing night, and now the sun was blinding him from its zenith. As he wiped the sweat from his eyes, he couldn't help but regret leaving the comfort of the cave and wished he were gripping the neck of a sake bottle instead of metal bars.

Women had gathered around as the day progressed, whistling at him and yelling profane compliments that made even Akkael blush.

"I like to see you above me, intruder!"

"Should have hidden at my place. I'd have treated you right!"

"Thanks, ladies," said Akkael, coyly saluting with his bound hands. "Appreciate it."

"If you had stayed outside the wall, you'd have been my go-to shag," yelled a woman Akkael couldn't see. A strange pride washed over him before he forced himself to remember that they weren't complimenting him, just some bandit he'd taken the body from. That good feeling quickly turned sour in his mouth.

Akkael's cage spun until his vision was eclipsed by the city's eastern wall from which he was dangling. When his back turned to the women, the whistling got louder.

"That's the view I like to see!"

After a few more moments of swinging, his vision split between the beige city wall and the amassing crowd of Sekandans; Akkael noticed some women preparing the plank stage to his left. Two flags were carried to the back corners of the platform, the blue circle of Sekando emblazoned on the red Edokand'i background. Guardswomen in blue cuirasses pushed the crowds back as someone placed a basket before a chopping block. A large, black-bladed axe was propped against the wall, and steps were rolled into place in front of the stage.

Akkael pressed himself against the bars of his cage and whispered to a guard below him. She wore a helmet with a spike on top and carried a spear inside her fist.

"Psst," said Akkael, knocking the bars. "Psst!"

The guardswoman ignored him, shuffling in her armour. Akkael used his body weight to slap his cage against the wall, metal ringing against the sandstone.

"Yes, that's it," said a woman in the crowd, "shake it!"

Akkael ignored the comments. "Hey, you! Yes, you in the tin shirt. Hey!"

"What, intruder?" asked the guard with a short intake of breath.

"Who's going to kill me?" asked Akkael.

The guardswoman looked confused. "Excuse me?"

"You know, who's gonna –?" Akkael clicked his tongue and ran his thumb across his neck.

The guardswoman squinted at the man she thought was a loyalist criminal. "Lady Ichika has asked to personally dispatch anyone bearing the emblem of you vultures." She gave Akkael a disconcerting smile. "And who is the Queen to deny such a reasonable request."

"Ichika?" Akkael smiled to himself. He'd planned to keep getting killed until he'd become someone who had sway with the Queen or even the Queen themself. But to be executed by their First Blade and most trusted confident on his first try, Akkael couldn't believe his luck.

Akkael felt guilty about the full bladder pushing at his abdomen. He didn't know the bandit he'd become. But, judging from the reactions of everyone Akkael had met since coming to Sekando, his fame warranted more than leggings full of piss, mercilessly getting jeered and mocked before being beheaded for a ridiculous crime he would never have committed if he were himself.

Drums were beating from the alleys that peered behind the crowd, standing as dense as a forest. The women had grown quiet, turning slowly and splitting a path from the centre alley where the noise was loudest. In the distance, Akkael could see more Sekandan flags. Warrior women carried the standards, walking three abreast, a few rows before and after an ornate palanquin that was thin enough to fit through the narrow street. There was no roof, just a blue velvet bench and gold inlay on the edges of the platform, carved into a feathered pattern.

On top of the bench sat Ichika, picking dirt out of her fingernails as she bobbed to the steps of those carrying her. She was wearing a lot of armour to execute someone tied up. Akkael thought he'd have to prepare for the weight difference as he shifted from his bandit leathers to her blue plate. But he'd always wanted to ride in a palanquin.

When the convoy made their way to the opening, the standard bearers spread out, lining the two sides of spectators. The palanquin stopped halfway between the alley and the stage and was placed on the path. Ichika stood from her bench, and the crowd exploded into cheers and screams. She grinned a little and raised her hands into the air. Everyone cheered louder before Ichika ran and jumped onto the lip of the stage. She turned to face the crowd, arms again in the air, which only caused more hollering.

Akkael, head still pounding from being knocked out and beaten, could have done without the theatrics but enjoyed seeing what passed for entertainment in Sekando.

"Women of Sekando City," said Ichika. Her voice was strangely amplified as if coming from the sky above. Akkael looked around and noticed a sage at the mouth of the alleyway who must have been using her powers to carry Ichika's voice.

The First Blade of Sekando continued. "The traditions of our city may be odd to some outsiders. *A capital city that only half the population can enter. How can such a place thrive as it has?"* She made her voice deep as if to imitate a man. "They imagine us behind our walls, look at the blue dot of our people, and think us strange. And maybe we are."

The crowd laughed as Ichika shrugged and folded her bottom lip. "We don't have to explain our ways to these outsiders. We don't have to tell them the justifications, the historical precedents, the reasons, and the stories that led us to become what we are today. We don't have to explain our traditions, but we must enforce them!

"Now, sometimes, the Queen is merciful. Not all men who enter our city face corporal punishment; that's a myth. You know this. Often, they are set free after a few days in the birdcage." Ichika pointed to Akkael, scowling at the man she thought he was. "But not the likes of him. The vultures have undermined the Queen's rule and the Queens before them. They use their emblem as a metaphor, saying they are picking at the corpse of Sekando. But, if you ask me, Sekando is very much alive."

The women in the audience erupted into hollers and applause, whistling at Ichika's words. After a moment of playing to the crowd, Ichika pointed back at the cage. "Bring him to me!"

The guardswoman Akkael had spoken to walked over to his cage and, with her spear, released the bolt that kept the floor of his cell in place. The bolt hit the sand with a whisper, followed by Akkael with a thud. Women laughed as the hatch of his cage squeaked above his head. The guardswomen and another Sekandan in armour linked with Akkael's bound arms and dragged him up the steps of the stage.

Akkael met Ichika face to face as she grinned maliciously. She had already retrieved the executioner's axe that rested against the wall, clutching it horizontally with both gauntleted hands. He still didn't understand why Ichika was wearing so much armour. She didn't wear any when she was with Koji's army.

"I've got a busy day ahead of me, intruder," said Ichika nonchalantly. "Do you have any last words?"

Akkael thought for a moment on some critical, final note. He spoke slowly, putting emphasis on each word. "Umm, I don't understand why people hate pears so much. They are a fine fruit."

Ichika squinted. "What?"

"Apples get all the praise," continued Akkael, trying to stifle a grin. "But the pear is a decent fruit and deserves equal, if not more, acclaim."

From the corner of his eye, he saw one woman in the crowd nod to herself, breaking Akkael's composure.

Ichika rolled her eyes, turning to the women who were restraining him. "Put him on the block."

They pushed and pulled Akkael until he was in line with the chopping block, and then they kicked the backs of his knees, causing him to kneel in front of it. Ichika lined up to where Akkael's head would be. "Neck where it needs to be, or I'll have my warriors keep it there. This is your chance to die with dignity."

Akkael obliged Ichika's demand, laying his head where the axe would fall. The First Blade continued. "In the name of Their Royal Majesty, Queen Kazar Kya, the city's protector and lone pillar of Sekando, I sentence you to die."

Akkael could feel the wind move as if it had been given its marching orders, following the path of the axe. The crowd and the city behind them were frozen in a pastel blur. Some turned away, and some watched with expressions Akkael couldn't focus on enough to make out. Then the axe was brought down, and the last thing Akkael heard was a hurricane whirring just behind him. The wind charged like a vanguard, hitting the block before the axe sliced through the bandit's neck.

Akkael saw through Ichika's eyes before the head hit the basket. The state change made Akkael feel nauseous, but he tried hard to keep a steady stomach. He looked at the crowd, all eyes on who they assumed was the First Blade. He threw the executioner's axe to the stage, trying to employ the same theatrics Ichika had done to keep up appearances.

"The man is slain!!" The crowd erupted into raucous applause as Akkael lifted Ichika's arms. "It is a deep and paramount shame to leave after such a grand spectacle," continued Akkael, trying desperately to remember how Ichika talked, "but alas, I must depart. Farewell, my fellow women. Fare thee well."

The audience was silent until one woman spoke out. "Why are you talking like that?"

Akkael froze in silence before replying. "Goodbye," he said before hastily declining the stage steps. The palanquin bearers had already lifted the platform when

Akkael approached. He stepped on, sitting in the same blue seat Ichika had on her way to execute him.

Since Wu Wei, Akkael has been met with constant challenges and unprecedented situations. He smiled, finally feeling that things were going according to plan and he was one step closer to his revenge.

"So, my lady," said the closest palanquin bearer. She wore a sapphire doublet and leather gloves for a better grip. "Now that the execution is over, are you looking forward to your duel with Astrid?"

Akkael felt his heart skip a beat, and the palanquin seemed to stand still despite the buildings that passed by. "Astrid?" he asked, hoping he hadn't just heard his wife's name come out of the carrier's mouth.

"Yeah, Astrid Torne," she said, straining to get a better grip. "There's been a lot of chatter about your duel of sway. The Northmen are ruthless in battle, but my money's on you, my lady."

"I'm fighting Astrid Torne in a duel of sway?" Akkael said through the heart beating in his ears.

The palanquin bearer paused momentarily, confusion changing her face before she sighed and rolled her eyes. "Ichika, you know I don't like playing this game."

"What's the duel of sway about?" Akkael blurted out. "Why is Astrid here?"

The palanquin-bearer just sighed again. "I'm sorry I tried to show interest in your life, cousin. You do this every time."

Akkael was taken aback, deciding not to ask Ichika's cousin any more questions to keep his distance from the real-world implications of his abilities. He let the wave of dread wash over him once again as he pictured being in the duelling ring with his wife. He never expected to face her after what happened to Alani.

Every worry and tense scenario played in Akkael's head as his hand trembled. He thought about how much he'd let her down, failing the last request she had given him. He led their daughter to her death, and he got himself killed, leaving her alone in the world without considering how devastated she would be. He'd dwelled on Alani's death with self-pity, self-destruction, and self-loathing, not allowing himself to think of Astrid because he couldn't bear her ire as well as his own.

His pulse beat at his neck and chest like a captive trying to break down a locked door. He could feel his breath scraping against his teeth as blood rushed to his head, hotter than the magma that engulfed his daughter. His hand was cramping as if Alani were still squeezing it, terrified. The mountains flashed into his head, and his vision blurred until he felt like he was looking through a keyhole.

Akkael still had enough self-control to conceal his panic attack, despite every muscle telling him to run and never stop. He just sat there as the palanquin bobbed under him, leading him closer to the woman he'd married; back when he was himself.

[CHAPTER 23] — THE DUEL OF SWAY

Astrid could not remember the last time she blinked. The nights had allowed her little sleep, and her days granted little rest. Most of the time, she enjoyed that exhaustion. It was numbing and kept her from thinking for too long. But she worried it would hinder the duel, and she knew this was her best chance to get the revenge she craved.

She watched from atop the balcony of her guest room like a gargoyle, overlooking the arena where she'd fight in the duel of sway. Stands slowly filled with Sekandan nobles, skin made to look as white as marble, with expressions too rigid for stone. Her lips were locked tight, and her nostrils never wavered. People might have wondered if she was breathing if she weren't alone.

Hours had passed, and Astrid's green eyes were now fixed on Yuri, already at the arena, training with her steel weapons next to the platform. She was too far to focus on skill or technique, so she just stared thoughtlessly at her opponent, waiting for the other to arrive.

The duel of sway allowed the combatants three weapons and three shields. Yuri chose a geom, a katana, and a spear with a large blade. Everything was steel, including her blue plate-mail. She imagined Ichika would prefer a similar weapon set. Astrid chose two hand axes and her Urkanzan dagger. Her shields were fir wood covered in leather. The iron buckles on the front were the same quality as her axes.

The first horn blew, and Astrid was shocked at how far the sun had sunk. With ten minutes until sunset, she stood up from her balcony, turned into her guest room, now nearly pitch black, and went down to the arena.

The walk was made longer in her mind, feeling a weight weeks in the making. This was the best chance she would have of crushing Wu Wei. The Sekandans fought with Koji at the mountains but never spilt Solstic blood. The alliance would be tense, but that would abate. All that mattered was Wu Wei and the heaped rubble Astrid would reduce it to.

137

When she reached the platform, a chalk circle drawn onto a wooden stage, she made her way to the Solstic side of the stands. Shield maidens lined the dais, cheering while she moved along the ring. She noticed Queen Kya sitting in their box, a blue tarp concealing them from the elements. Lanterns lined the area, and flags fluttered in the night wind.

Yuri was finishing her drills, and Ichika sat in her corner beside two spears and a geom clasped in a frame behind her. Three shields identical to the ones in Yuri's corner were also hung up. Ichika stared at Astrid with an intensity that made her want to turn away.

Lindsay was fixing the shields to a rack when Astrid approached. She gave a warm smile which hid concern. "I put all your weapons in your belt, princess." Astrid winced at the moniker but chose to ignore it. "They offered you a weapon's rack too, but I thought you'd rather have everything with you when you fought."

Astrid nodded, clasping her hand on Lindsay's shoulder. "Thank you. You've been a great strength for me these long weeks, and I don't know how I'll repay you."

Lindsay just smiled. "You can start by winning."

Astrid giggled before moving over to her weapon's belt and clasping it around her waist. Axes at each hip, with her Urkanzan dagger clasped on her left side.

"Women of Sekando!" A sage spoke in the arena's centre, wearing purple robes and a blue sash. She amplified her voice with her gifts. "We are gathered here to witness a duel of sway. Each combatant comes with their own path, wish, and will. The outcome of this duel will decide which of these paths comes to fruition. The duel's outcome will be respected, as decreed by Queen Kya themself. Combatants, please choose your first weapon and shield, and make your way into the circle."

Astrid reached for the leather-bound shield Lindsay held out and made her way to the ring. Yuri was already standing in the centre next to the sage, with a one-handed spear in her giant left fist and a steel shield in her right. She was a foot taller than Astrid and was scowling at the top of the Northwoman's blonde head through the visor of a kabuto helmet.

Ichika paused for a moment, staring at the weapons she had chosen. She tentatively picked up the sword and a shield before turning and stepping into the circle, eyes locked on Astrid.

Astrid felt uneasy as if Ichika were readying herself to strike her. Yuri would probably do the same, so she knew she'd need to move first. Akkael was always better at duelling and had taught her to pick a target before the battle started. She met Ichika's glare, knowing where her axe would fly first.

"With the Seraphim's wisdom seeped into our souls, we go about our sacred tradition." There was still a light tinge to the sky, but the sun had disappeared on the horizon. "First, I must reiterate the rules. Each duellist has three weapons and three shields. If anything falls to the ground, they are no longer in use. The combatant may then leave the arena briefly to reequip. If they are out of the arena for longer than a minute, they are forfeit. If a combatant leaves the circle with a shield and weapon in hand, they are forfeit. If a combatant loses all weapons and shields, they are forfeit." The sage looked at each of the battle-ready women in turn. "You three must decide: is this duel to first blood, yield, or death?"

"First blood," said Ichika as the sage finished speaking. The crowd broke into confused murmurs, and Astrid furrowed her brow.

The sage didn't react, instead turning to Yuri for her vote. "Yield," said Yuri, also squinting at Ichika.

"Yield," said Astrid, as well.

"So, yield it will be." The sage turned to the Queen and, with their nod of approval, continued. "The stakes of the duel involve Sekando's stance in the war between Edokand and Solstr. First Blade Ichika is fighting on the side of neutrality. Councilwoman Yuri is fighting to join forces with Edokand. The foreigner, Astrid Torne, is fighting for Sekando's support. The duel's winner will sway Their Majesty's decision in this matter, who has made an oath to hold the outcome as law. Do all the combatants agree to these terms?"

All three women nodded.

"Then take your positions at the edge of the circle." The sage vacated the arena as the three women stood equidistant at the ring's circumference. A wind carried sand across the platform with the quiet grating of a distant whetstone slowly running along a blade as those in the stands fell silent. Astrid's heartbeat was like the rhythmic pounding of a hammer at an anvil, and the sky was coloured like the dying embers of a forge.

The sage looked at each woman individually. "In three..." she bellowed, her gifts still projecting her voice.

"Two..." The Sekandans shuffled in their armour. Astrid heard the pull of her leather tunic as she stretched.

"One..." She unbuckled an axe from her belt, holding it tight in her right fist. She tightened her grip on the shield, and pulled a breath into her lungs, exhaling slowly like a light breeze sneaking through the rafters. Her eyes met Ichika's, and she centred herself, making her first battle decision before it had begun. Astrid prepared to strike first, crouching like a cat ready to pounce.

"Fight!"

Astrid lunged.

[CHAPTER 24] — CHASING BIRDS

Akkael had heard of duels of sway from studying Edokand. He remembered a few instances where combat determined significant constitutional and military changes. A duel of sway led Wu Wei to expand across all five islands of Edokand and name them for their clan. It was also a duel of sway which ended that war.

Akkael had found a book about such events in the library at Skaldgard. Whenever he wasn't raiding or warring, he would sit in the dark of the library and read by the candlelight. Alani would join him, sitting on his lap and sometimes reading the pages aloud.

He closed his eyes, remembering those moments. The smell of the books, the flickering of the candle, the rustling of the papers as wind snuck through holes in the ceiling. Alani read Edokand'i faster than he could, her eyes dancing along the pages like the flame on the wick. He would sit there until Alani had fallen asleep against his chest, and sometimes, he'd just close his eyes and do the same.

"Fight!" yelled the sage, pulling Akkael out of his reverie, raising his steel shield to meet Astrid's axe.

The axe head scraped down the domed shield with a sound that went through Akkael. He hated metal shields and would have preferred the flat, round, leather one in his wife's fist. Akkael sliced at Astrid to create distance, which she blocked quickly.

She stepped back from Akkael just in time to see the brute, Yuri, charge into the gap, lunging her geom blade towards her. She parried, hooking the sword with her axe, and pulled it away before slamming her weapon into the centre of Yuri's armoured chest. Yuri stumbled back until all three combatants were two arm's widths from the next.

Akkael realised he had the advantage in this fight. He knew how Astrid fought, knew her weaknesses and strengths and had an intimate knowledge of her skill with axes and shields. When they duelled for fun, Akkael would win half the time, but that was because Astrid also had an equal understanding of how he fought.

141

However, Astrid thought he was Ichika, a woman she'd never seen fight. Akkael knew Astrid would conduct herself as if she were fighting any other Sekandan, not one of the Solstic.

Yuri was at even more of a disadvantage. She had probably seen Ichika fight, so she went into the ring with expectations. Estimation and assumptions get the best fighters killed all the time.

There was a gap in Yuri's armour under the shoulder, so Akkael swung for it. However, Yuri stepped back, only receiving a shallow cut from the tip of his double-edged blade. She took a fighting stance, hilt at her waist and hidden by her shield. The blade pointed towards the ground.

Astrid went for the left pauldron strap, exposed by Yuri's twisted body. But the councilwoman was quick, meeting Astrid's axe with her sword before lunging at her belly. Astrid raised her shield just in time, and while the fight had turned in her direction, Akkael swung for the same gap in Yuri's armour, slicing a deeper gash in her arm. The large woman yelped; head raised to the night sky. She swung her sword in an arch at Akkael, who dodged. Sand flicked up as the blade hit the wooden platform below their feet.

Akkael had to make an extra effort not to die. If Yuri killed him, he would become her. That was okay, but it might cause problems, as he wasn't sure how much value she enjoyed on the Queen's council. However, if Astrid killed him, Akkael would erase her from her body, and no revenge was worth that.

No one needed to die, either. If Astrid won the duel, the Sekandans would be fighting with the Solstic against Wu Wei, precisely what he wanted. Akkael didn't have to win. He just had to defeat Yuri and then surrender. He'd be on his way to Trim with an unbeatable force ready to lay the City of Disciplines to ruin. He ducked Astrid's axe as the thought made him smile.

Akkael spent the next few moments in defence, blocking the head of Astrid's axe and dodging the blade of Yuri's sword. He needed to get back on the offensive, but it became increasingly difficult as the two opponents kept on him.

Astrid clipped his shield and pulled it down before changing course, smashing her axe against his armour, denting the chest piece. Yuri then stabbed Akkael's torso but stopped just shy of the plate mail. The blade fell flat against his arm, scrapping the length of leather and steel towards his hand until Yuri's sword caught his own handle. With one movement, Akkael's sword hit the floor of the duelling platform.

Unarmed, he ducked and rolled out of the chalk perimeter the women had pushed him towards. He had sixty seconds to retrieve one of the spears from the rack and return to the arena. He counted himself as an all-round fighter with proficiency in swords, axes, and knives, and though he was the worst with spears, he could also wield them. However, the Sekandan spears were different to what Akkael was familiar with. They were shorter, one-handed poles with a large head shaped like a cleaver.

He pulled the first of the two spears from the rack and re-entered the ring at the furthest point from Astrid and Yuri. They had barely noticed his return, caught up in their dance that Akkael didn't want to interrupt. He just watched as his wife met each of the large woman's blows with an accuracy he'd always envied. She used to say she was terrible at one-on-one combat, but Akkael admired her. She was so in tune with her axe and was ready to parry moves ahead. He could watch her fight all day and still be amazed.

Yuri stumbled backwards when Astrid cut a gash in her leg, followed by a blow that knocked her helmet to the ground. Astrid moved closer as the Sekandan limped on her wounded leg. But Yuri was still quick, lunging with her geom at Astrid. She tried to dodge, but a gash ripped through her side and sliced at her ribs. She buckled to her knees.

"Just so you know," said Yuri, towering over Astrid, "this isn't personal. I have nothing against the Northmen. But you don't belong here, and I have dreamt a long time to see the last of your ships leave our shores." Yuri moved closer until her boot touched Astrid's knee, the Northwoman gripping her side. "Yield or –"

Astrid didn't let the large Sekandan finish. Akkael was making his way over to stop Yuri just as Astrid rose, swift like a geyser, launching a thick gash through Yuri's neck. She collapsed, dropping her sword and clasping her throat as she drowned in her blood. Akkael stopped, watching Yuri writhe like a fish out of water. After a few moments, she went limp, gurgling her last breath.

Astrid and Akkael both looked at Queen Kya in the stands. They had averted their gaze from the arena, mouth covered by a gloved hand and eyes filled with water. After a few seconds, they composed themself with a deep breath, turning to face the arena once more.

"Continue," they croaked, the sage enhancing their wavering voice.

Without a second's delay, Astrid leapt over Yuri's corpse and charged towards a frozen Akkael. He raised his steel shield just in time to stop the flight of her axe and backed off. They circled each other for a few moments. Astrid tightened her grip on her weapon, and Akkael spun his spear in his hand.

After a few seconds, Astrid stopped, which caused Akkael to do the same.

"My husband used to do that," she said, gesturing to the spear.

"What?" asked Akkael, trying to focus on his Ichika impression while speaking in Edokand'i.

"That," she said, pointing again. "He used to spin weapons like that when getting ready to strike. It was one of his worst tells."

Akkael remained silent, keeping the spear still in his fist.

Astrid squinted. "He also used to hold spears like that. Closer to the tip with the pole held tight along the forearm. You can't possibly fight like that, can you?"

Akkael didn't know what to say next. He moved his fist to the centre of the spear and, after a moment, replied. "Are we going to finish this duel, or are we going to talk more?"

Astrid's lip twitched. "Fair enough," she said. She let the axe handle fall slightly down her grip until her small finger met the ridge. She lifted it over her shoulder and launched it at Akkael. He was too slow to react, and the axe burrowed into his breastplate. It cut his chest but didn't go deep, held in place more by the armour than his flesh.

Astrid bounded towards Akkael, unhooking the second axe from her belt and swinging it towards his helmetless head. He ducked, parrying with a lunge from his spear. Astrid spun away. Akkael's next slice met Astrid's shield with such force it cleaved it in half, swinging loosely by the leather binding. She unleashed a barrage of blows at Akkael's shield intended to create distance. She succeeded before fleeing to the edge of the ring.

"Lindsay, shield!" Astrid yelled, unbuckling the broken one attached to her arm as Akkael removed the axe from his chest.

Lindsay removed another round shield from the rack and threw it to Astrid, who caught it with one hand.

Astrid turned back to Akkael, making her way towards him with the prowl of a wolf on the hunt. Akkael took the initiative, charging with his spear in front of him. Astrid redirected him with her axe. She swung for his back. She missed, allowing Akkael to turn and swing his spear around, disarming her again.

Akkael knew he should be finding ways to believably lose while still surviving the duel. However, he missed sparing with Astrid. Some couples danced. Some played games or sang. Akkael and Astrid were never more connected than when they fought each other. Each blow and block took him one step closer to the life he used to have when things made sense and the world was calm.

Astrid removed her Urkanzan dagger from her belt, repeatedly swinging at Akkael as he dodged and weaved out of the way. He started to smile, which visually angered Astrid. He knew it would have annoyed her even if he didn't look like Ichika, and that thought made him smile more.

Astrid yelled in battle rage after repeatedly being side-stepped and swerved. Her blade got faster; her steps got closer. Akkael kept his eye on the dagger's tip, watching and predicting its path, making it miss every time. After he ducked a swing to his face, he waited for the next move. Starting at the blade and waiting for a stab or slice that never came.

Instead, Astrid twisted her whole body and lifted her left arm, planting her shield where her axe had dented his armour.

She threw Akkael off his feet. All the wind left his body, and he gasped so hard his eyes went bloodshot. His ribs cracked from the shield's weight, and he fell with a crash, head smacking the wooden duelling platform.

When he opened his eyes, two rotating images of his wife holding a knife to his throat consumed his vision. "Do you yield?" he heard her say in a slow echo.

His eyes watered from the pain, and Astrid leaned her knee on his broken chest. "Astrid…" he croaked.

"Do you yield?" she repeated.

He looked up at the double, spiralling picture of her. Her green eyes and blonde hair looked so much like Alani's, it was as if Astrid were standing next to their daughter, and she was all grown up.

"I'm sorry…" he managed to groan.

"What?" she said, shaking her head.

More tears poured from his eyes as the pain grew. "You were right. We should have let her chase them."

"What are you talking about?" Astrid spat.

"I stopped her every time, but you liked to watch her. You were right." The pressure in Akkael's chest abated as Astrid removed her knee. Akkael continued to whisper. "I would let her chase them now. I'd let her chase them as much as she wanted."

Astrid paused for a moment. "Chase, what?" She asked, almost as quietly as Akkael was speaking.

Akkael's lip quivered, and more tears rolled off his cheek. "The birds," he said. "I'd let her chase those birds. She loved it so much."

The double image of Astrid merged into one as Akkael's vision focused. Her eyes were red, and her mouth was agape. The dagger fell to the platform as her shield arm sagged, her face wet. She shook her head slowly; her body trembled like a leaf in the wind as she prepared to speak. She could only manage one stuttered word.

"Akkael?"

Astrid said his name as if she were asking about the pronunciation of a foreign word. Akkael couldn't answer, moaning as he drifted into unconsciousness. His vision went black, and the last thing he felt was someone grab his hand, leading him into the darkness.

[CHAPTER 25] — HER SCARF

"We know you probably can't hear us, but it helps to talk to you. We always feel better with you by our side. Hopefully, having us here helps you too." A chair scraped against floorboards in the darkness.

"We don't understand what people are saying. The sage overheard your conversation with Astrid. Why were you talking like that? What did you mean? Astrid was pulled away from the fighting ring, screaming her husband's name. Was it some ploy? To put her off her guard and strike before you fell unconscious. Was that it? And the way you fought. We've seen you battle hundreds of times, but never that way. Why?

"We know you can't answer. Ichika, something is happening in our world that none of us fully understand. Mountains rising from the sea, Koji's army slaughtering each other, killing friends. Reports of dragon sightings are getting louder." Someone grabbed Akkael's hand. "Ichika, the thought of doing all this without you scares us. We... I can't do this without you."

There was silence, only broken by the occasional sniffling. "We must go. The Northmen are getting restless, and we must make previsions to march on Wu Wei. We will not leave without you, though. So, wake up soon. That's an order from your Queen. Wake up, and please... be you."

After a few more moments, light footsteps preceded the creaking of a heavy door. Once it was shut again, the silence caused Akkael to drift even further into unconsciousness.

Akkael dreamt.

He saw a young girl with bright, green eyes standing in a light beam. An ambient whisper, like a babbling waterfall, breathed serenity into the void as the little girl stood like a statue.

"Alani," said Akkael, lips quivering.

"Hello, da," she said in a flat tone.

Akkael took a small step closer. "Am I dreaming?" he asked, knowing the answer but hoping he was wrong.

"Oh, da," she said, with pity in her voice. "Of course, you are. I'm dead. How else would I talk to you?"

"Oh, yes. Sorry."

"It's alright." There was none of Alani's spirit in the apparition. But she looked like her, and that was enough.

"Can we talk for a while anyway?" asked Akkael.

"If you'd like."

Akkael looked for something to say, staring at Alani. Her face relaxed, like a person sleeping, with no discernible emotion. "I need you to know that I'm sorry. It was my fault, all of it. I blame myself for everything."

Alani just stood vacant as Akkael breathed heavily.

"Good," she finally said, nodding. "I'm glad we're on the same page."

Like a flash of lightning, Alani was replaced with a taller figure. The same blonde hair and green eyes burst into view as Akkael faced the image of his wife.

He was cast out of the void, and his eyes flung open, waking up in a cold sweat. His breath was the sound of lumberjacks heaving either end of a crosscut saw. Black, wet hair clung to his forehead. When he looked down, a tight bandage was wrapped around his torso, and his legs were covered by blue, embroidered bed sheets.

A calm, teal darkness swirled around him, slowly forming the interior of a bedroom as he recovered from his dream. He lay on a four-poster bed. To his right was a writing desk with a thick document in the centre, an inkwell next to it, and a dried quill on top of the bottle. Across from Akkael was a long mirror, blue bed sheets leading to Ichika's face staring back at him.

He sighed in relief when he saw Astrid hadn't killed him. He didn't know what to do if it was his wife in the mirror. He saw the colour of the sky through a silk curtain, heard the birds singing on Ichika's balcony, and realised it was dawn. Food from last night's meal had been left to cool on the bedside at Akkael's left. He

149

knew he probably didn't have long before it would be replaced with breakfast, so he had to prepare himself for whatever would come through the door.

It seemed strange, considering the powers he'd been given. Still, he hadn't been confronted with many situations where he'd had to act as the person he'd become. The shadow archer was the closest he got to it. When he was the bandit, he had to pretend he was a man who had broken into Sekando City, which was easy because he was a man who had broken into Sekando City. But this was different. He knew extraordinarily little about Ichika's personal life except for her job title and parts of her personality.

When Akkael was a child in Solstr, he saw a Rhaynese acting troupe in his uncle's great hall. He loved watching them, mainly when they performed plays that weren't written down. These improvised performances were so engaging, but, over time, Akkael learned the knack for them. He'd noticed one little phrase that the troupe repeated, which kept the performances progressing.

"Yes, and..." No matter what came through the door, so long as he remembered that phrase, he knew he'd be all right.

The door slowly creaked open.

"Mumma!"

Three figures entered the room. One was a young servant carrying a platter of food. The next was a shorter woman wearing a grey shirt and black leggings. She looked rather odd in her outfit, but her blue earrings and styled hair gave her away as someone of high status.

The third was a child no older than eight. She wore a blue dress, and her black hair was platted. Strange glass circles were held in front of her eyes by a metal frame, which was also stained blue. As soon as she entered the room and saw Akkael she smiled and ran for the bed.

"Mumma!" she screamed, jumping at Akkael's broken ribcage and clasping tight around it. "I missed you so much, mumma! Did you miss me?"

Akkael winced at the pain. "Yes, and," he said, trying to think of what else to say, "I dreamt about you every second."

The girl smiled widely before her face turned serious. "You've been asleep for three days."

Akkael's eyes sharpened. "Three days?"

The servant replaced the cold food with the breakfast platter and bowed before excusing herself.

"Yeah, you missed a lot." Ichika's daughter stood up from the bed and made a stern face. She began to count on her fingers everything that had happened since the duel. "Queen Kya has been with the Northwoman, planning to invade Wu Wei. The blossoms have started on the trees, which is really pretty. I got new glasses, see. They're nicer than my old ones. Oh, and people have been talking about a dragon a lot."

"A dragon?" Much had happened to Akkael since the mountains rose, but he still didn't know how that had slipped his mind. The black scales were like a sliver of the night against the day's sky. Its body was like a snake, pacing through the grass. He thought he'd just hallucinated from blood loss after the bandits had left him for dead. He wondered when, if ever, he'd stop being surprised by the novel experiences and changes.

"Mi-ok," said the woman in the grey shirt, "maybe you should give your mother some rest."

The girl pouted. "But she's been resting for days, and there is so much I haven't said."

The woman put her hand on Mi-ok's shoulder. "There are important matters I need to discuss with your mother, and they are not for a little girl's ears."

Mi-ok sighed and rolled her eyes. "Fine!" She gave Akkael one more hug. It hurt, but Akkael didn't want her to let go. He closed his eyes and imagined he was in the library of Skaldgard, hugging Alani.

Ichika's daughter pulled away, smiling. "I'm glad you're better. Bye, mumma. Bye, Moon."

"Bye." Akkael's voice sounded so small and much less stable as he wavered through the word.

151

Mi-ok left the room, and Akkael turned to face Moon. Her arms were folded, which showed off her muscular frame. She looked at Akkael like she was studying a text. "So, Ichika. Where did you learn to fight like that?"

Akkael could sense the mockery in her voice. "I guess it was just an off day," he said, trying his best not to fidget. "What did you need to talk to me about?"

Moon took a sharp intake of breath. "I need to see your report?"

"Report?" Akkael regretted intonating the question like that. He needed to pretend he knew what Ichika knew and couldn't question something's existence, which Ichika had full knowledge of. "Why do you need my report?"

"I got a warrant from the Queen to look over it." Moon's eyebrow rose above the other. "Where is it?"

Akkael looked around the room as subtly as he could. After a second, he remembered the stack of papers on Ichika's writing desk. "It's over there."

Moon sat at the desk and started flipping through the pages Ichika had written. Akkael had no idea what the report was about but needed to pretend he did. "What are you looking for?"

Moon remained silent, still flipping through the pages. Eventually, she stopped on a page Akkael was too far, off-angle, and supine to read. She scanned a little longer in silence before placing her finger on a passage. Then, Moon started to read aloud:

"*After interviewing the survivors that had found their way to Koseki, we could piece together some idea of what occurred on the battlefield. Captain Cheolsan, the only high-ranking officer who survived the carnage, gave the first statement. 'I watched men who loved each other kill each other,' he said. 'Brothers-in-arms, brothers-in-law, life-long friends, soulmates. Men I had watched drink and laugh together one minute had murdered each other the next. No secret agenda or political motivation could have caused this. There is no doubt in my mind that these soldiers were possessed by some form of demon, whose hatred for mankind is the greatest force of malice in our world.'*"

Akkael stayed silent, not trusting himself to speak first. He became very aware of the pattern of his breathing and the speed of his heartbeat as Moon stared at him.

"What's my job?" asked Moon.

Akkael remained still.

"Come on," insisted Moon. "We've worked together for years, Ichika. What's my job?"

His mind raced, trying to think if he'd ever heard of Moon. Ichika was the First Blade of Sekando's military and had a seat on the council. So, for Moon to have worked with her for years meant she was a part of one of those two establishments. Or both.

Then he remembered Moon had said that the Queen gave her the warrant to look at the report, which Akkael knew could only mean one thing. "You're the commander of the military police."

Moon smiled. "Good." She spoke as if congratulating a child for getting a trivia question right. "In the capacity of my job, naturally, I have to deal with many crimes. Men breaking into the city, theft, murder, treason, desertion. It's all the same. But do you know what I like about crimes? Sometimes, they are mysteries. You must use your brain to solve them, collect clues, and connect the dots. It's why the Queen gave me the job I have. I'm particularly good at mysteries."

"Okay," Akkael said, still as a statue.

"Do you want to know why I'm good at mysteries?" Moon didn't wait for Akkael to answer before continuing. "I have no shame. That sounds like a trait best utilised by jesters or prostitutes, but I assure you it's transferrable. I don't care how crazy my theories sound; if it connects the dots, I follow my gut. Most times, I get it right."

Akkael shrugged like he thought Ichika would have. "Great. What's that got to do with anything?"

Moon snickered before continuing. "Do you remember the ballad of Boksu?"

153

He knew Moon was testing him, asking him basic questions to see if he could produce an answer. Luckily, he had heard the song. He sang it dozens of times one night while drinking with an Edokand'i bard. "Of course, I know it," he said, trying not to sound too pleased with himself.

"Of course," repeated Moon. "Do you mind telling me what it's about?"

Rolling eyes can mean a lot of things. More commonly, it's to show disinterest or annoyance, but it can also show someone is trying hard to recall something. Akkael hoped Moon thought it was the former.

"It's a revenge tale," said Akkael. "An Edokand'i general kills Bok-su and her family. She returns as a ghost and hunts him down, returning the favour."

Moon had her arms folded as she nodded her head. "The motivation for most murders is revenge," she said, returning to the report. "The scorned lover, the wronged, the jealous. Most of the worst parts of history are caused by revenge. So, when Astrid gets pulled off the duelling platform screaming her husband's name, the part of my brain that connects dots starts spinning."

She placed her finger on the report. "If I combine this statement, Astrid's outburst, the strange way you were acting during the duel, and what the sage heard you say to Astrid after she knocked you to the ground, then I just can't stop myself."

"What are you implying?" said Akkael meekly.

"Let me paint you the picture in my head," said Moon, standing up from her chair and pacing around the room. "King Doran and his brothers go to Wu Wei. They leave Doran there and then go back to their camp. Then, bang! The world breaks. The two islands collide, and mountains rise. Akkael's daughter is killed by the explosions, and Akkael is killed by a shadow archer. The Northmen were betrayed by Hideo and Koji. So, like an act of some non-existent god, Koji's army implodes. They think it's a demon, but what if it's simpler than that? What if it's just revenge?"

Akkael felt a lump in Ichika's throat but tried not to gulp. "Revenge by who?"

Moon raised her shoulders. "Akkael Torne."

154

Akkael tried his best to give a convincing snicker. "Akkael Torne? A man you just said is dead?"

"I know it's strange," said Moon. "But consider it for a second. What if, somehow, Akkael, back from the dead as some form of spirit, is seeking retribution on those who wronged him? I don't know how, but I don't know how anything has happened recently. As crazy as it sounds, though, much more makes sense when we use that as our working theory. Don't you agree?"

Akkael's stomach sank, and his pulse was thumping against his temple. "So let me get this straight," he said, his voice hoarse as if he hadn't spoken in days. "You think that somehow, I'm not Ichika, First Blade of Sekando. Somehow, I'm Akkael Torne. The Northman."

Moon shrugged. "Maybe. Maybe not. Maybe not right now. That's what I've got going on up here anyway." She tapped her head three times before shrugging again.

"Wow," said Akkael, "You've gone insane in the three days I was out."

"Maybe," Moon laughed. "Maybe not. Maybe not right now."

Akkael sat up in the bed, the pain in his ribs shooting through his body.

"What do you think you're doing?" asked Moon.

"I'm leaving," he said, looking down at the blue carpet. "I've had enough of insane people for today."

"I'm afraid not," said Moon.

Akkael looked over at the captain of the military police. "Why not?"

"You're under house arrest until the Queen says otherwise."

Akkael sighed. "This is ridiculous."

"The Queen has a war to plan and relations with the Northmen to repair," said Moon. "After everything, your presence will be more of a hindrance than a boon. It's better this way. Hopefully, our investigation will be done by the time you heal, and you can join the Queen before they reach Wu Wei."

Akkael wanted to spend as little time with Moon as possible, so he resigned, hoping she'd leave sooner. It was scary how right she'd been about everything, and he needed more time to fake his innocence. "Fine. Just leave. I need some rest."

"Just so you know," said Moon. "I really hope I'm wrong."

Akkael remained silent and stared down at the carpet. He noticed a bundle of blue silk peeking out from under the bed. It looked almost like a geode, reflecting the light that peaked through the closed curtains.

"Is there anything you need?" asked Moon.

Akkael bent over, wincing at the pain as he retrieved the long silk scarf, translucent and beautiful as it unfurled in front of him like a waterfall. "Was the Queen here?"

"The Queen barely left your side for the last few days," Moon confirmed.

"Well then," said Akkael, holding the scarf out towards Moon. "This must be *her* scarf. Do you mind returning it?"

Moon just stood completely still. She remained silent for a long time, turning pale as if she'd seen a ghost. "Whose scarf?"

Akkael squinted at Moon's reaction, trying to understand where he could have gone wrong. "Sorry," he said, "I'm tired. I meant to say *her* majesty's scarf."

The wind howled outside the window of Ichika's room. Akkael's arm began to ache as he held the scarf out for Moon to take. She stood their eyes wide, breathing deeply as she stared, unblinking, at Akkael. "Ichika, I'm so sorry."

"What do you mean?" Akkael asked, his heart racing again.

"Two guards are standing outside this door," said Moon, ignoring the question. "If you try to leave, they will detain you."

"Detain me?" Akkael was lost, not understanding why things had escalated so quickly.

Moon just shook her head, laughing through a scowl. "I'm afraid you've given yourself away. Of course, I don't know if you are Akkael, but you certainly aren't Ichika."

"What do you mean?" Moon ignored Akkael's question, opened the door, and entered the hallway. Akkael could see an armoured fist clutching a spear through the aperture of the door and knew Moon wasn't bluffing about the guards.

She turned to face Akkael one last time. "I've known Ichika for a long time. Never have I heard her refer to Their Majesty as *her*."

He went to speak but couldn't think of anything to say that wouldn't make him look more guilty. He lowered his eyes to the ground and sighed.

"You took the body of a good woman," said Moon. "I hope for your sake we can get her back."

Moon slammed the door behind her, leaving Akkael alone in Ichika's room. He lay back down on the First Blade's bed, clutching his broken ribs.

For some reason, after a while of lying there, a feeling of relief washed over him. He'd failed, and there was a certain serenity in that. His revenge tale was over. He'd never see Hideo's life drain from his eyes and never learn how he changed the world and took everything.

Akkael began to feel his daughter's touch press against his left hand. He clenched his fist around that feeling, holding on to it as a tear left his eye.

[CHAPTER 26] — SACRAL

Skane sat on the cliffs of Skaldgard, watching the armada bobbing in the tide. Two hundred longships sat in the bay, polished wood glistening in the noon sun. Orange sails were strapped down, and the ships were tied together to keep them floating away from those moored to the beach. It was like a stage built in the sea, stretching like a manufactured peninsula. Further along the coast, tents and pavilions had been set up to accommodate the warriors who came with their boats.

The wind drowned out Skane's long exhale, not that anyone was around to hear. He wrapped furs around his shoulders, and his eyes darted across the scene like a moth around a flame. But, despite their lively watch, they were also heavy like stone. Skane knew that his worries would keep him busy. If anything, he desired to empty his head of everything but the thought that there was nothing to do or think about.

Skane was the type to lose himself in his mind, like an endless forest on a dark night. Or he would use it as a shield to guard against the gruelling world. This was the latter. He made every effort to ignore the noise of the Solstic below him. Their jolly yells and singing grated at Skane's heart.

He remembered those in his life better suited to the role he found himself adopting. Doran was always the best commander. Akkael was a good tactician. Even Magar would be better to an extent. He wouldn't let silly things like conscience cloud his mind. He'd relish the fight. But now, none of them could help him. He was all alone.

Skane took another deep breath, losing focus of the ships as he fought back his tears. He missed his husband, missed his friends. He forced the memories out of his head until they slowly began to fade to the dark depths of his mind, and the last blinking miscellanies of those thoughts were repressed.

Soon after, light steps came from behind him. Skane turned to the stairs that led from Skaldgard's stacked houses to the top of the cliffs. He saw three figures silhouetted by the light. Two were in furs, looking no older than sixteen, with bleach-blond hair and stubble growing around their chins. Their fists were clenched around spears. Between them was Rigpa, who Skane first recognised from the purple robes in the distance.

"King Skane," said one of the boys. Skane was still unsure of his title. Doran's hierarchy was an amalgamation of those found in Rhayne and Edokand, and Skane knew little about those systems. "We brought the Grand Sage, as you ordered."

Rigpa smiled despite her arms being restricted by the grips of the teenagers flanking her. "Leave us," said Skane. The soldiers let go, bowed, and retreated down the steps of the flats.

Rigpa waited until they were out of earshot before speaking. "So, what can I do for you, Skane?"

Skane appreciated Rigpa's deliberate decision not to call him king. He gestured for her to sit on the grass beside him, and she complied. "I want to learn more about the chakras. You said there were seven."

"That's right," Rigpa nodded.

"What's the next one, then?" asked Skane, locking his unblinking eyes on the sage.

"Well," she started, shuffling until her legs were folded under her, "after the root chakra is the sacral chakra. Like the first one, the sacral chakra deals with humanity's carnal, instinctual desires. It deals with the pleasure of all kinds."

She behaved coyly, as if embarrassed at what she was suggesting. Skane laughed under his breath before Rigpa continued. "However, it also shows the difference between man and beast. It balances human creativity with base desires. It is blocked by a concept that is also manmade; guilt."

"Guilt?" Skane repeated.

"Yes. Like fear, guilt can cripple those who do not have a grasp on it." She straightened her back and closed her eyes. "It can stop the pursuit of self-fulfilment and block one's path to betterment."

Skane was quiet for a moment. He thought about living a life without guilt, and it was like staring at a city's walls and being told to burrow to the other side.

"Is there really nothing you feel guilty about?" he asked the sage.

Rigpa tilted her head momentarily, furrowing her brow, eyes floating up in thought. "I've tried to lead a life of virtue and responsibility," she said before shaking her head. "But, no, I have some things to feel guilty about. But the chakras aren't there to remove these emotions, rather get more of a handle on them before they become a burden too heavy to bear."

"I don't know," he said, looking down at the grass. "I don't think I want to leave my guilt behind."

"And why is that?" asked Rigpa.

Skane shrugged. "Without the mistakes I've made and the weight they've left on me, what's stopping me from putting myself on that path again?"

Rigpa thought in silence for a moment before answering. "You may think that feeling this way keeps you from making the same mistakes, but all it does is prevent you from making any meaningful change." She shimmied closer and placed her hand on the giant Northman's shoulders. "You must accept that those terrible things you did have happened, but you must not let it consume you. All you can do is live every day trying to be a little better than the day before, and if you don't succeed one day, try harder the next."

Skane removed the old woman's hand and looked her in the eye, which was harder to do with every word he spoke. "I've killed so many people. I've burned homes where families had built their lives and stolen more food and trinkets than I think I've bought."

"You have," Rigpa nodded. "What did you do today?"

"You mean apart from organising the voyage of a massive invasion force to do more of the same shit?" he asked, pointing at the fleet floating in the bay.

"Yes, apart from that."

Skane thought. "I don't really know. I helped move some of the building materials for the orphanage and then just sat here."

"The orphanage that you approved?" Rigpa asked.

"I suppose," he said, bowing his head.

Rigpa continued. "The orphanage that, because of you, will feed and clothe both, Solstic and Edokand'i children?"

"It doesn't remove the bad things I did."

"No," Rigpa agreed. "Nothing will. All you can do is hope that, before the end, your contributions to this world were more good than bad."

Skane squinted. "That seems a pretty simplistic way of viewing things."

Rigpa bent her bottom lip. "Does it have to be more complicated than that?"

"I suppose it doesn't."

Skane looked back over the cliff edge. The tide was coming in. Some children played in the sea and threw stones at the boats. The sunlight formed a glistening bridge across the water's surface, and the shadows of seagulls ran along it. The feint outline of Tsul looked like a cloud lurking on the horizon, and rocks spat out the waves that lapped against the shore.

"I really like the view up here," Skane said, taking in the fresh air. "I feel so far away."

[CHAPTER 27] — THE COUNCIL

The council room was more extensive than any long hall in Solstr. Soaring ceilings were held up by wooden pillars, spreading out from a long dark-wood table. Blue pillows flanked the table for councillors to kneel, and a tea chest was positioned against the east wall, concealed by the columns that sprouted up like bamboo.

Astrid ran her free hand across the carved wood of the tea chest as she poured herself a cup. To the left of the teapot was a clay figurine of a creature that looked half lion and half frog. It glistened as if it had been doused in wax or varnish. As Astrid went to put the pot down, someone came from behind her and gripped her hand around the handle.

Resisting the urge to punch the woman, Astrid scowled, waiting for the councillor to explain. "You can't put it down yet. You must pour tea on the pet for a good and productive meeting. It's a tradition."

The woman slowly released her hand from Astrid's. She was getting pretty tired of Edokand'i traditions but obliged, raising the pot above the frog-lion and pouring a few drops on top of it. She watched as the tea trickled down into the stained cracks and rivets of the small sculpture. She looked back at the councillor, who nodded. Astrid placed the pot down, picked up her mug, and turned towards the table.

The Queen sat at the head of the table. Light from an open balcony silhouetted Kya as it peered inside, their face entirely concealed by shade. They had barely spoken a word since Ichika had been asleep. Astrid blamed herself for that. She caused panic and hysteria when she was pulled away from the fighting ring, yelling Akkael's name. Even thinking about it made her cheeks flare red.

She blamed the adrenaline and Ichika's words. Astrid wasn't aware Ichika had a daughter of her own. She understood now that she was just talking about her little girl chasing the birds. That had to be it.

"I'm Moon." Astrid turned to see the woman who had told her to pour the tea on the statue. She bowed to Astrid before continuing. "Well, Commander Moon. But, if you call me that, I'll have to call you Princess, and neither of us wants that."

Astrid snickered and bowed back. "Good to meet you, Moon." Astrid took a seat, kneeling next to Lindsay. Moon knelt to the other side of her, placing her tea on the table at the same time as Astrid.

"I haven't been to a council meeting since the mountains rose," continued Moon. "Kind of missed it, but I'm sure that feeling won't last long."

Astrid wasn't sure how to respond. "Council meetings can be a drag."

"You're telling me. It's even worse now all the fun councillors are gone." Moon took a swig of her tea, trying to speak through the gulp. "Not blaming you, of course. Yuri knew the risks of duelling a Northwoman, and Ichika was lucky to have just a few broken ribs. However, those two bickering made these meetings go much faster for me."

Astrid looked around the table, drawing similarities from her time on Doran's council. She thought of sage Jiro and Frode, arguing whether Doran should place Edokand'i noblemen on spikes outside Takakawa's pagoda or whatever moral issue irked them that week.

Only the relevant councillors had attended the meeting. Sekando's highest-ranking general sat opposite Astrid. Moon was the commander of the military police. She didn't need to attend but was filling in for Ichika, the Queen's First Blade and primary advisor. The chancellor of the treasury was also present, as well as the Queen's spymaster.

"I'm sorry about Akkael," said Moon, ridding Astrid of another quiet moment. "Sekandans are typically polyamorous, so not many people here will be able to relate. We tend not to fall in love." Moon took a deep breath, not looking at Astrid. "But I was in love once. I never felt pain like I felt when she died. Not before. Not since. I understand how you feel."

Astrid didn't speak, sitting in silence as the general prepared the meeting. Her name was Kwan. Her skin was pale, and her hair was cut an inch above her

163

shoulders. She turned to face the Queen. "With Your Majesty's permission, I want to begin the meeting."

The Queen nodded, and Kwan sat back down.

"So, the invasion force is set to leave within the week," She began, facing Astrid. Kwan liked to keep eye contact when she spoke, trying her hardest not to blink. "As previously discussed, three-thousand women will be sent to Wu Wei with you, a thousand more than we sent with Koji. I hope this will sufficiently demonstrate our solidarity, regret, and condolences."

Kwan waited for a response from Astrid. When none came, Lindsay spoke instead. "We are very grateful."

Kwan smiled at Lindsay before continuing. "Of course, we can't in good conscience leave Sekando undefended with a hostile army at our doorstep. The survivors of Koji's military blunder are held at Koseki mining town, less than thirty miles from here. A thousand men are stationed there. Not enough to take the city, but enough to do some damage if they are inclined to view our allegiance with you as a betrayal."

"What do you suggest, then?" asked Astrid, arms folded on the tabletop.

Kwan reached under the table and revealed a folded piece of old parchment. She unfurled it and placed it on the table. It was a map of Sekando, beautifully illustrated, with small drawings of Sekando city, Koseki, and other essential landmarks within the region. "Once we meet with Lord Skane at Sui Bay-"

Astrid interrupted her. "King Skane." She wasn't entirely sure if Skane was technically King or not. But the Edokand'i often used the word *lord* to insult Doran, insinuating he was less than he was.

Kwan bowed her head and corrected herself. "We'll meet King Skane at Sui Bay. With the soldiers he brings and the three thousand you have outside our city, we will send five thousand women with you. We will then make our way to Koseki."

Kwan used her finger to indicate where they would be on the map, and Astrid watched intently. She saw the drawing of an opal-coloured sea serpent in the east ocean of the map and wondered if something like that existed.

"You will help us set up a siege of Koseki. Once that is complete, two thousand women will remain at the mining town to ensure the army doesn't march on the capital."

She ran her finger north to where the words 'Sui Bay' were written. "Then we will return to your ships and sail around the mountains to Trim." She folded up the map and placed it next to her leg. "Does this work for you?"

The chancellor of the treasury spent the entire demonstration writing, rubbing her forehead as she priced provisions and calculated the logistics of conducting a siege and an invasion simultaneously. The master of secrets just sat still, leaning back on her hands. Astrid didn't know why she memorised the General's name but not the others. Maybe a life of military prowess was far more noteworthy than those who built careers on money or deceit.

"Why don't we just take these people out, so you don't have to start a siege?" asked Astrid.

"Koseki is built on a volcano due to its abundance of natural resources," stated Kwan. "The up-hill battle puts us at a disadvantage. Also, the people there are loyal to Wu Wei, so if we do try to take the town, we'd be fighting the people of Koseki and the army sojourning there. The population may not be militarily trained, but they've lived hard lives. We'd lose more than it is worth."

To the left of Astrid, Moon sat up, shifting into her peripheral vision as she leaned over the table. "Also, the army there were the only witnesses to what happened to Koji's army," she said, looking between Astrid and Kwan with wide eyes. "I want no harm to come to them until I get to interview them."

"Hasn't Ichika already conducted interviews?" asked Kwan.

Moon glanced at the Queen, who was silent as a statue in the balcony light, before returning to Kwan. "You have your orders, General."

165

"No harm will come to the sentinels unless they try to rush us," confirmed Kwan.

Moon paused for a moment before nodding and leaning back out of Astrid's line of sight.

"Okay, so now we've cleared that up, let's move on to the battle at Wu Wei," said Kwan. She shifted in her seat, elbows firmly planted on the table.

However, before she got the chance to continue, Moon interrupted her. "Actually, Kwan, if you don't mind, I'd like to use this natural lull for a recess. A lot of information is being floated around, and I want to be fully focused on what you have to say. Shall we reconvene in twenty minutes?"

"That's a longer break than the meeting so far," said Kwan.

"I apologise," she said, giving a disconcerting smile.

Kwan looked around the room at anyone who would meet her eye. When no one did, she sighed before turning back to Moon and nodding. She stood up, faced Queen Kya, bowed, and left the room. The paper doors slid closed behind her.

The chancellor of the treasury also stood up, as well as the master of secrets. "I don't know how you expect me to get these provisions in such a short amount of time," said the chancellor of the treasury, looking at the Queen. Kya just stared back, and the treasurer rolled her eyes. "But I'm excited about the challenge." She left the room, followed by the silent spymaster.

Astrid went to stand up, but she felt a hand clasp down on her left soldier. Lindsay was already standing before she noticed Moon holding Astrid to the pillow under her shins. Moon lifted herself off the ground, using Astrid as leverage, while Lindsay slowly sat back down.

"If you don't mind, Your Majesty," said Moon, not looking at the Queen, "I have an update about Ichika that I would like to discuss with the room."

Kya moved for the first time since the meeting began, leaning out of the overwhelming light so Astrid could see their face. They had black rings around their eyes, and their make-up looked like they had slept in it. "Is she awake?"

Moon ignored the Queen, instead turning to the Northwomen. "Astrid, why did you think you were speaking with your husband after the duel?"

Astrid rolled her eyes. "Not this again," she said, sighing. "Look, it's been a long couple of weeks. I was filled with adrenalin, remembering how it felt to spar with him, and I got confused. It was nothing."

"I appreciate that," said Moon, nodding. "But what did Ichika say at the moment that made you think she was Akkael?"

"I've already told you," said Astrid, feeling her blood pumping and her voice getting louder. "She said that her daughter liked chasing birds, which reminded me of Alani." Astrid caught a lump in her throat.

Moon snapped her fingers. "That's the first part of this that didn't make sense to me. Mi-ok is a brave soul and a warrior, just like her mother. But she's ornithophobic."

Astrid blinked rapidly before shrugging. "Is that contagious?"

Moon snickered. "It means she's scared of birds. Has been since she was a toddler. She will attack men thrice her size with a wooden sword but won't go near a pigeon."

"We don't understand your point," said Queen Kya. "Is Ichika okay or not?"

"Your Majesty," said Moon, now looking at the Queen. "I do not believe Lady Ichika is herself."

Astrid's heart skipped a beat.

"What do you mean?" asked the Queen.

Moon cleared her throat. "This may sound ridiculous. But Ichika's working theory for what happened to Koji's army was some form of possession. I was sceptical, to say the least. But now, not only do I believe her, but I think whatever possessed the sentinels is here in Sekando. I believe it is inside Lady Ichika."

The room was silent. If this were just over a fortnight ago, the idea of human possession would be absurd. But the world has changed a lot since then.

"Are you sure?" asked Kya, a slight shakiness to their voice.

Moon shrugged. "No," she said, walking over to the balcony window.

The Queen furrowed their brow, turning their whole body to face Moon. "So, let us get this straight," they snapped, "You halt a war meeting to bring forward baseless, absurd allegations with no evidence. Is that correct?"

"Ichika's acting strange." If Moon was flustered by the Queen's ire, she didn't show it. Instead, she was perfectly still, standing in front of the window like a painting in a frame.

Kya scoffed. "She's not the only one who's acting strange."

"She called you *her*." The Queen opened their mouth but slowly shut it again before their head lowered, eyes darting across the floor.

"So," said Astrid, voice croaking as if she hadn't spoken in days. "Are you saying Ichika has somehow become... Akkael?"

Moon took a deep breath turning to look out the balcony window. "I really don't have the answers. I just thought you both should know where my investigation has led me. Maybe I'm wrong." Her chin fell to her chest, making her silhouette look decapitated. "Maybe I'm wrong, and Ichika is still getting over her injuries, but I don't know. That's the thing about ignorance, though. We strive to overcome it no matter how comforting it might be. I promise you both I'll find the answers, or they will find me."

Just as Moon finished talking, the sky began to bellow like the clouds were playing trumpets. The sound was slow but repetitive, like sleeping breath. Astrid and Lindsay stood and moved to the window, looking at the blue, almost cloudless sky. The Queen also stood, staying by the table. Suddenly, a large shadow enveloped the palace grounds below them, making the midday feel like twilight.

The wind picked up, rustling the trees violently as if something were hurling gusts like a child throwing a ball. Distant screams erupted from below them, evolving slowly into a panic. Moon and Astrid looked at each other as they went to lean over the balcony, scanning for any cause of the hysteria they were hearing. Then the shade started to move, and the sunlight hit the backs of their necks. They looked up just as two black wings emerged from behind the palace roof, beating the air like a hammer beats a nail.

Moon lost balance as a gust of wind hit the balcony. More of the creature began to arise from behind the pagoda. The two wings were in the centre of a long, worm-like body, black as night with scales that reflected the sunlight. Its head was obscured as it flew, but Astrid could make out a thin, white streak of hair protruding from its snout. It had no other appendages, making it unclear where the body ended and the tail began.

Branches snapped from the trees and plunged deep into the earth, just as gazebos cracked under the pressure of its flight. The shadow it cast moved out of the palace grounds as the point of its tail was revealed from behind the overhang. It kept flying, shattering roofs and stalls with the beating of its wings.

Astrid watched with unblinking eyes as the unmistakable figure of a dragon shrank into the distance. Her hand was clamped firmly on her empty weapons belt as she turned to face Lindsay, Kya, and Moon.

Astrid could only think of one thing to say in that heart-racing moment.

"What the fuck?"

169

[CHAPTER 28] — WINGS AND SCALES

Magar scraped dried blood from his knuckles with his fingernails, tasting iron as a red streak ran from his nose to his smirk.

"Anyone else?" he bellowed as Godvar was carried out of the perimeter of planks and broken twigs that acted as a fighting ring. One of the boards had a nail still sticking from it, which had become so infamous over the last couple of days that it even had a name; Shriek-maker. Magar nodded at it with reverence whenever he entered the ring, which was often.

His mug of mead sat on a plank, another obstacle to anyone who fought against the giant lump of Magar Torne. Frikr had knocked it over when she stumbled out of the ring and hadn't woken up since.

"Come on!" yelled Magar. "Two-thousand pounds of gold for anyone who can beat me. Who wants to try?"

Magar had fought four fights since sun-up, which usually meant it would take a few hours before anyone risked trying again. The battle in Wu Wei was more important than breaking a fighting arm in some vanity brawl against the King.

Magar grunted. "Cowards."

He left the makeshift arena, retrieving his mug. He took a swig which stung as the mead passed over the gap in his teeth left from Godvar's luckiest blow in the fight. It felt like a decade since his brothers had died, and he knew he was doing fine. The brawls were precisely what he needed, despite what everyone had told him. He was happy. He was free.

Skane kept pushing him to talk, but Magar had nothing to discuss. Every time he fought, he forgot a little more, and he would keep doing it until he had forgotten that Akkael and Doran had ever existed. That was the right thing to do, and the fact Skane couldn't see that made Magar wonder why he'd ever married him. Just that thought made him want to punch someone.

Magar walked into an opening surrounded by tents. On a pile of food crates sat Trygve, also drinking. He was regaling several young men and women with his tales. He spun his knife against the wood under him as they sat and looked up at him in awe. Magar loomed behind him and listened.

"We landed on Sui Bay. You have to understand this was early in the war. We didn't know the difference between Sekando and Edokand back then. A city filled only with women; half the population completely absent; should be an easy raid, right? We didn't make it two miles.

"We only sent a thousand warriors for the raid. Our goal was to pillage the surrounding areas, not hold cities, so we didn't need many. We came across a small village built on a hill near the sea. We noticed the trees surrounding it were cropped at the top, so those on the hill could see the ocean and watch as we approached. Genius.

"That was when I met her. Ichika sat on her horse before as many women as we had warriors. Going by how easy the goutuizi were to kill, one of us should have been worth five of them." Trygve shook his head and giggled. "She killed dozens of us on her own. My warriors dragged me away as I watched her clean her katana. After several failed invasions, Doran ordered us not to stray into Sekandan territory. He said they'd stay away from us if we stayed away from them." Trygve snickered again.

He looked up from his knife at the young Solstic soldiers sitting before him. "But, ever since that day in the village, I knew that it was my fate to kill Ichika." He lifted his blade. "One day, I will drive this knife through her throat. I have dreamt of it. I have memorized every detail of that defeat and know it's my destiny to have revenge. It is inevitable, like breathing."

The young fighters sat as still as possible while Trygve smiled.

Magar coughed before speaking. "Sekandans don't use katanas. They use geom."

Trygve turned, grin like a trimmed fingernail. "What difference does that make?"

"I thought you memorized every detail," shrugged Magar. "She didn't have a katana."

"Yes, she did," said Trygve.

Magar took a sip of his mead. "No, she didn't."

Trygve dropped his smile for a moment. "How do you know? You weren't there."

"Just do," said Magar, shrugging again.

Trygve stood from the crate he was sitting on and squared up to Magar. The King dwarfed Trygve like a cat standing over a mouse. Magar grinned just as Trygve had, one step closer to getting the fight he wanted.

However, before Trygve could speak, he heard a sound like a trumpet blowing in the sky. Suddenly, the tents of their encampment began to ferociously billow, and pegs were plucked from the ground like weeds. Barrels, weapons, and other effects were knocked over as men and women failed to keep their balance. Even Magar had to plant his feet firmly to avoid falling as Trygve stumbled into his chest.

A large pavilion stood between Magar and Sekando city. He and Trygve ran in opposite directions around the tent as warriors ran for their weapons and horses pulled against their ropes. Before Magar met Trygve on the other side, he could see what caused the commotion. A giant black dragon floated above the city, wings flapping like tornados, sending tsunamis of sand in every direction. Black scales caught the sun like they were on fire, and its long body curled as it stayed level in the sky.

Its back was turned to Magar's camp; he and Trygve froze in awe of the beast. After a moment, Magar turned sharply to the Jarl. "Get the best archers to the fence."

Before Trygve could answer, Magar ran into the large pavilion. He had used the tent as a war room and had left his bastard sword resting against the crates they used as a table. He strapped it to his back quickly, fastening the straps tighter than was comfortable against his bare torso. Then he went back outside, watching as the first archers ran past with their bows and quivers in hand.

The Solstic army didn't have many bowmen. However, Magar could see the city walls filled with the figures of Sekandan women, who were famous for their long-range proficiency. "Get ready to bring that thing down!" yelled Magar as he reached the stake fences, hoping to be heard over the beating wings. "Warriors, charge it when it hits the sand."

The dragon didn't falter in its flight, hovering in place as both sides amassed a force to fight it. The wait was unbearable, every inch of Magar's being telling him to run through the sand that separated him from the city. He could reach its head and cleave it in two if he jumped from atop the wall and couldn't understand why no one had done it yet.

After a few moments, the dragon finally moved. It flew to an extensive dune equidistant from the city and the shanty town Magar had made camp. It landed, resting on its tail, coiled under itself like a corkscrew. Wings were still unfurled but no longer flapping as the dragon balanced on its lower half.

Then, it opened its maw and spoke. Its voice was less like the growl Magar had expected. There was a deepness to it, but it sounded almost dignified. The voice that wise kings have in all the stories.

"I mean to bring no harm here." Its voice carried across the dunes as if a sage amplified it. "My presence is mere altruism, if slightly selfish on the part of my intrigue and impetus. There are troubling things, novel to the archipelago you share. I wish to aid, not hinder, the alliances being drawn here. Not with my intervention, but with my information."

Magar struggled to follow what the dragon was saying. He thought its words were designed to quell peoples' hostility, but they only made Magar want to swing his sword at it even more.

"However, before I can impart my knowledge upon those of both parties, I must also learn from you. I wish to interview an agent I do not understand, currently residing in the palace of Sekando."

The winged wyrm turned to face the city, raising itself higher by its tail before leaping back into the air, Magar reaching for his sword instinctively. The dragon spoke again, louder than before.

"Please," it said, speaking between the blasts of its wings. "Bring me Akkael Torne."

All eyes shot at Magar as his sword sang from the sheath. Clasped in his fist, he stared at the long, thick blade, vision unfocused until he saw double. He was speechless, gasping for breath as if he'd run for hours.

For the first time, the dragon looked towards the shanty town. Magar raised his head as the sound of the wings began to calm. Magar couldn't tell if they were getting quieter or just being drowned out by the thoughts in his head. But one thing was sure; the dragon was looking right at him.

Any doubt he heard wrong faded as he stared back at it. He had not mistaken the beast, no matter how impossible. It said his brother was alive.

[CHAPTER 29] — CATS AND BAGS

There was a saying about cats and bags in some parts of the world. Akkael didn't quite understand it, but as Moon trundled him from Ichika's bedroom, he felt the phrase was fitting. She didn't speak to him except when beckoning him to follow. The guardswomen with Moon were breathing heavily, and there were stares from everyone he passed.

Eventually, they left the palace to a carriage with no windows. Black horses were tied to a black stagecoach with a woman dressed all in black wringing the reigns. Moon indicated for Akkael to enter, her eyes burrowing into the back of his head as he passed by.

He put a foot on the step, turning back to the palace. He had no idea where he was going, but he was worried it would be the last time he would see the Sekandan palace and wanted to savour it.

Looking back, he saw a broad figure in one of the windows glaring at him, eyes as agape as her mouth. Eventually, he recognised his wife. Her blonde hair shook from the breeze which entered through the opening. Akkael froze, looking back at her through Ichika's eyes. Something about how Astrid looked told him she knew who he was, but something in her expression shouted that she couldn't believe it. He entered the carriage, refusing to look back at the window as others entered the car.

Moon sat opposite Akkael, and two Sekandan guards also journeyed with them. Moon held her hand out, and one of the guards handed her the shackles from her belt. Akkael instinctively held out his wrists, and Moon lent in to secure them.

"Why didn't you do that back in the room?" Akkael asked.

"What, and drag the First Blade of Sekando through the palace in handcuffs?" Akkael heard the screeching of the gates as the windowless coach exited in haste.

"What's going on?" asked Akkael.

175

"You'll see," said Moon. Akkael realised she couldn't look him in the eye. "I'm not allowed to be present, but you will be watched the whole time. Try and run to your friends to the west, and you will be put down."

Akkael appreciated the bluntness. "Am I leaving the city?"

"You have a meeting," said Moon.

"Who with?" Akkael squinted.

Moon smiled, holding Akkael's gaze for as long as she could stomach. "I love that you don't know."

Realising he wouldn't get more of an answer, he rested his head against the wall. The city was big, so he knew he would sit in awkward silences and tense exchanges for a while. The carriage was going fast, though. Akkael wondered what the rush was for.

"How did you do it?" asked Moon after a few minutes of quiet.

Akkael opened his eyes and lifted his head. "Do what?"

"This!" She gestured to Ichika's body, shaking her head as her hand scanned the form of a woman Moon used to know very well. "How did you move into Ichika's body?"

"I don't really know," he said. "When someone kills me, I become them. That's all I know."

"Ichika didn't kill you; a shadow archer did." Moon's eyes were darting back and forth.

"That was the first time; I've been killed lots of times now." Akkael had no idea why he was divulging this information. Maybe it was because he knew he'd ruined Astrid's plan to ally with Sekando and wanted to do his best to mend ties. Perhaps he wanted to see if Moon had information he didn't and was hoping for a mutual exchange of information. Or maybe it felt good to finally talk about what had happened to him. Regardless, he saw no reason to lie, and the last few days taught him he was terrible at it anyway.

"I was the man Ichika executed before the duel."

After a long exhale, Moon continued. "But how?" Moon pushed. "How is it possible? What gave you this ability?"

Akkael thought of the creature he'd seen in the dark prison. The floating eyes in the green, pulsating smoke. The tentacles and the warped, sharp grin. The harsh whisper and the wailing captives it had driven to madness. Akkael's voice broke as he spoke. "You wouldn't believe me if I told you."

"You have no idea what I'd believe right now," she said. "Try me."

Akkael was now the one unable to make eye contact. "It was a living nightmare," he managed to breathe.

After a few moments, Moon looked for more but reclined on her bench and spent the rest of the journey silent. Eventually, the carriage came to an abrupt stop. From outside, Akkael could hear the heavy jogging and rattling of dozens, if not hundreds, of armoured soldiers. One of the guardswomen open the carriage door, gripping Akkael's shackles and dragging him out after her.

Every alley and street was cordoned off by women with spears and geoms. Akkael looked behind the horses and saw steps to the parapet of Sekando's wall. Blue armour leaned over the crenellation to watch as the sentinels led Akkael to the top, Moon following close behind. The wall was so crowded, Akkael worried someone might fall off as his escorts pushed through the crowd of warriors.

"Why are there so many soldiers here?" Akkael asked Moon, being pulled too frantically through the throng to face her. "What is going on?"

Before the last question left his lips, he was brought to a stop, looking over the wall at the vast sand dunes of Sekando.

"That is who you're meeting with," stated Moon. Akkael looked at her before following her line of sight.

According to stories, when the Northmen first landed in Rhayne, the people there looked out to sea at the approaching armada and saw… nothing. The sight was so beyond their understanding that they couldn't comprehend what they saw. Akkael looked over the wall. It was windier than usual, with sand blowing in all directions. The tufts of long grass lay flatter against a darkened sky. That was all Akkael could compute to start with. It wasn't until it stretched its wings that Akkael could register the massive dragon on a large dune to the west.

Its scales absorbed the light and shimmered in the heat. When it yawned against the hillock, its maw looked like a small, jagged range. The beast's eyes were closed, fidgeting in its sleep. Akkael was sure this was the dragon he'd seen fly over him after the bandits had left him for dead. But even though he was closer and more lucid, he still wasn't convinced it was real.

"It's funny," said Moon, staring unblinkingly at the winged anomaly. "I was worried I would lose my whole career on the million-to-one hunch you weren't Ichika, but a dead man in her body. But when that thing asked for you by name, part of me wished I was wrong."

Akkael looked at his feet and noticed a hoist contraption. "General Kwan has ordered all gates to the city to remain closed," Moon shrugged. "You know, in case the fucking thing forgets that it can fly."

The lift was nothing more than a plank, scaffolding, and ropes. Akkael was prodded onto the platform and felt it creak under his weight. "You pushed me a bit hard for a plank with no railings," he complained.

Moon ignored him. "Archers, notch your arrows."

Akkael turned around and noticed for the first time that everyone behind him had a bow.

"As I said," continued Moon, "you run, we shoot."

"I told you," said Akkael, "I become whoever kills me, so it's not the most alarming of threats."

"Who the fuck said anything about killing you?" Moon was doing a stoic job of repressing her resentment towards Akkael. No matter the extent of her fascination with what he was, Ichika was her friend, and Akkael had ripped her from her own body. Akkael decided to stay silent. He nodded, turning towards the dragon nuzzling against the sand as the hoist lowered him.

The lift sent up a small spray when it touched the ground. Akkael stepped off and trudged into the dunes, trying to walk on the tufts of mud and grass so the sand didn't slow him down. He stared at the dragon as he walked. It didn't get larger as he approached, as if perceiving it any bigger was impossible. He struggled to judge the distance between him and it. He had no idea how long it took to reach the dragon, anyway, consumed by trepidation and intrigue.

The scales were so dark he struggled to make it out. White whiskers descended from the dragon's jowls, and its eyes were orange orbs as they opened, fixed on Akkael. Akkael knew a bit about dragon lore from his readings. As the dragon wriggled up from the sand, Akkael saw no arms or legs to use as props, making it an Amphithere, or, as Alani used to say, an 'am-theatre.' The mythology was indigenous to Edokand, though, much like gods, no one believed in them.

"So, Akkael Torne, I presume," said the Amphithere. When it spoke, its mouth didn't make the shapes of sounds. It just opened and closed as if the words were like wind through the aperture of a cave. However, Akkael found something strange in the words; they were of his own people.

"You speak Solstic?" asked Akkael.

"No, you just hear it because it's familiar." Akkael thought about the sages. They also knew and could seemingly speak every language. "It's part of my condition to be understood by all living things."

"Condition?" Akkael cocked his brow. "If this is some kind of sickness, I would love to know how you catch it."

The dragon scoffed. "Humans always aspire to positions they know frighteningly little about."

"I suppose that's true," Akkael shrugged, eyes still betraying his curiosity. "What do I call you?"

"My name is Seravex," it said.

Akkael nodded and bent his lips. "That's a good name for a dragon."

"A happy coincidence, I assure you," smiled Seravex. At least Akkael thought it was a smile. "I didn't always look like this."

The word *condition* made more sense to Akkael. "How did this happen to you?"

179

The dragon delayed before it shook its head and spoke. "I will inform you in due time. First, you must respond to my questions."

Akkael hadn't been briefed about the meeting with Seravex, but he could assume what it was about. The dragon wanted to know about him, and, in return, it would exchange information that could help the Sekandans. Akkael smiled at the simplicity of those motives. He still couldn't work out why the creature with the tentacles had given him his powers, so a deal with purposes that were easy to understand was a welcome relief. "Ask away."

"Firstly," started Seravex, "I must know when you came across Seradok. How did your paths cross? Did he come to you or bring you to him?"

"I don't know who you're talking about," said Akkael.

The dragon sighed. "You do, but you may not know his name. He made you what you are."

Akkael's eyes widened as he considered the monster again. "I met him after... after the land broke apart. I was killed."

Seravex nodded. "The rules of his existence are strangely arbitrary," he stated. "He can interact with those who have died. Through them, he can bestow profound changes upon our world."

"You seem to know a lot about him," said Akkael through thinning eyes.

Seravex let the air stay silent for a while before lowering its long neck and staring at the sand. "He is my brother."

"Well, I can't say I see the resemblance," Akkael said in an increasingly curt voice, realising he judged the meeting's simplicity too soon. "Why does your brother want to 'bestow these changes, ' as you put it?"

"It's not a want; it's a need," said Seravex.

Akkael's head bent to the side. "I don't understand."

"It's hard to explain." It sighed through its nose, kicking up the sand below it. "Just know it's not his fault. He couldn't help it, like a thirsty man lapping at the rain. He needed to create you, just like he needed to make what forged those mountains."

"He's helping Hideo?" Akkael said slowly. He knew Hideo was involved; there was no doubt about that. But would Hideo have sunk so low as to rip apart the country he loves to destroy the Northmen? That question was swiftly answered when Akkael considered how far he'd gone for revenge.

"A few weeks ago, Lord Kazar Hideo of Sekando attempted seppuku to protest the peace talks between the Emperor and your brother."

Akkael's eyes went wide. "He what?"

Seravex continued. "Seradok interrupted him and gifted him an invention that set the wheels of disequilibrium in motion."

"How do you know that?" asked Akkael.

"It is my duty to know everything," said Seravex, almost sullenly. "When landmasses merge, the suture forms a mountain range. This process takes millions of years. However, Lord Hideo and Seradok caused the process to occur in hours. I had to learn."

"And that's why you're here now." Akkael hadn't realised how much his hand was aching. "You want to know how else your brother fucked up the world."

"I don't want to know. I *have to* know." There was a pain in the dragon's voice.

It took Akkael a moment to understand why Seravex had bitten his words. "Lapping at the rain?" he asked quietly.

Seravex nodded at the ground. "We were human once," he whispered. "It feels like yesterday and ancient history. Before you, before your people started voyaging. Before Alawa."

"Alawa?" Akkael had read a lot about Edokand but had never heard that name.

The Amphithere took a sharp breath and looked back at Ichika's face and the Northman behind her eyes. "I promise I will tell you my piece of this puzzle. But I need your part first. I just have a few more questions."

Akkael was quiet for a while. He walked over to a mound closer to the dragon and sat down. "Okay."

He told Seravex everything. He recounted the moment he died, trying to ignore the pressure in his hand from where his daughter had held on. He talked about the dungeon he woke up in and his meeting with Seradok. Seravex had flown over Koji's army, and Akkael told it what happened. He tried to remember every death in as much detail as possible but settled on the important ones that brought him here.

Seravex sat silently for the most part until Akkael had finished. Then, it spoke, voice croaking as if it'd not spoken in hours. "It's a shame we can't work out the limits of your power without killing you."

"Yeah, real shame," said Akkael sarcastically.

The dragon ignored him, lifting its body higher. Lost in thought, its eyes scanned the surroundings without looking at anything. "If you die of starvation, will you just die or become the last person who denied you food? If you die in prison, do you become the warden or the man with the keys? Or even the person who accused you of the crime that put you there? Or the judge that sentenced you? What happens when you kill yourself?" The dragon was hyperventilating, circling Akkael like a snake as it ranted.

It cycled through all sorts of hypotheticals; euthanasia, falling from a great height, killing blows from multiple people at once, dying after the killer. With each one, Seravex seemed to get irate, breaths getting faster and shorter until, suddenly, the dragon stopped. It looked at Akkael and moved back to its original position.

"I'm sorry," it said. "This is why my brother needs to be stopped. The world must return to the path of predictable chaos it had been put on a long time ago."

Akkael didn't understand the connection between Seravex's strange episode and Seradok's interventions but moved on anyway. "And how do we do that?"

"Well, coming here to see Sekandan-Solstic peace talks were promising." The dragon inhaled slowly, still trying to calm itself. "With any luck, it will hold, and you can make a unified stand against Hideo and my brother. Your unfortunate misstep with Ichika was not good, but from what I know of Queen Kya, they are practical. So long as nothing more damages the alliance, we should be fine."

"ICHIKA!!" Akkael turned toward the bellow to see Magar trudging through the sand alone, dragging his massive sword behind him. His face was red and wrinkled with anger, and his voice was a deep growl.

"Oh shit." Akkael sighed.

"Who's that?" asked Seravex.

Akkael rubbed his forehead. "My brother."

"WHAT THE FUCK HAVE YOU DONE WITH MY BROTHER?" Magar screamed, "WHERE'S AKKAEL?"

Without waiting for an answer, Magar began to charge, his sword raised above his head as he ran up the hill at Akkael and the giant Amphithere.

Seravex turned to Akkael. "I'm sorry."

"For what? "asked Akkael.

"For this." One of Seravex's white whiskers rose as if it were carried by the wind. Akkael watched as it floated towards him, going cock-eyed before it connected with his forehead. As soon as it touched him, his eyes rolled to the back of his head, and his vision went black. The battle cry of his brother was muted as Akkael fell to the ground, unconscious.

[CHAPTER 30] — CHUTON

A train of a hundred sentinels tailed Hideo, each equally as clueless as he was. The same question rattled in his brain for the whole ride to Chuton; why had Seradok made him come here? What did the creature have planned?

Chuton was a military fortress a few miles north of Wu Wei – or Jin Bu. It was built for its strategic position. When Edokand was split into clans, all ambitiously vying for complete control, the region's topography meant invaders would be funnelled towards Chuton before ever making it to the capital. Dense bamboo forests and perilous volcanic geography were too hard to traverse for an army.

This advantage helped throughout history. Hideo liked to think, if the Sekandans or Northmen had ever decided to strike the capital, they would have been spat out by Chuton's fortress.

The fortress clung to the steep incline at both sides of a V-shaped valley. The stone walls looked as if they were built first before the hills were dropped on top of them. Three circular walls with two thick timber gates leading to the valley's well-beaten paths surrounded a round, black tower in the centre. Sentinels with bright red armour marched on the parapets like clockwork, each only ten paces apart.

The valley's north side stretched straight for miles, with watchtowers, manned with ten sentinels each, atop both hills at quarter-mile intervals to limit the possibility of a surprise attack. However, the same could not be said for the south entrance. The hills were winding, blocking lines of sight, and since Wu Wei was to the south, it was useless erecting watchtowers to warn of their own side's approach. Hideo was half a kilometre from Chuton before the determined sentinels broke their march and looked over the crenellated battlements at the approaching horses.

Hideo heard the horns blow, signalling their arrival, but once at the gate, it took the best part of twenty minutes for them to open and for those inside to greet him. An impatient Ieyasu rode up to Hideo as he sat still, vacantly staring at the patterns in the wooden gate.

"Forgive me, my lord," said Ieyasu, "but maybe it would have been wise to send someone ahead to announce our arrival."

When Hideo didn't respond, Ieyasu turned around, leaving the Second Pillar of Edokand to follow the darker swirls in the oak. Hideo didn't mind waiting. The longer they took getting ready, the more whatever Seradok had planned would be delayed.

After a few more beats of Hideo's heart, the gates were pulled open to the yells of pacemakers, ordering soldiers to yank the iron chains in repetitive intervals. Hideo could see the two further gates through the crack in the first gate opening to the same pattern. Five silhouettes made their way on foot when the gates were fully opened. Ieyasu trotted up to Hideo again with a sage to his right.

Lines of red armour flanked the five approaching figures. In the centre was General Kho, the thickset man in charge of Chuton. With him was also a sage, two other sentinels with trimmed armour denoting high ranks, and Ponzu, Hideo's steward, who was sent to Chuton after they met with the Torne brothers.

When Kho's party reached the front gate, Ponzu ran to Hideo's side, startling his horse slightly. He gestured towards Hideo as if he'd arrived with his caravan, clearing his throat before speaking to the men he came with.

"You are in the presence of Lord Hideo Kazar, the Iron Hand of Wu Wei and the Second Pillar of Edokand." Ponzu looked at Hideo like a dog who wanted a treat.

After a moment of silence, General Kho spoke. "Lord Hideo, we are honoured you are here. But we would have preferred some warning of your arrival." Hideo just stared, not blinking, before Kho continued. "What do you want?"

Hideo sighed, reaching down into the saddle bag of his horse. He opened it and retrieved a sealed scroll. Hideo stretched his hand out. After a while, Kho sent one of the decorated Sentinels to retrieve the letter. He hesitantly took it and brought it to the General.

"The Emperor's seal," said Kho, with a tone and a raised eyebrow that gave his suspicion away. He cracked the wax and unfurled the parchment, reading silently as his eyes sunk deeper into his skull. "You want me to evacuate Chuton?"

Hideo slowly nodded. "Only for an hour."

"It doesn't matter how long," yelled Kho, visibly irate. "There are two-thousand men here. Chuton has never been unmanned."

"You'll be right outside if someone decides to attack for the first time in centuries." Ieyasu and the sage fidgeted on their horses next to Hideo. He understood why. Only Seradok knew why they were at Chuton.

Kho's head lowered. "You know, Hideo, I've heard rumours about the capital," he said, avoiding calling the city by its new name.

"Rumours can be entertaining," said Hideo. "Even if they're false."

Kho snickered. "I heard the Emperor hasn't left his chambers in weeks. I heard you're running things now, and those who oppose you either put a sword in their belly or you do it for them."

The wind whistled through the valley as Hideo sat upon his horse, unblinking as he glared at the General. He yawned into his elbow before he spoke. "Well, I guess you have two outcomes to consider, don't you, General," said Hideo, no muscle moving on his face. "Either that letter is an order from your Emperor. In which case, you should do what it says, or face the consequences." He fiddled with the strap of his false hand before continuing. "Or the rumours are true. I took the capital, usurped the Emperor and rule in his stead, killed Akkael and Doran Torne, broke the earth, and rose mountains from the sea."

He looked up, meeting Kho's hazel eyes that seemed less focused. "In which case, General, you should obey the letter or face the consequences."

The General tensed and stood taller. "Is that a threat?"

"That's definitely one possibility."

"My Lord," exclaimed Ieyasu, shaking his head in Hideo's peripheral vision.

Hideo took a deep breath. "As the Second Pillar of Edokand, I already outrank you," he said calmly. "If this was my order, I would have commanded it myself."

Kho considered that a little longer, reading over the letter, scanning the Emperor's signature and seal, looking for anything that would indicate it was a lie. Hideo knew his type. He was honourable, but unless he had explicit evidence that something was afoot, he wouldn't act. He would reluctantly go along with it, telling himself he was biding his time. However, he knew deep down it wasn't true. He knew he treasured justice less than a safe and comfortable life. The world was changing; why create more unnecessary turmoil?

Kho sighed. "Give us until dusk."

"Fine," said Hideo.

The wait was excruciatingly long for anyone besides Hideo. Jin Bu was less than a day's ride, so the sentinels only brought provisions they could carry. Now they were probably staying the night outside Chuton, and the one-hundred men Hideo had travelled with were beginning to pout. The food and water would be enough but not abundant. The valley was also rocky, and nobody had brought tents or rolls to sleep on.

Hideo couldn't remember the last good night's sleep he had. Even before Seradok, the living nightmare had come into his life, Hideo struggled to sleep. He couldn't even remember when his sleepless nights began. Was it when he lost the hand he used to rest under his head or when the Northmen had begun their invasion? Was it when his wife died and left his bed cold, or when he was kicked out of the first home he'd ever known, never allowed to return? Did he learn it young, staring at flickering candles and pondering ways to make his mother proud of the son she'd never wanted? Had he ever truly slept?

Hideo had spoken to no one since the waiting started. Even Ieyasu was avoiding him. Ponzu, who had stayed outside with the men from the capital, had tried to start conversations . But, after a dozen or so grunts, he took the hint and slunk away. The moon was pale in the dark red sky when the last sentinels in Chuton had funnelled out the northern gate. A smaller group, led by General Kho, had made their way out of the south entrance to join Hideo's men, still outnumbering them five to one.

"It is done," said the General after approaching Hideo, sitting in the same place on the hill as he had been for hours. "The fortress has been evacuated. What now?"

Ignoring the General, Hideo stood up, dusted off the back of his armour, and looked apprehensively at the fortress. After pulling in a breath, he made his way inside Chuton. It seemed almost haunted. The rings of each wall cast dark shadows where the outlines of crates and training dummies made him feel like a child, seeing figures in the dark and imagining monsters. Spears and katanas were left leaning against the first wall. It was harrowing to see Chuton empty, like walking through an apocalyptic prophecy.

The courtyard beyond the third wall stood at the foot of the stone fortress in the heart of the military base. Two-thousand men slept, ate, trained, strategised, cooked, and drank every night within the large, round castle. Hideo cricked his neck, trying to see the crenellated top, his gaze running up the thin slits that were unwelcoming excuses for windows. No torches were lit except the ones that made the yellow streaks in the tower so noticeable, like tiger eyes in a dark forest, sending bright pink stripes across a lone cherry blossom tree.

It was so dark that when Seradok appeared, its dark green hue made Hideo wince. Tentacles stretched into the night like roots that had grown above ground. The moving eyes and sharp maw were even more menacing, as if they could float boundlessly in the endless blackness. As soon as Hideo noticed it, the open gates leading out of Chuton slammed shut, and Hideo was left alone with the creature he feared.

"Well done, Hideo," said Seradok in a gruff whisper. "I am proud of you for getting us this far."

Hideo remained silent. He barely ever spoke when it was around.

"Don't fret," it said, placing a tentacle on Hideo's shoulder. "After tonight, you will never doubt my intentions again. You and I will be famous friends."

Hideo couldn't help but recoil from Seradok's smile. After a moment of more silence, Seradok backed away from Hideo, leaving at least a yard between them. Then, a noise that sounded like fingers snapping echoed against Chuton's walls and, in between Hideo and Seradok, a small black object plummeted to the ground. It was the metronome, ticking away inside Seradok's green light.

"Here you go," said Seradok, still smiling. "Your salvation; your dream; everything you have spent four years fighting for, is mere heartbeats away. Pick up the metronome, stop the hand, and claim your destiny."

Hideo looked up at one of Seradok's eyes before his head tilted back towards the metronome. A small crater where the device had landed buried it a finger-joint length into the dirt. Hideo walked over and, using his good hand, picked the metronome up before placing it in the palm of his fake one. The rod ticked relentlessly, rocking itself as it sat unevenly in the iron hand.

A breeze ran through the circuit of the courtyard, but the shiver down Hideo's spine was caused more by fear than by the cold. He looked at Seradok one last time, its grin getting thinner. He let himself breathe heavily, like turning the crank on a music box, knowing nothing would stop it from starting once he let go. He counted in his head, clasped his eyes shut, and, once he got to zero, reached for the device.

Hideo pinched the rod of the black metronome. The ticking stopped, and the fortress was bathed in a deafening silence. When Hideo let go, the rod stayed still. After a few heartbeats, he heard the noise that kept him awake. It was faint, like several false starts to light kindling with flint and steel. The metronome fizzled and clicked before the sound slowly petered out. Then, the world erupted.

The sound was intense, like being in the eye of a storm as it raged around him. As his eyes adjusted to the chaos caused by the metronome's magic, he started finding patterns. Plants around him began to wilt, die, and regrow rapidly. The cherry blossom tree lost its blossoms, fruit, and leaves before starting the cycle over

189

again. Cracks in the stones began to form before they were filled in. Scaffolding was erected and then disappeared, becoming new buildings as the grass under his feet turned to gravel.

He couldn't comprehend anything he was seeing. The tower's windows flashed as if the candles inside were being lit and unlit rapidly. Objects appeared and disappeared before Hideo could even identify them. Slices tore through the training dummies before they were instantaneously replaced, only to spawn new tears.

They got replaced again, accruing holes too small to be from a sword. He couldn't tell what weapon made those wounds in the dummies. Spears, maybe? New buildings arose with architecture he'd never seen, built from the original round tower. Then the sounds stopped, and the world ceased to change.

The metronome returned to its ticking, its hand waving back and forth to a reliable beat. Seradok was still there; its grin was larger than Hideo had ever seen. Its tentacles spread out from its body, indicating its surroundings. Hideo turned to see Chuton, unrecognisable from the one he'd walked into.

The centre ring of the fortress was no longer just a tower. It was a complex. Buildings stretched to the inner wall that surrounded the round castle. The new buildings looked strange. Made from wood carved too well and bricks cut too straight to have been done by hand. New flags hung from the fortress, yellow lines crossed vertically, horizontally, and diagonally on a black field. Hideo had never seen a flag like it.

He looked around the new compound, slack-jawed, until his eyes met a new inscription carved above the gate. The first few words were in a language he didn't understand; *Rhulian Orientem Dominia*. Underneath those words were Edokand'i characters he did recognise. But that familiarity was somehow more harrowing. It was a date.

Thirteen, Iron, Ox.

He could feel his heartbeat in his ears. He knew his maths couldn't be correct. But he came to the same result every time he worked it out. He shook him, involuntarily covering his mouth. It took him a while to admit what he was looking at. Still, inevitably, he resigned himself to the horror hanging above him.

The date was almost two-hundred years in the future.

[CHAPTER 31] — ALAWA

Akkael woke up lying in a shallow puddle. His eyes adjusted to the brightness of his surroundings before he groggily spun onto his side, got on his knees, and lifted himself from the ground. Despite moving in the water, it was undisturbed, like sitting inside a mirror. He looked down at himself and was shocked to see… himself. The blue eyes he was born with, the dirty-blond hair in unkempt locks. He stared at his face for a long time before rising onto unsteady legs.

He looked around. Despite the brightness, he couldn't see the sun. The calm puddle stretched into the flat horizon and was hard to distinguish from the white sky. He turned around, and, to his shock, a cow stood in the pool behind him. It grazed on a small patch of grass that protruded from the water.

Akkael stood, stunned, staring at the bovine, the only other being as far as the eye could see. "Where am I?" he said to no one, smiling at the sound of his own voice. He didn't realise how much he missed being him.

A growl emanated from the sky above him. "You are in my mind." The voice was Seravex. Akkael looked around, trying to locate the source to no avail. "That's the easiest way to describe it. It is a universe I can design any way I wish, unreachable by mortals unless I allow your admittance."

Akkael remembered the dungeon that the tentacle creature, Seradok, had taken him to before it gave him his power. Seravex's world was a lot less terrifying than his brother's. A cow peacefully grazing in the light replaced the prisoners that bellowed and screeched in the blackness.

"It's bland for a world of your own design." Akkael pointed at the animal. "What's with the cow?"

The dragon's voice seemed to soften. "Cows fascinate me."

Akkael scrunched his brow. "You are aware you're a dragon, right? In the rock, paper, scissors-esque hierarchy, dragons beat cows every time."

"My Amphithere form is not my original body," said Seravex. "Even still, cows intrigue me more. Think of the life of a cow. Humans manipulate every part of this creature. You eat their meat, drink their milk, and turn their hide into clothes. You even use their waste to grow crops. When religions existed, some cultures believed cows were sacred. Can you blame them? If a turnip gained sentience, would they pray to the farmer that cultivated them or the cow that made their existence possible through tilling the land and fertilising the soil?"

Akkael shook his head. "There is a special kind of mushroom in Solstr. This conversation reminds me of it."

The dragon's laugh reverberated in Akkael's chest before it continued. "Despite their usefulness, they are completely oblivious to their function. Imagine creating a garden, being the reason people survive, and having no idea you were doing it."

Akkael folded his arms, trying to think of a way of moving the conversation along. "Was Alawa a cow?"

Akkael heard the dragon scoff. "No," he said. "She was infinitely more."

With that, the world around Akkael started to change. The cow disappeared, replaced by wooden beams. Stained tables sprouted from the placid water, which had changed to dark wood planks. Soju cups and pint mugs dropped onto new coasters, and fists materialised around the handles. Blue flags unfurled from the rafters, descended from the bar, and stretched across the room's far end. People began to take shape, and Akkael recognised his surroundings as a bustling tavern.

At first, Akkael thought most of the patrons were Edokand'i men. But then, the spattering of disgruntled women in blue cuirasses and the flags made Akkael realises they weren't Edokand'i men. They were Sekandan, and they were celebrating.

"Originally, Edokand was nothing but a small clan in the west corner of Trim." No one in the pub seemed to hear the dragon's voice. "However, they were expanding their control rapidly. Trim fell in a year. Then, they set sail for Tsul. The Sen clan, Haiyen clan, and Takakawa clan also lost. The only two clans left in the archipelago were Edokand and..."

"SEKANDO!" Yelled one of the young men at a beer-stained table, soju spilling on his hand as he raised his cup. The rest of the men also cheered.

"The Edokand'i will break against our walls!" said another, to a cacophony of more cheers.

"Walls?" said Akkael. "Are we in the city?" The males mostly looked young, but some had too much facial hair, wrinkles, and greys to be under sixteen. "I thought men weren't allowed here."

"They aren't," agreed Seravex. "The war forced the Queen at the time to give these men sojourn. Hence the celebration. This was bigger than any victory, finally welcomed home after so many years of exile. It felt as though the world changed for the better. They finally welcomed us inside the city we were born."

"We?" asked Akkael, furrowing his brow.

"Vex, get up here." The man who had yelled first stood on a table, beckoning for someone to join him. They were both young, with the same straight black hair and brown eyes. However, the first man suited the white-toothed smile that shot across his face, whereas the other donned a dower, serious look.

Reluctantly, Vex joined the first man on the table. The smiler then turned to another person in the crowd. "You too, Phim."

Phim rolled his eyes and joined the two men. He was shorter but still resembled the others.

"In Sekando, the family name comes first," said Seravex's ethereal voice. "This story starts very similar to your own, with three brothers and a war."

Sera Vex. The first part was the family name. Akkael thought the smiling man must be Sera Dok. He remembered the sharp, frightening grin that floated amongst the dozen or so eyes in the green smoke. Akkael had to think hard to identify the third brother. Phim. Sera Phim.

It struck Akkael like lightning when he realised. The Seraphim, the being that reincarnated into the Grand Sage and gave them his power. The unfathomable being stood at shoulder height next to his human brothers, only differentiated from the crowded inn by the fact they were standing on a table. No tentacles or wings. Just alcohol in their hands, raised in celebration.

"What happened?" Akkael asked.

The dragon took a while to respond. "You'll see," he croaked.

Sera Dok spoke jovially, his cup still aloft. "Many of us never thought we'd live to see it; men entering the great capital of our clan with open arms. Yes, I said capital. Many Edokand'i already call us their 'second city.' They pretend it's a compliment, but don't be fooled; they mean it as an insult. Together, women and men of Sekando, we will fight for our land. Only together will we prevail. This marks a new chapter in the history of our people. An era of unity. For Sekando!"

The inhabitants of the tavern cheered, even the women, though more reluctantly.

From an outsider's perspective, Sekando may look divided. However, in the four years Akkael had been in Edokand, he realised Sekando was more equal than most places he'd seen. Edokand doesn't allow women to fight, and though Sekandan women only fight alongside men when the Queen's guard is not present, it does happen. Also, both men and women have places in society. The women are the scholars, politicians, and warriors, whereas the men are the labourers, traders, craftsmen, and ambassadors. Lord Hideo had been sent as an official of Wu Wei when he was cast from Sekando.

Akkael was lost by history. He knew about Edokand's expansion and the ensuing civil war but struggled with the little details. He decided to focus on the three brothers as to not get overwhelmed by his ignorance.

"Why does everyone listen to your brother?" asked Akkael. "Is he important?"

Akkael could hear the contemplation in Seravex's voice. "Yes and no," he replied. "He was the head of the student's union at the Male Academy. Since the beginning of the war with Edokand, he'd debated with traditionalists about letting men help fortify the capital. He even debated before the Queen; many people credited him for this. He always had ambitions to change the world, even when he was human."

Akkael watched as the three brothers, Dok, Phim and Vex of the Sera family, drank, laughed, and sang in the dingy, dimly lit tavern. The dragon was silent, as if getting lost in the reverie, allowing the smiling faces of his brothers to play for longer than was necessary. Vex choked on a shot of soju, and his brothers laughed at him. Then Dok tripped over a stool leg, and there was more laughter. Phim's voice cracked during the chorus of an old song, and they mocked him with smiles. It reminded Akkael of nights with his brothers, and he watched the Sekandans dance with a lump in his throat.

"Seravex," said Akkael softly. "Why are you showing me this?"

After a moment, the dragon spoke. "Just wait."

With that, Dok clasped his arm around Vex's shoulders. "Psst, Vex," he whispered. "Look over there."

Akkael followed his eye line to a woman sitting alone in the corner of the room. She had straight black hair, her ears poking like little crescents. Her eyes were brown, with black bags and bloodshot streaks as she stared at the table, littered with empty beer mugs and soju bottles. Her lips were red, and her skin was pale. She barely moved except to bring her drink to her mouth and paid no attention to Dok's gaze.

"Look at her," he said to his brother.

"She looks sad," said Vex.

"War makes everyone sad," said Dok before raising his eyebrows and smiling. "Maybe I can cheer her up."

Vex shook his head. "Leave her be; she clearly doesn't want to be disturbed."

"Tomorrow's round says I'll be making her breakfast in the morning." Dok held out his hand to make the deal.

"I'm not making that bet with you," said Vex. "Your breath stinks, and she's content drinking alone."

Dok winked. "We'll see."

Vex rolled his eyes, following his brother to the woman's table. She barely registered Dok as he pulled out a stool opposite her and sat down. Vex sat next to his brother, slightly further from the table.

Dok rested his back against the wall beside him, smiling at the woman. "Hello, sweetheart. My brother and I noticed you looking a bit maudlin. I was hoping there was something I could do to cheer you up. What's your name?"

She looked up for the first time, her tired eyes darting between Dok and Vex before answering. "Alawa."

"Nice to meet you, Alawa," Dok responded. "I'm Dok, and this is Vex."

Alawa grunted. She looked back at her drinks and mouthed something as she moved her finger between a half-empty beer mug and a newly opened bottle of soju. She landed on the beer, finishing the cup in a few gulps. She then looked back at the soju and shrugged, drinking some of that as well.

Dok's mouth was slightly agape as Alawa wiped her mouth dry. "Thirsty?" he asked.

Alawa snickered. "What gave it away?"

"Hey, Phim," Dok yelled to his younger brother at the other side of the room. "Grab us another round. One for the lady as well. My tab."

Phim rolled his eyes before walking to the bar.

Dok turned his attention back to Alawa. "Are you from the city?"

"No," she answered.

"Where then?"

"Far away."

Dok nodded. "I get it. The war has displaced a lot of people. You don't have to talk about it."

Alawa's head shot up, startling the brothers slightly. "War?"

"Yeah," said Dok. "The one between us and Edokand."

"You're fighting a war?" Alawa's voice was getting louder.

Dok cocked his head. "That's why we're celebrating."

"You celebrate wars?" She was almost shouting now. "What sort of people are you?"

Dok lifted himself from the wall and broadened his shoulders. "Who are you to judge?"

"I'm…" Alawa stopped herself, her eyes slowly sinking to the tabletop.

Dok was breathing heavily, as Alawa looked strangely sullen. Vex awkwardly scanned the scene before him and carefully considered his words.

"It's not the war we're celebrating," he said, getting Alawa's attention. "Life has been hard lately, and we take what we get. My brother has spent months using this war to improve many people's lives. Wars are disastrous, but they can be used for good if, like Dok, you have the drive for it."

Alawa considered Vex for a moment. "You seem smart," she finally said.

Vex shrugged. "I try to be." Dok lightly kicked his brother's leg under the table, inciting a slight smirk from Vex's lips.

With a thud, Phim dropped four mugs onto the table. He handed each person a drink before sitting and sipping on his.

"What about you?" Alawa turned to face Phim. "Why do you celebrate wars?"

Phim looked like a deer watching the moonlight bounce off an arrowhead. He gulped at the three pairs of eyes looking his way.

"Nice to meet you," he said coyly.

Alawa tilted her head as if she didn't understand what Phim had said. The room was silent as the woman waited for an answer. Eventually, Phim began searching the Deep recesses of his mind for something to say.

"I don't know. I like this city; I'm glad I don't have to leave yet. But that's not why. I guess, now there are more people here to defend the city, the less chance Edokand will break through the walls, the less chance of people being slaughtered in their homes. Even if Dok doesn't get his way and men are cast out again, I will leave knowing we did our best to save the most. Does that make sense?" Phim looked to his brothers for approval. Vex smiled and nodded back at him, and Phim took a deep breath.

"So," said Alawa. "We have the smart one," she said, pointing at Vex. She turned to Phim. "The kind one. What does that make you?" she asked Dok.

"Wars change the world," he answered, arms folded and back straight. "That's just how it works. Sometimes for good, sometimes for bad. Edokand wants to take our home, our autonomy. The only people who should rule anywhere are those who are there. I won't apologise for being happy every time victory moves further from their grasp."

"Dok," said Vex, "calm down."

Silence fell over the table for a while, the brothers quietly drinking as Alawa stared inside her beer. "I think you're right," she finally said before lifting the tankard to her lips. "The only ones who should rule are the ones who are here."

To avoid another silence, Vex segued to a new topic. "Since you don't know about the war, I assume you're not from here. Where are you from?"

"Far away," repeated Alawa. She began to smile, staring up at the ceiling. "My people are magnificent artisans, craftsmen; you could also say gardeners." Her smile turned bitter as she changed drinks, wrapping her hands around the soju bottle. "We made a garden, but it went wrong. It was an accident. We abandoned it, and it grew wild. But it wasn't our fault; we didn't know. We didn't know."

"Hey, miss, are you okay?" said Phim, tracking a tear that rolled down Alawa's cheek.

"I'm fine," she said, wiping it away and wrapping her lips around the neck of the bottle. Eventually, she came up for air and spoke. "Do you have religions here?"

"Old ones." Vex seemed to love talking about religions and old history so much that he barely registered how strange the tangent was. "Dead ones, really."

"And in all of those religions, there was a creator," she said, moving her arms emphatically. "Maybe a pantheon of creators."

"Yes," Vex nodded.

199

"But some people didn't believe in these gods." She moved her drinks to the side, leaning closer to Vex. "Despite the wondrous things around them, every way these gods showed their influence, it was too farfetched for them to take seriously."

"I think all people feel that way now," scoffed Dok.

"What if there were gods?" she whispered as if she were divulging secrets. "What if there was a pantheon that created everything around you? What if, instead of you not believing they exist, they didn't believe in you? What if you were abandoned by creators who find your existence too farfetched?"

Dok squinted at Alawa. "How much have you had?"

Vex ignored his brother. "How could this pantheon not believe in something they made?"

"Does a cow know where its manure goes?" Alawa smiled, taking another swig of beer.

"Well, these metaphors and thought experiments are fun, but I must be going," said Dok, rolling his eyes. "It was lovely to meet you, uhm..."

"Alawa."

"Right, Alawa. Anyway, see you." Dok scraped his stool across the wooden floor and went to stand up. However, he found he couldn't move. He couldn't lift himself from his seat no matter how hard he tried. "Why can't I stand up?"

His brothers tried to stand as well to no avail. After a moment of struggle, the tavern around them began to darken. People disappeared into shadow, and furniture sank into a void that engulfed everything in sight until all that was left was their table, drinks, and them.

Alawa slowly reached for her beer and downed the contents. "You were right," she said softly. "The only people who should rule anywhere are those who are there. My people are not here. There are no gods in Edokand."

"Your people?" Dok gasped, still struggling to stand.

Vex was the only one still paralysed by fear and confusion while his brothers fought to escape.

200

"But what is a god anyway?" shrugged Alawa, ignoring Dok. "What personality really defines one? Creativity? Intelligence? Kindness?... All three at once?"

"Let us leave," barked Dok.

"I'm sorry, but no." Alawa stood, walking around the brothers as if taunting them. "I tried too long to make amends for my peoples' failings. This is the last resort. If it's any consolation, you'll live. I wish the same could be said for me."

"Dok!" yelled Phim, eyes red and full of tears as he pulled against the invisible restraints. "Vex!"

"Goodbye." With Alawa's last words, their heads shot back, eyes rolling into their heads as their bodies contorted. Akkael didn't have long to see what happened before everyone before him vanished. Like a curtain descending at the end of a play, the white sky and shallow puddle floor returned slowly.

Akkael's eyes were wide as he looked around the empty dreamscape. "What happened?"

"Different things," said Seravex, still an incorporeal voice. "Those traits she mentioned – Creativity, Intelligence, Kindness – became the urge and essence of our existence. Phim, overwhelmed by a need to help, gave his life and powers to humanity. Every reincarnation of the Grand Sage is him hoping to help humanity live better lives. Dok's curse is creation. All those things he's done: the mountains, Hideo, you. It wasn't his fault; he physically couldn't help himself. He wanted to change the world, so Alawa ensured he did."

Akkael's eyes darted back and forth, trying hard to comprehend what he was being told. "What about you?"

"Me?" Seravex scoffed. "My drive is intelligence. I need to learn. When Alawa's power coursed through me, I sent myself to the beginning of time and studied everything. I excruciatingly revised every second of existence. I watched atoms merge for the first time. I watched how suns expanded and how every substance was made. I watched the first planets form. I watched as landmasses broke apart and moved, and seas ebbed, flowed, froze, and boiled. I watched humanity evolve, and I watched civilisation start. It took aeons. But the need kept eating at me. I thought I learned how to control it, but then the mountains rose, and you... and here I am again."

Akkael's head hurt. He sat in the undisturbed water, eyes floating between every thought in his head. He opened his mouth to speak but couldn't think of anything to say.

"Tell your companions this story," said the dragon. "Join forces with Sekando and stop Hideo before he changes this world any more than he already has."

Akkael turned around as if he expected Seravex to be there. "I understand why you're helping me. You don't want the world to change because, if it does, the need to learn about it will eat at you. You're helping yourself."

The dragon was quiet for a while. "Our motives align." Akkael opened his mouth to speak again, but Seravex interrupted him. "Goodbye, Akkael Torne. And good luck."

With that, Akkael began to fall. The water swallowed him with a slight ripple, the only one on its unbroken surface. He looked down into the white void until he fell unconscious, replacing the clean, bright world with darkness.

Akkael woke up in the garden of Sekando's palace. He heard shouts from guards and approaching footsteps as his vision slowly came together. He looked at his hands, smaller and less calloused than his old ones, and saw he was back in Ichika's body. It was night, but torches and lanterns lit the palace as much as the sun.

He didn't bother sitting up, just lying in the grass and staring at the stars. When he saw stars for the first time in his life, there was no wonder. No intrigue, or peace, or even apathy. Only fear. He feared what he did not know. It was a novel concept to Akkael, as for most of his people. It was different from his fear of Seradok. Despite being unfathomable, it existed. Akkael couldn't deny that the monster was real. But there was so much he didn't know, and now he wasn't sure he wanted to find them out. When he looked up and had no answers as to what he saw, it was the scariest thought in existence.

[CHAPTER 32] — EMPIRES

Hideo stared at the engraved plaque above Chuton's inner gate. He knew what the metronome could do, but he'd never seen it up close like that. Two-hundred years of history skipped in a matter of seconds. The rest of the world unaffected except this spot, propelled through time by a device that fit in the palm of his hand.

"Thank you," said Seradok. It was a strange kind of *thank you*, genuine relief gliding on its grating voice. "See what we can create together! You are unstoppable with me beside you."

Hideo was silent, eyes fixed on the date for a few more seconds before he placed the metronome on the new gravel, turned around, and entered the tower building. The furniture was different inside from when he had been to Chuton last. However, it had been years since he last visited so he couldn't be sure what it looked like before the black metronome's magic. He did know the furniture was strange. Nothing that couldn't be made in the present. In fact, the lack of colour almost made the place look drab compared to the vibrant interior the tower used to have.

Mounted animal heads and pelts gave variety to the texture of the dining room, clashing with the light wood tables and chairs. Pronged cutlery and tin cups were scattered across tabletops, along with cards and dice organised in the structure of some game he'd never seen. A large pot hung above a stove, and the door to a larger kitchen was opened a crack. He ignored it however and ascended the stairs to his left.

The steps were carpeted, black wool concealing the smooth stone. He remembered the first few floors were bunks for sentinels and, other than the arrangement and colour scheme, it was pretty much the same. The top floor led to the general's room; a large, iron-rimmed door replaced the red sliding one with paper windows that Hideo remembered. He entered.

It was like the colour had been washed away from a wet canvas. The desk was in the same place, as was the bed and the bookcases. But, instead of the pigments that decorated his country, they were replaced with varnished wood and leather browns. The only thing that had colour was the strange flag he'd seen outside, with the yellow, inter-crossing lines and the black background. It hung behind the leather desk chair.

Hideo noticed a book in the centre of the bureau. It was bound with tanned goose skin, which Hideo recognised from the bumps in the cover. He flipped through it, but the writing was in the strange language he had read above the gate. He closed the book, discarded it back on the desk, and walked over to the closest bookcase.

He ran his fingers along the tomes, looking for anything that was written in Edokand'i. After scanning three shelves, he found one, and removed it. The spine read: '*General Kazar Shigeru's diary.*' Kazar? He wondered if this was a descendent of his, living two-hundred years in the future. Hideo opened the book to the last page of writing and began to read:

... It's the first day of the fifth moon of the Thirteenth Iron Ox. The empire is at our gates. They blasted through the outer wall an hour ago. Most of the second wall has been reduced to rubble as well. Many sentinels are dead, and the rest are retreating through the south gate. Maybe that's a good thing. Maybe they can save Wu Wei from this fate. The fate that Skaldgard, Takakawa, and Sekando have now all fallen to...

Hideo squinted at the pages, trying hard to make sense of what he was reading. Eventually he paused, a long breath forcing itself down the Iron Hand's throat. He read his own name. Slowly, he reread the excerpt:

I've been thinking a lot about history. My ancestor, Lord Kazar Hideo, struggled against the Northmen centuries ago. He fought against what he saw as an invading force and committed seppuku as a final act of defiance against them. Is this how he felt? Even the descendants of those Northmen have fallen to The Rhulian Empire. Some of which were my friends, now killed defending our cities. Ours: those of Edokand'i and Solstic descent. But now those places are theirs. And this place is too.

I meet the same fate as my misguided ancestor. Hopefully, they don't burn this book. It will be the last thing I ever do. I would be lying if I said I wasn't scared.

It will be a slow, painful way to kill myself. I could use one of those Rhulian guns and end it quickly. But a bullet to the head is their way. Seppuku forces you to stare death in the face, hold its gaze and say, 'I'm not scared of you.'

Those last thoughts will be a lie, but no one will know but me.

Hideo Looked at the blank part of the book where nothing had been written. The walls outside weren't ruins as Shigeru described. The Rhulian Empire must have rebuilt them. That was the only thread he wanted to connect from the book in his hand. The others were too hard to lift, and too painful to think about.

"This is a glimpse of what could have been," said Seradok, who had appeared in the room without Hideo realising. "If I hadn't stopped you that night, you would have killed yourself, and nothing would have changed. The Northmen would get the territories they wanted. Your own descendant would consider them friends: equals. And that weakness would coalesce into... this. Complete submission to a foreign empire. The Rhulian Empire would have preyed on the weaknesses your absence would have nurtured."

He looked back at the flag, eyes following the diagonal lines that crossed over the next. Emotions overwhelmed him until he began to shake.

"Where is the Rhulian Empire?" asked Hideo.

"It doesn't exist yet," said Seradok.

He looked back at the book, scanning the page as his breath got louder and louder. His attention fixed on one word that made a vein pop from his temple as he shuddered in apoplexy.

"'*Misguided*,'" he muttered. "How dare he call me 'misguided.' He failed. A gross insult to what it means to be Edokand'i. He let that flag get hung there! Not me. Him!"

"Exactly." Seradok's grinned widely, its eyes more buoyant than usual as they danced in the green mist.

He looked outside, heart racing. "It won't stop. People will come here forever and try to subdue us. Erase our culture." A tear rolled off his chin. For the first time in weeks, that sentiment meant something. Before they were just words that he felt like he should say. But now they were more than that. They were facts. "If it's not the Northmen, it's this Rhulian Empire. If it's not them, it'll be someone else. They will keep trying to take everything from us."

Seradok rose above Hideo. "I have something to show you. Come down to the armoury."

Hideo nodded, leaving the generals quarters and obeying Seradok. He descended the carpeted stairs and left the tower. Seradok was waiting outside one of the new Rhulian buildings in the complex. Hideo walked over to him and stood outside the closed wooden door. The building was short, with white, stone walls and another Rhulian flag hanging from the bamboo guttering. Hideo looked at Seradok, who was holding out one of his tentacles. Indicating to the door.

Hideo turned the handle and entered the armoury. Steps led down to a large vault; dirt barely concealed by the bricks. It might have looked like a pool dug into the floor if it weren't for the strange devices hanging on racks. He walked down the plank steps towards one of the frames.

The devices had long iron tubes almost the length of an arm. A hole in the front suggested a complex interior, leading to where the construct bends down and widens into a wooden triangle. A trigger like those found on a shadow archer crossbow rested underneath a lever-like contraption and was guarded by a metal strip.

Barrels were also laid across the armoury. Some were full of a thin black powder, while others contained small metal balls. Seradok was floating in the doorway as Hideo investigated.

"What am I looking at?" asked Hideo, shrugging.

Seradok smiled. "These weapons are what the Rhulian Empire will use to swiftly capture the entire world. They are the key to your victory."

"Gentlemen, please. There is no need for violence here." Ponzu was standing between the two sages, the only three people outside Chuton's south gate who hadn't picked a side.

Ieyasu and the one-hundred men that Hideo came to Chuton with were standing in front of the gate, which had slammed shut just before the unexplainable events that had occurred inside the fortress. Lines were drawn quickly, as Ieyasu prevented Kho from interfering with whatever Hideo had done.

Kho was standing twenty feet away with his men. The rest of the sentinels were outside the north gate, probably as confused. Every blade on their side of the valley was drawn.

"Ieyasu," said General Kho. "This is your last chance. Move away from the gate and let us inside."

"I won't do that," said Ieyasu.

"No one has to die today." Kho pleaded, lowering his weapon and stepping forward. "You have to understand. We have more men on the other side of this fortress. You won't survive this."

Ieyasu looked either side of him and shook his head. "The valley is too steep and treacherous on that side to climb. They might come through the gates but the fact that they haven't yet probably means they won't, or they can't."

"If you don't think they can get through the gates," began Kho, "why are you risking your life to stop us?"

Ieyasu shrugged. "Just in case."

"You can't still support that monster," said Kho, raising his voice. "You know what he's done better than anyone. And who knows what he's doing to Chuton."

Ieyasu didn't speak, instead lifting his sword.

"Lord Hideo is loyal to the Emperor and the people of Edokand," said Ponzu, standing off to the side, away from any potential conflict. "Let us not resort to violence where there need not be any."

"I understand your loyalty," Kho said to Ieyasu, ignoring Ponzu. "You two against the world must be an appealing sentiment. Loyalty isn't a crime, but you don't need to be on the wrong side of history. Let me pass."

"Lord Hideo!" Ponzu yelled.

All eyes turned to him, standing atop Chuton's outer wall listening to the sentinel's quarrel. The metronome rested in his iron hand as the ticking echoed faintly in the valley.

"What have you done, Hideo?" shouted General Kho, scowling up at the Second Pillar of Edokand.

"I have won the war." He said, grinning. "I have won every war."

Kho furrowed his brow. "You're crazy."

Hideo just laughed, before his expression turned dark. "Here is the deal," he said to everyone in the valley. "I don't want to hurt anyone with Edokand'i blood. But if you betray me, I will not hesitate to cut you down. If you wish to follow me to victory over the terror our people have been submitted to: if you wish to stop the cruelty of the Northmen, then stand over by Ieyasu. I promise no harm will come to you."

No one moved.

Kho laughed. "No one here wants to follow you Hideo."

Hideo smiled. "Have it your way."

With his free hand, he pinched the rod of the rocking metronome. It began to sizzle and pop before going completely silent.

After a few seconds, Kho shrugged. "What was that supposed to ach-" He was interrupted his own cough. He instinctively went to raise his elbow to his mouth before he realised how heavy it felt. He tried to clench his fist inside his gauntlet, but it was stiff, like a wheel trying to move in the mud. He shook off his armoured glove to find a hand more spotted and wrinkled than his own. He looked around at the sentinels he knew well. All of them looked older as they stared at each other's gaunt faces in disbelief.

"What have you done?" Kho croaked to a sinister looking Hideo.

The paint of his armour started to peel off as the soldiers behind him fell to the ground, the skin that hung loose on their skull slowly melting away. Kho collapsed to his knees. The straps in his armour started to break as if they had been worn, and pieces of his sentinel garb fell to the grass, more orange than red now.

Then, when he couldn't hold himself up any longer, he collapsed to ground as his life faded away.

There was no noise in the valley. Hideo looked at nothing but a pile of stained bones and rusted armour. The tense quiet was only broken when the metronome began to tick again, echoing even louder than before, since there was no one left to block the sound from bouncing along the hills.

Hideo stood over the rest of the sentinels all staring in disbelief. As if by magic, the gates opened under him.

"Come in," said Hideo, smiling. "Come and see what I've given you."

[CHAPTER 33] — SUI BAY

Skane could see fires and tents on Sui Bay as his armada approached. Blue material was a promising sight. He hadn't heard from Magar or Astrid since Takakawa, so he hoped everything had gone without a hitch. It was nearing night, so he welcomed the brightness of the camp as he and the Northmen rowed to shore.

Every ship had another in tow, empty for those on the beach to occupy. In total, two hundred ships littered the ocean, each with orange sails that had been lowered and shields that were clasped to the side. Skane was in the largest ship, capable of being manned by one hundred and fifty. It was their oldest ship. Wool was escaping the gaps in the planks, and the scratched hull showed its age. Dragon figureheads on prow and stern scowled at the land and out to sea. Skane had his back to the shore, pushing his oar against the tide.

Three men helped him attack the waves and sat on the same oar benches as dozens of identical teams rowed in time to the continuous drumbeat of the pacemaker. Rigpa sat in front Skane. He was on the last oar bench, so Rigpa could rest against the ship's rear and still dangled her legs in Skane's foot well.

"The third Chakra is arguably the most important," yelled the Grand Sage over the drumming and violent sea. "Though as a scholar and sage, I am supposed to say they are all equally as important as each other."

Skane felt his back muscles burn as he heaved the oar out of the sea and submerged it again to the drum rhythm. "Can't this wait until we are moored?"

"It can't," she said indignantly. "The solar-plexus chakra concerns our individual willpower and innate drive to achieve. It is blocked by rage."

"Ahh, I see," said Skane, trying to massage his shoulder with his chin. "So, you're getting me angry as a practical exercise."

"No, that's just a happy coincidence." Rigpa smiled, and Skane couldn't help raising his lips in return. "In life, we have many ambitions and obstacles between us and our goals. When these obstacles seem insurmountable, we either persevere or give up and blame these obstacles for our failure. We become resentful."

Skane was only half listening to the sage as she spoke over many drumbeats. "Okay, so don't get angry at stuff. Got it. Chakra: complete."

The sage rolled her eyes and continued. "This chakra also deals with shame."

Skane squinted. "Didn't the last chakra deal with shame, too."

"Yes and no," replied Rigpa. "This shame is more immediate. The kind of in-the-moment shame that blocks you from moving forward. Letting people down or not doing something you feel you are supposed to."

"Okay, so no anger and no shame." His biceps burned. The tides were calm, but he hadn't rowed in a long time.

"As I said, the chakras aren't about neglecting negative feelings. They're about knowing how to act when confronted by these scenarios." Rigpa sat up and looked Skane in the eye. "We don't know what has happened since we've been away. Maybe it'll be straightforward, but maybe it won't. We must work out how to overcome obstacles if we are met with them."

"Why are you telling me this now?" Skane asked.

"I don't know," shrugged the sage. Rigpa looked over the boat at the approaching land, furrowing her brow. "I'm too far away to feel anyone's emotions. But I feel something. The curse of my gifts is that I've never really known whether I'm being irrational. But there is tension over that beach. Something's changed."

Skane had let the others on the bench do his work as he listened to the Grand Sage.

"Skane!" a shield maiden yelled at him as she squinted in pain. Skane nodded at the sage and went back to rowing. Rigpa lent back against the ship, leaving the Northmen to approach the shore.

They had reached Sui Bay, rowing in reverse to bring the ships to a stop. Skane dropped his oar and stretched his arms before climbing out of his ship to help with the docking. Some tied the boats to one another while Skane went to the shore and helped drive pegs deep into the sand for mooring. Some of the Northmen from the camp came to help, embracing their countrymen before taking up mallets and securing the stakes. Anchors were dropped from the larger ships, and when Skane looked out at the armada, it was little wonder why whole civilisations feared the sight of them.

Every muscle in Skane's body hurt, reminding himself of his age as he grimaced. Age was a thing to be revered unless you were the one who was old. He was older than Magar by eight years. Older than Akkael by six. He wondered if there was a chakra that was blocked by a longing to be young again because, if so, Skane would never open it.

"King Skane." He turned around to see the source of the call. It was a shield maiden from the house staff at Skaldgard, Lindsay. Her straight blonde hair was separated by braids, and she wore leather armour. She approached with a smile. Skane tried to smile back, but he could only pant and sweat.

"Lindsay," he managed to say. "Is Astrid here?"

"Yes." Lindsay delayed before continuing. "Queen Kya requests your presence."

"Where are they?" he asked.

"They're by the cage." She looked down to the sand.

"Cage?"

"Astrid and Magar are also with them." Lindsay paused. "You need to go now."

"But the mooring." Skane looked back at the immense number of ships.

"The Queen has ordered some of their women to help." Skane looked around but couldn't see any Sekandans. "Please come with me. A lot has happened since you've been gone."

Skane left with what he hoped those around him would perceive as reluctance instead of relief, following Lindsay through the pavilions. He couldn't help but feel happy as he watched Sekandan women alongside Solstic warriors. They were day drinking together and having friendly competitions despite the language barrier. The Tornes and many Northmen learned Edokand'i in the four years of the war, but a lot hadn't.

Eventually, Skane, still sweating but less exhausted, had made it to a clearing, still tailing the housecarl. Sekandans, swords drawn, lined an alley between two large tents. They looked forward, not acknowledging Lindsay or Skane's presence. The housecarl kept walking, beckoning Skane to follow. He was painfully aware that he was unarmed and not wearing his armour. Still, he followed.

He saw Queen Kya first; their white make-up and long, black hair were stark against the blue dress they wore over their chain mail. To their right was Astrid, black bags under her bloodshot eyes making it look like she hadn't slept in days. Magar looked much the same, but cuts and bruises on his face reminded Skane of how he'd been spending his free time. There were a few Sekandans that Skane didn't recognise, standing next to a cage on wheels.

Wooden wedges kept it from rolling away. The cage was large, with a mattress and blanket in the corner under a long chain. Skane followed the two-metre-long shackles and saw the rusted cuffs clamped around a woman's wrists. He recognised the woman instantly, eyes as sharp as blades and black hair tied in a wolf's tail. It was Ichika, the First Blade of Sekando.

"This is King Skane," announced Lindsay.

The Queen looked him up and down. Their eyes were tired, too. But it was a different tired as if they had been fatigued from tears that the make-up hid. "It is a pleasure, King Skane. We are assured you have amassed a large force for our journey to Wu Wei."

"Yes, Your Majesty," said Skane, with a small, respectful bow. "Five thousand strong."

"Excellent," they replied. "However, before we go, a few pieces of business need to be discussed."

"Of course." Skane hadn't realised he was doing it but was avoiding Magar's eyes. The red streaks and purple blotches across his face hurt too much to even look at. Also, Skane was too fascinated by the prisoner. "If I may, why is Ichika in chains?"

"In due time," exclaimed the Queen. "Firstly, we must discuss Koseki."

"Koseki?" asked Skane. "Isn't that a mining town?"

Kya nodded. "There are currently over a thousand sentinels sojourning there. Before we sail with you, you will help us design a siege of the town so when we do go with you, our lands are protected from those who might do it harm."

Skane thought for a moment. It sounded reasonable enough, so he nodded.

"Good," said Queen Kya before indicating to one of the strangers closer to the cage. "This is our general, Kwan. She will review our plans in more detail once this communion is adjourned."

"Sounds good." A strange silence spread over those in the clearing. "What's next?" said Skane, sucking his teeth.

The Queen looked at Astrid, giving her permission to speak. When she did, her voice wavered like someone who hadn't spoken in days. "Well, the thing is, this war isn't normal." She coughed as if she were stalling to decide her following words. "If I told you everything at once, it would be overwhelming. It's overwhelming anyway, but…"

Astrid trailed off, looking back at the cage with a scowl and leaving Skane to wait.

"Come on," he said. "It can't be stranger than mountains rising from the sea, can it?"

Astrid glared.

Skane gulped. "Can it?"

"We think we should start with our brother," said the Queen, emphasising the word 'our' as if to say, 'not your brother.' Skane didn't have a brother, so he didn't quite understand the intonation. "A dragon visited Sekando City a few days ago."

"A dragon?" Skane was conscious of how high his voice had gotten.

"This would go much faster if you didn't interrupt us." Skane nodded slowly, and Kya continued. "This dragon told us that our brother, Lord Hideo, has acquired some sort of device that can control time within a certain radius."

"Control time?"

Kya shrugged. "Apparently, if we had waited a million years, those mountains would have risen naturally. Hideo messed with the tempo of time, speeding it up to create a barrier between Tsul and Trim. We don't know what else he's used this device for. Still, those mountains have decimated the Sekandan coastline, making it an attack, not just on the Northmen, but on our people, too."

Skane couldn't understand why he thought this, but it seemed Kya spoke in a way that suggested they wouldn't be here by choice.

"We can't allow our brother such power," they continued. "It's an abomination of our world." They looked at the cage for the first time as if ready to spit before looking back to Skane, still glowering.

Skane met Ichika's eye line. She sat strangely, shackles resting on her knee as she leaned against the bars. She stared at him with a chillingly blank expression.

"Why is Ichika in the cage?" Skane asked again.

Astrid turned her eyes to the ground, and Magar wrung his hands together like they were around a neck. Another Sekandan that Skane didn't recognise stepped forward to continue for the Queen. "Hello, Skane. My name is Moon."

"Hi, Moon," said Skane, trying to remember Rigpa's advice and not get irritated. "Are you going to answer my question?"

Moon snickered. "In a moment." She put her hands behind her back and began pacing in front of the cage. "According to this dragon, it has a brother, too. I know, it's all about brothers." Moon laughed to herself before continuing. "Its name is Seradok. For some reason, this creature likes to bestow these chaotic gifts on those about to die."

Skane raised an eyebrow. "Hideo was going to die?"

"Apparently, he was," said Moon, shrugging. "Anyway, so did the person in the cage. Many times, in fact. This Seradok has also enhanced him, giving him a corrupt immortality."

"Him?" said Skane, looking at the woman in the cage.

Moon turned to the person in the cage. "Go on, Ichika," she said, spitting out the First Blades' name. "Tell your friend a story."

Ichika slowly blinked, looking down at the hay carpet of her cage and sighing. Then she followed Moon's command. "It was winter. We sat on the Urkanzan Plateau. You were nervous about your wedding, so you wanted some encouragement. I was bad at it. I just kept going on and on about Magar's flaws. His anger, constant brooding, and monotone grunts, which you informed me, follow him into the bedroom. Didn't need to know that. But, despite my barrage of complaints about my brother, that conversation was exactly what you needed. You always want to help people; make people better. You were the best thing that had ever happened to Magar."

Skane was hyperventilating as if he were about to pass out. He looked at Astrid and Magar, both grimacing at the ground. Queen Kya was almost snarling, and Moon held her arms out as if she were unveiling an art piece.

Skane stuttered as he spoke. "Akkael?"

Ichika smiled. "Hello, Skane."

Skane took a deep breath, and his eyes rolled to the back of his head. His pulse bulged from his neck as he looked back at the cage.

"So, anyway," said Moon, her grin fading, "Welcome to Sui Bay."

[CHAPTER 34] — AN OVERDUE REUNION

Astrid couldn't sleep, which had become routine for her. She spent most of her nights lying down for hours, staring open-eyed into the dark. But this time, she was restless, switching positions regularly as she became too conscious of her breathing. After hours, she got up, hoping a walk would clear her head.

She paced along the bay; sounds of the sea crashing against the rocks mingled with the whispered conversations of those still awake in the thirteen-thousand-strong camp. The smoke of fire swirled with the scent of sea salt and the taste of frigid air. The ships knocked against each other as they bobbed to the tides. It always reassured Astrid that the sea looked the same whether you were in the tundra of Solstr, the deserts of Urkanza, or the volcanic landscape of Edokand.

After a few laps of the beach, Astrid made her way through the camp. The Solstic tents were closer to the ocean. She walked past furs hanging from clotheslines and axes strewn across the ground. She played with the pommel of her Urkanzan dagger as she walked.

Most of the people in the camp had no idea Akkael was alive. Skane was the last who needed to know. Trygve was told at the same time that Magar found out but had refused to go near him. Instead, he spent the whole journey to Sui Bay complaining that he wasn't the one to kill Ichika while Magar and Astrid dawdled in silence.

The tents began to turn blue as Astrid walked into the Sekandan sections of the camp. The round pavilions huddled under tarps and were much bigger than the Solstic ones. It was much cleaner than the Solstic part, too, with no weapons or mead horns littering the path.

After everything that had happened since the mountains rose, Astrid still couldn't believe Akkael was alive. He had let her mourn over his body, weeping as she tugged at the cloth under him, and, all the while, he was alive. Their daughter had died, and he wasn't there. Astrid clenched her fist around the dagger.

Before she realised, Astrid found herself outside Queen Kya's marquee, only a short walk from Akkael's cage. Two guardswomen stood outside the tent, fists around spears. As Astrid approached, she noticed one of them huffing irately.

"All I can hear is you breathing," said the first guard. She had a large scar across her face.

"I'm not even breathing that hard," said the second woman, with a massive dent in the centre of her breastplate.

"Yes, you are," replied the first speaker. "It's like you're sighing."

"Well, I'm sorry." The Sekandan emphasised each syllable in her sarcastic apology. "My nose is blocked because of allergies, not that you care."

"You're right, I don't."

"I had a sneezing fit this morning," continued the woman with the busted breastplate. "Fifty-three."

The sentry with the scar shook her head. "That's not true."

"It is, I counted," said the guard with allergies. "Seonhwa was there too, she saw."

"Wouldn't your eyes fall out if you sneezed that much?"

"What are you talking about?" she squinted.

"I don't know," shrugged the scarred woman. "I thought your eyes would fall out."

"No, that's if you sneeze with your eyes open," she scoffed. "You know nothing about sneezing."

"I know you didn't sneeze fifty-three times; that's what I know."

"You are such a… Lady Astrid!" The guardswomen corrected their posture, backs straight and chins high.

Astrid held her hand out for them to relax before she spoke. "I'm here to see the Queen," she said. In truth, she had no idea why she'd come.

"My apologies, Astrid; Their Highness is asleep," said the sneezer. "If you want us to pass on a message, we'll be happy to."

Astrid peeked behind the guards.

"The candles are lit," she stated, pointing at the iridescent fabric.

"The Queen just informed us they didn't want to receive any more guests tonight. I'm-"

"Send her in." A voice bellowed from inside the tent, interrupting the guard.

The two sentries looked at each other before stepping aside and allowing Astrid to pass.

Astrid pushed aside the flaps and was greeted by an explosion of candlelight. A four-poster bed pushed the grass back into the ground, and a complete make-up stand was set up against the west fabric wall. Chests of clothes and other belongings lined its circumference, and a full-body mirror pushed against the conical roof next to the bed.

Kya sat on a studded-leather chair facing the entrance of the pavilion. They wore a blue nightgown, with their hair above their neck. They held a wine glass loosely, with a bottle of red on a small table next to them.

"Are you going to travel to Wu Wei with all this?" asked Astrid, still scanning the tent's interior.

"We doubt the bed will fit on one of your ships," smiled Kya. "But why not keep the grandeur while we can?"

"I suppose," agreed Astrid.

"So how can we help you," asked the Queen.

Astrid thought for a moment, leaving the silence to be broken by the flickering candlelight. "Honestly, I don't know why I'm here. I found myself at your tent, and I panicked."

Kya laughed. "We see. You should sleep; we have a long march ahead of us."

"You're not sleeping either," said Astrid.

"I suppose we aren't." Kya sighed deeply, looking at the ground and swilling the wine in their glass. "Help yourself to some of our wine and a seat."

Astrid did just that, taking one of the wine glasses next to the bottle and pouring some for herself. She pulled a chair from under the make-up table, took a sip, and tried to find something to say. "Why do you talk like that?"

"Like what?" asked Kya, taken aback by the question.

"With *us* and *our* as if you're multiple people," said Astrid, taking another sip.

"We have to say, we are not used to people with your lack of courtesy." Astrid raised her glass, causing the Queen to smile before continuing. "It's tradition. That's how all future monarchs learn to speak."

"And calling you *they*," said Astrid. "Is that part of these traditions?"

Kya sat silent for a while, taking a sip from their glass. "No," they finally said. "That was Ichika's idea."

Astrid remained quiet as Kya stared unblinking into their wine.

"We were never comfortable," they said. "Being Queen means we are held to an extremely high standard. We have to be the cleverest, dignified, and beautiful. It's exhausting. We enjoy wearing make-up, we enjoy our dresses. But this world, it forces you to ask questions. Would we have liked those things if we were born a man? Would we like our hair more if it were short or our body more if it were flatter?"

The Queen looked over at Astrid, flushed cheeks breaking through the foundation still caked on their face. "Anyway," they continued, "we told Ichika this; told her we didn't want to be ourself, but we didn't want to be anyone else either. This is Sekando. We knew the alternative was exile. It's what happened to our brother, Hideo, and all men in Sekando City. She had the idea of having people call us 'they.' That way, we were neither."

A tear tore a streak through the Queens' make-up. Astrid felt her throat dry up and clutched her wine glass tightly. "I'm sorry about what happened to Ichika. She meant a lot to you, and it wasn't a good death."

"No death is good," stated the Queen.

Astrid nodded. "I meant she deserved better."

They sat silently, sipping at their wine in the dancing candlelight. Eventually, Kya finished their glass. They briefly considered the bottle before shaking their head and putting the glass on the table beside them.

"We are going to get some sleep, Astrid," said Kya. "We suggest you do the same. It's a long journey to Koseki."

Astrid downed the rest of her wine and stood up, replacing the chair under the desk. She was halfway to the exit before she froze in her tracks. Suddenly she realised why she had walked all this way.

"Before I go, I want permission to visit Akkael."

The Queen's face betrayed no emotion as they stared through Astrid. Eventually, they took a deep breath and shook their head. "Why not? We've already given Skane permission to visit him. He should still be there."

Astrid bowed. "Thank you," she said. "Goodnight, Your Majesty."

Kya didn't respond, just waving their hand and dismissing the Northwoman. Astrid left to see the sky was lighter than when she'd entered the tent. The clouds were going pale, and seagulls were already beginning to squeal in the distance. Astrid walked behind the Queen's tent to a small opening where Akkael's cage was wedged. A few small trees and faint torched decorated the alcove, and the light danced off the two Sekandans' armour as they stood to watch at the edge of the opening.

They allowed Astrid through, and she saw Skane standing before Akkael's cage. It was strange to see them laughing. Before, it seemed like laughing was half of what Astrid and Akkael did together, but now, watching her husband smile through a new face, seeing Skane raise his head and chuckle at the sky, Astrid wondered how it had become so strange so quickly.

"I'm telling you, it's true," said Ichika; Akkael. It was still hard for Astrid to see him behind that face. "I was sharing a hill with a twenty-foot dragon; at least twenty-foot. Then, I heard someone yelling at the bottom of the sand dune. Of course, I recognised the voice immediately. I turned, and there he was, your husband, my stupid younger brother, sword drawn, charging."

221

Skane grabbed his side, massaging a stitch as he struggled to get words through his laughter. "How did the dragon react?"

"It just looked sort of confused," said Akkael. "No one looks good running uphill through the sand with a sword waving above their head, least of all Magar."

Skane wiped a tear from his eye. "What a fucking idiot."

"I wish you could have seen it." Akkael leant back against the bars behind him.

They took a few moments to catch their breath before Skane sighed. "Oh, Akkael. I've missed you, my friend."

Akkael smiled. "I missed you too. It's been a funny few weeks."

"That's a euphemism and a half," said Skane. "But at least you're not dead. You make a bad corpse."

Akkael snickered. "I may as well be dead. I will rot in a Sekandan prison for the rest of my life."

"No, you won't," said Skane, shaking his head. "We can find ways to smooth things over with the Queen."

Akkael shrugged, staring blankly into the distance. "I don't know. Maybe I deserve it, you know. I was so focused on my own concept of victory that I nearly ruined all of this." He indicated to the Sekandan camp.

Skane looked down at the ground and shrugged. "Yeah, well, you were just doing what you knew. That kind of war of attrition, running at a wall until you break through. In your case, keep dying until you become someone who puts you before Hideo. Doran always said if we were going forward, we'd need peace and alliances. It's only recently I realised how smart he really was."

Akkael took a deep, stuttering breath. "Yeah. He was good."

Astrid watched the conversation before her and felt her heart beating faster as her body shook. She didn't know how Skane could do it. He'd seen Akkael's corpse as well. It was flat and cold on a clothed table. He was gone. Astrid clenched her fists. She hadn't allowed herself to blink for so long that her eyes began to sting, staring at Ichika and waiting for her charade to collapse and for everyone to realise it was all pretend.

Astrid unfurled her hands, watching the two talk a little longer before turning around. She wasn't ready; she waited and listened to Akkael's voice again. It wasn't the right pitch, but it had the correct cadence and pattern. Every pause was how Akkael broke his speech. Every emphasis was on how he would speak. She waited for him to finish whatever he was saying before walking away.

She took one step, then another, and then, with the next, a tree branch snapped under her foot.

"Astrid?"

She froze, and the stick ends propped up on either side of her foot like antlers. Astrid slowly turned to see Skane looking at her, as well as Akkael, through Ichika's eyes.

Before Astrid could say anything, Skane turned to Akkael. "It's getting late; I should go. Good talking to you, my friend."

Akkael couldn't stop looking back at Astrid. He nodded to Skane in response.

The big Northman left the clearing, tapping Astrid on the shoulder as he walked past her. Astrid heard his footsteps fade away, staring silently at the Sekandan face Akkael hid behind.

"Hello," he finally said, breaking the silence.

Astrid didn't reply for a moment. When she had composed herself enough to speak, she found herself filled with rage. "How are you alive?"

"I told you and Queen Kya everything I know," he said, keeping his voice low. "I'm sorry I didn't tell you sooner."

"Tell me sooner," she repeated, eyes wide. "When did you want to tell me? I could have killed you in that duel. Would you have become me then?"

"I'm sorry." Akkael was looking down at the floor of his cage.

"I suppose it's fitting," she said. "You took everything else from me; you may as well have taken my life as well."

Astrid knew what she said was wrong, but the silence she got from Akkael only made her anger worsen. She picked a stone from the ground next to her foot and launched it at him. It bounced off one of the cage bars, so she got another one. This time the stone flicked Akkael's cheek. After that, she noticed a tree branch resting against a trunk. She paced over to it and clenched it in her fist.

"You abandoned me." She charged to the cage and began striking it with the stick. "I. Lost. Everything!" Each word was punctuated by a strike on the bars. Her face grew red, and her eyes began to sting. She screamed, hitting the cage faster and harder until the branch snapped. Her eyes tracked the half that spun in the air, landing in a pile of rotting blossoms.

She noticed how heavy her breathing was. Her chin hit her chest, and she watched tears fall onto the ground, dimly lit by the twilight.

"Why?" she started. "Why didn't you come to me first? We could have worked everything out. We could have done it together."

Akkael delayed before speaking. "I don't know," he finally said. "I didn't think you'd believe me, but that wasn't why. I was afraid. I couldn't face you after what happened to Alani. If you showed me a fraction of my hatred for myself, it would have broken me."

Astrid looked up. "Were you worried I would attack you with a tree branch or something?"

It took Akkael a while, but eventually, he started to laugh, as did Astrid. However, it wasn't long before they stopped, letting the silence revert the tension.

Akkael's lips thinned, and his left hand clenched and unclenched. "I'm sorry I didn't look after Alani," said Akkael. "I'm sorry for not being there for you. I'm sorry I put you through all of this. I'm sorry for all of it."

Astrid couldn't bring herself to say the words she knew he wanted to hear. She just stared at him. It was easier to see Akkael. There was a rhythm to the way he spoke and the way his eyes moved was as unique as a fingerprint.

Astrid turned around and walked away, having said all she could. She felt Akkael looking at her as she walked away but said nothing as she turned the corner.

The sky was blue, and the pink of the trees was brighter than when she'd first arrived at the opening. She walked past Queen Kya's tent, noticing candlelight still leaking from under the pavilion.

She felt the heaviness of exhaustion all the way back to her tent. There was no use trying to sleep, though, as the camp was soon to wake and pack up for the long journey to Koseki. Astrid just lay on the bedroll and watched the light through her tent. She remembered Alani and smiled. There was humming, giggling, the pattering of unstable footsteps, and the fluttering wings of nearby birds in fearful flight. Her memories were almost like dreams.

[CHAPTER 35] — THE MARCH

The rain had died an hour prior, but the ground was still wet. Thirteen-thousand boots squelched deep into the damp, beaten mud. Rice paddies were the only signs of civilisation for miles, shoots submerged in water like they were growing in a mirror, reflecting the grey sky and the glistening lines where the sun was desperate to break through. The smell of thousands of wet, dirty people permeated the surroundings like a bog.

Sand was bunched in Skane's shoes from trekking the Sekandan dunes, so he welcomed the ease of hiking through the mire. He wore full plate armour, which sunk him deeper into the dirt, and two people's worth of luggage: his own and Rigpa's.

There were many horse-drawn carriages in the caravan. The Queen had their own, and one for all their dignitaries, such as Moon, Kwan, and some sages. The cage that held Akkael needed a horse too, which made Skane jealous of his imprisoned, cursed shield brother. The rest of the carts were for supplies like food and tents.

The Queen offered Rigpa a seat in their carriage, despite still being the Solstic army's hostage. Another prisoner of which Skane was jealous. However, the old woman politely refused, saying pilgrimages had been her training for these sorts of long journeys. Skane began trailing next to her when her head started bobbing in exhaustion. He offered to carry her bag the second time her legs gave way. She accepted his help after the third.

Skane carried her backpack on his left shoulder, leaving room for his rucksack. She didn't have much on her, just a tent and bedroll the Solstic had given her to not insult the Sekandans. The Grand Sage also carried food and water for herself.

"I'm not as fit as I used to be," she said after an hour of walking in silence at the back of the train.

"None of us are," replied Skane, trying not the show how much his lower back ached.

They began walking uphill, and Skane felt a pulsing pain in his back muscles. His breathing had already been laboured, but it was hot on his teeth. His own pack was a lot larger than Rigpa's. He carried his camping gear, weaponry, hunting traps, food, and drink.

"Why are you wearing armour?" Rigpa asked, looking the Northman up and down.

"Well, if I don't wear it, I'd have to carry it," he said. "If that was the case, who'd carry your shit?"

Rigpa snickered. "You could have left it at the ship."

"Armour is expensive, and we only left a few hundred soldiers to protect the boats. Lucky bastards." Skane tripped on a clod of dirt as if for emphasis.

"You were wearing armour on the day we met," continued Rigpa.

"I'm flattered you remembered that."

"None of your people wear armour," she continued. "Just furs or leather or nothing. Why do you?"

Skane shrugged, the pressure on his shoulders causing his muscles to burn. "Just do. Safer." Skane didn't know why but was compelled to change the topic. "I bet you regret not taking Their Majesty's offer."

Rigpa shook her head. "I needed the walk. It gives me time to think."

"Same for me," he grunted. "It's strange; you warned me I would be angry or feel, I don't know, dejected. Honestly, I wasn't really listening to you."

"I'm used to it," she said, rolling her eyes.

"But I didn't feel any of that," continued Skane. "As Akkael told me everything that had happened, I felt relief. Now he's alive, he can make things go back to normal."

Rigpa was silent for a moment before taking a deep breath. "I'm sorry, but that is a false emotion."

Skane squinted. "What do you mean? I'm not happy Akkael is alive?"

"That part's real," the Grand Sage nodded. "But believing he's going to fix all the pain in your heart is false. The only way to heal is to confront your biggest issues yourself, not wait for someone to come along and do it for you."

Skane was silent for a few steps. "I think you make everything a lot more complicated than it needs to be."

The old woman laughed. "Once you open your fourth chakra, you will see I'm right."

Skane groaned and shot his head back. "Can we not talk about chakras today? It's a long walk, and I don't feel attuned with my spiritual self or whatever."

"I thought you wanted to go through all of them," said Rigpa.

"I do." Skane looked like a child who didn't want to do his chores. "I mean, we're friends, right? Surely, we can go a day without talking about chakras."

Rigpa smiled to herself. "Yeah, friends," she said. "What do you want to talk about?"

Skane thought for a while. It was a long enough pause for the Grand Sage to forget herself and allow the actual conflict inside her to briefly show on her face. She knew what Akkael had learned about the Sera brothers and the person to whom she had dedicated her whole life. The Seraphim was not what she thought.

"How are you feeling about all the stuff Akkael said?" asked Skane, still watching her expression.

The reincarnation of Sera Phim just shrugged and folded her lips into a half smile. "I'm okay."

"*Okay?*" Skane snickered. "I get a thorough breakdown of every thought in my head, and all you give me in return is you're okay."

Rigpa grinned and chuckled through her nose before her face turned dower again. "I always knew there was something about the Seraphim we didn't fully understand. I look forward to learning more and uncovering the truth."

It sounded like a line she was being fed or a mantra that, if said enough, would become true. Skane looked straight ahead, adjusting the bag on his shoulder. "At least we know why the Grand Sage only appears in Edokand."

"Excuse me," said Rigpa, forced out of a reverie to which Skane wasn't privy.

"I asked you when you were in prison why you only reincarnate here," said Skane. "Now we know."

"Do we?"

Skane nodded. "Sera Phim is Sekandan. It makes sense he would stay here. He would miss home."

"I'm impressed," said Rigpa, grinning. "Understanding people's motives shows an empathetic character."

"I suppose I have you to blame for that." Skane patted the sage on the shoulder.

Rigpa's smile was so wide it made her eyes look closed. After a few more moments of silent marching, Rigpa spoke. "Do you ever miss home?"

"Uhm, yeah," said Skane, shrugging. "Yeah, sometimes. I haven't been there for over a decade now, though. I doubt I would recognise it."

"Did you ever think about going back?" Rigpa asked.

Skane looked down at the mud. "Not really. Magar was here. Before here, he was in Urkanza. Just wasn't in the stars."

"Duty." Rigpa gave a sharp sigh. "I understand that."

"Yeah." Skane tried to imagine it. The blanket of unbroken tundra stretched to the horizon. The boats floating in the fiord. Ice dyed pink by the setting sun. The forests where horror stories were sparked and fear was kindled. Wheat and barley waving to passers-by, and straw tumbling down the farm paths. The constant sounds of grinding mills and blacksmiths working, singing, yelling, fighting, and laughing. He tried to picture all of it, but it was like looking at a painting that had fallen in water; the shapes were still there, but the colour had run off and made it duller than before.

"Did you know I ran away from my temple when I was a young girl?" Rigpa asked, expelling Skane from his attempts at remembering home.

"Why would I know that?"

"It's true," continued Rigpa. "I was discovered as the Seraphim at just six, living in a small farming town in Trim. I went from rural life to a procession following me everywhere. My days were hard. I woke up before dawn, studied long hours, and was denied many of the basic necessities of young life."

"Sounds tough," said Skane.

"I had my first kiss at fifteen," Rigpa whispered, smiling like a mischievous child. "But we got caught. They couldn't exactly punish me. But him. I never did learn where they sent him. I still remember his face, though. He was very handsome."

Rigpa giggled, which brought a smile to Skane's face. After a moment, her smile faded, and she continued. "I was so angry when they sent him away that I cried for a week. Or so they thought. They gave me a lot of space for a time. I used that to plan my escape."

Skane laughed. "Even teenage monks have that angst, huh?"

"I had a book about Rhayne that I would read in my free time." The Grand Sage shook her head. "Can you believe that? I spent my days studying, and I used my free time to read more."

"I can absolutely believe you did that," nodded Skane.

"I smuggled myself on a ship and-" Rigpa clapped, slicing her right hand across the palm of her left before pointing with all four fingers into the distance, "-I was away. I had no idea where the ship was going, but in my head, I was leaving for Rhayne. There was no question about that. Why would this random ship bother going anywhere else? However, as the ship got further and further from the temple, I began to feel this dread." She clenched the torso of her purple robes. "It was like a sinking in my stomach, like something was pulling me back. Since then, I haven't tried to leave Edokand. My entire life, I've been too scared of that feeling. Too cowardly."

The Grand Sage bowed, watching her feet for a few paces. Skane let the silence fester for a moment before speaking. "How far did the ship take you?"

"Takakawa," Rigpa snickered. "I was caught by the sages within an hour."

The sun emerged from the clouds, and the sky slowly got bluer, though it was still mostly overcast. It reminded Skane of snow clouds in Solstr. As a boy, he noticed the clouds were dark when it rained. But no matter how much it snowed and how dismally cold it got, when he looked up and saw snowflakes in their dancing descent, he would look at a sky as pure white as the ground below his feet.

"I'd take you to Rhayne if you wanted," said Skane.

Rigpa squinted at the big man. "Really?"

"Yeah," Skane shrugged. "We have a large settlement there. Vineyards, villas, and views. You can have a vacation, and I'll bring you straight back. What do you say?"

Rigpa shook her head, looking down and the boot prints of those marching ahead. "I'm too old for adventure now."

Skane scoffed. "For the last few weeks, you've been trundled about all over the place as a prisoner of a foreign army. I'd class that as an adventure, wouldn't you?"

Skane loved making the old woman smile; it was a warming sight. "I suppose," she agreed. "Why don't you ask me again at the end of this war?"

Skane smiled back. "Okay."

They walked silently for hours watching as Sekando rolled past them; the rural landscape and the little homesteads lingered in Skane's view as they avoided the larger towns on the arduous march.

Magar was further ahead, deep in thought, despite his exterior. Trygve was also somewhere, probably still stropping that he wasn't the one to kill Ichika. Astrid stalked Akkael's cage, fluctuating between intense anger and extreme relief. But Skane allowed himself a reprieve from the complex world around him. He just watched the simple beauty of the Tsul landscape and counted himself lucky to see this random corner of the world with his own eyes.

That was the greatest part of the life of a Northman. He and his kin broke a mould that had existed since the beginning of history. He was one of the first of his people to look at the rice growing in the fields or the smoke rising from the stoves in the villages. Never again could a Northman say they were the first to see the hills he walked past, or the cherry blossoms scattered under the pink trees to his left.

The pain had moved from his back to his neck muscles, which made him realise that, as long as it took the sun to sink from its zenith to the horizon, he had forgotten it was even there.

[CHAPTER 36] — MUSKETS AND CANNONS

Hideo watched the men of Chuton train with the new guns, as the books named them, from atop the central tower. Explosions like thunder emanated from the ground as the small, metal bullets bolted through the straw dummies and splintered the wooden targets. They pierced anything they touched, and Hideo imagined these shots burrowing through a Northman's chest.

According to inventory logs, translated through the gifts of the sages, there were two types of new weapons in Chuton. The long, handheld weapon that fired the piercing bullets were called a *musket*. Some of these weapons had bayonets clipped on the front, which Hideo assumed was for close combat if the shooting failed.

Unlike the musket, the *cannon* was too large to hold. Eight spread evenly across Chuton's wall. They looked like giant metal cylinders which fired larger balls at less accurate targets. They cratered the valley during practice.

The flammable substance that made all these weapons function was a grey powder, like ash. The barrels that stored it took up most of the armoury. Sacks filled with it lay in crates to use with the cannons or left loose to pour into a hole in the muskets. Then the projectile was forced into the aperture of the weapon. Musket bullets were suppressed by a long stick before they could fire. A trigger, like those on a crossbow, ignited the powder. However, with the cannons, a fuse set the powder alight.

The sages translated how these weapons worked from what appeared to be a training manual. Hideo had sages pouring through every Rhulian text he could find. The only maps he found were of Edokand. Nothing told him the location of Rhule or anything about the heart of the future empire.

Hideo turned away from the window, looking into the General's quarters. The metronome sat on the desk, facing him as it slowly ticked, drowning out the explosions from outside. The Rhulian flags had been lowered and burnt, except one, which Hideo kept as a desk cloth. The thin yellow lines slicing through the black field were the only colour in the room.

His head was filled with enemies. The shadow archers that killed his son were all but extinct. However, three remained. He would hunt them until they were all dead. The Sekandans. The sentinels of Koji's army. The Northmen, soon to be lying in the grass with bullet holes and vacant looks. The Emperor, trapped in his room. The politicians that opposed his coup rotted in prison. The Rhulian empire from two-hundred years in the future, each moment bringing them closer to the day they will invade.

As Hideo was locked in his spiral of hate and vengeance, there was a knock at the door. He sat down on his studded chair before calling to the knocker.

It was Ieyasu, the new General of Chuton. Hideo wanted a commander that he could control.

"My Lord Hideo," said Ieyasu, bowing. Hideo waited for a little too long before offering him a seat on the sofa next to the desk that technically belonged to Ieyasu.

"What do you want, General?" asked Hideo, yawning. He hadn't slept since coming to Chuton.

Ieyasu cleared his throat before speaking. "I want to discuss the progress of our training routine."

"If you fail me, it won't just be your rank that you'll lose," said Hideo in a calm, off-putting tone. "You know what I expect from you."

"Of course, my lord, everything is going exactly as planned." Ieyasu wiped the sweat from his brow as he looked down at the metronome. Hideo could see the thoughts behind his eyes. The fear of the contraption that Hideo used to wipe out Kho and his men. He continued, "However, we have been forced to improvise with these new weapons and have devised a strategy that utilises all of our strengths."

"What are you talking about?" asked Hideo, leaning back on his chair.

"Well, as with any weapon or military equipment, these guns take a lot of training," Ieyasu smiled to relieve the tension. "Even though we have enough muskets to train everyone to use them, the time it would take and the resources it would waste would make it pointless."

Hideo saw the logic in that and nodded, which made Ieyasu sigh in relief.

"So, what do you have in mind?"

"Well, the accuracy and speed to find a target are transferable skills for most archers," said Ieyasu. "There are fifteen-hundred warriors left in Chuton after... after Kho and the rest of them betrayed you."

Once Hideo reduced Kho and his men to ash, he made his way to the other side of the wall where most of Chuton's sentinels stood. Most abandoned their late leader in return for their lives, but some were still loyal. They met the same fate.

"Luckily," Ieyasu continued, "all of them are proficient in archery and sword combat."

Hideo yawned again. "Can you hurry up and get to your point."

"Absolutely, sorry, my lord." The fear was dripping off Ieyasu like wax from a candle. "I have opted to train only two-hundred men in these new weapons. For each musket, I will appoint two bowmen."

"Why?" asked Hideo. "Surely the muskets are more powerful than the bow."

"That is astute, my Lord." The grovelling was beginning to irritate Hideo. "However, reloading these weapons takes a long time, three times as long as the shadow archer crossbows. Instead of having pockets of muskets firing intermittently, which will be hard to choreograph and easy for the enemy to predict, we want all the muskets to be firing simultaneously. Then, as they reload, the archers will shoot, creating an almost endless barrage of projectiles."

Hideo could imagine it. The muskets would pierce the shield walls, and the archers would pick them off once their shields were abandoned. Hideo smiled.

"So," said Ieyasu, "because of our frugal use of these weapons, the remaining muskets and the five cannons, not immediately facing the valley, will be sent to the capital with you."

235

Hideo's eyes widened. "Why? Are you not expecting to win? Are you predicting you will fail?"

"Not at all," smiled Ieyasu. "It's just a caution. Also, when you take all these weapons to Jin Bu, the people there will see you as their saviour. These weapons will be like banners; they will mean hope. And once we win here, no one can deny your greatness. Stories of your ingenuity will filter through the streets, and people will say, '*Lord Hideo Kazar, the hero of Edokand.*'"

Hideo stayed still. He didn't blink or move in his chair, and his chest didn't expand with his breath. Ieyasu looked down at his wringing hands, avoiding Hideo's line of sight. With the silence, the ticking was allowed to fill the room, the black metronome rocking to its own momentum. Hideo's eyes moved to watch the hand sway back and forth. He placed his stumped arm onto the desk and reached for the metronome with his hand, stopping the rod between his finger and thumb.

After the metronome fizzled and clicked, Hideo looked up at Ieyasu, still staring at his hands. It would take a deft eye to notice how he had been affected by the metronome's magic. Half open, his eyes blinked at the speed of a snail's sprint. His nostrils expanded with a deep breath that would take a while to finish. He looked frozen in time, but Hideo understood he had just been slowed, the metronome changing his tempo until every second of his life would take an hour to complete.

He watched Ieyasu for a moment before sighing and shaking his head. "I don't remember the last time someone got my name right," he said, speaking down towards his handless arm. "It's Lord Kazar Hideo. I'm Sekandan; the family name comes first. It shouldn't bother me, but every time I hear Hideo Kazar, all I can think is how that's not my name."

The metronome's ticking had begun again as if inviting someone to stop it. Hideo had a few moments to let the beat consume him before he heard a whispered voice behind him. "What are you going to do next?"

It was Seradok, Hideo knew. However, he didn't turn to look. "What do you mean?" he asked.

"I know what you think about it," Seradok continued. "The Northmen, the shadow archers, everyone who betrayed you."

"I've already told you," Hideo snapped. "I want to wipe out the Northmen the right way. I want to watch the last one die and history to say I was the one to end them."

"I know this," said Seradok. "But what about everyone else? You know exactly where the Sekandans are and the sentinels who let your son die. History won't care what happens to them."

Hideo shook his head. "That's not true. History will remember how Sekando falls. They need a proper death, too. And Koseki..." Hideo trailed off, thinking about the mining town where the dregs of Koji's army were hiding. The town was a great exporter of iron, which is easy to find near volcanos.

Hideo remembered his son. People always said they looked alike, but Hideo never understood why. He had the face of his mother. Koji wore a peacock feather on his helmet. He said it was to set him apart from his father. Now, that helmet was sinking into the mud, his son's decaying face melting into the iron of his armour.

Hideo's breath got heavier as he cursed the soldiers that left him there. Those who had arranged to kill him were probably hiding amongst the cowards, silently pleased that their mission had been completed. All of them deserved to die.

Hideo pictured Koseki, built onto the volcano's slopes, and reached for the metronome. He stopped the arm again, closing his eyes and imagining carnage. The metronome spat and sputtered before continuing to tick.

"Good work," said Seradok.

Hideo turned around and saw nothing but the window, muskets still firing in the courtyard below. He turned back to Ieyasu, still frozen by the metronome's magic. Hideo stopped the metronome once more to free him.

The General raised his head as if nothing had happened.

After a few moments, Hideo smiled. His grin felt like Seradok's looked; thin, stretching the width of his face.

"Continue," said Hideo. "Tell me the rest of your strategy."

He pretended to listen as Ieyasu explained how he intended to break the Northmen. The sound of musket shots and ticking and cannonballs cratering Chuton's valley melded together as Ieyasu spoke. The only image in Hideo's head was Koseki, and the one less name in his quest for revenge.

"How does that sound?" asked Ieyasu. Hideo had no idea how long he was speaking.

Hideo smiled at the General. "Perfect," he said, nodding with Seradok's grin still stretching across his face. "Everything is perfect."

[CHAPTER 37] — KOSEKI

Akkael sat in his cage and twiddled his thumbs as those around him prepared camp. They had reached Koseki a few hours prior, though Akkael hadn't seen much of it except the volcano's peak through the breaks in the bamboo.

They set up camp within the forest while designing a siege line of trenches closer to the town. If they had asked Akkael, a large army camping in a forest was a perfect opportunity for the enemy to pick them off one by one, especially with the dense layers of bamboo. But no one had asked him, and why would they.

There were thirteen thousand in the army, a mix of eight thousand Northmen and five thousand Sekandans. However, from overheard conversations, he knew two thousand Sekandans would stay behind to continue the siege. At the same time, the rest would sail for Wu Wei.

Akkael still hadn't come to terms with what Seravex had shown him. The power of a god altering three Sekandans and warping their human bodies. He never even considered gods were real. No one had. He was still in denial about what he saw; however, with everything that had happened since he'd died, Akkael felt he was much more experienced in dealing with these things than those around him.

Trygve was the worst. He hadn't spoken to anyone since he'd learned who inhabited Ichika's body. On the road, Akkael would spot him skulking behind his cage, and when there were breaks in the soldiers, Akkael could see Trygve staring at him, twirling his knife between his fingers. Then, when Sekandans would fill the gaps again, he would disappear, and Akkael would find him doing the same thing in another spot.

The cage was near the Queen's tent at the commander's end of the camp. Next to Their Majesty's giant blue pavilion was their General's tent, Moon's, and a strategy tent. The Queen only allowed certain Northmen to set up near them. Astrid, Skane, and Magar erected their patchwork, domed tents next to the pristine, blue-silken marquees of the Sekandans. Akkael tried not to look too long in their direction, the same way Astrid had purposely averted her eyes from him. He just

239

stared down at the hay-laden floor of his cage, watching his thumbs dance around each other.

"Do you remember our game?" Akkael looked up and locked eyes with his brother, Magar. The skin around his eye was still blue, and his face was littered with cuts. They hadn't seen each other since Akkael explained everything to Skane at Sui Bay.

Akkael's voice was hoarse, not having spoken in days. "What game?"

"When we were kids," Magar continued quickly. "The one father taught us."

Akkael assumed Magar was being so vague because he was double-checking it was really him and not Ichika.

"The rhyming game?"

"Yes." Magar had been so used to scowling that when he smiled, his cut bottom lip opened, bubbling a little with blood. "I've been thinking about that game."

Magar wasn't generally good with words, but whenever the three of them, including Doran, played as kids, he would take it more seriously than war. "You're good, despite your vocabulary."

The rules were simple: competitive rhyming couplets. "It's easy, like cutting an artery."

Akkael winced. "That was a stretch."

Magar grunted. "This power suits you: you needed a new face."

Akkael snickered, as did Magar. He looked up at the bars above him, thinking of a good response. "I was a work of art; you're an ugly disgrace."

"Disgrace?" said Skane standing behind Magar with folded arms. A smug grin spread across his face as both brothers turned to face him. "Says the one in yet *another* cage."

Akkael grinned at his brother-in-law before speaking. "Kept on display," he started, raising his arms with grandeur. "I was born for the stage."

Skane rolled his eyes, smiling. Before anyone else could throw another line, Akkael noticed Astrid approaching the men. His eyes went wide, as did Skane's. Akkael hadn't seen Astrid since Sui Bay, their last conversation was short but hurt more than most of the deaths he had felt.

For a moment, she was still, like the bamboo around them. But eventually, she opened her mouth to speak. "The stage? You suck at acting. That's why you're here."

Akkael shrugged. He didn't have a response to that; he was a lousy actor. He couldn't even pretend to be Ichika for one day, and his life depended on it. He thought long and hard about something to say, looking at his wife and hoping to hold on to this moment.

"Everyone's a critic, it would appear," he said, feigning insult.

"Try puppet shows," said Magar, sanguine lips reaching ear to ear. "You can hide in a box."

Akkael turned his attention to his brother. "Like you could do better with your head filled with rocks."

All four laughed. Akkael imagined they were back at an inn, in his old body, with his hand wrapped around a mead horn. All he would need was one cup, and he'd be drunk enough to stand on a stool and sing. Astrid would have her cithara, and Skane would drum on the table. Doran would make some drunken speech, and Magar would sit quietly, his arms folded, smiling.

"What's going on here?" Akkael and the rest of his family were cast out of happy reveries, turning to see Queen Kya flanked by four guardswomen and Moon. They had their arms folded, staring at each of them in turn.

"Sorry, Queen Kya," said Astrid, stepping before the cage. "We were just playing a Solstic children's game. Nothing else."

"We have respected your authority over your own prisoner," they responded. "Despite the Grand Sage's importance, we have let you keep her in your custody. Respect the boundaries we have placed on ours."

241

"Of course," said Astrid after a moment's delay. Magar stood up and walked away without a word; Kya sucked their teeth as he left without being dismissed.

"What was the game?" asked Moon.

Skane and Astrid looked at each other before responding. "It's a poetry game," said Astrid.

"Poetry?" Moon scoffed as if she found barbarians doing poetry as funny as a cat fetching a ball.

Queen Kya stepped forward, locking eyes with Akkael. Their disgust mingled with their mourning. It was the same look they gave him whenever they looked his way. "The thief plays his games:/ The killer hides the remains./ The noose greets them both."

Silence followed as the Queen's eyes darted across the body that their friend once occupied.

Skane spoke to alleviate the dense tension. "Is that a Sekandan poem?"

"Yes," they spat, not taking their eyes off Akkael. "But our poetry isn't for childish games. It can be as sharp as a blade if honed enough. It's art." They turned around, moving within an inch of Skane. "Here, things are sacred./ Time, and death, and timeless death./ We don't play with these."

Again, a quiet that was thicker than blood filled the camp. Akkael could only see the back of Kya's head, but even still, he felt the intensity of their fiery gaze. Akkael looked at Moon. She was already staring at him, scowling.

"Skane!" The yell made Akkael almost jump out of Ichika's skin. Everyone near the cage turned, noticing Rigpa emerge from her tent. She began running, lifting her robes to not slow her down. When she reached Skane and the Queen, Akkael noticed her eyes were filled with panic and her face was covered in fear. "Something's happening."

Skane turned all his attention to the Grand Sage. "What's happening?"

"I don't know." She shook her head, scrying the ground under her feet. "It's like back at your camp. It is quick. Something bad is about to happen."

Akkael turned around in his cage. Kya had brought some of their own sages with them from Sekando City. Akkael also saw them approaching with the same fear on their faces. However, they didn't have time to reach Kya before Akkael heard the explosion. Every face turned east towards Koseki.

They couldn't see the town through the bamboo, but the tip of the mountain it was built on peaked over the trees. Or it would have if it hadn't been engulfed by a billow of black smoke. Rocks were flung from the top as the volcano opened like an egg. A red hue, like the one that swallowed Alani, shone through the dense miasma. Akkael's hand began to hurt as he watched the eruption, standing hunched inside his cage with the same slack jaw and wide eyes as those around him.

Then, as everyone watched in stunned silence, the red magma leaked from the smoke and descended the hill toward the mining town. Koseki, the place they had spent hours setting up to besiege so those inside couldn't escape, was about to be engulfed.

[CHAPTER 38] — THE VOLCANO

The ground rocked like ships at sea. It was as if the thunder came before the lightning. Everyone knew the rumbles beneath them were meant to be the prelude, warning those around about the calamity. But since that warning came later, Skane watched the magma sprint down the mountain towards the unsuspecting town.

The delayed earthquakes seemed more violent than they would have been. Like congestion, there was too much going on at once. Tents collapsed, and barrels of water fell, spilling across the encampment. Men and women were brought to their knees as Skane stumbled clear of the tree line, with Magar, Astrid, and Moon close behind, followed by Queen Kya and Kwan.

The sight of Koseki was worse than Skane had predicted. Lava had already seeped into the highest mine on the volcano, leaving him to fear for the fates of those inside. The magma itself wasn't smoking, but the more it touched, the denser the blanket of ash got. Pillars of smoke shot up, closing in on the town.

This was the first time Skane had looked at Koseki in person, and without the orange hue above it, it reminded him of his home village. Mines dug deep into the mountain. Houses with bamboo roofing and loosely fitted walls made from the black volcanic rock were scattered, unburdened by the patterns of roads. The gate was worn by time and stood in the aperture of a large blue gatehouse with a shingle roof that reminded Skane of the pagoda at Takakawa. The palisade fence was barely taller than a man and resembled spiked scaffolding more than a solid defence. The two watchtowers were the height of a two-story inn.

Trenches on the siege line were shallow, but Skane still worried it would slow the escape of those inside. When Skane considered the town, it was hard to see it as anything but kindling. It would all burn.

"What should we do?" Astrid was the first to speak, almost yelling over the sound of thirteen thousand men and women forming ranks in front of them.

"They'll take the opportunity to charge us." Magar was stone-faced, monotoned. "If we let them, they'll take out a huge chunk of us. We should ready archers to shoot in case they come our way."

"Excuse me?" The words left Skane's mouth before he noticed he'd turned to face Magar.

"Most people in that town are our people," said Kya curtly. "We will not sacrifice them for the sake of a thousand sentinels."

"If your people are smart, they'll run to the river south of that hill," said Magar, shaking his head and pointing to a freshwater stream they had thought to use for drinking water. "Only the soldiers will come this way."

Magma was filling the town like a bath, destroying homes and livelihoods.

"We are standing on the closest incline, and most of the path towards that stream is declining farmland," Skane pointed out. "The rice will slow them down, and lava will slide directly to them."

Moon pointed between Skane and Magar. "Look," she whispered.

Everyone turned their heads as the gate to the city flung open, men, women, and children pouring out of the city towards them as the liquid fire nipped at their heels.

"The people of the town know we are here," said Kwan, Kya's General. "They will come this way thinking we will help them."

Skane noticed it first, but Magar was the one to speak. The glint of red sentinel armour was distinct against the drab clothing of the townspeople. "They are using the people as cover to mount an attack."

"They're not attacking; they're fleeing," observed Skane. He felt himself clasp Magar's arm and watched his expression change to fear at Skane's scowl.

Skane let go. "We need to help them."

The lava began to reduce the wall and exit the town; nothing resembling homes could be seen above the glowing mass, like slurry, rolling and pouring simultaneously. The screams of those running away were now close enough to be heard over the chattering of the soldiers in front of them.

"Those aren't battle cries," said Moon.

They had spoken enough, all turning to Queen Kya and awaiting their orders. "Kwan, Skane, run to the captains at the front line and tell them to remove every weapon from every sentinel before we allow them up the hill. Children are given priority, then our people."

Without bowing, Kwan sprinted down the hill. Skane and Astrid followed. The survivors began clambering over the trenches. Some had tripped, unable to get up before the lava dove in after them. Some had remained inside the trenches to help friends and loved ones to their feet. Most had met the same fate.

Skane relayed the Queen's instructions to the Northmen, some looking genuinely dismayed as they replaced their weapons in their belts. The front flanks kept their weapons drawn to deter the Edokand'i from reacting to those barricading their escape.

But, as the land began to plateau, the magma slowed down, crawling behind the villagers as they gained some ground.

"Stop where you are," yelled Skane, pushing to the front line.

The crowd from Koseki, beleaguered and panting, were slowly brought to a quiet halt; only the sniffling of children could be heard.

Eventually, a sentinel pushed to the front of the new refugees, gold gilding on his armour showing him to be a captain. Probably the only one left from Koji's army. "Barbarians!" he screeched. "Let us pass!"

"Insulting us is no way to get aid," replied Skane, no weapon in his folded arms. "There may be Sekandans with us, but we are the bulk of this force."

Sweat trickled down the captain's forehead. "There are children with us. Let us through!"

"Discard your weapons, and we'll let you through," said Skane. "Children first, then Sekandans, then sentinels."

The captain scoffed. "Let ourselves be at the mercy of the likes of you? No chance."

The earth growled, shaking as civilians behind the captain started to scream.

Skane spread his legs out to keep his footing, unfolding his arms for balance. The sentinel nearly fell over, only just managing to stay on his feet as he buckled to the left.

After the shake, Skane spoke. "Drop your weapons. Children first."

The sentinel turned, looking past the townspeople at the engulfed mining village. He looked down at the grass under his feet before unbuckling his belt and throwing his katana. The sentinels who had not emerged from the throng saw their captain and followed his example. Then they ushered the children to the front.

Over time, they found an easy mechanism for the process. Children walked in slow fear through the imposing height of Solstic warriors as sentinels were stripped of their weapons. Some resisted for a moment. However, each time the ground shook like it might give way, more relented, stepping over their swords and waiting their turn.

The Solstic civilians reacted with gratitude and disgust as they walked through the corridors made by the Northmen. As the adult refugees were processed, Skane's job changed from humanitarianism to managing potential unrest.

"Let me take him." Skane heard a feint protest from behind him as the now refugees were being led in single-file columns to the top of the hillock. He turned and saw one column being held up by a skinny old man facing a large Northman. The elder had tattoos up his neck, and, in his arms, he clutched a ferret on a lead. The ferret was fatter than the man, with white fur and red eyes.

"What you want a lemur for?" asked the Northman slowly, trying to piece together what little Edokand'i he'd learned.

The tattooed man puffed up his chest. "It's a ferret. His name is Lee, and he just survived a surprise volcanic eruption; thank you very much. He's seen more than most ferrets, and he's coming with me."

The Solstic warrior scratched his bare chest. The old man had spoken fast, and the warrior clearly hadn't understood anything he'd said.

"Just ditch it," said a woman in line behind the man.

"Quiet, wench," said the man.

"Don't talk to me like that; I'm your wife," said the woman.

The man shook his head. "My wife knows how much I love Lee. She would never tell me to discard him. He's like the son I never had."

"You have a son," said his wife.

"Yeah, and he's a prick."

The woman gasped. "You know what. Bring the rodent. You call it Lee; I call it lunch."

"You eat Lee, I eat you!"

Skane intervened, barging in front of his kinsman. "It's okay; you can take the ferret."

"Harrumph," The man barked, scowling as he walked up the hill. His wife followed behind him, still bickering.

The rest of the process went on without a hitch. Children had been separated from their parents as they were led into the forest, and some had been injured in the panic. But those who'd made it found their way to the camp that had still not been built. The lava had stopped as the land began to rise. Some of it had rolled further up, but most had begun to crust over, trading the iridescent hue for an almost scab-like colour.

Skane noticed Magar's absence when he returned to the top of the hill. The sun began to set behind the bamboo forest. Fires still burned, and the ash and soot pouring from the mountain drowned the pink and orange above him as if the volcano had emptied into the sky.

There was still a lot to be done, but he decided to sit in the grass and let the noises of those around him sink away. He looked out at everything that was destroyed and felt guilty. He didn't feel bad for looking or about what had happened. He felt terrible for just how beautiful he found it.

[CHAPTER 39] — THE AFTERSHOCK

Astrid sat close enough to the Queen to see they were shaking. It wasn't from the occasional aftershocks rocking the ground beneath their feet nor the chill of the early morning hours. It was subtler. The kind of shakes that vibrated in the bones and numbed the skin. The jitters came more from the mind than anything physical. Astrid recognised the pattern of their trembling like an old friend's handwriting. It didn't come from shock or fear at what had happened in Koseki. Astrid had felt the same way when she heard that Akkael was alive. It was anger. Simple rage.

Almost two-dozen people crammed into the small tent used as a council chamber. A small wooden table, laden with maps and inventory lists, was positioned in the centre. Most of the chairs were removed to make space, with the only person sitting being the Queen. Sekandan flags, the blue dot on the red background, surrounded them like eyes watching from every corner.

Astrid, Kya, Moon, Skane, and Magar occupied the tent. The Queen's general, Kwan, was also there, with Lindsay, who accompanied Astrid, and the Grand Sage, Rigpa, who accompanied Skane. The captain of the goutuizi also attended, as well as two other sentinels and the mayor of Koseki. His name was Min, and he had the right sternness and build for the leader of a mining village. The rest of those crammed into the pavilion were Solstic and Sekandan soldiers, standing guard.

Despite the weeping, sniffling, and loud complaints of the refugees outside, the tent was silent, all waiting in bated breath for the Queen to speak.

"Where's Jarl Trygve?" the Queen finally asked. "Isn't he somewhat important? Why is he not present?"

Astrid hadn't seen Trygve since Sui Bay. He was always strange, but he had been particularly elusive lately.

Astrid prepared to speak as if she'd forgotten how. "I don't know. It's best to assume he's not coming."

The Queen scoffed. "Is this some form of Northern insult?" they asked. "Not attending us as a way of making us feel lesser."

"No," Astrid said quickly. "I promise you that's not what he's doing."

"Trygve is just a Jarl," said Magar, arms folded and voice flat and calm. "I'm King of the Solstic. I'm all that matters."

Astrid realised this was the first time Magar had referred to himself as king. Queen Kya seemed to accept Magar's response, bowing their head towards the table.

Astrid noticed flaws in their make-up. Cracks and smudges appeared in the foundation, and the mascara had disappeared from one eye, making it look uneven.

Kya sharply glanced towards the Rigpa. "Grand Sage, your order is blessed with many gifts, you most of all. How far are you able to sense the ground beneath your feet?"

The old woman squinted. "Forgive me, Your Majesty, but that's not really how it works," she said, averting her eyes. "It's more like an extension of my own sense of touch. It's like the earth is another extremity, and the further away something is, the more numb the extremity feels. Like an arm falling asleep."

Kya took a deep breath to not lose their temper with the Grand Sage. "Okay, so was Koseki, as you put it, numb?"

Rigpa shook her head. "No. I wasn't close enough to know the exact population, but I could feel it."

"So, how didn't you know the volcano would erupt?" The Queen raised their voice slightly. After directing their ire at Trygve, they directed it at Rigpa. Astrid could see they just wanted someone to blame.

"I felt this once before," said the sage. "At the Solstic camp just before the islands began to merge. It was as if one second, silence, and the next, there was chaos."

"We know who made the mountains rise," said Skane, taking over from Rigpa, who was too much of a monk to lay the blame for the calamity at anyone's feet. "Lord Hideo has the power to alter time within a particular radius. Maybe the sages couldn't feel the volcano about to erupt until the last second because it shouldn't have. Not yet."

Everyone had considered that as an option. The similarities between Koseki and the mountains were apparent. But no one could answer the question of why. Hideo couldn't know they were nearby. Things had moved quickly, making communication between the two, what used to be islands, harder.

"Excuse me." The captain of the goutuizi stepped forward. "I'm confused. Are you suggesting Lord Hideo has some form of... magic? And he's used it to destroy a peaceful mining village. That's slander."

Astrid turned to the captain, her eyebrows almost touching. "Shut the fuck up, goutuizi."

The rest of the sentinels stepped forward. "How dare you speak to me like that, Northman!"

"Captain," yelled the Queen, "take her advice. You're so ignorant and inconsequential to everything here that we and most here don't even know your name. Step back and stay silent, or you will be escorted out of the only important meeting you have ever been privy to."

If the sentinel had a tail, it would be tucked between his legs.

An earthquake shook those in the tent like leaves. As they all waited for the tremor to pass, Kya's head and eyes flicked back and forth as if they were reading something with paragraphs widely and randomly spaced. When the quake finished, the Queen's face changed, raising one of their perfectly kept eyebrows. "Sentinel, did you send word to Lord Hideo of your location?"

The captain, regaining his footing, looked around a little to confirm he had permission to speak. "Yes. Almost as soon as we arrived in Koseki."

It was as if the whole room groaned in unison. "Well, we know why he attacked. Some form of revenge," Moon spoke. She stood closest to the Queen, elbow almost touching their shoulder. "You failed him on the battlefield."

"Lord Hideo would not use this time magic to sentence his own men to death." The captain straightened his back and hardened his expression. But, despite

251

that, there was a weakness in his tone that didn't quite believe his own words. "Besides, we didn't fail him; it wasn't a battlefield. It was as if those men were-"

"Possessed, we know." The Queen waved their hand for the captain to slink back to where he was standing. She then looked over to their general. "This wasn't just an attack on the sentinels. This happened on Sekandan soil. This was a declaration of war against us. Against us."

Astrid knew the first us meant Sekando, and, with the latter, they meant themself. It was easy to forget that Lord Hideo and Kya were siblings. They may not have grown up together but they shared the same blood.

Over the weeks Astrid had gotten to know Kya, she had grown rather fond of them, with their silent strength and subtle stoicism. They insisted on travelling with their army to Wu Wei, as with Koji's army. In the four years of the war, she rarely witnessed Hideo set foot on the battlefield after his defeat at Skaldgard, and, as far as she knew, the Emperor had never left the palace.

"This war will end," said the Queen, clenching their fist. "This stupid, pointless war. We will end it."

Their eyes were bloodshot, making Astrid wonder if they had slept since leaving Sekando City.

"Yes." Skane nodded, speaking softly. "We will end it."

The Queen looked up at Skane, peering from beneath their brow. "I meant me. I will end it."

The tension held in the air, the Queen's eyes rapidly pacing in their skull as Skane, holding their gaze, remained silent, trying to keep a face of stone like everyone around him.

The Queen's staring was so encapsulating Astrid barely noticed the giant figure step forward from behind her. "What about us?" Astrid turned and noticed the mayor of Koseki. It was strange to see a male leader in Sekando. Still, men were usually labourers, so it made sense for a mining town to elect someone they knew would understand their work. "Our people have no home. Your people. Will you help?"

"You will show respect to Their Majesty," said Moon, like she was reluctantly disciplining a child.

Kya turned away from Skane to face the mayor. "We will give you the means and supplies to rebuild, and labourers to help you. The Sentinels will stay and aid you. Two thousand of our own warriors will also stay. We will send word to Sekando City to supply the needed materials."

"Eun won't like that," said General Kwan. Eun was the Queen's treasurer, already pulling her hair out trying to finance a siege and a war simultaneously.

Moon scoffed as the Queen laid out their commitments to the people of Koseki. They spoke for a while, leaving Astrid the time to think. The entire time she'd been in Edokand, she never understood why Doran was so determined to stay here. The war was slow and brutal. With the other Solstic settlements around the world, the people either supplied them land in return for their strength, or they had won land so swiftly that the inhabitants had no choice but to let them stay.

Edokand was different. In four years, they had won less land than any other colony and had torn the country apart in the process. Those proudest of their nation are burning it or altering it forever to keep the Solstic from achieving Doran's dream. Astrid felt a twinge of guilt knowing that, once a bystander in the war, Sekando was dragged into the fight by lies and fire.

But the guilt faded quickly. Hideo killed her daughter. She would rip the world in half to kill him. As Astrid's thoughts turned sour and violent, she felt a hand touch her elbow. Astrid shuddered initially before realising it was Lindsay. Astrid sighed, returning Lindsay's smile, though a little shallower than her companion's reassuring grin.

As Kya finished laying out their commitments to Koseki, a Sekandan soldier barged into the tent, causing everyone to face her in annoyed unison.

"Your Majesty," the soldier said, bowing quickly to correct her rude entrance.

"What?" said Kya, breathing deeply.

The soldier took a moment to catch her breath. "It's Ichika." *Akkael.*

The Queen straightened their back in their seat. "What about her?" Most had heard rumours about why Ichika was in a cage, but only those who needed to know were told the truth.

The soldier failed to answer fast enough, leading the Queen to repeat themself more curtly. "What about her?"

"My Queen," said the Sekandan, averting her eyes. "I'm sorry. She's dead."

[CHAPTER 40] — TRYGVE

Akkael sat up in his cage, watching in the distance as people rushed around, supplying the refugees of Koseki with food and water. His cage was moved away from the centre to accommodate those in need. The darkness engulfed him as he desperately stared at the warm torches, the light and heat he wanted.

Earthquakes had loosened the wedges that kept his wheels in place, and with each tremor or gust of wind, Akkael's cage shook as if a child was trying to guess what was inside a boxed gift. The cold breeze made him shiver and his teeth chatter.

He could only see the eruption, not the destruction the magma caused. The grey, black smoke was still visible against the midnight sky, and the trembling refugees were evidence enough of the carnage. He watched as figures in the distance huddled together.

He remembered falling into Magar's arms as he emerged from the ash and recalled the fear of those around him when Tsul and Trim collided. When he heard the weeps of those who had lost people, he remembered Alani. His hand ached with the phantom pain that had followed him since he had let go of his daughter.

He heard a twig snap to his left, and Akkael turned his head towards the noise. He noticed a skinny figure. Under one arm, the silhouette held a small, wooden keg. In their other hand were two mugs pinched between their fingers. As the figure got closer, Akkael noticed two knives held in a belt around their waist.

"Trygve?" said Akkael, fidgeting to face the Jarl of Takakawa.

"Mmmhmm." Trygve slumped down, back leaning against the cage. He fell so clumsily he moved the carriage. Akkael gripped the bars as Trygve collapsed into a further recline.

They corrected their posture before Trygve spoke. "Crazy day, right?"

Akkael moved slowly closer to the bars where Trygve sat. "Shouldn't you be in the Queen's meeting?" he asked. "It's probably important."

255

He knew everyone with a title was currently in the war tent, probably discussing how to proceed after the plans of a simple siege had gone awry.

Trygve shrugged. "Skipping it. Want some mead?" he asked, holding up a mug.

Akkael nodded without a moment's delay. He watched as Trygve clamped the cup between his legs and upturned the keg. He got more on his thighs than in the mug. Once he finished, he handed the mead through the bars to Akkael before repeating the process for his drink.

Akkael brought the cup to his lips. He didn't know if it was because he hadn't had mead in a while or if it was a good brew, but it was the best thing he'd ever tasted. The sweet honey sent a shiver to his stomach and a comforting warmth into his belly. He pulled it away from his lips and couldn't help exhaling slowly, closing his eyes, and smiling.

Trygve was less graceful. Pulling away from his mug, he let out a deep burp that echoed against the bamboo.

"How much have you drunk?" Akkael asked.

Trygve shrugged again. "Two. Three."

"Mugs?"

"Kegs."

Even though Trygve wasn't looking at Akkael, he seemed to sense the wide-eyed shock from inside the cage. "They weren't full kegs," Trygve clarified. "I had to share it with the sad saps of Koseki because Their Majesty didn't think to bring enough soju for everyone."

Akkael looked over at the camp where those who'd had their homes destroyed would lie awake all night, unable to rest. "Always be prepared to drink your sorrows."

Trygve raised his mug. "Ya ki da."

Akkael repeated the Solstic phrase for *cheers*, raising his mug as well. He looked at the back of his friend's head as they both took another sweet sip. "You can't look at me, can you?"

Trygve delayed before speaking. "It's not you that I can't look at."

His hatred for Ichika was widely known. Every time her name came up since his failed raids in Sekando was followed by a pledge of revenge and a promise of her death. Still, Akkael was disheartened by his friend's evident discomfort.

"Why did you ditch the Queen's meeting and come by my cage if you can't even look at me?"

"First, they're not my Queen," Trygve said, holding up his index finger, "and I wouldn't have gone to that meeting if they paid me. Second..." He trailed off after raising a second finger.

Eventually, Trygve's hand dropped. He took a deep breath. "Did you know my home was the first place Doran came when recruiting people for Edokand?"

Akkael shook his head before realising Trygve couldn't see him. "I didn't."

Trygve sighed again. "Annakat. It was a trade port on Solstr's southern coast. On one end, a fjord stretched for frozen miles. On the other, the Vicious Woods where only danger lurked." He took another sip of his mead before continuing. "Like most places in Solstr, we had no king. Anyone wealthy enough usually scampered to the Rhaynese or Urkanzan colonies. They'd pretend it was a raid, so we'd hold out for a few years. But, when it became painfully apparent that they weren't coming back, we'd elect another prick to abandon us come Autumn.

"I was thane, so I was in charge until a king was appointed. From an outsider's perspective, your brother picked a dreadful day to come to Annakat for recruits. Of course, winter was approaching, but all signs pointed to it being the easiest one we'd had in a while. Wolves were too distracted with the good harvests up north to venture south, and many wandering warriors had come to sojourn in Annakat for the winter. There are plenty to defend us from great bears and act as a good deterrent against raiders. We were comfortable, eating well, and drinking late into the night. Until the day your brother's ship arrived."

He took a long gulp of mead, finishing his mug. Akkael waited patiently as Trygve poured more into his cup and over his lap. After taking an even longer sip from his newly refilled drink, he restarted his story.

"I was outside feeding the pigs when I saw it. My father always said to watch the tops of the trees. You must keep an eye on the trees. I noticed the tips of the pines were snapped. The wind was strong the night before. Religion may be dead, but I prayed it was the wind. That's when I heard the screaming. In the early hours, three eagles the size of a horse swooped down, ripped away the straw roofs, and plucked five children from their beds. They didn't even wake a mouse.

"That's the Annakat your brother arrived at. It was easy to convince those people to leave their homes and never look back. So easy, in fact, that he left me to do it. He just got on his ship and told me he'd return soon, and I had to prepare men and women to bring their families to a place they'd never seen. Even those parents who had their children stolen the night before. I did such an excellent job wrangling the broken community that Doran said I could lead them in every battle we fought."

Trygve emptied his mug again, looking inside at the dregs at the bottom. "I don't think any of those people I brought with me are alive today. Some died in Skaldgard, and some in Takakawa. But the bulk of them..." For the first time since the start of their conversation, he turned to look Akkael dead in the eye. "They were killed by Ichika."

Trygve wasn't grinning. Akkael had never seen his face without a smile slashed like a scar across his face. The bold laugh he usually brought with him hadn't bellowed in the dark as it would have on other drunken nights, and the jokes he couldn't stop himself from making were tight behind his lips. This wasn't the same Trygve he's seen numerous times before. However, something told Akkael the man in front of him was more sincere than the one he was familiar with. This was the Trygve he hid behind jokes and smiles.

"I didn't know any of that," said Akkael softly.

Trygve looked back at the mug, rotating it in his hand, before nodding and discarding it. He stood up, still facing Akkael, a slight wolf's snarl on his lips as he looked at Ichika's face.

"People deserve revenge," he said. "Some may be big and lucky enough to look those who've wronged them in the eye and forgive them. Some may not even need that to move on. Some may want revenge but are never able to achieve it. None of that stops the fact that everyone deserves it. Every time."

Akkael felt his hand twinge and thought of Lord Hideo.

"Every time," Akkael repeated.

Trygve removed a dagger from his belt, jolting Akkael from his thoughts. "You should be the one to kill Hideo," said Trygve looking down at the blade. "And, after tonight, it's clear someone needs to do it. No one has a better chance than you."

Akkael knew exactly what Trygve was thinking. Akkael had told everyone how his power worked back at Sui Bay.

"But Trygve," Akkael started, "it'll kill you?"

Trygve's grin was slicing further across his face every second. Akkael knew at that moment his friend was scared.

Trygve stepped forward, holding the knife outward. "How would you like to die?"

Akkael considered the dagger before locking eyes with its wielder. He didn't want to kill his friend and didn't understand why he would willingly choose to die.

Then, Akkael looked down at his hands: at Ichika's hands. The person Trygve had devoted his life to killing was in a cage right in front of him. It may be Akkael's mind, but it was Ichika's face. Ichika's heart was still allowed to beat. Ichika's hands were drenched in the blood of those she'd killed. Trygve wasn't doing it on the off chance Akkael could escape and kill Hideo.

He was doing it for himself.

"Everyone deserves revenge, right?" said Akkael. Looking back at Trygve. "How would you like to kill me?"

Trygve's face displayed a range of emotions, from shock to excitement and pleasure. "Come." Akkael did so, still kneeling on the floor of his cage so they were at eye level. Trygve clenched the dagger and brought it closer to the bars. "Good luck, Akkael."

Those were the last works Trygve uttered. He plunged the knife into Akkael's throat, pulling it out just as quick. Akkael tried to keep the gurgling as quiet as possible as he drowned in Ichika's blood. Still, the instinctual shock and fear caused him to thrash as he fell to the floor of his cage, rocking it back and forth as he tried to breathe. Eventually, he lost so much oxygen that he couldn't even fight for his life. Warm blood poured from his neck as his hands dropped away from the wound.

Trygve watched as Ichika's eyes became bloodshot and her face turned red. Akkael could see a smile, smaller than the one he usually displayed, curve his lips. Trygve closed his eyes briefly and took a long, cathartic breath. He watched for a few more moments at Akkael's slow, agonising death before walking away, leaving him to die alone.

Akkael's last thoughts in Ichika's body were of what Trygve had said after his story. Everyone deserves revenge. Everyone, every time.

[CHAPTER 41] — TO SEA

"Tell the Queen it doesn't matter how angry they are; the Sekandans can't sail these ships."

The army was back at Sui Bay, returning to the five hundred men and women left behind to guard the floating island of boats in the northern sea. On the journey back, the tensions between the Sekandan and Solstic armies were high. Camps were segregated, and there was barely any fraternising between the two peoples.

Trygve, or Akkael in Trygve's body, still hadn't been found. Despite the tension and distrust that Trygve's selfish, vengeful decision caused, Skane couldn't help mourning the loss of an old friend. Skane had only met Trygve during the journey to Edokand, but the four years of war had cemented them as brothers in arms. However, trying to hold his disparate army together didn't leave him much time to think about his friend's death.

Moon and Astrid were the only envoys that could communicate with the Queen and pass on messages from them. Skane stood on the beach, passing luggage and supplies down a chain of men leading to the furthest boats. Rowing benches had been unclasped and used as planks connecting the ships. Men were removing tethers and raising anchors to get ready to depart. Due to the sheer number of boats, they sent them in waves, with the first wave already starting the day-long voyage to Trim.

"Wu Wei is west," Skane said to Moon. "That means that we have to sail two-hundred ships around Tsul, rowing most of the way, past the volcanic islets near Skaldgard and the shallow rocks near Takakawa."

Moon, arms folded, nodded as Skane spoke. "Yes, I understand the journey."

"Oh, you do," said Skane, throwing another rolled-up tent to a man standing precariously on one of the planks with such carelessness that he nearly lost his balance. "I just thought I'd clarify since this is maybe the eighth time we've had this conversation. Sekandans can't sail Solstic ships. That's just a fact. There are three

261

thousand Sekandans, so that's at least thirty ships, which is a lot to lose to Their Majesty's hubris."

"The Queen will not feel safe surrounded by Solstic warriors," said Moon.

"That's not my problem." Skane sighed, rubbing his eyes with one hand and massaging his back with the knuckles of his other. "Look, if the Queen wants to take their army and go, no one will blame them. A lot has happened since the duel; we will understand if they break their oath."

Moon looked down at the sand, then towards the blue tents being dismantled on the grass. "Their Majesty is determined to take their revenge on Lord Hideo. They blame him for what has happened as much as they blame Akkael."

Skane paused before nodding gently to himself. "If you're going to blame any two people for what has happened..." He trailed off, looking back at the ships, the second wave clasping their shields to the gunwale and getting ready to depart. "Best I can do for the Queen is this; the Sekandans will leave in the last three waves. I will captain the flagship of the first, and Astrid will captain the third wave. On every ship that carries Sekandans, your people will outnumber my people. Our weapon belts will be stored under our benches, and you can do whatever you want with yours."

Moon considered it for a moment. "What about King Magar? Shouldn't he captain one of these waves? His importance to your people will put our minds at ease that there will be no pointless bloodshed."

"He left with the first wave," said Skane, stepping up to Moon. "Trust me, if we wanted you dead, we'd have killed you days ago."

Skane regretted the words almost as soon as he said them. He knew they were stupid and only served to sow fear. Luckily, Moon seemed to ignore the comment or at least contemplate its logic.

"I will bring this compromise to the Queen."

Without saying goodbye, Moon turned and walked towards the bank. Skane waved to the back of Moon's head before turning around and kicking a bedroll at his feet. It went further than Skane expected, flying over the closest boat and landing in the sea on the other side.

"Hey," yelled a Northman further up the beach. The sides of his head were shaved, and spiralling blue tattoos bloomed from his ears. "What you do that for? That was my bed."

Skane immediately felt the pangs of guilt. "I'm sorry."

"Great, cheers, mate. Ruined my day." The man turned to his work, but after a few more moments, he threw the mooring rope, which he had just loosened and moved up the beach to sit in the sand. Another Northman came over to comfort him.

"Hey man, chin up; he didn't mean anything by it," said the second.

"I know," said the one with the head tattoos, looking up as if to stop tears. "Just been a long couple of weeks."

Skane turned away, guilt sinking into his stomach. Suddenly, his heart started racing as all the sounds of his surroundings invaded the last bastion of solace in his angry, turbulent mind. The hammering of the mast bolts as the third wave of ships getting ready to depart mingled with the emerging anchors sending ripples across the water and the creaking of the gangplanks. Shields were slotting into place along the rim of every ship with a feint ticking. At the same time, men and women yelled instructions to their peers along the extensive network of vessels.

A thought hit Skane every so often. It was one of those thoughts that could fade into the back of his mind, not entirely forgotten, but almost. Or it was a typhoon, able to rip the armada in front of him to smithereens until nothing remained but splinters and shreds of sailcloth. It was an obvious thought, but that didn't abate the damage it could cause.

They were sailing towards war, bloodshed, chaos, and death. He would kill people and exist as another link in an endless chain.

Skane was leaning against the prow of the closest ship. The wood was lacquered with a dark sheen, and a deer skull was used as the masthead. Many of the ships built in Edokand were more ornate, with carved dragon heads looking out to sea. However, the first ships were more spartan. Most had no mastheads, used chiefly for transporting cargo between the various Solstic settlements worldwide. Those were the ships the Tornes brought, but only the warriors from Solstr still had use for the fearsome warships.

Skane looked into the hollow eyes of the skull, wondering if this was one of the boats Trygve had brought with him from his homeland.

His forehead slammed against the prow, rolling it over the groves in the overlapping planks. He breathed so deeply the sand could be kicked up by force, and he gripped the ship's edge so tightly it might crack like the earth at the foot of the mountains. He would have stayed like that for hours, massaging a headache with a ship's figurehead. But before too long, he felt a light hand clasp down on his shoulder.

He turned suddenly, heart jumping, until he saw the purple-robed old woman standing behind him. Rigpa brandished her signature kind smile, tucking her hands into her long sleeves. Skane pushed himself from the boat, standing in silence as he looked back at his friend with a blank expression so taut it was like a child trying to conceal something in their fist.

Eventually, Skane sighed, sitting in the sand and sidling the ship behind him. Rigpa followed him, folding her legs under her and sitting opposite him.

After staring at the brightening sky, Skane decided to speak first. "Our culture worshipped war back when we still believed in gods." Skane didn't know why he chose to discuss the dead religions or why it was the first thing that came to mind. "Victory meant just as much to us as death in battle. Anything to increase our battle fame and impress the gods. Religion may be gone, but it still feels like we're chasing their approval."

Skane wasn't looking at Rigpa, but he could hear the smile in her voice. "You do not seem like someone of a warrior religion."

Skane chuckled. "Thanks, I guess."

Rigpa shuffled in the sand to sit closer to Skane. "In our old faith," she said, "we would bury our dead with a clay bird figurine so that, if their soul was light enough, they would use the bird to fly to heaven. To this day, the Emperors of Edokand are still buried with these birds."

Skane squinted, sitting up to look at the Grand Sage. "Why?"

Rigpa shrugged. "For the same reason, the sages occupy the temples of the old faiths. Religion is gone, but the quirks and unique aspects of our culture are not so easily scrubbed away."

Skane rolled his eyes, using the ship's side to lift himself off the ground. "Even if it breeds war-hungry animals?"

"That's not how I see your people, and you shouldn't either." Rigpa tried to follow him but struggled to lift herself off the ground. Skane gave her his hand to help her to her feet.

"You were there at Koseki," said Skane, looking down at the blowing sand. "You saw Magar. He was ready to wipe out those refugees for the sake of a few soldiers."

"Is that why you didn't talk to him before he left?"

Skane looked at Rigpa from the side of his eye before returning to his boots, folding his arms across his chest. In the distance, he heard a horn blow on one of the furthest ships in the bay. "Second wave, depart!" yelled a Solstic woman as oars were plunged into the waves.

"There are many reasons why I haven't spoken with him." Skane finally whispered loud enough to be heard over the distant rowing.

Rigpa and Skane watched as two dozen warships turned west, keeping the land to their left as they journeyed to Trim. After watching the mesmerising pattern of nearly fifteen hundred men and women rowing in unison, Rigpa restarted their conversation.

"I think it's time we discuss the fourth chakra," she said.

Skane looked around at the many ships sitting in the sea, being loaded by those still busy at work. "Right now?"

"I will be brief," said the Grand Sage, turning her body to face Skane.

265

Skane blinked a few times, shrugged, sighed, and faced the nun. "Okay, where is it then?"

"In your heart," she said, pointing at his chest. "This chakra deals with love and is blocked by stress and conflict."

Skane followed Rigpa's finger, looking down as if he would see his own heart before looking back and trying to hide how foolish he felt.

"Love is the emotion that comes most naturally to humans," Rigpa continued. "Most of the dead religions had love gods. It can take many forms. Familial love, the love of a friend, a patriotic love, or a love of a good book. But most commonly, the chakra faces its biggest challenge in romantic love."

Skane shook his head, his foot fanning in the sand. "Look, I know what you're doing. Magar and I will be fine. We've been together for a long time. I know him better than anyone; he's the love of my life. We'll get through this, just in our own time."

She gave Skane a look as if he were a naive child. "The longer you wait, the harder it will be to have the necessary conversations."

Skane averted his eyes, taking a moment before raising his shoulders. "Time heals all wounds, right?"

"In Edokand, we say that differently." Rigpa walked around to face Skane again. "Time is medicine."

"I don't see the difference," said Skane with a taut brow.

"You can salve a wound to make the pain disappear, but a scar will still be left behind." She moved close again, arms tucked in her sleeve. "Time is just the salve. You can't rely on time, Akkael, or me, to fix the problems in your life. You must do that yourself."

Skane wanted Akkael's return to help Magar, but it didn't. Magar was still angry and sad, and there was nothing anyone could do for him. Skane didn't know if anything could bring back the man he loved.

"What if I can't?"

Rigpa was now an arm's length away, and she used the closeness to reach up and rest her hand on Skane's cheek. "The first time I met you back at your camp, you greeted Magar with a kiss. I was reminded of the stories told at Wu Wei's court about the giant couple that incited terror across the country. When Skane Brick-Chest and Magar Torne fight in the same shield wall, the earth quaked under their feet as they charge."

Skane couldn't help the grin forming in the corner of his mouth. "Skane Brick-Chest?" he said, having never heard his nickname.

Rigpa ignored Skane and continued. "Since that moment, I have only known bitterness and animosity between you." She removed the hand from Skane's cheek and looked him dead in the eye. "You are a famous couple, and your love has been seen on every battlefield in Edokand. But, to my misfortune, I have not seen it."

The Grand Sage turned away from the big Northman. She took a few steps before turning her head and talking beyond her shoulder. "I hope I get the chance to one day."

She made her way down the length of the beach, leaving Skane to his thoughts. He looked back at the sea to the west. The second wave had disappeared behind the hills, chasing those further along the voyage. They were rowing towards Magar. Skane breathed the cold, sea salt air and considered the work that needed to be completed.

The Sekandan tents were all lowered and brought to the beach. The third wave was ready, and luggage littered the border between the damp sand and the approaching tide. Skane got to work loading the remaining ships. The sooner the jobs were done, the sooner he'd be following Magar's ship's turbulent wake.

[CHAPTER 42] — HORSE THIEF

When Akkael took over Trygve's body, he was standing beside the horse pen. He was also suddenly very drunk. Trygve had hidden it well while talking, but he was seeing double and barely able to walk straight.

Luckily, just like the cage, the horse pen hadn't been watched due to the chaos at Koseki. The horses were tied individually to trees nearby, with another rope to keep them penned in. Akkael untied the rope around the perimeter and stumbled onto the closest horse, like an old dog clambers onto its owner's chair. He leant over, nearly falling off, to cut the horse's tether and spur it away from the camp.

That was a week ago, and, despite being a wobbly, drunk fugitive, riding slowly away from a camp of thirteen thousand soldiers, Akkael went undetected. He decided to give them the benefit of the doubt and blame the confusion brought on by that night instead of allowing himself to believe the Solstic and the Sekandans were that unreceptive to sneak attacks and scouts.

Since then, he'd made his way slowly south, keeping the sun on his flanks as he rode alone. He tried to keep away from any signs of civilisation. However, as he hit Sekando's more fertile land, it became increasingly difficult to avoid farm villages. The rough terrain and poor weather forced him to stay on the road for fear of losing his way. He got some looks from those he had no choice but to pass. A Northman on a well-kept horse was an odd sight and clearly not permissible.

Forests and hilly land were a gamble. The roads often winded, so he couldn't always see ahead. Though there was no room for farmland, the odds of crossing a town of some kind were never zero.

Akkael suddenly thought of the horse he'd left at the shanty town outside Sekando city. He hoped to return to that horse but doubted he'd ever return to the loyalist child's livery. Over the week of travelling, he'd grown fond of his new horse and decided to call him Knarr. It was the namesake of Akkael's last horse, which was the namesake of his father's ship. Solstic traditions didn't allow for much diversity with names.

Eventually, Akkael hit a small homestead in a dense brush. A red and blue torii gate sat at the entrance, with a sign hanging from it reading '*Halju.*' A fence encapsulated the town, with huts made from straw and stone. It was a simple-looking place, with a long, cobblestone path leading to an identical gate on the other side of the homestead.

Akkael saw a man working at the entrance. As he got closer, he noticed a few imperfections on its posts. Carvings of people's initials encased in hearts, and other, more lewd designs littered the torii gate. Some of the drawings and writings were done with paint or charcoal. That was when Akkael noticed two buckets next to the man. One was steaming with soapy water; the other was full of red paint.

The worker, a short, balding man with a bushy moustache, turned to face Akkael.

"Hey," he yelled, swiftly getting up from where he was scrubbing. He delayed a moment before pointing a sponge at Akkael. "You speak Edokand'i, Northman?"

"Yes," said Akkael, holding up his hands while gripping the reins. He had found some rope to steer his horse but was still riding without a saddle, wreaking havoc on his thighs. "I mean no harm; I just need to pass through."

Akkael could see the feint charcoal where the balding man had been scrubbing. It was a three-line poem with a pattern Akkael recognised as a haiku. It read: *Women, I leave you./My privates are now for men./ Weep for what you've lost.*

Akkael scoffed, remembering Queen Kya's insistence that Sekandan poetry was a *superior* art.

"What's your business?" said the cleaner.

Akkael shook his head. "No business, just need to go south."

The man stroked his moustache, raising one eyebrow, which had patches missing. "I heard Queen Kya was in business with the Northmen, though. Are they behind you?"

"No," said Akkael. "They've gone north." Akkael tried to keep what he was saying as vague as possible. He didn't know much about what Kya and Skane were planning since he had spent his time with the army as a prisoner.

"Hmm," groaned the man. "Well, good. Didn't want Their Majesty to see what some rapscallions had done to our gate. I'm Chin. You?"

Akkael thought for a moment. Even though he was in a Solstic body, he still couldn't give his own name because he had been too famous in life and was famously dead. He couldn't use Trygve's name either. As well as also being famous, Akkael didn't want to give his friend's name in case news that Trygve killed Ichika had made its way here. He gave the first Solstic-sounding name that came to mind. "Knarr."

"Nice to meet you, Knarr," said Chin, bowing. "And your horse?"

Shit! Akkael realised just how bad he was at naming things. He spent so long thinking that he didn't have a name prepared when Chin spoke again.

"It's a mighty fine horse anyhow," he said, stroking his moustache again. "But it hasn't got a saddle or reigns. Did you steal that horse, Northman?"

Akkael gulped, subtly reaching for the dagger in his belt. However, before tensions could rise any further, Chin threw up his hands.

"Hey, none of my business what you steal or don't steal, anything to challenge the established laws, am I right?" Chin winked, with a grin concealed by the hair on his lip, suds pouring from his fist as he clenched the sponge. Akkael was very confused. Chin continued.

"Did you know if you steal a horse, the government cuts your hands off?" He rolled his eyes as the word *government* left his mouth. "But, if you kill a horse, all you have to do is pay the owner its value. Doesn't make sense, does it?"

Chin was determined to wait for Akkael to reply. "No. No, it doesn't."

He turned, throwing his sponge, which Akkael had forgotten he was holding, into the water bucket, so hard it nearly tipped over. "Come with me. I'll guide you to the other side of town."

Despite being able to see the exit of Halju from where he was, Akkael decided not to object, riding closely behind Chin as he spoke.

"Laws make no sense," he said, shaking his head. "Rules are inconsistent and, because they make no sense, they incite criminals to challenge them."

"Absolutely," said Akkael, hoping that agreeing with the man would make the conversation quicker.

"You know whose fault it is?" Chin didn't leave enough time for Akkael to answer before continuing. "It's the Queen. The Emperor's no better, either. You know what kind of society I want?"

It was challenging to know which questions Akkael was meant to answer and which he wasn't, but the delay was long enough that Akkael decided to give it a go.

"Democracy?" he suggested.

"Democracy!" Chin scoffed. "Democracy just invites nonsense laws. One guy raises the tax on bread, and the next lowers the tax on the cake. Makes no sense."

Akkael wondered why, every time he spoke to a random civilian, they happened to be strangely political. It was either bad luck or how everyone was in Sekando.

"No, what I want… is *anarchy*." Chin turned to Akkael, raising both eyebrows twice as he slowly nodded. "Pure, unspoiled anarchy. No laws, no government, no military. Just people living their lives and doing what they want."

Akkael nodded back, hoping that was a good enough response.

Suddenly, Chin collapsed to the ground so fast he slightly startled Knarr. "See this?" he said, pointing at a thin crack in the cobblestone path. "This has been here since the mountains rose. The earthquakes caused cracks up and down this path. Now, if we lived in anarchy, I'd go home, make some mortar, and fill these cracks. Or I'd dig up the ruined rocks and replace them. That makes sense, right?"

Akkael knew that Chin's delay meant he should answer. "Right."

"But not in this nonsense society." He rolled his eyes again, sharply blowing towards his moustache. "I'd have to go to the magistrate's office that way

271

and ask some toff for permission to fill this in. Then, I'd have to wait weeks for the bureaucracy to give me the slip telling me I'm allowed to do what I could have done straight away. They knock on my door and tell me to clean the torii gate; no problem, happy to do my bit. But if I want to take the initiative and take matters into my own hands, I have to twiddle my thumbs, waiting for some guy I don't respect to give me permission."

Chin stopped talking, looking up at Akkael from his hunched position on the ground. "It doesn't make sense," said Akkael, hoping to appease his strange guide.

"Doesn't. Make. Sense." Chin slapped the stone to emphasise each word. Eventually, he stood, beckoning Akkael to follow along. Akkael noticed Chin massaging his hand, red from where he'd hit the stone.

A short while later, Akkael had reached the other end of the town. The brush around them had thinned, and a clearing followed the exit. The mountains dominated the skyline, stretching as far east and west as Akkael could see. It was the first time Akkael had seen them this close without a veil of smoke and ash.

"There you go, Northman," said Chin, stepping aside to make way for the horse. He looked back toward the mountains stroking his moustache, then back at Akkael. "If you don't mind me asking, where are you going?"

"I told you," said Akkael. "South."

Chin scoffed. "There isn't much more south you can go. Unless you plan on climbing."

Akkael looked at Chin with silent intensity.

"Wait." Chin moved into the horse's way. "It's dangerous to go near the mountains. Haven't you heard? Dragons are living up there."

"One dragon," said Akkael, shrugging. "I've met him."

"Wha…" Chin was left speechless for the first time since they'd crossed paths.

"Goodbye, Chin," said Akkael before silently spurring his horse on, making his way towards the mountain range, and the revenge he deserved.

[CHAPTER 43] — THE HEART CHAKRA

Skane lay on his bed roll, staring up at the darkening hue in the fabric of his lonely tent. It was twilight outside, the sky purple through the canopy. A few weeks had passed since he left Skaldgard, and everywhere Skane had travelled, he'd slept alone.

They were on the coast of what used to be Trim, their island of ships bound to the beach and stretching deep into the ocean. Skane had only made the voyage to Trim once before, but the two journeys could not have been more different. Where there was a welcoming strait dividing the two islands, a mountain range now stood. Skane knew that, but it didn't make rowing past them any less harrowing.

Kya's rage had made the Queen forget their earlier hospitality, so the camp was again segregated into Solstic and Sekandan areas. Skane was close enough to the sea to hear the drumming of the ships smacking against each other and the tide's desperate attempts to reach the rocks on the shore.

He had tried to get a good night's sleep after rowing, mooring, and setting up camp. His lower back was pulsing with pain, and his biceps were numb. He was too tired to take his armour off, his full plate mail making the comfort of the bedroll redundant. However, no matter how much he tried, he couldn't sleep. After an hour of trying, he gave up.

He left the tent and looked around the camp. It had the circumference of some cities, with the smaller, dark-coloured tents of the Northmen butting up against the affluent quarter of blue marquees in the Sekandan area. The Solstic no longer mingled with the Queen's army, as they had cracked down on any affiliations that weren't mandatory to defeating Edokand.

The tent adjacent to Skane's belonged to Rigpa. She was still a prisoner and, though given permission to sleep near the Queen, decided to stay in the far more dangerous camp. Skane entered her tent without announcing himself.

Rigpa's tent was sparse. A bedroll was laid at the far end, and her rucksack was left by the entrance. The Grand Sage sat in the dome's centre, legs folded and positioned between two candles. Her eyes were closed as she breathed slowly in meditation. Skane imitated her position.

After a moment, Rigpa sighed. "What can I do for you, Skane?" she asked.

Skane was taken aback. "Are you busy?"

"Not necessarily." She opened her eyes and smiled at Skane.

Skane grinned back. "I was wondering if we could continue with the chakras."

Rigpa tilted her head like a confused dog. "What do you mean?"

"The fifth chakra," Skane said quickly. "What is it?"

The Grand Sage locked eyes with the Northman. "I'm sorry," she said, almost disappointed, "I thought you wanted to do this right."

"I do," Skane nodded.

"Then we can't move on to the fifth chakra until you've unblocked the fourth." She unfolded her legs, tucking them under her. "The heart chakra."

Skane tried to keep eye contact, but his gaze fell to the floor. "I don't know how."

"You will work it out," said Rigpa.

"Can't we just move to the fifth and double back?" Skane asked.

Rigpa laughed, shaking her head. Skane sighed.

"I think, if you want to open the heart chakra," said Rigpa, placing her hand on Skane's shoulder, "I am not the person you need to speak to."

Skane looked into her dark bark-coloured eyes, building the confidence he knew he needed. The last time he'd spoken to Magar, he had threatened to fight him. The last time they'd embraced, Magar was covered in blood. The last time they'd kissed was just before the mountains rose. Skane's heart sank as if the distance and lack of intimacy had suddenly caught up with him.

"I'm sorry for disturbing you, Rigpa," said Skane, standing up.

Rigpa shook her head. "You're never a disruption."

Skane nodded his head as a goodbye before leaving the tent. He stood still for a second, looking out at the sliver of the sea he could see above the ships as the bright hue as the drowning sun clung to the horizon. He sucked in a large breath, clutching his eyes shut before launching them open and heading towards Magar's tent.

Magar slept far away from Skane. He was nowhere near anyone he knew and had been especially quiet since Koseki, keeping to himself on the road and in the ship. Or so Skane had heard.

After a few moments of wandering between the sweet smell of mead and the loud laughs of those playing games, Skane found Magar's tent. He was sat outside, sharpening his giant blade with a whetstone. Furs covered his shoulders as the sword rested on grey breaches. Skane stood out of sight, taking slow, meticulous breaths, building up the confidence to approach.

However, before he could, a Solstic man stood above Magar. The warrior was bald, his bare chest littered with scars and had a yellow beard kept in tight braids.

"Magar," said the bald man. Magar grunted in acknowledgement, and the stranger continued. "Wanna fight?"

Magar raised his head, and the warrior smiled.

"Thought you would," said the stranger, vigorously scratching his beard. "You slow?"

Skane couldn't see Magar's eyes, but he imagined they were squinting with the same confusion.

"I cricked my neck a few hours ago and don't wanna move my head too much. It's good if you're slow." The bearded man rubbed where his neck hurt. "Also, I think I'm coming down with shin splints, so I don't want to move around too much, either. And nothing to the legs. Oh, and I had a big dinner, so nothing to the gut, either. I don't wanna shit myself."

Magar just sat silently, placing his bastard sword back into its sheath.

"Also, I pulled something here when rowing." He rubbed the side of his torso, hand bumping over the scars. "Nothing here but the left side's fine. Wait, no, the right side. The right side's fine. That all good for you?"

After a few seconds, Magar stood up. He looked the man up and down. He was much shorter than Magar, his bald head reaching below his neck. Then, Magar grunted, gripped his sword by the sheath, and entered the tent. The stranger stood for a moment before he shrugged and walked away. When he was out of sight, Skane followed Magar into the tent.

It was just as sparse as Rigpa's, with the only addition being a clay bowl full of salt water and dirty rags resting on a small crate. Magar locked eyes with Skane as soon as he entered. They stood in silence for a long time as if they were strangers, despite almost a decade of marriage.

Skane spoke first, words like water droplets being coaxed from an empty flask. "Hey."

"Hey," Magar whispered back.

To Skane's right, he noticed a large tree trunk bound with rope and tied in such a way as to make handles. It was almost longer than the tent. "What's that?" Skane asked.

Magar considered it for a moment, then shrugged. "Battering ram."

"Right," said Skane, raising an eyebrow. He looked back to Magar, tracking the crusty brown scabs littering his face. "Your wounds are healing nicely," he said, trying to make conversation. "Doesn't look like anything will scar."

"Hmm," Magar grunted, placing his sword on the ground.

"And I bet you got a few good wins," Skane continued awkwardly. "Must have been fun."

"Do you want something?" Magar said, rapidly twisting his head away from his blade.

Suddenly, Skane felt stupid for coming. His heart sank, and he hoped it was just the embarrassment. "No. I'll go." He turned around and lifted the flaps of the tent.

"Wait." There was an urgency in Magar's voice, but once Skane dropped the fabric and faced him, the energy in his voice left as his expression sank. He walked over to the battering ram and sat on it, staying silent momentarily, leaving Skane to wonder if he should stay or go.

"Do you hate me?" Magar asked.

"What?" snapped Skane, maybe a little loudly. "Of course not. Why would you think that?"

Magar shrugged, looking down at the grass. "We haven't talked."

Skane moved before his husband and threw his hands into the air. "We've been in different places."

Blue irises peered under Magar's thick, blond eyebrows. "I saw the way you looked at me in Koseki."

Skane couldn't deny it. He remembered the disgust he felt towards Magar's actions and felt guilty. "I'm sorry. I was scared. A lot was going on."

Magar looked back at his feet. "It's because you're better than me."

"I didn't say that," he said, violently shaking his head.

"I know," mumbled Magar. "I did. You were always smarter than me and kinder. I'm just a warrior. Stupid and bloody."

Skane responded quickly, like instinct. "That's not how I see you." He felt better about himself when he realised, to his relief, he still believed what he said.

"Yes, it is," Magar barked.

"No, it's not." Skane knelt, trying to catch Magar's eye line. "I see a strong, complex man. You're unstoppable, stubborn, and immovable. When you choose a path, you stick to it no matter how hard the terrain gets. You never back down, and you never give in. I see your loyalty and stoicism and the man I love."

Magar was quiet for a moment before looking up. "What's stoicism mean?"

Skane couldn't help smirking. "It's sort of bravery. It means you can endure anything."

Magar shook his head and looked back at his feet. "I can't. Seeing your face. Seeing what's happened to Akkael. It made me realise how much I fucked everything up because I don't have *stoicism*."

277

"You haven't fucked anything up." Skane touched Magar's leg, but Magar quickly removed it.

"You left me." Magar's voice broke slightly, and his eyes became shiny.

Skane thought of Magar every day, but this was the first time he considered how everything was affecting him. He lost two brothers and his niece in a matter of minutes, as well as friends and shield brothers swallowed by the earth. He had needed Skane, but all Skane did was get as far away as possible.

"I am so sorry," Skane said, something caught in his throat.

"I'm not angry," he said, shaking his head. "I was an arse."

"You weren't an arse." Magar looked sharply at him, and Skane wiggled his head. "Well, you were."

Magar gave a breathy laugh, and Skane smiled, placing his hand back on Magar's leg. This time it wasn't removed.

"But you were just lost. I was lost too. But I'm slowly getting better, and I want to be able to help you as well."

Magar took a deep breath. "You've never left me alone before."

Skane's eyes stung a little. "I won't ever again."

Silence lingered in the tent as the night settled outside. No candles had been lit in the tent, but there were lanterns outside, creating enough light to help Skane's eyes adjust to the rest of the dark. Magar placed his large hand on Skane's steel pauldron. He looked at the metal he was touching without blinking. "I know why you wear armour."

Skane squinted. "Pardon?"

"I never understood it before," Magar continued, "but I do now. It's so, when you are at war, there is less chance you die and leave me alone. I fight. I risk my life in war, and I love it. But I never think about the consequences, about leaving you alone."

"It's okay," Skane said through a thin smile. "You're better at fighting."

Magar moved his hand to Skane's cheek, stroking him with his thumb. "This is our last war. No more. You've been doing this long enough."

Skane's eyes widened. "Really?"

"Really," Magar nodded, smiling. "This is our last settlement. I would rather not have war than not have you. I've lost both before, and losing you is worse."

Skane felt his heartbeat in his throat. He remembered confessing his greatest fear to Rigpa at Skaldgard. Having to fight war after war scared him more than death. What Magar said overwhelmed him. He rose, kissing him.

He didn't want to pull away. They hadn't kissed or held each other in so long; it was like a man in the desert ferociously lapping at an oasis until he couldn't breathe. Magar wrapped his arms around Skane, and they both rose to their feet, eyes closed. Then, Magar pulled away to lift the furs over his head before his lips met Skane's again. He began fumbling with the straps of Skane's armour, visibly irritated by how long it took to loosen.

"Fucking armour," he exclaimed.

Skane laughed, leaning into Magar's neck before pushing away from him and removing his plate-mail.

They moved over to the bedroll, still standing as Magar pushed Skane against the canvas wall so hard one of the pegs on the other side was plucked, and the tent nearly toppled over. They lowered to the ground, lying on top of the bed covers.

The night marched on and on as they forgot what time it was, where they were, or everything but themselves. They were entwined for hours, the bed smelling sweet from sweat. They stayed above the covers. It had been a month of cold beds and lonely nights, and even though they wouldn't sleep much, neither would spend the night alone.

[CHAPTER 44] — THE MOUNTAINS

The mountains stood proud before Akkael as he scanned the grass and forestry cascading towards him like magma. Trees as tall as he'd ever seen sprouted from the range, and tall brushes and diverse plant life made it seem as if they had always been there, not just for mere weeks but millennia. The peaks were diverse, some as sharp as fangs, some were flatter, with rivets and crenulation like seashells. Paths beaten by nothing swerved around the infant mountains, with the grass flanking the mud as if it knew from instinct not to infringe past the unnatural limits.

His eyes, a brighter blue than the ones he was born with, fixed, unblinking and wide, on the south as he twisted Knarr's reins in his lap. He had seen a lot of dreadful, inexplicable things since he was here last, but it was then Akkael knew; nothing in the world would bring him more discomfort than the mountains that rose from the sea.

He stood at the foot of the mountains for almost half an hour staring at the landmark that had swallowed his daughter, the incline that shattered his ships, his camp, and his whole life. It was strange, feeling hatred for a landmass. It was like shouting at the old, forgotten gods or something else that didn't exist. He tried to picture Hideo as if his face were carved into the mountains. Finally, after pressing the leather of the reins and Trygve's obscenely long fingernails into his aching hand, he gained the energy to spur the horse towards the virgin yet beaten road.

The incline was gradual, but it felt like Akkael's heart would fall out of his body. Knarr felt uncomfortable too. It was subtle, but the slight jitters, false steps, and nickers from the horse were enough to give away his unease.

The tree cover was almost like climbing up a tunnel. The sun was just pinpricks in the canvas above him, with circles of light passing over Akkael as he ducked under the lower branches. After barely half a kilometre, Akkael stopped at a tree that caught his eye. The roots emerged from the dirt in the vague shape of a dragon's skull. One knot was perfectly placed to be the eye, and a thick root stretched like a snout.

Akkael was still, looking down with a furrowed brow. He didn't know why, but it reminded him of Solstr. He never thought of home very much, as he spent most of his youth in the various settlements his father and uncle had established. However, he suddenly remembered playing in the woods where he used to live. They were a vast, thick maze, but he and his brothers always knew how to find each other there.

In that forest, there was a tree with roots that breached the earth. They were long and stretched down a short ridge like the bars of a cage. No matter how late in the day, Doran, Magar, and Akkael always knew the way to the prison tree.

For some reason, that thought made Akkael sad. These mountains plucked aeons from their own time, were stolen from the children who were the first to play in them. The people who would climb just for satisfaction and personal achievement. These mountains, objectively beautiful, would have probably been a place for joy, where people cheer at the highest point, and kids race to the tree with the dragon's head. But Hideo stole that and they will forever be marred by fear and dread; the mountains that burst from the ocean in flames.

Suddenly, the world around Akkael became less clear as his eyes unfocused. The real world gave way to the world he painted in his mind:

He heard the sea behind him, the creaking boats in the dock. The cliffs that flanked the city were covered by wooden flats and scaffolding, which housed most of the population. He was in Skaldgard, the first place in Edokand that the Solstic had captured.

"Come on, Da." Alani was in front, dragging Akkael by the left hand up the wooden flats at the side of Skaldgard's cliffs. "Muma said we would meet her by the crying giant."

Akkael snickered, trying not to trip on the steps as Alani stomped up three at a time despite her little legs.

"Crying giant?" he smiled. "What are you talking about?"

Alani wasn't facing him, but Akkael could still feel her eyes roll. "Don't you know anything?" she scoffed. "It's a waterfall. The water pours out of a cave and looks like a big eye. Muma said it was a giant, but of course, I know it's not."

Akkael was ejected from his memory as quick as he was dragged into it. He wiped a tear from his cheek, still looking at the knotted eye of the tree root dragon. The horse was subtly shaking its neck against the reins. Akkael took a moment to collect himself before spurring Knarr and pressing on.

The path was straight to start with but got more twisted the higher he reached, causing him to pull Knarr left and right, sometimes in rapid intervals. This added to the horse's frustration, nickering more intensely with every change in direction.

Eventually, they emerged from the tree cover, reaching a rockier terrain as the mountain began to plateau. There was still a while to go before reaching the summit, but the flatland gave Knarr a little reprieve from the steep climb. Akkael decided to dismount, giving the horse some rest as they strolled.

Akkael, one hand clasping a lead, the other stroking the stead's mane, began to see the beast gradually calm.

"Don't like tree cover, do you, boy?" said Akkael.

The horse whinnied as if to confirm.

Akkael reached into the bag tied to the side of the horse, stolen from a nearby farm. Salted pork and carrots were left inside, along with a makeshift rabbit trap and what remained of last night's dinner. Akkael took a piece of pork for himself and a carrot for Knarr, who swallowed the whole thing before he even saw it. Akkael smiled, trying to decide if he preferred horses to boats.

But before he could decide, the wind went from a gentle breeze to a frenzied storm. The trees behind him began to bow as the stones and rocks on the plateau began to roll. Suddenly a shadow fell over the field. Akkael looked up just in time to watch a large, black wing glide over him.

The scales of the dragon's body looked like burning coals as they caught the sun's light. When Seravex's tail passed over Akkael's head, it beat its wings again, causing the grass and dirt to uproot. Pebbles were carried by a shockwave as the force brought Akkael to his knees.

Knarr was on his hind legs, writhing against the lead as he snorted and brayed. Akkael fell to his side, trying to keep hold of the reins as Knarr's hooves landed on either side of his head. The horse dragged him a short distance across the plateau until a rock rolled under his ribs, and he let go out of pain. The horse bolted back towards the forest when Akkael lost his grip on the lead.

"Knarr!" Akkael yelled. "Hey!" He tried making noises with his mouth, but they came out as poor imitations of whistling since he didn't know how. He watched, lying on the ground, as Knarr galloped out of sight.

Once his horse was gone. Akkael sat up, watching Seravex fly off to the west as it surveyed the mountains. After a stunned silence, Akkael threw his arms into the air.

"Least you can do is give me a ride to Wu Wei," Akkael shouted, knowing the dragon wouldn't hear. "You prick!"

Akkael wasn't aware Seravex was still investigating the mountains. It told Akkael it had an unnatural need to learn after being given some of Alawa's power. But how much could it learn from flying over the same range?

"If you really wanted to learn something new, try talking to your brother with the tentacles." Akkael shook his head, realising how absurd that sentence would have sounded not too long ago.

After a moment, he stood up, dusting himself off and massaging where the rock drove into his ribcage. He looked up at the closest peak, contemplating his situation. He had no food, water, or ride, was alone and was hundreds of miles from Wu Wei. If Astrid were with him, she'd laugh so hard she'd struggle to breathe. Akkael smiled, thinking about the pleasure his wife would have at his misfortune, and continued up the mountain.

Trygve was older than Akkael, so the aches he felt in his hips, back, and sides were made worse by Jarl's ageing body. As Akkael limped, one thought entered his head. He definitely preferred boats to horses. Ships could crash, sink, and splinter, but they wouldn't run away at the first sign of danger. Sailing across the strait that was once under his feet was much easier than dragging a frightened beast up something it didn't want to climb.

It took almost an hour to reach the top. If the mountains were left in their own time, the view would be an unsullied beauty that the entire world would envy. Valleys and paths looked like the veins and sinew of some giant that people would've worshipped back when there were religions. As Akkael's eyes scanned the south, he remembered his first time coming to Trim.

He'd almost forgotten, but the Emperor's invite to Edokand's central island was a massive step in the four-year war. No Northman had ever set foot in Trim, let alone seen Wu Wei, the City of Disciplines, the prize of the East. A few weeks ago, he would have relished the chance to return. His intrigue, Doran's desire for a settlement, and Magar's lust for war were the tent poles that propped up the whole Edokand campaign for almost a decade.

But that was gone. Doran was probably dead, and Akkael only had one desire left. Revenge. He had felt the phantom pain of his daughter's grip since Seradok gave him his curse. But, looking toward the object of his ire, the pain had never been so intense.

"It's nearly over," Akkael said to no one.

He took his first step on the descent, eyes fixed towards Wu Wei. "Don't worry, Alani, it'll be over soon."

[CHAPTER 45] — HEIYANG

Astrid was getting tired of meetings. Since stewarding over Skaldgard, she had sat through half a dozen diplomatic and strategic councils. Each one was as boring as the last.

They sat around a bonfire, Magar, Skane, and Astrid on one side, Queen Kya, Moon, and Kwan on the other. Surrounding them were armoured women and Solstic brutes in case things turned.

The posturing stunt was designed by the Queen and exacerbated by Skane's caution. The relations between the two armies had been driven to the edge, and paranoia ruled everyone's hearts. Astrid was the only Solstic person who allowed any direct contact with Kya, but even that was sparser than before.

Astrid's bitterness towards her husband and disdain for Trygve made her scowl whenever it came to mind. Akkael almost destroyed the relations between the two nations after what he did to Ichika. Then, with the considerable army heading for Wu Wei, he and Trygve worked directly against the best interest of their fragile alliance. Akkael was going around puppeteering Trygve's corpse, and Astrid knew if she saw him, she'd be hard-pressed to restrain herself from killing him again. Consequences be damned.

Kya was drinking wine, determined to finish their glass before allowing anything to commence. It was a strange but compelling power move. The fire crackled in the centre of the group, counting the seconds and minutes where everyone sat in bated silence. Once the last drop of wine poured from the glass into Kya's mouth, they wiped their lips and stood, passing it to one of their soldiers, who had no idea what to do with it.

The fire in front of them shone in Kya's eyes, and the light and shadows danced across their stony face. After a few moments of standing like this, they spoke.

"Wu Wei is a two-day march from this camp," they said, looking between each of the Solstic faces in front of them with the same scolding expression before fixing on Astrid. "However, before we make it to the city, we must take the fortress of Chuton at the heart of the valley."

Magar removed Skane's hand from his lap and stood. Even though the fire separated him from the Queen, the height difference still granted him a looming presence. "Why?" he said, shrugging his shoulders.

General Kwan stepped forward. "The terrain means the only path through the valley leads directly to the fortress. We could go along the hills, but that might add days to our journey and make it impossible to go undetected. Even if we made it to Wu Wei without getting ambushed, having two thousand well-trained soldiers behind us as we try to capture the greatest city in Edokand would mean a lot more casualties."

Magar thought for a moment and nodded. He sat back down.

Astrid stood up next. "So, what's the plan?" she asked.

Kwan continued to speak. "Chuton is well fortified, but the hills make it susceptible to arrow fire. The valley is lined with watchtowers; they know our armies are working together. The main force will walk straight towards Chuton while four-hundred archers sneak along the hills, two hundred on each side. As we launch a well-advertised attack from the front, we'll rain arrows on them from above."

Astrid shrugged. "Seems a little simplistic."

Kwan scoffed, trying hard to hide her offence. "Simple tactics often work, Princess."

By now, everyone knew how Astrid hated being called by her titles, and she knew Kwan said it to get a rise out of her. She sat quietly, trying not to bite at the insult.

Moon stepped forward, noticing the deliberate quiet between Astrid and the General. "King Magar," she said, looking at the two men in each other's arms. It was nice to see their relationship mended, though it made Astrid's chest ache.

Magar grunted, and Moon continued. "I understand you have been working on a ram for the gates of Wu Wei." The subtleties of Magar's communication were harder to distinguish in the firelight. After what might have been a nod, Moon continued. "There are three gates on either side of the fortress leading to the centre. We may need the ram to get through."

Magar nodded more clearly. "We'll bring a boat too." Astrid could see the Sekandans squint in confusion.

Skane clarified what Magar meant. "We'll use the hull for cover as we break through the gates."

Everyone's eyes widened in realisation. "Great idea," said Moon.

Magar nodded, leaning back into Skane. Astrid and Akkael never admitted it to each other, but their relationship wasn't perfect. Alani made it essential, and there was love between them. But even before everything that had happened, they weren't the kind of couple that felt comfort from each other's presence. They wouldn't lean into each other or hold each other close despite the eyes of everyone around them. Astrid blamed herself for that. She knew she wasn't a warm person. Akkael always said it was why he loved her, but she could see sometimes that he needed more.

Looking at Skane and Magar was the first time Astrid wished she had something like that. It might have meant little, but Akkael's touch would have soothed her for a time.

"Right," said Queen Kya, still standing in the glow of the flames. "We will attack tomorrow. No sense in delaying. The sooner we get to Wu Wei, the sooner we can go home."

General Kwan nodded. "I agree, it'll be a tough fight, but it should be straightforward enough. We greatly outnumber them, and our soldiers are also well-trained. Chuton will fall."

Astrid stood up again, followed by everyone else around the fire. "Great, we'll arrange our forces at first light and move out as soon as convenient." She bent her head towards the Queen. "Goodnight, Your Majesty."

Astrid's eyes looked towards the kindling, then back at the Sekandans. However, as she raised her head, she noticed a gentle fog blocking her vision that hadn't been there before. The light dissolved inside the smoke, only managing to escape it in short strands. Astrid couldn't pinpoint why the smoke in front of her was separate from that emerging from the fire. Then, just as suddenly as the plume appeared, it dissipated in all directions as an Edokand'i man Astrid did not recognise emerged from the centre of the spiralling mist.

Astrid's heart jumped into her throat as adrenaline coursed through her body.

"Fuck!"

Before she knew what she was doing, Astrid's fist launched at the man who spawned in front of her. His eyes widen just before Astrid's fist connects with his jaw, and he collapses unconscious at the feet of Magar and Skane.

Metal sung as swords left the sheaves, and axes left their belts. A second man appeared from a similar mist. He had his hands raised above his head, eyes widened with fear. He wore the same crimson leather as his unconscious partner, signalling them as shadow archers.

The shadow archer that was still awake, began slicing his palms horizontally in front of himself before knocking his right palm twice against his forehead.

"Wait!" Moon began to scream. Skane held his arm out to the Solstic, who were ready to unthinkingly kill the shadow archer, and Kwan held up her fist to her more disciplined warriors.

The atmosphere began to calm as the shadow archer repeated the same gesture, slowing the pace of his hand movements.

"What the shit was that?" bellowed Astrid, struggling to bring her heart rate down.

"He's saying he's no threat," said Moon.

Astrid scowled through the flames. "Seemed pretty threatening, appearing out of nowhere like that."

The shadow archer tilted his head at Moon. He rapidly made a series of gestures, which Moon responded to by bobbing her fist in front of her.

"What's he saying now?" asked Queen Kya, eyebrows fleeing behind their fringe.

"He's asking if I can translate him," answered Moon. "I said yes."

Shadow archers had their tongues removed in the ritual that gave them their abilities, along with other parts. They developed sign language for the thirteen of them to communicate. Since there could only be that many shadow archers at a time, the masses didn't need to learn the language, so it was lucky that Moon understood it.

"The shadow archers are subjects of all the realms of Edokand, like the sages," said Moon. "Since they follow Sekando and Wu Wei, we needed someone to communicate with them, so I learned."

The shadow archer made more hand signals, which Moon responded to before translating.

"He says he is sorry his brother startled you, Astrid. They thought appearing in the open would be less threatening."

Astrid rolled her eyes. "Good plan, dickhead."

Suddenly, a third shadow archer appeared from behind the one signing and next to the unconscious one. He was taller, and his leather seemed cleaner. He had a scar on his top lip that stretched across his cheek like a leafless tree. He was the only one carrying the crossbow of his order, five bolts clipped to its underbelly. The other shadow archer turned and bowed his head to the taller man before receding behind him.

The scarred archer signed with a fluid elegance; each finger prepared for the next sign like perfect choreography. This time, Moon translated his meaning before offering a response. "He says his name is Heiyang, shadow lord of the Order of Shades. He has come to offer his services to the Queen of Sekando."

All eyes turned to Kya, their face like a stone as they considered what to say. "Where is the rest of your order?" they asked.

In amongst the barrage of hand signals, Astrid saw one used repeatedly. Heiyang dropped his index and middle fingers vertically. When he made the sign,

Heiyang's lip twisted, and the tree-shaped scar curved in the scowl like it was blowing in a storm. Despite not knowing the language, Astrid knew what that symbol meant.

"They died," translated Moon. "One was killed by Akkael, two died with Koji's army, and seven died at the hands of Lord Hideo."

Queen Kya's eyes widened briefly before they fought to retain their stoicism. "We guess Lord Hideo blamed your order for his son's death. We, too, were confused as to why a man of your order broke ranks to assassinate the heir to the Second Pillar of Edokand."

Heiyang scowled again.

"That's not what happened," said Moon, translating the shadow lord. The unconscious archer stirred, blinking and groaning as he woke. The second shadow archer ran over to him, pulling him behind Heiyang.

"We were there," continued the Queen. "We saw the dagger leave your man's hand and find its way into our nephew's neck."

Heiyang delayed before responding, signing more slowly than before.

"If that is true, he worked on his own accord," reiterated Moon. "The Order of Shades had nothing to do with it."

Astrid didn't understand why the Queen was keeping up this charade. Everyone around the fire knew the shadow archer who killed Koji was possessed by Akkael. Maybe she wanted to find out what Heiyang knew or withhold information, but it seemed like a waste of time to Astrid.

"The last time three shadow archers appeared out of nowhere, we nearly died." All eyes turned to Magar, his bulky frame dwarfing the tall yet lanky shadow lord. "Why should we trust you?"

Heiyang's eyes met Magar's, not fazed by the thinly veiled threat.

"If you want us to apologise, we won't," said Heiyang through Moon. "We followed our orders. We came here because we saw how the Northmen forgave the Sekandans for their role in what happened at the mountains. You knew they were not to blame; you know we are not to blame. Wu Wei is to blame."

Magar didn't flinch, his stillness showing Heiyang had not convinced him.

"If you want to refuse our fealty, then fine," Heiyang signalled to everyone around the fire. "But trust me when I say if you march on Chuton without us, all of you will die."

Astrid scoffed. "We outnumber them five to one. We will overrun Chuton and all its little watchtowers before the next sunset."

Heiyang turned to Astrid and signed. Moon delayed a moment, squinting before she translated.

"The watchtowers have been abandoned."

"Why?" asked the Queen.

Moon's confusion raised the pitch of her voice as she read Heiyang's hands. "The fortress has too little men guarding it."

"Two little men guarding a whole fortress?" Magar sounded genuinely confused.

"No." Moon shot him a look that could fell a tree. "Hideo has reduced the soldiers there by a quarter. The watchtowers have been unmanned to bolster their diminished forces."

"Even easier!" yelled Astrid throwing up her hands.

Heiyang remained still, smiling with his chin lowered to his chest. The silence raised everyone's heartbeat.

Kya spoke next, their voice lowered to almost a whisper. "They have fewer men and no scouts to alert them of our arrival. Why, then, do you say we will lose?"

Heiyang turned back to the Queen before he answered.

Moon translated as Heiyang signed. "They have new weapons. More deadly than our crossbows. They are so powerful no shield can defend against them. We've watched them work. Louder than a thunderclap, faster than wind, and more destructive than a battering ram. You may outnumber them five to one, but trust me, if you face these weapons without our help, they will annihilate you before you decimate them."

Once Heiyang finished signing, and Moon finished speaking, another silence fell wherever the firelight touched. Skane stood up next to Magar as Kwan whispered to Kya.

"How do we know you're telling the truth?" asked Skane, with no venom or hint of distrust in his voice, as if he was only speaking to give the shadow lord more chance to strengthen his argument.

Heiyang returned with a calmly delivered answer, though there was a hint of solemnness on his face.

"My order is destroyed because of Hideo," signed Heiyang. "He killed those sworn to protect him based on a vicious lie. I will have my revenge."

The other shadow archer behind Heiyang checked his brother for a concussion. Astrid thought about revenge. It had led Hideo to do what he did. He raised the mountains from the sea because he wanted revenge, killing her daughter. As a result, Akkael took revenge and used the shadow archer's body to kill Koji. That caused Hideo to take revenge on the shades, which has led them to take revenge on him, just as the Solstic and the Sekandans have also sworn.

It was a cycle, like falling leaves. As soon as the season is right, they all lower themselves to the dirt.

"Why don't you just kill him then?" Astrid's voice was hoarse, and she barely recognised it as her own. "You can teleport. Why don't you just go to Wu Wei and slice his throat?"

Heiyang looked almost offended by the suggestion. "We may be three, but we are an honourable order. The moment we kill a pillar of Edokand is the moment we are outlawed, especially after what happened to Koji's army. They can always make more of us, and my family will grow again. Hideo needs to die the right way."

Astrid exhaled loudly and raised her head towards the sky. She hated council meetings, and she looked forward to this being short. Everyone knew their role and plan before meeting around the fire. The summit was just a formality the night before the war. It would have been short.

But Heiyang's appearance made one thing increasingly more apparent, to Astrid's dismay: This gathering was far from over.

Kya met Heiyang's eyes. "Tell us more about these weapons."

[CHAPTER 46] — YONG THE BRAVE

After Akkael had received the mountains, he came across a small village. It was so close to the mountains that some huts had collapsed. Others were temporarily propped up with poles or left to ruin. Cracks in a cobbled wall, that encircled the hamlet, showed further dereliction caused by the rising range. Ash was still heaped outside the walls, collected into mounds like hay.

When Akkael saw the village, his stomach growled, and he felt how dry his lips were. He hadn't eaten or drunk since his horse got scared off by a dragon, which, as a man who spent most of his life on or around ships, was not something he ever imagined would happen to him.

He began rummaging on his person for anything he could sell. Trygve's daggers were relatively ornate, with good leather straps and strong steel that might fetch a decent price. His belt buckle was metal too, and his boots were probably newer than most shoes in the village. If he could trade them for worse boots and a bit of food, he'd be much more content.

He took one step towards the village before he stopped himself and sighed. "Fucking wars," he breathed, looking down at his Northman hands. He was in Trim now, not Sekando. His appearance would be seen a lot less favourably unless his head was on a spike. Almost as soon as that thought hit him, he spotted an Edokand'i sentinel standing atop the village wall. His armour was duller than the military's, but he looked well-fed.

Akkael sighed again. He thought if he allowed the goutuizi to kill him, he'd take over his less hungry body and have the influence to get another horse. But a pang of guilt stayed him. He knew he couldn't stay in Trygve's body forever but wanted to give his friend a decent death. When people talk about Trygve, he wanted his story to meet a stunning, well-fought end, not outside a random village.

Then his stomach growled and cramped as a cough tore through his dry throat.

"Sorry, Trygve."

Akkael approached the walls of the village. He got surprisingly close before the sentinel noticed him, and it took a little longer for him to recognise Akkael as a Northman. This worried Akkael a little, wondering what inhabiting a body with a defect like short-sightedness would be like.

Once the guard noticed the blond hair and blue eyes, he visibly tensed. "Stop! Northman!" He reached down and grabbed a horn, which released a deep bellow like a cow in a tunnel. He blew the horn twice fast and once slow, which Akkael assumed was the colloquial signal for a Solstic intruder.

After setting the horn down, he moved to the right and retrieved a bow resting on the ramparts. There was a barrel of arrows next to the goutuizi that Akkael only noticed from the red feathers peaking over the top. The sentinel notched an arrow and pointed the undrawn bow at Akkael.

"Begone, Northman! You have no business here," said the sentinel, broadening his shoulders to look more imposing.

Akkael was trying to think of ways to antagonise the sentinel so that he would kill him rather than arrest him.

"How do you know what my business is?" said Akkael.

The sentinel squinted, lowering his bow slightly. "You speak my language?"

"of course," said Akkael. "Which is already one more language than your dumb arse can speak."

The guard scoffed. "A true Edokand'i wouldn't debase themselves to learn your barbarian tongue."

"There's always an excuse for stupidity." Akkael knew he focused too hard on insulting his intelligence. Still, he was too tired and hungry to think of anything better that quickly.

"What's your name, Northman," asked the guard.

Akkael took a deep breath before bringing himself to say his friend's name. "Trygve. What's your name?"

"Yong," said the guard.

"Fuck you, Yong," said Akkael, stomach growling.

Yong pulled the string of the bow. "Enough of your insults. Turn around, Northman. No one must die today."

Akkael felt slightly guilty that the sentinel was being so tolerant and merciful. But he was also a little impatient. "Just kill me already," he breathed.

"What did you say?" asked Yong, tilting his head to the left.

"You couldn't kill me anyway," he yelled.

Yong just shook his head, sniggering to himself. "Trygve, right?" he waited for Akkael to nod before continuing. "Trygve, we may be a small village, but we outnumber you hundreds of times over. Once I call for these gates to open, the brave men ready to defend their home will charge through and kill you before my arrow can even loose from the bow."

"Wow," said Akkael. "You must be a really bad archer, then."

Yong straightened his weapon. "I can kill you at any moment, but I want the people to have the satisfaction of ridding one more of your kind from the world."

"Oh, I see. You let them do the work you get paid their taxes to do."

Yong paused momentarily, but Akkael could tell he had gotten under the goutuizi's skin. Akkael smiled.

The more he thought about it, the more fitting this death was for Trygve. Annoying someone to the point of getting himself killed. All those times that Trygve laughed like he did and dedicated his day to telling jokes at everyone's expense. It made Akkael happy that his friend died for his revenge, but even more pleased that he would be remembered in this small nameless town for dying doing what he loved.

"You know what," said Yong through his teeth, "You've convinced me."

Akkael let his smile reach each ear. "Ha!" he bellowed, making the best impression of his friend.

The sentinel drew the string back and released, sending the arrow hurtling towards Akkael, entering through his left eye.

The transition was almost instantaneous, barely feeling the pain of death before he was standing on the parapets in Yong's place. Akkael's first reaction to being in the sentinel's body was the change in vision. He couldn't comprehend how someone with such bad eyesight was such a good shot. He could barely make out Trygve's corpse lying in the ashy grass.

He was still tired but no longer hungry. On the contrary, he felt extremely bloated, as if the sentinel had eaten a feast just before their meeting. However, Akkael was most shocked once he turned around. A sea of blurry Edokand'i stood below the wall, looking up at him. He could make out the concentration on the faces of those in the front row but nothing as he looked at those standing further along the path.

Someone in the throng broke the silence as Akkael looked over them in shock. "So," they said, "is it done? Is the Northman dead?"

Akkael took a few more seconds to speak, trying to regain his composure and enter the character of the goutuizi soldier he had become.

"The intruder has been dealt with."

The villagers were silent, those in the front tilting their heads slightly.

"He's dead," Akkael clarified.

Everyone Akkael could see, and more he couldn't, began to cheer and clap. After a moment, the erratic celebration focused on a chant. "Yong the Brave! Yong the Brave! Yong the Brave!" The village repeated this in unison, filling the dirt-clad streets.

"He's dressed in armour, red! He's better than the rest! Yong the Brave! Yong the Brave!" yelled a few men in a monotone rhythm.

"He defends our little village! From those who want to pillage! Yong the Brave! Yong the Brave!" screamed another group.

This continued for a few minutes while Akkael stood with a wrinkled forehead, one eyebrow higher than the other. His power was strange, not just because of the actual process of it but because of the interactions he had with the people who knew those he had removed from their bodies.

The worst consequence of his gift was usurping the hard-earned reputations of those he possessed and utilising it for his own gain. Whether it was a child who

297

loved them or a village who worshipped them, they left a mark forged from a lifetime. It was unnatural to uproot that in the blink of an eye just to sit in the hole they left.

However, there was another part of him, the part that had a shattered heart and a hand aching for Alani's grip. That part knew it was necessary. Every time someone dies in war, a community is torn, and people are sad. It's normal, and no matter if it's by the sword or by Akkael, it is just what war breeds.

Akkael descended the steps of the wall, holding his hand up to stop everyone from chanting. "I appreciate your praise, but I'm afraid this is not over yet." The crowd ebbed to make way for him as he walked to the centre of the amassed crowd. "I am worried that this Northman has come with a raiding party."

Gasps erupted from the crowd. "How do you know?" asked one of the villages close to him.

"Don't question Sentinel Yong!" another villager yelled at the first. "Has he ever led us astray before? When that pack of wolves was praying on our farms, was it not Yong's insight that rid us of them?"

"And when the thieves were hiding in our forests, it was Yong who found them and chased them away."

Akkael raised his hand. "Thank you, my friends. But it was a valid question. I can't be sure. Which is why I need someone to ready me a horse. I shall scout the area myself and report what I find."

Without a second's hesitation, a man, a woman, and two kids left the circle and made their way deeper into the town. Akkael assumed they were stable workers, and after a few moments, they returned with a mare. She had a white coat with patches and a mane of black hair.

"There are provisions in the saddle bag for you," said the man holding the horse's reins.

Akkael put his right foot in the stirrups and launched onto its back. A few of the more excitable villagers gently clapped.

"Yong!" screeched someone that Akkael couldn't see. "What if the Northmen kill you? How will we cope without your protection?"

A silence spread across the crowd as all heads turned from the speaker to Akkael, awaiting the answer of Yong the Brave.

Akkael wanted to play the hero role, trying desperately to think of some stoic one-liner that all the old heroes in the stories used to say. He scanned the crowd, keeping his chin high and his chest broad.

"The question isn't whether I will survive. It's who I will allow to survive."

There was a pause. Then, the crowd erupted into a raucous celebration. Some flung their arms into the air, screaming at the top of their lungs. Others began chanting again. "Yong! Yong!! Yong!!!" The energetic throng broke as the village pulled the gates open for their triumphant hero to exit onto new glory, not knowing that, as soon he was too far to see, it would be the last time they would set eyes on their protector.

Akkael galloped out of the village, simultaneously feeling guilt and satisfaction at having reduced the morale of one Edokand'i settlement. By the time the constant cheering was a faint whisper behind him, he had reached Trygve's body, lying in the scorched dirt that had only managed to grow back in patches, some of the grass still smothered by ash.

The red feathers of the arrow that was lodged in Trygve's eye ruffled in the wind. The other eye, glassy blue and lifeless, stared directly at the sun, and the muscles in his face were so slacked that he barely looked like himself.

Akkael slowed the mare as he looked at his old friend. "I hope they are kind to your body," he said, trying to find more to say but falling short of anything profound.

After a few moments of nothing but the sound of the horse's breath and the whistling wind, he pried his eyes from Trygve, spurring his horse onwards.

He headed west towards Wu Wei, hoping the roads led to the City of Disciplines. He looked down at his third horse since the mountains rose. Fourth, if the one he had borrowed on his first journey to Wu Wei counted. He leaned over and scratched behind her ear. "I hope you like the name Knarr," said Akkael. The horse whickered, almost in confirmation.

Akkael raised his head and let his smile fade as he looked towards the last leg of his journey. The last steps towards his revenge.

[CHAPTER 47] — THE BATTLE OF CHUTON

Initially, they had planned to attack at first light. But, with the information Heiyang had provided, it was well after dusk before lines were drawn in front of Chuton. This was one of many changes they had made.

It was pitch black, and the silhouetted figures against the torchlight on Chuton's wall were enough to confirm the shadow archer's report.

The architecture was different to how the Queen and Kwan had described it. They had said three disconnected concentric walls surrounded a fortress in the middle. However, Skane could see towers connecting one bulwark to the next. Also, extensions to the outer wall made it just closer to the incline of the valley. Each of these new platforms held one of the new weapons. The larger one; cannons.

The crenellated wall and ground barricades concealed those with the second new weapon: the muskets. Skane kept watch, hoping to glimpse one poking from behind the barriers. Archers were also two for every musket, according to the shadow lord's reconnaissance. Four-hundred archers shared between the wall and the ground, which meant two hundred musketeers. That left nearly a thousand soldiers, probably infantry, ready to pick the Northmen off once the guns had done their damage.

The full force of the Solstic stood behind Skane as they stared silently across the half-kilometre stretch of valley. The high hills were almost claustrophobic. It was the perfect funnel to pick off an army one by one, especially with projectiles that their shields were useless against.

Despite primarily being redundant, everyone Skane could see, and thousands more carried a round shield in their fist. The only person Skane was aware of that wasn't wielding one was Magar, but it was impossible for him to forgo his two-handed bastard sword.

The winds blew slowly as the two forces stood still, and Skane grew increasingly impatient. He looked left, then right in the direction of his husband, who was too far to see, before directing his eyes back towards the fortress.

301

He adjusted his armour to check its fitting before taking a deep breath, feeling the whole army's anticipation for the words that would soon follow.

"Shield wall!" Everyone in the front line placed their shields to their chests in unison as those behind clambered to add theirs to the building defence. By the end, the shield wall was four rows high, covering them like a tsunami enveloping the land.

Skane could sense the smirks of those in Chuton, wringing their new weapons in their hands as they awaited the slaughter they knew was about to come. They thought they had the element of surprise against the Northmen, but there was little satisfaction for those in the shield wall who knew they were about to be slaughtered.

"Charge!" Skane yelled before he realised the words had left his lips. Battle screams erupted from the Solstic as they pushed forward almost in a sprint. Skane struggled to keep his position in the wall as the armour slowed his pace, his mind trying to map the landscape he couldn't see and the distance left to go.

Then, Skane was pulled out of his thoughts by an eruption that sounded from Chuton like thunder strikes. The explosion half a kilometre away was replaced by smashing wood as the balls from the muskets shattered their shields. Skane heard the projectiles fly by his ear and watched warriors around him collapse, blood seeping from holes in their bodies as they slowly lost the light from their eyes. The shield wall became derelict in a matter of seconds as the Northmen behind tripped over hundreds of their newly dead.

Skane did not have time to consider the carnage around him. The shadow archers who had spied on Chuton's tactics informed them of what was coming next. The muskets took a long time to reload, so to fill the interim, the two archers on either side of each musketeer kept up the onslaught.

"Stop moving!" bellowed Skane. "Shields up!" He raised his shield above his head to block the rain of arrows about to fall. He looked up at the round wooden shield clenched in his fist. He stared through the hole from a bullet that narrowly missed his flesh, the moon like an iris in the crack.

He didn't see the arrow but felt its force as it planted itself in the oak planks blocking its fall. Some more Solstic fell or joined the cacophony of screams around him. Then a second spate of arrows found soil, shields, and skin.

He lowered his shield before the last arrows hit their targets. He looked around at his army, a much thinner vanguard than just a minute ago. He watched as those around him made desperate attempts to repair the shield wall.

"Forget it!" said Skane to those who could hear. "Save your shields for the arrows. Just sprint."

The message passed down the line through word and example as the Solstic ran at full speed towards the fortress. The vanguard began to outrun Skane, his legs older and his body anchored by armour. The blast of the muskets echoed through the valley again. All Skane could make out from the carnage were the bodies being released from the dense crowd and the flecks of blood and bone catching the moonlight before ricocheting off the warriors in front. A streak of blood burst across Skane's face, which was warm against the chilly night air.

As the last musket shots found their victims, those alive raised their shields above them, still maintaining their charge. More men fell to the arrows than last time, but they covered more ground. It took another barrage of musket shots and a wave of arrows before Skane's foot found a hole. He almost tripped on the pocked earth, and his heart skipped a beat. The shadow archers had also warned them of this. They were now in range of the cannons.

The blast was louder, deeper, and more terrifying than the muskets. He may not have seen the impact but swore the ground rocked. Over the heads of those around him, he could see sprays of dirt, blood, and limbs from where the cannonballs had hit. He knew Magar was far from the sites, but his heart felt heavier than his armour.

Skane understood how war technology evolved. The Solstic could settle in every corner of the world because of their advanced ships. The Edokand'i had better swords and crossbows, the Urkanzans had smarter tactics, the Rhaynese had trebuchets, and the Sekandans had the best bows in the world. These cannons and muskets were far beyond anything Skane had seen but not out of the realm of possibility.

The only question Skane had about these weapons was *why*. How could people manufacture such destruction? There was no honour to these muskets. You didn't have to aim for a gap in the armour or places where organs hid. You would just point into a crowd and watch as other humans fell. The cannons were worse, launching iron the size of heads with reckless abandon. Skane had no idea how many of his kinsmen were dead, and he didn't want to guess.

After the cannon blasts, the Sekandans took their cue. Skane watched the hills as Kya's women, half the force on each side, emerged from the valley's ridges, and he couldn't help but smirk. The sky was too dark to see the Sekandan arrows firing at Chuton, but the Solstic made great distance before the musket shots could be heard again. Skane saw fewer men fall this time as more muskets turned towards the hills.

If the shadow archers were doing their duty, the three would pick off the musketeers and cannon men the moment the Sekandans rose above the hills. The feathering and the assassinations distracted the goutuizi, making the bullets and arrows more sporadic until Skane was only a few feet from the walls of Chuton.

The musket shots came with the arrows this time, their battle structure off kilter due to the chaos. Most of the arrows landed in the shields still held aloft. The bullets then thinned the men in front of Skane like a curtain giving way until all he could see were corpses, scared sentinels, and the walls of Chuton, cracked under the weight of time it had never seen. Skane removed the axe from his belt, ready to engage with the goutuizi outside the gates.

Some sentinels already had katanas in their hands by the time the Solstic got into fighting range. Those who didn't were the first to die, still fumbling with their muskets just before a rusted axe head opened their throats. Skane looked around, wide-eyed and covered in blood, trying to find the first victim for his axe.

There was a sentinel backing towards the sizeable dark wood gates of the fortress. He clutched his musket and pointed it towards any Northman who got too close, not firing the weapon for fear of losing the only bullet in the barrel. Skane made for him, pointing his axe at the enemy as he got closer.

When the soldier noticed Skane approach, he pointed the musket towards him, trembling. Skane ducked as soon as he saw the weapon, charging to tackle the sentinel. He heard the weapon fire above his head as he brought the man to the ground. Skane felt the musket roll down his back. He sat on his enemy's chest, raising his axe before forcing it into his skull.

Then, in his peripheral, he saw another charge at him, sword at his side. Skane rolled out of the way before the katana could sink into his flesh. He got to his feet as the next swing of the sentinel's blade fell. He dodged two more swipes before he saw the opportunity to slice at his opponent. The force of the slash spun his helmet, hiding half of his bleeding face.

As his enemy fell, Skane turned just as a shadow archer appeared, sending a knife flying into another sentinel's neck. He couldn't make out which shade it was, as his mouth and nose were covered by a mask. As the men of Chuton gurgled on their own blood, the archer and Skane caught each other's eye. Skane looked around to see how easily the overwhelming Solstic force had cleared the front gate of goutuizi and was awaiting the next stage of the plan. Arrows and bullets still rained from the wall, but they were distracted by the Sekandans on the hill.

Skane turned back to the shadow archer. After Heiyang had told them all of the new Edokand'i weapons, they quickly abandoned the ram and the boat, knowing it would slow down their charge. Instead, the shadow archers would teleport to the other side of the gates and remove the bars that kept it locked.

"Get the doors open!" Skane yelled to the archer. The shade nodded before disappearing in smoke.

After giving his command, Skane looked around at the men he just charged the fortress with. They may still outnumber the Edokand'i, but the army seemed thin. The gaps in their ranks were too frequent, and those still yet to get their weapons bloodied were red with their dead kin. Skane dreaded having to count those lost. He peered into the distance, the ground more corpse than grass.

305

Skane's distraction allowed a sentinel to knock him to the ground, causing Skane to hit his head on the rocky path, weapon and shield discarded. A buzzing resonated in Skane's skull as he tried to lift himself up, getting to his hands and knees. In his stunned state, he found clarity in the confusion. He couldn't understand why the sentinel was taking so long to kill him. Glancing behind his thigh, Skane saw the goutuizi was delayed by a sizeable Solstic man, who had swiftly darted to his defence. As his eyes regained their clarity, he recognised his defender. It was Magar.

Skane gained enough focus to watch the killing blow, Magar cleaving through the armour of the man in front of him, almost cutting him in half. After wriggling his large blade free from its victim, Magar made his way to Skane, holding out a hand and dragging him to his feet. The two smiled at each other, touching foreheads to be heard over the battle chaos.

"See," said Magar. "I told you armour was useless."

Skane snickered. "It got me this far."

Magar kissed Skane's bloodied forehead before pulling away, still smiling.

But the smile jolted from his face as a thunderclap burst from atop the wall. A musket peered over the ridge, releasing a bullet through Magar's bare shoulder and out of his bicep. He dropped his sword into the mud. A second blast made a hole in Magar's right thigh, and a third scrapped his other leg.

Before Skane's face could change, his arms were outstretched to catch him and soften his descent. Cradling Magar in his arms as the giant writhed in pain, Skane's eyes began to swell before he could say anything.

"Magar," he whimpered, cupping his hand over the exit wound in Magar's arm.

The gate of Chuton was starting to open as Solstic filed past Skane and Magar to push the doors ajar. The Solstic men and women sprinted into the fortress, giving them a wide berth as Skane clutched his injured husband.

Magar's eyes began to flutter as the pain and blood loss drove him unconscious. All Skane could do was repeat Magar's name, rocking back and forth as tears streamed down his cheek.

[CHAPTER 48] — A SIMPLE NOD

Astrid lay on the grassy hill watching as those below flooded into Chuton. Arrows flew over her head, some so close that her hair lifted in the updraft. Chuton was beautiful from her birds-eye view, and the architecture stolen from the future made it unbelievable. The round towers that jutted from the original fortress were clearly disparate from the castle and its original circular walls. New structures connected each wall together, like a spider's web.

"Your people have made it through the first gate," said Moon, ducking under the arrows behind Astrid. "It's time."

Astrid saw the first axes fell their first victims within the walls before she nodded. She turned around. The Sekandan archers were a few yards behind her, making room for the sea of prone women that hid in the grass. A thousand on each side of the valley, made of Sekandan warriors and Solstic shield maidens, were waiting under the constant barrage of blue-flight arrows. The Sekandans rarely fought alongside men, so this was the only compromise Queen Kya would entertain.

Astrid met Moon's eyes as she clutched her sheathed geom tightly in both fists, as her iron shield rattled on her back against her blue armour.

"Bring the bridges," Astrid commanded.

Moon nodded, turning to pass the same instruction behind her. When the signal reached the rear, those at the back of the line began passing log bridges up to the front. There were ten bridges on each side of the valley, Astrid's arms aching from spending all afternoon making them. Three felled trees, bound with iron and rope and eight handles along the length, made up the bridges, with hooks on the ends for securing them to the hills and the walls.

The bridges were placed lengthways at even intervals along the prone army, so they would be easy to grab when it was time to descend. Astrid wrapped her left fist around one of the handles of the bridge before turning back around. She didn't look at Moon this time, instead locking eyes with the only Solstic archer not drawing their bow. Astrid nodded to her, and she nodded back.

Astrid was getting bored of all the nodding going on. She had nodded when the first musket shots had sounded, her signal to make their way up the hill. She had nodded for the Solstic archers to start firing when Skane and Magar's forces got in the cannons' firing range. She had even nodded to the shadow archers when it was time for them to assassinate those below. She knew it was trivial, but Astrid promised herself that next time she was at war, she'd try and find diverse ways of evolving a battle strategy that didn't involve moving her head.

The archer she had signalled to reached into a barrel of arrows at her feet and pulled one out. The tip was wrapped in cloth, dowsed in oil. Reaching into her belt pouch, she removed some flint and steel. She held them out for the archer to her right to take before notching the arrow and drawing her bow. The second Sekandan, her own bow placed over her shoulder, used the flint and steel to light the arrow. Then the archer raised her aim, launching the fire arrow into Chuton.

Astrid turned back around and waited, watching Kya's side of the valley with unblinking eyes. After a few moments, a second flaming arrow joined the torrent from the adjacent hill.

Astrid closed her eyes and focused on her heartbeat. If her people still had gods, this would be the time for prayer. If she were an inspirational leader, this would be the time for a speech. But Astrid Torne was a warrior, and, for warriors, these times were for battle cries.

"Charge!" she shrieked, letting a scream follow her as she got to her feet. The Solstic shield maidens followed her example, allowing their war cries to fill the air. Even some Sekandans joined the concert as they all stood, bringing the bridges up.

The shield maidens and Sekandans cascaded down the hill like a stampede. The torch lit fortress looked stunning as their view of Chuton lowered like they were running into a wildfire. Astrid noticed a thousand women follow suit on the opposite side of the valley, bellowing their battle cries and clenching their bridges as they descended. The Queen had not charged with them, probably still crouching under the arrows of their bowwomen.

The confusion of the goutuizi on the walls was palpable, not knowing where to point their weapons as they were attacked on three fronts. Eventually, they had gotten so far down the valley that Astrid could no longer see inside Chuton. She was moving too fast to stop herself as they approached the first wall, so she braced herself by moving side-face and using her left shoulder to block some of the impact.

The log bridge hit the wall first, sending a shockwave through her whole body before she smacked into the stone herself. The pressure of those behind her, also unable to stop their descent, pressing her into the wall made her feel like a bellows as all the air left her body. They quickly peeled away from each other as they considered the height of Chuton's outer wall.

Once Astrid confirmed she was okay, she wasted no time giving the next order. "Bring up the bridge!"

Astrid moved under her bridge, pushing it further up the wall as those behind her pushed it forward, the iron hooks scrapping the stone as it ascended. Eventually, the logs were vertical, standing the length of the wall and half again.

Astrid turned to face Moon, who she didn't even realise was still directly behind her. Her eyes were wide like a deer hearing a hunter break a twig under his foot. Moon was the Commander of the military police in Sekando. It wasn't a comfortable job by any stretch. But she had not seen war the way Astrid had.

Astrid looked over Moon's shoulder at the Sekandans behind her. "Pull out!"

The women began to ascend the hill again, bringing the bridge to rest diagonally on the crenellated parapet. They kept moving until the hooks on the end of the bridges gripped the bricks at the top and were dug into the mud at the bottom. The logs were still more vertical than horizontal but were less steep than the hills they had just run down.

"Up!" screamed Astrid. The women at the foot of the bridge began to climb single files on all ten bridges that had been erected.

As the Sekandans and shield maidens began to funnel towards the closest bridge, Astrid could see the mad scramble of the sentinels to remove the bridges from their walls. However, the hooks in the hills and the weight of those climbing made them hard to push, exasperated by the sheer lack of men that stood atop the walls.

Arrows and musket balls found some of those climbing to the top, and they had managed to lower one of the bridges, crushing a few warriors as it hit the ground. But, as soon as the first shield maidens and Sekandans made it onto the wall, securing the bridges and pushing the goutuizi back, it was only a matter of time until the women would flood the top.

Astrid was waiting her turn to climb the bridge. Those still at the bottom were thinning as hundreds were already fighting on the wall. Moon stood before her at the foot of the bridge, still as a corpse.

Astrid could see the fear dripping off Moon as she delayed the ascent of those behind her. After a moment, Astrid spun Moon around, causing her chest to heave and her body to flinch.

"What's wrong with you?" Astrid yelled.

Moon couldn't look into Astrid's eyes, instead looking either at her feet or at the grass. A musket fired, and Moon jumped. Eventually, she spoke. "I'm not a fighter; I'm a politician. I'm not meant to be here."

"Meant?" Astrid spat. "You're here; get over yourself. You're a fighter today."

"But…" Moon began before Astrid removed her helmet and slapped her across the face.

"I'm going to climb that bridge," said Astrid as Moon rubbed her cheek. "If you're not behind me, I will rip one of those muskets from the first corpse I make and shoot you between the eyes."

Astrid pushed past Moon and up the bridge towards the fortress. She didn't bother looking back, feeling the bridge's tension as Moon climbed behind her.

Astrid placed her hand on the stone and vaulted onto the battlements. The shadow archers had already opened the second gate, and the ground assault had made short work of the sentinels below. Some of Skane and Magar's force had charged the steps to the ramparts and were already clearing the walls.

After checking Moon had gotten onto the wall safely, Astrid tried to find someone to fight. The Edokand'i forces were so thin there must have been twenty allies for every one of them. Astrid could see a small group that had bundled near Chuton's castle. Astrid didn't count each man, but there couldn't have been more than a hundred behind the safety of the third wall.

Astrid ignored them for the moment, instead focusing on the unstructured smattering of goutuizi, not hiding away. Pulling the axe from her belt and the shield from her back, she stepped onto the wall, using the crenellations like steppingstones to get through the congested walkway.

Eventually, she could see the blue armour of the Sekandans begin to break away, replaced by Edokand'i red. Twenty men stood five abreast: the front two lines wielded spears with muskets resting on their shoulders from the rear.

The enemy was so focused on those in front of them that they didn't notice Astrid sprinting along the wall until it was too late. When she got close enough, Astrid launched from the wall, shield first, into the spearmen. She felt like one of the cannon balls as she knocked down most of the Edokand'i rank. Some dropped their spears, one fell over the wall, and some musketeers misfired, hitting stone or nothing or even their own.

Astrid drove her axe into the face of the closest sentinel lying next to her as the Sekandans took the opportunity of the faltered formation to charge. She killed three before they were all dead. Her second kill bled out from his neck. For the third, she repeatedly brought her axe down on his chest until his breastplate caved in and his ribs pierced his lungs.

With adrenaline coursing through her, she stood, face covered in blood and eyes frantically darting for the next kill. She didn't realise she was smiling until it started to fade, unable to see anyone wearing red armour that wasn't huddled near Chuton's castle. The promise of the new weapons made Astrid forget how small a force of fifteen hundred was. Part of her knew leading the second phase of the attack meant that she wouldn't be seeing much fighting but knowing that was different to experiencing it.

Astrid stood, sulking as the Sekandans filtered past her, moving further along the wall, down the steps, and across to the second wall. She could tell the women passing her were frustrated by Astrid standing in their way as they stepped over a pile of corpses, but she didn't care. She just scanned Chuton, watching the aimless Solstic and Sekandans struggling to find any fight in which to engage.

Then, Astrid noticed something peculiar happening in front of the central castle. The two hundred or so sentinels began to move to the rear gate. The north and south gates of the first and second walls had already been opened, leaving the central northern entrance and the rear gate leading towards Wu Wei.

From one of the newer structures in the central complex, a goutuizi brought out a brown horse. Quickly, a sentinel mounted it as others began pulling the chains on the steel doors, allowing the rider to gallop south towards the City of Disciplines.

Astrid ran below, sprinting between the pierced training dummies and bored soldiers waiting for a fight. Luckily, she wasn't running long before she saw Heiyang teleport a few feet from her. He pulled an Edokand'i soldier from behind some barrels and stabbed him in the throat.

"Heiyang!" Astrid yelled to him as the sentinel collapsed, gurgling on his blood. She pointed towards the other end of the valley. "Rider."

Heiyang looked south as if he could see through the stone walls before returning to Astrid and nodding. He teleported away.

She moved in line with the rear gates to see the horse galloping with no rider, the sentinel lying dead in the valley's centre, Heiyang already gone. Astrid smiled, turning towards the central castle as the sentinels inside tried to desperately close the gate.

However, the door was still cracked when it had stopped closing. Astrid squinted, moving closer until she could hear screaming from inside. As she approached, she noticed fighting through the aperture of the entrance. Her eyes widened, and she dashed towards Chuton's castle, moving side-faced to squeeze through the gates.

As the Edokand'i were distracted, the Solstic flooded through the Northern gate and overwhelmed them. They were already mostly corpses by the time Astrid had entered the fray. She wasted no time, charging towards the closest sentinel, axe and shield held tightly in her fists as she gave a blood-curdling scream. The sentinel turned, fear in his eyes, as Astrid charged him, axe aloft.

However, before Astrid reached him, the sentinel collapsed, a spear standing in his place and embedded in his spine. Astrid stopped, seeing a Solstic man stand unarmed behind him. He nodded to Astrid before removing an axe from his belt and moving on to his next victim. Astrid growled.

Another sentinel stood alone, trembling with fear. Astrid smiled as she made her way towards him. She was only a few feet away before she felt an arrow fly past her and watched it burrow into the goutuizi's face. Astrid turned to see a Sekandan archer standing atop the central wall. She also nodded at Astrid, which made her blood boil.

The next Edokand'i that Astrid saw had his back against the castle. His eyes frantically scanned the carnage around him through slits in a demon mask, which slotted into his kabuto helmet. Astrid wasted no time marching towards him. When the sentinel noticed Astrid, rage in her eyes, he dropped his katana to the ground.

"I yield," screamed the sentinel, muffled in his mask. "Chuton is yours. I yield!"

Astrid just smiled. She used her shield to press the goutuizi against the castle. All the air left his body instantly as Astrid spat in her enemy's face.

"This will be fun," she grinned. She wound her shoulder back, ready to drive the axe head through the sentinel's mask.

Then Astrid felt a fist clench around her wrist. She turned to see Moon standing next to her, expression stern.

"Don't kill him," said Moon. "This is Ieyasu, Hideo's right-hand man. We need him alive."

The scowl on Astrid's face started to hurt as her eyes darted between Moon's. After a few moments of an intense, unblinking glower, Moon tried to reassure Astrid with a nod.

Astrid immediately dropped her shield, placing the ridge of her axe on Moon's breast. "Don't nod at me!"

Moon furrowed her brow. "What?"

Rolling her eyes, Astrid discarded her axe and walked away from Moon and Ieyasu. A chorus of cheers and chants erupted from those around her as they realised there were no more sentinels to fight. The fortress was secure, and the battle was won, leaving Astrid with nothing to do but clean the blood from her face and clothes, wishing she were covered in more.

[CHAPTER 49] — THE AFTERMATH

Rigpa leaned over Magar's unconscious body, checking his temperature and pulse. He had bandages around all three wounds, discoloured by blood. Skane had replaced the bandages twice already but was wary of how many were needed for the rest of the injured that filled the room.

After the battle, Skane sprinted to the shore where their boats had been moored. Five-hundred warriors were there to protect the ships and the Queen's sages and servants who had no place in war. Rigpa was also there. Skane rushed into camp, forlorn and panicked. He demanded the sages be brought to Chuton immediately, as well as two hundred more warriors.

Skane sat opposite Rigpa on the other side of Magar's bed in Chuton's dormitory, which they used as an infirmary. Her robes were mud-laden and filthy from her trek to Chuton. Skane wasn't wearing his armour, but blood was still crusted on his face from the fighting. It had been days, and his bloodied axe was still resting against the foot of Magar's iron bed. Black bags, like burlap sacks hanging from a horse's saddle, had formed under Skane's eyes, and every so often, he would clench his jaw to stifle a yawn.

Skane watched as Rigpa ran her hands above Magar's body, using some of the sage gifts Skane didn't understand. Eventually, she leaned back in her chair and gave Skane a warm smile. "He'll be okay," she said. "A few weeks of rest, and he'll return to full health."

Skane breathed a sigh of relief, allowing himself a brief grin. "Thank you, Rigpa," he said. "You're a very useful prisoner."

Rigpa scoffed. "An epitaph for the ages."

Skane shook his head into the palm of his hand, hunching over in his chair. "I don't want to think of epitaphs right now."

"At my age, you don't have much else to consider." She leaned back in her chair. "It makes me wonder."

"About what?" asked Skane, still hunched as he watched his sleeping husband from the corner of his eye.

Rigpa shrugged. "How people will remember me when I die. When scholars write about my time as Grand Sage, what will they say?"

"How old are you?" Skane asked.

"I'm seventy-two," Rigpa answered.

Skane raised his eyebrows, bending his bottom lip.

"What's wrong?" Rigpa asked, folding her arms. "Did you not expect me to answer so willingly? Why would I care if you know how old I am? It wouldn't change reality."

"No, that's not it. I'm just impressed," said Skane. "I watched you march miles to Koseki and back, and you didn't complain once."

"Well, as I said, at my age, all you think about is the history books." She unfolded her arms and smiled again. "I don't want some pock-faced student writing about how I bitched across Sekando."

Skane laughed so loud he distracted the other sages and servants, tending to the rest of the injured fighters. "Rigpa! I didn't know you were allowed to swear."

She giggled, covering her mouth like a naughty child. "I'm not."

They laughed together for a moment before Magar started to stir in his sleep. Skane quickly went silent, fixing his eyes on him.

Rigpa breathed deeply, but Skane was too focused on Magar to see what her face was doing. "I told you; he'll be okay."

"I know, I just…" said Skane before trailing off and looking down at his feet. "I keep thinking of what I could have done differently."

"Didn't we already open that chakra?" asked Rigpa. "Don't let guilt block it once again."

"Okay." Skane nodded, trying desperately to collect himself. He could still picture the moment Magar went down. It was like a nightmare. He could see all three bullet holes pumping blood like a spring. He felt pathetic remembering how he tried to shovel the blood back into Magar's body. His tears had turned to steam as they hit the red liquid streaming down Magar's body like lava.

"I'm surprised, actually," said Rigpa, ejecting Skane from his memory.

Skane squinted. "Why?"

"Well, we've been sat alone for a few minutes, and you haven't once asked me about the next chakra," she said.

"Well, I've had other concerns," replied Skane, gesturing to the bed in front of them.

"Good."

"Good?" Skane asked, confused.

The Grand Sage huffed, adjusting herself in her chair until her back was straight and her hands were tucked into the purple sleeves. Skane was still slouched.

"Do you want to know how to open the last chakra?" she asked.

Skane squinted. "I thought there were seven. Aren't we only on number four?"

"Yes. But let's skip ahead."

"Okay," said Skane, slowly, looking around to see if the other sages were reacting to what their leader had suggested.

The Grand Sage continued. "The last chakra requires you to abandon all worldly attachments. Do you know what that means?"

"Sort of," said Skane, moving his head side to side. "You don't have any belongings or a home of your own."

"That's part of it," Rigpa nodded. She paused briefly before speaking. "I've only kissed one boy in my life. I've never had close friends, my own space, or anything that links me to this world. If I weren't Grand Sage, no one would remember me. I would fade away like a statue eroding into dust."

"That doesn't sound like a good life," Skane admitted.

"It is at times." She smiled, but there was a sadness behind her eyes. "It isn't at others. It is why only us sages manage to unlock the powers of the Seraphim.

We give up attachment to attain his gifts. It's a long, arduous, and lonely process. A process you would not be able to walk down, and I'm glad for it."

The two paused for a moment, looking at each other, down at the floor, at the unconscious king between them. Both were hunting for something to say.

"Well," started Skane, "I was thinking I'd be getting magic powers."

Rigpa scoffed. "It's not magic."

They both smiled at each other.

"You're wrong, by the way," said Skane.

Rigpa looked at him from the side of her eye. "About magic?"

"No," he said, shaking his head. "About you not having any close friends. You have one."

Rigpa's smile widened, and Skane copied it. Suddenly, the unconscious Magar began to stir between them. He groaned, tossed, and turned until, finally, his eyes fluttered open, the blue iris swarmed by bloodshot red lines like a sapphire entangled in red ivy.

"Magar," said Skane, moving closer to him.

Magar's eyes darted towards Skane. "Skane," he said in a hoarse voice. "Where am I?"

Skane placed a hand on Magar's arm, just above the bandage. "You're okay. You're in Chuton. We won the battle. Rigpa has been nursing you to health." Skane looked up to see Rigpa had gone. He looked around and noticed her tending to another patient.

"Did I miss it?" asked Magar, regaining Skane's attention.

"No," he smiled, "you were great."

Magar tried to sit up in his bed before grunting in pain.

As soon as he heard Magar moan, instincts brought Skane to his feet as he attempted to guide Magar back to a prone position. "Don't move. You were shot badly."

Magar groaned again, determined to sit up. "This bed is shit."

Skane snickered. "Nothing I can do about that now."

319

"Pillows?"

"All taken."

Magar grunted and rolled his eyes before adjusting and getting comfortable in his iron-framed bed. As Skane looked at Magar, he was surprised by a tear that leaked down his cheek. He wiped it away as soon as he noticed it and averted his gaze. After a moment, Magar's giant hand clamped onto Skane's arm as he tried to hide his face.

Skane looked back at Magar. "I thought I lost you," he managed to say through a log in his throat.

Magar bent his neck, trying his best not to look ashamed. "Armour doesn't sound so stupid now."

Skane laughed. After it faded away, he shrugged. "It wouldn't have helped anyway. Those muskets would have pierced straight through it."

Magar grunted in agreement as Skane looked around at the room full of injured. Most were in the makeshift infirmary with small bullet holes in non-threatening places. The muskets pierced through them like a knife through paper. It was hard to think of them as the lucky ones, some still writhing in pain as sages tried to cure infections and remove the shards of musket balls from their bodies.

"When are we going to Wu Wei?" Magar asked, breaking the contemplative quiet.

Skane's head spun to face Magar so fast he cricked his neck. He hid the pain behind his shock.

"You're not going anywhere," Skane decreed.

"Yes, I am," said Magar so calmly it annoyed Skane even more.

"No, you're not," Skane repeated. "You're staying in this bed until your wounds heal."

Magar sighed, keeping his voice low. "This is my last war," he said. "We agreed."

"We did." Skane nodded sarcastically. "That was before you got injured."

"I want to see the end of this." Magar punctuated his sentences by punching his own leg. "I need to see the end of this."

Skane saw the despondence on Magar's face. After everything they had been through, and the despair Magar had felt, Skane felt slightly guilty taking this away from him. He took a deep breath before continuing. "Look, we've got a few days left here. We'll talk about it another time."

Magar growled his agreement, and the two men sat in silence for a time. After a few moments, Skane moved closer to the bed, placed his head on Magar's chest, and wrapped a hand around his waist. Magar winced a little from the pain but, before long, had also enveloped his injured arm over Skane's shoulder.

Skane felt a kiss on the top of his head and smiled. He had no bearing on how long they had stayed like that. His eyes were closed as Magar held him tight. He must have dozed off briefly, as the room had grown a little darker when he opened his eyes, and more candles were lit. He was woken by Magar jostling his shoulders, and when he sat up, he saw Lindsay standing at the foot of the bed.

"My Kings, I'm sorry to disturb you." She bowed like one of the Sekandans. Skane wondered if that was something Astrid would have picked up from her time with Queen Kya, too. "Your presence is requested in the war room."

Skane squinted. "Astrid knows Magar is bedridden; he can't…."

Before Skane could finish speaking, Magar was already pushing himself out of bed. Skane noticed how blood-soaked the bed covers were and how pale Magar was. He stood up from his chair, looking panicked as Magar struggled to sit up.

Magar looked at Skane, sighed, and stopped trying to raise his body. He threw up his hands and spoke. "Are you going to help me stand?"

"You need to lie down," stressed Skane.

"I've laid down enough," said Magar.

"No, you haven't."

"Fine," spat Magar. "If you won't help."

Magar began to pull himself up again, face contorting from the pain.

"Wait," said Skane, worrying he would break some of the gut that bound his wounds. He sighed. "Fine, I'll help."

Skane walked to the other side of Magar, wrapped his right arm behind his back, and pulled him to his feet. Magar dropped his left arm on Skane's shoulder for leverage as the two men reached the door, followed by a concerned Lindsay.

"You're a stubborn old man," grunted Skane as he carried him to the steps leading to Chuton's war room.

Magar scoffed. "Less stubborn and younger than you."

[CHAPTER 50] — IEYASU

The war room made up the entirety of the penultimate floor in Chuton's castle, three flights above the dormitory where Magar had been resting. Large pillars rose like jungle trees and were engraved with strange symbols that Skane had not seen in any of the cities the Northmen had occupied. It partially resembled other war rooms in Edokand. Still, it was a lot blander, with dark, drab décor as opposed to the vibrant reds and accompanying colours that usually brightened the room.

According to Astrid, Sekando had a similar war room to Skaldgard, with a low table and pillow to kneel on. Takakawa's table was higher, but there were no chairs until the Northmen moved in and brought them. To Skane's dismay, this room was the same. Everyone stood around the dark wood table. They watched as Skane lugged his ailing husband up the last few steps.

Kya sat at the furthest head of the table, with Moon behind them. Astrid stood to their right, and General Kwan was to their left. The three shadow archers were also present, skulking in the corner with a smattering of Sekandan women in full armour against the walls. Lastly, their prisoner, Ieyasu, sat on his knees in front of the table. He was still in his armour, but his hands were bound. Dirt and blood clung to his face.

Skane held Magar upright, feeling the strain in his back. Every woman around the table stared at them in silence. Skane considered the Queen. He couldn't tell if it was the filter of simmering rage that took everything antagonistically. Still, he thought he noticed a hint of amusement on Kya's face.

Skane did his best to hide his scowl but knew he wasn't doing an excellent job. "Queen Kya, Astrid," he said, facing each of them in turn. "I must admit I am a little pissed. King Magar needs rest after his injuries."

Kya's eyes lit up before they spoke. "Magar is a big boy," they said in a patronising voice. "We are sure he can muster the strength to walk up a few flights of stairs."

Before Skane could let his rage boil from his lips, Moon beckoned to one of the shadow archers next to Heiyang. "Get Magar a chair," she commanded.

The shadow archer bowed before disappearing. He reappeared behind Skane and Magar with a leather studded chair, the same bland brown as the rest of the furniture. After helping Magar into the seat, the shadow archer returned to Heiyang's side.

Once Magar was comfortable, Skane looked up and caught Astrid's eye. Eventually, he took a deep breath and spoke. "Why are we here?"

Kya pointed to Ieyasu, still kneeling on the ground with his head facing the floor as if the weight of being the only survivor in Chuton was too heavy for his shoulders.

"General Ieyasu has said some very interesting things," said Kya. "Repeat what you told us to the Northmen."

Ieyasu raised his eyes. His natural hatred for the Solstic was overshadowed by the fear on his face. He looked between the two in front of him before his eyes landed on Magar. Then he spoke. "Your brother Doran is alive. He has been imprisoned with the Emperor."

Magar sat up in his chair, ignoring the pain as Skane's jaw dropped. "What?"

Skane squinted, unable to understand. Questions flooded into his head until there were too many to keep silent. "Why is he being kept alive? Why wasn't he executed?"

"He's not being kept alive," said Ieyasu, confusing Skane more. "At least it's not a choice."

"Start from the beginning, traitor," Kya spat from the other end of the table.

Ieyasu paused briefly, sighing down at the floorboards. "There was a coup," he muttered. "Hideo took control of the capital, and we executed any noble who said anything against his rule."

"We know this," said Skane. "So, Doran and the Emperor have been imprisoned?"

"Not imprisoned." Ieyasu paused, looking back and forth as if searching for the words. "Frozen," he eventually stuttered.

"Frozen?" Skane tilted his head.

"Hideo's magic," said Astrid. "The one the dragon warned Akkael about."

"It's a metronome," Ieyasu spoke louder, each word more laboured. "It's so simple looking. But I've seen it work. It changed Chuton. I watched it turn men to dust. He used it on me." Skane was close enough to see beads of sweat trickle from Ieyasu's forehead.

"A metronome?" asked Skane softly.

Magar leant towards Skane, speaking quietly. "What's a metronome?"

"It's a time-keeping device," Kya answered, a smugness in their voice after overhearing Magar's ignorance. "It's used to teach children how to play music."

"So," began Skane, "if we get our hands on this metronome, we can free Doran and the Emperor?"

"That's probably easier said than done," Astrid scoffed. "What's stopping Hideo from using this magic on us the moment we arrive at Wu Wei?"

"Jin Bu," whispered Ieyasu. "It's Jin Bu now."

"We don't really know what's been stopping him from using it on us so far anyway," continued Skane. "We know he doesn't need to be nearby because he was nowhere near the mountains or Koseki."

"It is pointless wondering about things beyond our understanding," Kya interjected. "First, we must get into Wu Wei."

"Jin Bu. It's Jin Bu now."

Skane looked down at Ieyasu, sweat pouring from his forehead as his chest seemed to convulse. His mouth was open, and his breaths grew heavy. Skane looked down at him with pity. He knew what panic looked like.

"My battering ram," Skane heard Magar suggest.

Kya waved their hand in front of them. "We left that at the ships. It would take too long to retrieve."

"Then why did I make it?" Magar asked.

Kya shrugged. "We don't know. Regardless we want to march on Wu Wei soon."

"Jin Bu," Ieyasu started. "It's –"

Kya spoke so loudly, and suddenly, it made Ieyasu jump. "Heiyang. We have no more use for Ieyasu. Kill him."

Ieyasu's eyes widened. "No, please!"

"What about the cannons?" Kya continued, ignoring Ieyasu's pleading and Heiyang's teleporting. "Is there any way to transport them to the city?"

Heiyang appeared behind Ieyasu with a knife in his hand. He was only in front of the table for a brief time. Enough for him to grab Ieyasu by the top knot, drive the blade into his neck, and disappear. The whole room watched Ieyasu die. After he drew his last breath, Kya cleared their throat, reclaiming the room's attention.

"We have the bridges," Astrid said as Skane struggled to remember what the Queen had just asked. "If we make them into platforms, we can drag the cannons on them, destroy the gates, and charge into the city."

Kya nodded. "Good."

Skane stared down at Ieyasu's body. He was fed up with watching people die, and he couldn't understand how everyone else was happy for the meeting to continue as blood was still pumped from Ieyasu's body. He watched the last of it trickle from the pale corpse and tried hard to think about how close they were to ending this war.

He tried to ignore how slim the chances of true peace were. Even if they won in Wu Wei, it would be a conqueror's peace. Fragile and brief.

Skane was drawn to optimistic thoughts. He couldn't achieve everything he wanted. But, as he looked at the corpse, maudlin and dower, something that felt more concrete than hope came to mind.

Skane stepped forward, only a few inches from the puddle of blood. "As harrowing as what Ieyasu said is, it also gives us an opportunity."

Kya tilted their head. "What do you mean?"

Skane pointed at Ieyasu. "He used the word '*frozen.*' We know the metronome manipulates time in some way. If the Emperor and Doran are still alive, chances are the metronome froze them in time or slowed it down, so weeks for us feel like seconds for them."

Kya shook their head. "What did we just say about speculating on things we don't understand?"

Skane ignored them. "If that is true, they would still believe they are still in peace negotiations. They have no idea what has happened since."

"What are you suggesting?" asked General Kwan.

"Instead of going to Wu Wei as conquerors," Skane started, "we can frame our attack as a rescue mission. If we free Doran and the Emperor, then there is no reason peace negotiations can't continue."

"I think an army of Northmen storming the capital of Edokand will look like an invasion regardless of intent," said Moon.

Skane looked to the ground, thinking for a moment before continuing. "We will escort the Grand Sage and the Queen into the palace to show this isn't just a Solstic attack."

Astrid leant in, facing the Queen. "No offence to Their Majesty or Rigpa, but they probably won't fair well on the battlefield."

"As Queen, we have been present at every battle our people have fought," said Kya indignantly.

"As a leader," said Astrid. "Not as a warrior."

"Once the main bulk of our force has taken the city," said Skane, wading through the blood, stepping over the corpse, and resting against the war table. "I, along with a thousand warriors, will escort the Queen and Rigpa up the volcano to the palace."

"I will lead the vanguard in the initial assault," said Astrid eagerly.

Magar sat up in his chair. "So will I."

Skane whipped around to face him. "No, you won't."

"I will go to Wu Wei," Magar bellowed, slamming his fist on his leg.

After a moment of tense silence between the two men, Astrid spoke. "You can join Skane and the escort."

Skane, conceding, closed his eyes and lowered his head. He turned back towards the table just in time to watch Kya shake their head.

"We will not trust our life to a force of a thousand Northmen," Kya insisted.

Skane sighed. "We'll split the force then. Half Solstic, half Sekandan."

"And, apart from Skane and Magar, the Solstic escort will be entirely made of shield maidens," Astrid interjected when Kya seemed nonplussed.

After looking at each face around the table, Kya bowed their head. "Fine."

Three finger snaps came from the back of the room, and everyone turned to face the shadow archers. Heiyang stepped forward and signed towards Moon.

Moon began to translate. "He says Wu Wei has twice the men that Chuton had, as well as more cannons and muskets."

Kwan chimed in. "Also, there'll be cavalry, infantry, archers. We would struggle to take the city even without the new weapons."

Skane shrugged. "They may have muskets and cannons, but so do we. Chuton trained for weeks with these weapons. Wu Wei hasn't. Their reload time will be slower, and shots will be less accurate. Plus, we know what we're dealing with this time."

Astrid nodded in agreement. "We're not fighting the whole Edokand'i army. We're fighting the city sentinels. Akkael destroyed half their fighting force when he destroyed Koji's army. They may have more than Chuton, but we still outnumber them."

"Also, we must remember this is a usurper's army," said Kya, clenching their fist. "Our brother, Hideo, will have filled the city with people he deems loyal to him. Even if he had called the banners of Trim to aid Wu Wei, the rumours of their coup would have staved off large-scale support."

"And the noble heads mounted on the palace walls would also be a deterrent for any lord invited to the capital," said Moon.

Kya nodded before turning to Heiyang. "You and your shades must go to Wu Wei and scout the size of their force."

Heiyang nodded.

"In three days, this war will be over," started Astrid, staring at each face in turn before stopping at Skane. "I know it."

[CHAPTER 51] — LANTERNS

Akkael walked into the City of Disciplines, and no one said anything in protest. It was a strange feeling. He remembered the first time his father took him to the Urkanzan capital, Ukbul. It felt wrong, like rain in the desert or grass in the tundra. He knew how out of place he was meant to feel, even at such an early age. As he got older, that feeling of not belonging was overshadowed by intrigue and pride. No Solstic had entered Wu Wei except for Doran. That would have excited him, and a grin wouldn't have left his face.

However, even though he looked like a goutuizi, he kept his head low, walking in lockstep with his horse as if to hide behind it. Farmers from the fields that butted against the walls streamed into the city frantically as if Magar and Kya were visible on the horizon. The urgency Akkael saw only happened in a city caught off guard when conflict is imminent.

Sentinels lined the path, ushering the dirt-clad men and women into the city. As he approached the gate, he noticed a few goutuizi watching him and nodding their heads as they caught Akkael's eye.

The buildings were all jade coloured, making it look like Akkael was seeing the city through a morning fog. Smoke from lanterns swirled into the cherry trees. The air smelt of burning coal, and the sweet aroma of rotting blossoms browning on the cobbled ground under his feet. Leaves of dark green grew strong on the branches and made the muted colours of the buildings look even more distant and faded.

As Akkael followed the funnel of people down through the gates of Wu Wei, he saw a city preparing for war. Goutuizi rough-handled stall owners, telling them to dismantle their shops and leave the district. They hauled barrels of arrows up the steps and distributed swords and spears to the goutuizi stationed behind the gates.

"Bring the cannons," yelled a goutuizi on the walls.

Akkael looked up, raising one eyebrow. Pallets were being lifted onto the walls with rope. Akkael's new, near-sighted eyes couldn't distinguish what was on them, but it looked like a large steel drum. He saw a large aperture at one end and a wooden crank on the side. Akkael didn't know what he was looking at. He squinted to try and get more details of it, but then he was nearly knocked off his feet.

"Watch out, soldier," the sentinel bumping into him yelled. Akkael gained his footing quickly enough to see the weapon the goutuizi held. It was a strange wooden pole. Another much smaller aperture was at the top of it, and it widened towards the bottom. Metal fixtures decorated the weapon, but Akkael couldn't determine what it was for.

He wanted to take more time to look at what the goutuizi held, but Knarr began to snort, pulling on the reins balled in Akkael's fist.

"Whoa, stranger!" Someone approached Akkael. He was wearing sentinel's armour, with a sashimono on his back signalling him as a captain. His moustache cascaded loosely around his lips, and a helmet held tight under his arm, leaving his balding head open to the elements. "All horses need to be kept aside for the cavalry. Where are you stationed?"

Akkael looked at him like a deer in a hunter's sight. He pointed up to the volcano that Wu Wei was built on. "The palace," he managed to say.

The captain scoffed. "It's alright for some," he said, holding out his free hand. "I'll take the horse from here. We'll need all the help we can get after losing Koji's army, and now Chuton." He sighed, cutting himself off.

Akkael tried to stifle a smile. Skane, Magar, and Astrid had successfully taken Chuton. He tensed his jaw to hide his genuine feelings.

"Don't worry, soldier," said the balding guard, wrongly interpreting Akkael's tenseness. "Chuton is one thing. But Jin Bu will never fall."

Akkael tilted his head. "Jin Bu?"

The captain laughed again. "You really are new here. Just hand me the horse."

He handed the sentinel Knarr's reins, not wanting to talk to him any longer. After bowing to each other, they went their separate ways. The captain left towards the gate while Akkael made his way up the mountain and deeper into the city.

After a moment of walking, the crowd of refugees began to thin. The city still had a hustle as shopkeepers boarded their doors and windows, and others flooded into the old temples and schools to hide in bulk. The temples were in much better condition than the ones Akkael had seen in Tsul. Like the rest of the world, their religions were dead, and gods were forgotten.

Most traditions and rituals were gone, and the buildings were derelict. But the temples in Wu Wei, *Jin Bu*, or whatever they were calling the city now, were well kept. Akkael had heard that the sages lived in most of them, as well as the shadow archers. Some were turned into tourist sights, university lecture halls, or pubs. Akkael had seen the remnants of every culture's religion. Still, none had incorporated them into their modern societies like Edokand had.

The structures started to turn red as Akkael found his way to the richer districts of the city. Akkael could tell by the drainage at his feet, which led all the sewage to the poorer quarters. The buildings were higher, and bakeries and grocers' stalls turned into banks and restaurants. There were spaces reserved for parks, with benches and bright green grass that didn't seem natural on the side of a volcano.

Akkael took a detour through one of these parks. The blossoms hid in the tall blades of grass, and the trees were already growing fruit. The smell of petrichor and morning dew filled the air, and the gravel path sang with a satisfying crush under Akkael's feet.

But what drew Akkael to the opening were the lanterns. Lines of coloured paper lights hung waist height in front of him from large wooden frames. Each row was a different colour, like a rainbow, and the flames inside flickered, causing vibrant shadows to dance across the grass. Akkael knelt, the brightness encompassing his vision until all he could see were the lanterns swinging in the light breeze.

The lanterns led to a temple, to which the gravel path Akkael was walking also led. The temple was just as colourful. Red beams held the corrugated roof, with teal and yellow patterns climbing up the building like ivy. A wind chime hung from the door, a soft melody emanating as the air ran past. The temple roof was overhung and crested like wings, and stone statues of old forgotten gods stood in unkempt vigil outside.

Akkael crouched for a while, watching the layered lanterns flow in the wind like a gentle wave. He took a deep breath, closing his eyes for a moment as a strange calmness filled him. Akkael opened his eyes again, vision still overcome by the slow pendulum swing of the coloured lamps, his ears filled with the quiet moan of the wind and the wind chimes, drowning out the odd sounds of the war preparations at the bottom of the volcano city. He had a lot of questions about the sight in front of him, but they were overcome by the feeling of calm and peace he allowed himself to feel.

"Are you lost, sentinel?" Akkael clambered to his feet, his heart almost jumping from his chest. He turned to the source of the voice and saw a young man smiling in front of him. The purple robes gave him away as a sage, as did the kind smile and straight posture. His arms were hidden by his sleeves, and he wore a hood that his brown eyes were barely visible behind.

Akkael panicked. Sages had gifts that he didn't really understand. He knew they couldn't read minds, but they could read emotions, and he had no idea to what extent his emotions would give away his true purpose in Wu Wei.

"Sorry if I'm trespassing," said Akkael, trying to keep emotions out of his expression and voice. "Which way is the palace?"

The sage tilted his head, smiling even deeper. He pointed to the top of the mountain. "Up," he said. "It's a pretty straightforward city."

"Right," said Akkael, bowing his head.

"You're not trespassing, though," clarified the sage, turning to face the lamps. "Our lanterns are for everyone to enjoy and feel solace in their beauty."

Akkael turned back to the display. "What are they for?" he asked.

The sage sighed and bowed his head. "No one knows anymore. The traditions and festivities they were associated with died with our religions. Modern superstitions use them for good luck. We light them for good fortune, the health and safety of loved ones. That sort of thing."

Akkael felt the eyes of the sage turn towards him.

"This is your first time in the city." It wasn't a question but a statement.

"Yes," said Akkael rigidly.

The sage sighed. "I wish you had visited at a better time."

"So do I."

The sage squinted as if his gaze were burrowing into the side of Akkael's head. Akkael stepped back from the lanterns getting ready to make his way back down the path.

"I can sense you have a troubled mind," stated the sage, smiling widely, which Akkael's paranoid mind could only view as disingenuous. "There is a lot of grief and sadness in you. Is there anything I can do to help you?"

Akkael paused but eventually shook his head. "Not anymore."

The sage just snickered. "Cryptic. Most people are with sages. It's a strange juxtaposition. Our only function is to help people: the body and the mind. But whenever anyone sees our purple robes, they close up like a snail in its shell."

Akkael found the sage's tone sad, as if he viewed his life as a curse. Still, all Akkael could do was shrug. "Well, magic is an uncomfortable thought."

"Magic." The robed man scoffed. "More like superstition. It's strange, isn't it? The superstition that leads people to fear what we don't understand is the same that designed this in the pursuit of good luck." He gestured to the beautiful lantern display.

"We are hypocrites by nature."

The sage smiled and took a deep breath like he was taking in the fresh air of a new spring day. "That's a nice thought."

Akkael squinted and tilted his head. "Is it?"

"Of course," said the sage in a very matter-of-fact way. "A man who hates with every fibre of his being might still perform acts of kindness to the object of his ire. A woman who morally opposes someone will still wave in greeting."

"I don't think that's what hypocrite means," said Akkael, raising one eyebrow.

"Perhaps," shrugged the sage.

A breeze waved the lanterns and sent a song across the wind chimes. The flames in the paper lamps danced as they gently knocked against each other, a cloud's shadow clambering over the display. The murmurs of war at the foot of the mountain seemed so far away as if a fight wasn't imminent, the city wasn't about to be raided, and Akkael had time to stand still and let the peaceful scene wash over him.

There were thoughts he couldn't voice. Fears and plights the sage either wouldn't understand or would give away that Akkael was an imposter. He couldn't talk about people he missed or creatures he'd seen, or even the consistent torment of the curse Seradok had given him. However, there was one concern he didn't realise he had.

Akkael hadn't even expected to give it voice until it leaked out like a stream between rocks. "I have this strange feeling like I'm going to die today."

The sage turned to face Akkael, a stoic expression across his face. "That is a natural worry this close to war."

"I suppose," said Akkael. However, after a moment, he shook his head, something still giving credence to his intrusive thought. "No, I've been in a war before. This is different."

"Why do you think this way?" asked the robed man.

Akkael turned to face him and shrugged. He couldn't talk about the deal he made with a giant tentacle monster in the torture dungeon he had woken up in after he was killed. Sages are tolerant people, but even he would assume Akkael belonged in an asylum. He made a deal that he'd be given ample opportunity to exact his revenge. But once he'd gotten it and Hideo was a corpse at his feet, what happened then?

Akkael took a sharp breath, eyes stinging as he clenched his jaw. He turned away from the sage, facing the temple instead. Then, something caught Akkael's eye. A staggered breath leaked from a dropped jaw as he stared unblinking at the foot of the temple's steps, pointing at the objects that captured his attention.

"Those pots." They were typical clay jars, nothing too complex in their design except the streaks of yellow that ran across them like veins.

The sage followed Akkael's line of sight. "Ahh yes, pretty, aren't they? It's an old art form, mending broken ceramics with –"

"Gold." Akkael felt the phantom pain in his hand blossom again as he remembered his daughter. He recalled Alani holding her pot just before the mountains rose, explaining it how she explained everything that fascinated her, with unbridled wonder and a fierce command. "My daughter taught me about it. Even when everything seems irreparable, it can be made into something beautiful."

The sage folded his bottom lip and nodded. "I like that interpretation."

"Interpretation?" Akkael sounded almost defensive as if he were trivialising Alani in some way.

The sage continued to nod. "I've always seen it as something different," he said, still facing the pottery. "The jars were beautiful on their own, and there are many ways to seamlessly repair them. To me, it shows how we all eventually shatter. We can either hide our broken pieces or show the world what made us whole again."

Akkael thought about that, but the idea butted against his memory of Alani like reason and sense and all reminiscences had recently.

"But that only works if it breaks a certain way," scowled Akkael.

The sage turned to face him. "What do you mean?" He asked.

He gestured to the pots before continuing. "You could fix them with gold because the shards were big enough to stick together. The pieces still resembled the larger whole. But sometimes it's not like that. Sometimes things are so broken, so smashed and ground, that the only thing they resemble is ash."

The man in purple robes considered Akkael for a moment. He could feel him scrying his emotions like a beast ripping him open with claws to see what was inside.

"We can derive meanings from such simple things," replied the sage. "But our outlooks always harken to our hearts."

Akkael couldn't get Alani out of his head or the ache from his hand. "My daughter's heart was in everything she saw. When she would chase the birds, talk about a new thing she'd learnt, or find a giant's head in the side of a cliff where others would just see the stone."

"She sounds like a wonderful child," smiled the sage.

"She was," Akkael confirmed, watching the wind make the blades of grass dance at his feet.

"She's why you're in this city." Akkael looked up as the sage's face twisted into emotions Akkael couldn't read. There was confusion on his face. Maybe concern. Akkael watched the sage's appearance contort. Eventually, he spoke. "You don't belong here, do you?"

"I..." Akkael was stunned, his hand instinctively gripping the katana at his side. The wind seemed to have picked up. The wind chimes rang in a constant drone as the lanterns frantically pulled against the beams to which they were bound. Akkael watched the sage's face turn stoic as his arms wrapped across his torso, hiding in the sleeves of his robe.

Tension filled the air, and the two men stood still inside it for a while. Then a drum erupted from lower in the city, breaking the unblinking moment of tension. The sage's eyes followed the sound, as did Akkael, removing his hand from the sword. They were high on the mountain and could see beyond the city's walls, but the hill blocked the north. Still, Akkael had been in enough battles to know what that sound meant. The Solstic and Sekandans were approaching.

"Well, I suppose you better be going," said the sage, turning back to Akkael, who was still in shock. "If you're wrong and this is not the day you die, you are always welcome here. I would like to hear more of your story, though I doubt I would understand it. Goodbye, sentinel."

He emphasised the last word before turning around and slowly approaching the temple. Akkael was fixated on the back of the purple robes until the sage entered the building and was out of sight. He let out a long, laboured sigh, clenching his fist where he could feel the pain that Alani had left too long ago.

337

He looked up to the top of the volcano. The palace was tucked into the caldera, but he knew it was there, like a gem in the pommel of a sword. He steadied himself before walking back down the gravel path. Then, he followed the incline of the city, listening to the drums still beating at the bottom of the mountain that signalled the start of the battle.

[CHAPTER 52] — JIN BU

Astrid thought if it weren't for the army behind her and the empty farms that encircled the city walls, it would feel as if she were visiting Wu Wei as a tourist. The calmness in the air contrasted with the violence that was soon to come. The lack of goutuizi between her and the gate made her feel like she could stroll in unhindered. She had to really try to see the heads of the sentinels that lined the city walls, and, now the bells that announced their arrival had stopped, the stillness would placate the more naïve.

But Astrid knew what awaited her if she took one more step. Arrows and musket balls would rain down. Cannons would fire. A cavalry would charge from the gates, two hundred strong, and foot soldiers would follow closely behind them. Heiyang had told her what to expect and how each of the three-thousand sentinels was being utilised. She knew how much the soldiers behind the walls despised her people and knew there would be plenty of chances to redden her axe.

She clenched the Urkanzan dagger in her belt with one hand, tightened the grip on her round shield with the other, and smiled. "I've been waiting for this."

At that moment, Heiyang and the other shadow archers appeared next to Astrid. Moon was behind with the Sekandan line, so no one could translate what Heiyang was saying.

Luckily, Astrid was already aware of what Heiyang had been scouting.

"Where are the cannons on the walls?" she asked.

Astrid followed Heiyang's finger to the tops of both gatehouses.

She squinted. "I thought you said Wu Wei had five cannons," she said. "Where are the other three?"

Heiyang shrugged.

Something about that made Astrid's stomach sink, but she didn't let herself think too hard about it. "Okay. Muskets?"

The shadow lord pointed along the walls on either side of the gate.

"How many?" she asked.

She watched as Heiyang rapidly unfurled all ten of his fingers in quick succession. When he stopped, Astrid just stared at him, blinking rapidly.

"Helpful," she said sarcastically.

The shadow archer replied with a gesture that Astrid understood without knowing sign language.

Standing at Astrid's right with an axe and shield in her fists, Lindsay faced her. "Should we bring our cannons forward?" she asked.

Astrid turned around. The assault would be far more straightforward than the attack on Chuton. One force. One direction. The bulk of the army were the Solstic ready to charge the gates, with the Sekandan archers prepared to notch their arrows, as well as draw their geoms once the vanguard had reached the city. After that, it was Queen Kya and Rigpa's escort, led by Skane and Magar.

She thought through every step in her mind, ensuring she knew it by heart before turning to Lindsay and giving her the command. With that, Lindsay dove into the sea of barbarians excited for war, and the shadow archers teleported away. After a moment of shuffling, three platforms emerged along the Solstic front line.

On each platform sat a cannon with a rope threaded through a loop on the back. When the gun fired, the force of the shot would repel it backwards, so the rope restrained it. There was also a backstop on the platform so the weapon would rebound into place. The long, metal tube sat inside a wooden frame with four wheels made redundant by the platform.

Two barrels, one with a dozen steel balls, another filled with silk sacks stuffed with the strange explosive powder, were nailed to each stand, along with a box of tools that were also part of the contraption. Ropes hung off each platform. Astrid thought pulling these log pallets would be a lot easier and quicker than one person pushing the cannon by its shoddy wheels along the rugged terrain.

They were too far for the cannons to touch the gates, but that didn't stop the sentinels at the top of the wall frantically getting ready to attack.

"Shield walls around the cannons!" yelled Astrid as she raised her own and made her way in front of the closest platform just in time for the first barrage of arrows to fly from the walls. Most landed in the gap between them and Wu Wei, with the rest planting themselves into the shields.

In the interim, Astrid bent down and grabbed one of the ropes attached to the pallets, indicating those around her to do the same. Lindsay had again found her way to Astrid's side, holding her rope with her axe hand. Once Astrid and those in front of the cannons were ready to pull, and the subsequent flurry of arrows had landed in the dirt and shields, Astrid yelled her next command, the one she had been waiting to give since she began preparing for this battle.

"Charge!"

It was less of a charge and more of a quickened hobble, as the cannons were heavier than she predicted. As soon as they began moving, Astrid heard the eruption of musket fire echo along the open terrain. Shields shattered as men and women began to fall around her.

She knew the reload time was high with the muskets, so she strained herself to pull the platform faster as arrows descended from the city's walls. She only slowed when an arrow dove into her shield, and the head pierced through until it was an inch from her nose. But she didn't let it halt her for long, gritting her teeth and continuing to march towards the city.

Astrid didn't have another narrow escape for the subsequent few arrow storms and musket barrages. The Sekandan archers did an excellent job of slowing the pattern of the Edokand'i assault, and the enemy was aiming above the front line to stop those actively attacking them. Astrid was beginning to believe it would be an easy walk into position. Then she tumbled into the pockmarked ground.

She quickly got to her feet, holding up her shield just in time to catch another arrow. She knew what the holes in the ground meant. There were fewer outside Wu Wei than at Chuton, but they still meant the same thing; they were now in range of the cannons.

The cannons on top of the gatehouses had a higher elevation, so Astrid knew she had more to go before they could bring down the walls. She heard the first explosions from atop the towers and watched as dirt and blood shot above the heads

341

to her left. Another cannonball hit her right, and she heard a quiet thud hit the platform behind her. Astrid turned around and saw a bloody, severed arm wrapped around the barrel of metal balls.

Trying not to overthink the carnage around her, she quickly resumed pulling. She peeked over the steel brim of her shield just in time to watch a goutuizi fall from the crenellated top of the gatehouse. Astrid smiled. The cannons would already have been loaded before the Solstic began their charge, so there would have been no way to avoid the first attack. Like the attack on Chuton, the shadow archers used the first shots as their signal to teleport up and attack.

Astrid kept her eyes on the towers; the only signs of struggle she could see were the occasional tufts of smoke that signalled the shadow archers' appearances. Then, Astrid felt her shield get yanked upwards just in time to stop another arrow's descent towards her. She followed the arm gripping the bottom of her shield and saw Lindsay staring wide-eyed at her. Astrid winked at her in thanks.

When the Solstic were past the shallow craters, Astrid indicated for those around her to stop pulling. She considered the distance between the cannons they were lugging and the walls of Wu Wei and nodded to herself.

"We're close enough!" she bellowed to anyone who could hear her. "Get the cannons ready."

Astrid jumped onto the platform. She had spent the last few days practising with the cannons and trying to understand the weapon's range. Though, Astrid didn't feel confident as she got into position. After she kicked the severed arm to the side, she dragged the cannon until its barrel was aligned with the city's gates.

Lindsay got onto the platform as well. She reached for the barrel containing the bundles of silk-wrapped powder, taking one before placing it inside the cannon's aperture. Astrid then knelt to open the box of tools at her feet. She retrieved a large, thin rod from the crate and thrust it into a small hole at the top of the weapon. She felt each blow pierce the silk sack inside as Lindsay hoisted a metal ball into the mouth of the iron tube.

A thin wick was placed into the same hole as the poker, and Astrid got off the platform just in time for a musket shot to sink into the log where she stood.

The cannon to her left fired first, biting through a chunk of the parapet. Astrid retrieved the last tools from the box. She pulled out a pole with a thick rope entangled around it with one hand, gripping the flint and steel next to it with the other. Hunched over with the rod clenched between her thighs, she grated the flint against the steel to try and light the rope.

"Shields!" someone yelled near her. Astrid quickly moved the lighters into one hand before retrieving her shield, still leaving her axe in the dirt. Nothing hit her as arrows rained down. She threw her shield to the side and began trying to light the rope again. The cannon to her right fired, but it fell short of the walls. Then there was another explosion to her left, the cannonball blasting a hole in one of the gatehouses.

Astrid growled, kneeling in the dirt as she frantically tried to light the rope. Musket shots began peppering the frontline again. Astrid didn't even look up as those around her fell. She beat the flint against the steel, rock chips flying with the sparks.

"Ahh, fuck it!" Astrid screamed. She stood up as another barrage of arrows fell. She returned to the platform and tried to light the wick inside the cannon. It caught fire almost immediately.

However, Astrid was the first to realise the importance of the rod. The flame ran down the wick so fast she barely saw it move. The platform lifted like a ship over a storm's wave as the cannon emitted a deafening eruption. It recoiled into Astrid's chest, and she was repelled back, tripping over the backboard of the platform and landing with the buckle of her shield digging into her side.

Astrid inhaled so hard she thought her eye might bust out of its socket. Her vision was blurred, and a sharp pain ripped across her chest.

An arm wrapped around her shoulders as Lindsay's face burst through the miasma of hazy colours and darkening peripherals. She had broken a few ribs, she thought, which was the only thought she was able to have since the blast. She didn't

343

know how long she had been lying there or why fuzzy figures were dashing past her until Lindsay's voice began to come into focus through the ringing in her ear.

"You did it," she said like an echo at the end of a tunnel. "The gate is down."

Astrid tilted her head towards Wu Wei, but her vision was blocked by countless Solstic figures dashing towards the volcano.

"Can you stand?" asked Lindsay.

Astrid didn't realise she was seeing double until her vision began to focus. She let Lindsay help her to her feet. Wu Wei's gate was still blocked by the Solstic men and women pouring in front of her, but she could see the Edokand'i on horseback. Astrid grinned; the battle had well and truly begun.

A sharp pain still tore through Astrid's chest and side. She gently pulled away from Lindsay's grip, ensuring she was stable before turning to face her. Lindsay smiled, bending to retrieve Astrid's shield and axe. Astrid felt for her Urkanzan dagger, checking if it was still secure in her belt. It was.

The muskets exploded across the parapets. "Ready when you are?" said Lindsay, the two women smiling at each other as the influx of warriors began to thin.

Then, Astrid heard a sound like a bird taking flight. It sliced through the wind with a flutter until it stopped, an arrow digging itself through Astrid's shoulder. Astrid growled in pain as she collapsed to her knees. Her eyes cocked at the tip of the arrow protruding from the top of her breast.

Her axe and shield had been expelled from her hands again, so she brought the dagger from its sheath. With one clean cut, she severed the tip from the shaft before reaching behind her and pulling the rest of the arrow out of her back. She looked down at the blood-streaked stick and snapped it with a balled fist.

The shock and adrenaline drained out of her, but the pain across Astrid's torso was ever-present and overwhelming. However, when she turned back around, something made her forget her pains almost entirely.

Lindsay was kneeling on the ground, hands cupped as blood leaked through the gaps in her fingers. An arrow was lodged in her neck, a red feather on one side and a red tip on the other. Astrid rushed to her friend's side, wrapping her arms around Lindsay and reclining her in her lap.

Lindsay's eyes were wide with fear as she tried to push Astrid away. It was as if she thought Astrid was preventing her from saving herself. She could survive if she could pool enough of her blood in her hands. Astrid had seen it before. The desperation of someone about to die abandons reason or sense. There were no shame, pride, or gods to impress. Just a desperate urge to keep herself alive.

Lindsay wriggled in Astrid's arms as she got weaker and weaker. Eventually, she was still, her eyes rolled back, and her chest stopped heaving. Astrid held back the water in her eyes, leaning over to kiss Lindsay's forehead. She gently placed Lindsay's body on the ground and wiped as much blood as possible from her drenched leather slacks.

Staggering, she looked down at her shield resting in the trodden grass. She didn't have the strength to bend over and pick them up, and the hole in her shoulder meant she couldn't lift anything with that arm anyway. She still had her dagger clenched in her other fist, which was enough.

Astrid sprinted down the battlefield, over Lindsay, past the cannon's platform and towards the chaos of war. The pain was excruciating, but she ran through it, passing some of the Solstic warriors in the last file. Tears poured down her face, and she bit hard inside her mouth to distract herself with the taste of blood.

The battlefield was hectic by the time Astrid joined the fray. Any semblance of the structure had been abandoned as soldiers from different armies swirled together, only differentiated by the uniform red armour of the Edokand'i. The goutuizi infantry had joined the fight, outnumbering their mounted counterparts nearly ten to one.

The closest enemy to Astrid was a mounted soldier, red armour gleaming in the sunlight. A mound of corpses lay in front of the horse rider. Astrid vaulted off the bodies with laboured breaths and blinding pain, leaping at the sentinel and tackling him off his horse. Astrid's dagger had already found a chink in his armour before they landed on the other side of the mare. The blade had pierced his lung, and he writhed in the dirt, sodden with blood.

It took Astrid a moment to muster enough strength to lift herself from the ground. When she managed it, she noticed another cavalryman riding towards her, sword aloft. She didn't have time to wonder if the fall had broken another rib or if it had lacerated any of her organs.

She leant over, pulling the Urkanzan blade out of the first sentinel before getting to her feet. She considered the enemy riding towards her.

Akkael was much better at throwing daggers and axes than Astrid, but she didn't have much choice. She lined up her shot, trying to time it with the bouncing of the horse's head. Then, she let go. The dagger flew into the sentinel, and he went slack, dropping his grip on the reins and his katana.

Astrid stepped aside, waiting for the horse. Before the dead sentinel had time to fall, Astrid gripped the steed's reins, put her foot into the stirrup and lifted herself onto its back. She removed the dagger from the goutuizi's face and flung him from the saddle, placing herself in the seat.

She saw the whole battle from atop the horse. Solstic warriors pulled terrified sentinels off their horses as others held the Edokand'i infantry at bay. Corpses decorated the field. They were mostly of her army, but red armoured bodies were in no small figures. The Sekandans at the back were still firing arrows at the walls, and the goutuizi were firing back. Astrid watched as the shadow archers teleported along the parapets, murdering anyone holding a musket.

The stench of death filled her nostrils as she gripped her aching chest. All she could hear were explosions, singing weapons, and death rattles. Astrid turned her horse towards Wu Wei, and, for the first time, she saw a hole where the city gates should be. Wood lay shattered and splintered in the tunnel to the city, Solstic warriors already lining the entrance.

Astrid thought of all the people she was fighting for and all the pain and hurt that would end today. She thought of Lindsay, dead behind her. Doran, trapped in time. She remembered what Akkael looked like before his curse. Handsome and strong and, although she rarely remembered it, he had the face of the man she loved. She gritted her teeth and cursed whatever took it away from her.

Lastly, but the one that hurt the most, was Alani. She didn't know her daughter was dead until sometime after. She was in Skaldgard, imagining holding her, dreaming of her smile, and waiting for her to come back and chase the birds. It seemed like so long ago.

The sentinels sent out to stop them were already depleting, and many warriors flooded the city. Astrid didn't speak. She didn't yell a command or dedicate her fight to anyone she'd lost. She just spurred on her horse and, with Alani in her mind, galloped towards Wu Wei.

[CHAPTER 53] — THE ESCORT

Skane could still hear the cacophony of war, but it was further away. He couldn't see the walls of Wu Wei, just the tip of the volcano. At first, Skane was basing his knowledge of the battle on the slowing musket shots, the dying cannon blasts, and the quieting battle cries. The Sekandan archers used to be in view, and Skane saw them as another milestone in the fight's progress.

The Sekandans had charged towards the city, which meant the Solstic had already breached the walls. It also meant that the battle was in their favour, for if it looked like they were losing, the Sekandans would be retreating, and Skane would be dead. He looked at Queen Kya, hoping his face didn't show paranoia.

The escort group comprised Queen Kya, Rigpa, Kwan, Skane, and Magar. There were also half a dozen sages, all encircled by female warriors, split evenly between Sekandans and shield maidens. Everyone was silent for different reasons. The warriors were paid to be so, and Kwan was in quiet contemplation of the effectiveness of her strategy. Kya was as cold as they had always been in the presence of any Northman that wasn't Astrid. Their eyes had been fixed on the top of Wu Wei from the onset of the fight, and they never wavered. Rigpa could feel the pain and building angst in those around her and probably thought it best not to speak. As for Skane and Magar, they remained still for the same reason: Doran.

Skane still couldn't believe Doran was alive. It had been a fact that Doran had been dead since the mountains rose. Many decisions that had been made since were based on the unequivocal knowledge that the Solstic King had been killed during peace talks. Skane hadn't even entertained the idea his friend might still be alive. It made peace possible. It made war worth it. It made...

Skane turned to Magar and sighed. None of the thoughts floating in Skane's head meant anything to Magar. He just wanted his brother to not be dead again. Skane placed his hand on his back. He used a crutch to walk, and bandages still concealed his healing wounds.

"We'll save him. Don't worry," said Skane.

Magar gave Skane a half smile but remained silent. After a shared glance, Skane peeled away. The perimeter of warriors gave those inside fair room to walk around and for a few Sekandan flags to be erected. Skane felt remised by not bringing one of Doran's new banners with him to Trim. The three black snowflakes on the white cloth might have been nice for Doran to see, after being trapped in time.

He paced across the patch of open grass, playing with the loose pauldron on his left shoulder. He tried to tighten the straps behind him but couldn't reach them. Instead, he would just readjust it whenever it had descended his arm.

After a moment of aimless pacing, Skane gravitated toward Rigpa, as he had been doing a lot lately. She sat on the ground, her purple rope getting grass stained under her folded legs. As soon as she noticed him approach, the old woman smiled.

Skane hadn't thought of a reason to come over to the Grand Sage, so he tried to make one up. "How does it feel out there?" he asked.

"The last of the Sekandans are making their way into the city," she said, scrying the earth under her feet.

"Okay, good," nodded Skane. He was still impressed by the gifts of the sages. A lone magpie flew overhead, which was louder than the remaining signs of battle Skane could detect. "Is Moon on her way?"

Rigpa searched again. "I can't feel anyone coming towards us yet."

Skane breathed in sharply through his nose. "Even if the last warriors get past the walls, we don't move until Moon arrives. We'll do this right and slowly."

"I know." Rigpa stood up as Skane adjusted the pauldron again. "Is your armour loose?"

Skane sighed. "Just this strap. It keeps rocking, and I can't reach it."

"Do you want me to help?"

Skane paused for a moment before shrugging. "If you don't mind."

Rigpa walked out of her circle of sages, each one donning a panicked expression they tried to hide. Skane turned around, allowing the Grand Sage to pull the strap on his shoulder. She had not bothered to retreat behind her disciples once she was finished.

"Thanks," said Skane, testing the fastening of the pauldron.

"You're welcome," said the sage with a bow.

Skane began to turn back towards Magar before Rigpa spoke again.

"I was scared."

The statement caught Skane off guard. He glanced over his shoulder, squinting at the sage. "Excuse me?"

Rigpa took a deep breath before clarifying what she meant. "As Grand Sage, I try to abandon prejudice. But I'm old, and some of my ways are too."

Skane had adjusted his stance until he was again facing the old woman, whose gaze was brushing across the grass at her feet.

"When I first arrived at your camp, I thought my heartbeat was loud enough to hear," she continued. "Then I was imprisoned, threatened, and told I would die. To my shame, I wondered if the Northmen were as brutal and villainous as the stories suggested. But then I met you. You taught me the truth I had almost forgotten."

Skane breathed out a chuckle. "What truth?"

"That everyone is the same," she shrugged. "Everyone is human and deserves the benefit of the doubt. I'm telling you this because I think you need to hear it. You're a good person, Skane, and I'm thankful to whatever gods or fates truly exist that I was able to meet you."

"You're talking like this is the last time we'll ever see each other," said Skane, tilting his head.

Rigpa looked up from her feet and stared at Skane. The following silence was only broken by the wind rustling in the flags above them. He didn't know why, but his eyes began to sting.

Eventually, the old woman's lips curled like Skane had often seen them do. "Who knows what the future has in store for us," said Rigpa quietly.

Skane tapped Rigpa on the shoulder, sharing her smile when he heard Kya scoffing over their shoulder. Skane turned to watch them walk further out of earshot,

Kwan following them closely. He shook his head. Wars always end, but those who carry the ire off the battlefield allow conflict to fester. The Queen had every reason for their hatred and anger to have developed; he just hoped they found a way to come to terms with the pain and loss inside them.

Once that thought faded, he snickered, mocking himself for thinking like a sage.

Suddenly a plume of black smoke, as clear as a brick wall in the light of the cloudless day, materialised in the centre of their sentried space. Everyone in the circle turned to face it in anticipation just as Heiyang appeared. His crimson leathers did well to hide the blood beginning to dry on his clothes, but the red above his face mask was stark against his skin.

Heiyang faced Queen Kya and began to sign. He held out an index finger, moving his other hand away from it as he balled it into a fist. Then he moved the same finger across his body, stalling it at four intervals, before taking an outstretched palm and swinging it over his shoulder.

It was clear from everybody's expression that no one knew what he meant.

Kya, with an eyebrow raised, addressed the shadow lord. "We don't understand. Where is Moon? Has she fallen?" They spoke slowly like they would to a child, which made the shade's eye twitch.

Heiyang waved his hand horizontally away from his body, which Skane recognised as the sign for "no." He then paused before repeating the same motions as last time, but slower, head tilting to display a patronising tone and placing more emphasis on the last sign.

Skane was convinced everyone had blinked in unison, still utterly ignorant of what Heiyang was trying to say.

Eventually, the shadow archer threw his hands in the air and rolled his eyes. Skane was partially relieved he at least knew what that meant. Heiyang then disappeared, leaving the escort group even more confused than when he was trying to communicate.

351

When he returned, he was gripping Moon tightly in his arms. Moon was covered in less blood than Heiyang, but her blue armour was less adept at hiding it. As soon as she appeared, her geom fell from her fingers. She broke the shadow archer's grip just in time to turn, hunch, and vomit over her boots. She heaved three times as Skane watched with a slack jaw.

Moon wiped her mouth on her gauntlet when she was done before returning to Heiyang. "Don't ever do that to me again!" she yelled, her flushed cheeks the only colour on her pale face.

Heiyang signed, emphatically pointing at the dumbfounded faces surrounding them.

"Well, if you had told me that, I could have written something down for you," said Moon, her voice still raised.

Heiyang mimed writing with a pen before waving his hand across the air.

"Oh, I see," said an exasperated Moon. "So, you can teleport me two miles, but you can't just go find me a pen."

The shadow archer thought for a moment before he shrugged and nodded. Moon turned away, gobbing yellow spit on the ground before she turned to Queen Kya and bowed as if she could regain her decorum.

"Your Majesty," Moon began, "the lower precinct of the city is secure. It's time for the escort mission to move on."

Skane felt a jolt of anxiety course through his body. The plan was objectively absurd. They had lain waste to the Emperor's city, killed his men, destroyed vital architecture, only to turn up in his house, tell him he had been frozen in time, detail all the devastating ways his country had changed, then ask him to continue negotiations with the enemy he was surrounded by. And the notion that the face of the Grand Sage and Queen Kya, two people with no overt loyalty to his throne and one whose very title is an act of defiance against his empire, will somehow ease him into compliance.

Skane rubbed his forehead as Kya gave orders. "Kwan, lead the procession. Moon, you stay by our side as we march into the city. Heiyang, return to the battle and-"

Before Kya finished speaking, the shadow archer teleported away. Moon retrieved her geom with a shaking hand as Skane returned to Magar's side. The sages moved around Rigpa again, and when everyone was in position, Kwan yelled marching orders from the front. The Sekandans walked in time to her commands while the shield maidens walked casually beside them. As the rear of the all-around defence got awkwardly close, those inside the perimeter began to move.

Skane still stressed about all the minutia of the mammoth task ahead. Accusing the Second Pillar of Edokand of high treason and telling the Emperor how mountains rose from the sea. Explaining how a vast army led by Koji travelled to Tsul without his knowledge and was wiped out by Akkael Torne, who had gained the power of possession.

He knew he probably shouldn't start with Akkael, but where else? The dragon, or what the dragon had said about gods and magic? The volcano at Koseki or the weapons at Chuton? Are Akkael or Hideo's magic powers more palatable to someone completely ignorant of any such thing?

"It was your idea," said Magar. Skane took a sharp breath, startled by his husband's sudden ability to seemingly read minds.

"I... I know," he stuttered.

"Then it'll work." Magar had two arms clutching his giant crutch as the massive sword on his back flapped like a flag. Skane had tried convincing Magar to bring a lighter weapon, but it was useless.

Skane looked at him under a furrowed brow. "What do you mean?"

Magar shrugged, keeping pace with the rest of the convoy despite his injuries. "Your plans work. I've never heard one that didn't."

A smile broke onto Skane's face as he stared at Magar's profile. He leaned in to kiss Magar's cheek but missed and landed on his ear. Magar recoiled at the wet sound of it, but he carried a grin for a while after.

353

Skane couldn't see over the heads of the women in front, but two things told him he was getting close to the city. First was the view. He started seeing the poorer districts' turquoise and teal clash with the reds and golds higher up the mountain. Also, instead of just seeing a blur of indefinable buildings, he could differentiate between some temples, shops, inns, and apartments as he got closer to Wu Wei.

Second was the corpses. Solstic men and women lay with arrows in their chests, bullet holes in their heads, and axes as dry as when they were forged. Skane couldn't help but sneer at the back of Queen Kya's head. He knew it wasn't their fault. He knew that, given a chance, they would make things go differently. But, as he stepped over those he had sailed to Edokand with and fought beside for four years, he couldn't help noticing none of the dead donned the blue armour of Sekando. They waited until it was safe. They waited until it was convenient. They waited until everyone who was going to die had done so already. Skane forced the scowl off his face.

As they approached the city walls, everyone was on high alert. Skane could hear Solstic voices on top of the wall and saw the glint of blue armour from further away. He knew they had secured the walls of Wu Wei, but he was still nervous. The city's gates lay in a splintered mess at their feet as the escort's formation shifted to fit through the arch. Stone as smooth and silver as steel surrounded them on all sides before they left the tunnel and entered the city.

The smell of muskets and cannons filled the air as the Edokand'i and Solstic dead were scattered across the cobbled ground. Crows were already landing in the streets with curiosity and perching on the roofs of the teal apartments and shops. The guttering that filtered waste from the top of Wu Wei to the poorer bottom was red. Weapons and body parts blocked the drainage, causing blood to slither through the cracks in the paving. The walls were stained, and corpses lined the route.

"Something is wrong." Skane turned to see Rigpa frozen in the street, eyes unfocused. All those within earshot stopped too.

354

The female warriors that surrounded them continued to march to Kwan's commands.

"Halt!" screamed Skane, waiting for Kwan to repeat his order and for the procession to stop.

Queen Kya turned with fury in their eyes. "What is the meaning of this!" they barked before noticing the Grand Sage still behind them.

"The army hasn't made their way into the caldera," said Rigpa. "Something is delaying them."

"What?" asked Skane.

"I don't know, I can't see that far."

"Is something wrong?" yelled one of the Solstic men from atop the wall, their Sekandan counterparts standing in dutiful silence.

Skane thought for a moment as those around him whispered concerns and ideas.

"Hello," said the same Solstic man. He was strong looking, with blue writing tattooed by his eye and war paint on the sides of his head that stretched behind his ears. "Can anyone hear me?"

"Moon," said Skane, turning to face her as she stood in front of the Queen. "Do you know your way around this city?"

Moon's face twisted as she shrugged. "I mean, I know the palace is up."

"Oh, that's just great," bellowed the Solstic warrior. "The ones in charge ignoring the voice of the common foot soldier."

Skane tried his best to tune out the man on the wall. "Okay, Moon, pick twenty of your soldiers. I'll pick twenty shield maidens, and we'll go ahead to see what's happening."

"I'm going too," said Magar, adjusting his grip on his crutch.

"No, you're not." Skane saw the desperate look in Magar's eyes and placed his hand on his giant shoulder. "You'll slow us down. We'll see what's going on and come straight back."

Magar stared at Skane for a while before grunting, which Skane knew was his way of conceding.

"You know, I got a stitch while charging the gates." The man on the wall was rubbing his side with his bloodied axe. "I know it doesn't sound like much, but if I knew-"

"Oh, shut up," yelled Skane, turning sharply towards the parapet.

"Did you see that," he said to no one beside him. "Silenced by the aristocracy." The warrior then proceeded to give a bow imbued with sarcasm. "Yes, my liege. Right away, my liege."

Skane rolled his eyes and turned his back to the burly man on the wall. "Come on, Moon."

Skane and Moon chose twenty warriors each and separated from the escort group. He looked over his shoulder just as Sekandan soldiers moved between him and Magar. Their eyes met momentarily before his vision was entirely blocked by blue armour.

He faced ahead again, moving to the front of the small group. Then he led the way through Wu Wei and up the volcano.

[CHAPTER 54] — AKKAEL AND HIDEO

Hideo stood on the palace's balcony, looking out at the courtyard and wringing the grip of his katana as the cold wind sliced at his face. He couldn't see the battle over the lip of the caldera but could hear the screaming and fighting carried on the air. It wasn't long ago that Hideo had stood on the same balcony where he renamed the city and declared the scourge of the Northmen over. Dead politicians that had protested his rule were now hanging from the palace walls, staining the stone with blood.

He wondered what the people were thinking. All the things he had done in the promise of ridding them of Doran's invaders seem futile now. He sighed as his eyes lowered to the railing he was leaning against. He needed to decisively repel the marauders at the gates, or his legacy would be thrown to the dirt.

After that thought, he heard footsteps behind him. He turned slightly and saw Ponzu in his peripheral. Hideo sighed again.

"My gracious Lord," said Ponzu, causing Hideo to grind his iron hand against the balcony.

"What is it?" asked Hideo. It was a while before Hideo realised he wasn't listening to a word Ponzu was saying, his voice quickly drowning into the back of his mind like the metronome ticking.

"…If, of course, it would please your lordship." Hideo managed to catch the end of what his servant was saying. He considered a vague response to make it seem like he had listened.

"Of course, whatever is required," said Hideo, hoping that would suffice.

"Excellent judgement, my lord," said Ponzu before bowing. "I'll send him in now."

Hideo's eyes widened as he reached out instinctively to stop Ponzu. But it was too late. Hideo clamped his eyes shut, regretting whatever he agreed to.

After a moment, two men walked onto the balcony. Hideo didn't know their names, assuming Ponzu had told him while he was tuning him out. He could say to

357

the man on the left was a captain, judging by the décor of his armour and the straps on his back to hold a sashimono. The second was a sentinel with no rank or title Hideo could gleam.

The two men bowed before the captain opened his mouth. "Lord Hideo," he said, "the Northmen-"

Ponzu jogged to Hideo's side, distracting the captain from what he would say. "You are in the presence of Lord Hideo Kazar," he said, panting. "The Iron hand of Wu Wei, general of the sentinel guard, and Second Pillar of Edokand."

Hideo vividly imagined throwing Ponzu from the balcony but fought the urge. The captain stared at Ponzu and blinked rapidly before returning to Hideo and starting again. "Lord Hideo, the Northmen have reached the upper quarter of the city."

Hideo's heart sank into his stomach as he shook his head and sighed. "How has it come to this?"

The captain spoke stoically; no panic or stress could be heard in his voice. "They brought the cannons from Chuton and obliterated the gates. I have ordered the second wave of our cannons to be moved on the palace wall, but we will not fire into the city unless there is no other choice, my Lord."

He turned his back to the captain, looking down at the courtyard as his heartbeat rose. "Why didn't you destroy their cannons before they got in range?"

"They have shadow archers, my Lord," said the captain. "Our men were picked off one by one."

Hideo collapsed his head into his hands, thinking of the three shadow archers that survived Ieyasu's attack on their temple. He wanted them all dead for what happened to his son, and now they were showing their true traitorous colours. He blamed Ieyasu for letting them live and his sister for betraying him. He blamed the shadow archers for starting this cycle of treachery, and he blamed his son for dying.

"Oh, come on," said a voice in Hideo's head. "There is only one person to blame for all of this. *You.*"

Hideo's breath was sharp. He tried to eject that voice from his head, thinking about everything he had done to serve his country. He did everything to free his people from those who wanted to steal their land. He was their hero.

"I'm sure that will still be the case," said the voice, "once you start firing cannons into the city."

"No," Hideo said aloud.

"My Lord," said Ponzu, panic in his voice.

He remained silent, back still to the captain and the sentinel. Hideo had wanted to defeat the Northmen fairly. He wanted history to discuss how the Edokand'i army overwhelmed the barbarians and cast them into the sea. But they flooded the city, and Hideo knew vanity was the only thing delaying him from using Seradok's gift. To save the city, he needed the metronome.

He turned around. "Captain, sentinel, escort me to my chambers."

Hideo barged past them, leaving Ponzu on the balcony alone. He walked through the palace, allowing the rattling of the armour to distract him from his thoughts. He took a slow, meticulous breath, his heartbeat so fast it was as if he were sprinting through the halls. His eyes felt heavy when he remembered how little he had slept as he marched towards his chambers.

He was only one corridor away from his quarters before he heard something that stopped him in his tracks. "Hideo!" someone bellowed from the other side of the hall.

Hideo squinted. After a moment's delay, he turned to see where the yell had come from. At the other end of the corridor was a sentinel. He was a little portly, and his armour was poorly kept, with more dirt than enamel in the trimming.

Hideo turned, facing the stranger. The two sentinels on either side of him followed suit.

"Can I help you?" Hideo asked.

The stranger just smiled. It was a horrifying grin, thin like a cut and similar to Seradok's. Hideo's jaw dropped a little as the sentinel on the other end of the corridor drew the katana at his hip and began slowly walking towards him. He let the sword grate against the stone floor, sparks jumping as the grinding sound took all the air from Hideo's lungs.

He backed behind the two men guarding him as they drew their swords. Hideo didn't take his eyes off the stranger, still grinning, still dragging his sword behind him, slowly approaching.

"Stop, or you will be executed," said Hideo, the sound of cannons and muskets erupting outside the palace.

As he got into fighting range, the captain and the sentinel protecting Hideo raised their blades. However, the man paid them no mind, all his attention fixed on Hideo. The Iron Hand of Wu Wei retreated further behind his protectors as the lone sentinel got closer.

The captain held out his sword until the tip was barely a foot from the stranger. As the sword was raised to his face, the sentinel flinched, stopping as he went cock-eyed and glowered at the katana's tip.

"Move one more step. You will lose your head," threatened the captain.

The stranger's grin got wider and thinner. He stepped towards the captain, now so close that the tip of the sword pushed into the man's cheek. After calling his bluff, the captain had no choice but to engage. He moved into a striking stance before arching his blade towards the lone sentinel. The stranger made no attempt to block or dodge the attack. He just smiled as the katana sliced straight through his neck.

Hideo watched as his head smacked against the stone slabs, followed by his knees and the rest of his corpse.

He stared at the body in front of him, shaking his head as he tried to comprehend what had happened. He looked up at the captain. "Thank you, my-"

Hideo looked up just in time to see the captain's sword swinging towards him. He managed to collapse to the ground as the blade glided above him, planting into the wood of the wall opposite.

"Captain?" yelled the other sentinel escorting Hideo to his chambers. As the captain freed his blade from the wall, he marched towards Hideo, paying the sentinel no mind. Hideo crawled away, panting, sweat beading down his face as his eyes fixed on the captain, who was grinning just like the stranger had been.

He pinned Hideo down with his foot, causing his head to smack against the floor. Hideo's eyes clenched closed from the impact. When he opened them again, he saw the katana hanging above him like a stalactite. Hideo raised his iron hand in front of his face as he anticipated his own death. He stayed like that momentarily before hearing metal slicing through flesh.

When Hideo looked up, he saw the captain, sword still aloft, with another blade protruding from his mouth. His sword collapsed to the floor, followed by his body, revealing the young sentinel behind him, katana red from the captain's blood.

Hideo rose to his feet, hyperventilating as he stared unblinking at the sentinel, looking down at the corpse he just made.

"Soldier?" Hideo whispered.

After Hideo spoke, the sentinel rose his head, meeting his eye. He didn't speak or move an inch. All the sentinel did was stare at Hideo as his lips slowly curved into a smirk.

Hideo's heart skipped a beat. Without another word, he turned and sprinted down the corridor, feeling the Seradok-like grin burrowing into the back of his head. When he turned the corner, he saw the door to his chambers across the hallway, as well as seven house guards, one on either side of his door and five lining the walls. All their heads turned towards him as he came into view.

"Assassin," yelled Hideo, still running as he pointed in the direction he had come from. "Protect me."

Part of Hideo was disgusted by his cowardice. He had seen war and killed many that had attempted to kill him. He didn't know why, but the casual walk adopted by everyone who had tried to kill him, the lack of fear in the face of their own deaths, and the smile passed to each assailant were worse than any horde or army he had faced. Hideo was ashamed of how spineless he turned out to be in the face of things he didn't understand, but after everything that had happened to him, it didn't come as a shock.

The guards held their spears out as the sentinel turned the corner. Hideo's breath ran out of him. He didn't understand what was happening. It was as if the man who first attacked them possessed the captain and now the soldier. But how?

The first kill was made by his aggressor. His sword drove under the armour and into the gut of the closest guard. Then, the young sentinel who seemed kind and naïve, the one who was suddenly on a path to kill Hideo, was speared in the leg by a guard behind him. He collapsed to his knees, sharp breaths grating across his tongue. The guard pulled his spear out of the sentinel's leg just as another man approached, spear also clenched in his fist.

Hideo's heartbeat rose as his eyes shot wide. "Wait, don't kill him!"

By the time the words left his lips, it was too late. The second spearman drove his weapon into the neck of the possessed sentinel until the tip pierced his heart.

Hideo watched speechless as the guard retrieved the sentinel's blade, pulled it back, and drove it into the eye of the man who assisted in the kill. Confused, the other guards looked on as the man who had been on guard shift with them began to attack.

He made short work of the first guard he reached, barely able to move his weapon before his throat was sliced by the katana. Then the possessed guard move to kill the next man closest to him. He swung his weapon without the training or discipline expected of a soldier of Edokand. He chopped and sliced with the untamed ferocity of a Northman, with no structure or beauty in how he moved.

The spearman dodged the first few strikes, but the attacks were too quick, close, and wild. Eventually, he was a corpse. Leaving only Hideo and the two guards nearest to his bedroom door.

Hideo didn't delay. He turned and ran toward his chambers, beckoning for the guards outside his door to open it. They pushed the double doors open, and Hideo didn't slow down until he was in his room. He retrieved his door key from the pouch of his armour and began pushing the door closed with one of the two remaining guards, the enemy hurrying forwards.

Just as the heavy doors were about to close, Hideo felt an air current blow past him. The second surviving guard had launched a spear through the aperture of the door at the pursuer. "No!" screamed Hideo as the doors closed with a thud.

He peeked through the keyhole. The guard that was chasing them was lying on his back. The spear was in his chest, and there was a rattling in his throat as air struggled to get passed the blood.

"What's your name?" the guard, still holding his weapon, asked his friend.

"What?" squinted the spear-thrower.

"You saw what we saw," said Hideo, still looking through the keyhole. "Answer his questions."

The guard gulped. "Jun-ho. My name is Jun-ho. Dae-sun, I was the best man at your wedding."

The one still with the spear was frozen, holding his weapon against a man he knew very well in case he wasn't him. It was a strange situation, but the paranoia was heightened each moment they were confused.

"What's my husband's name?" Dae-sun asked.

"Do-hyon," answered Jun-ho.

The guard lowered his spear, breathing a sigh of relief. However, Hideo wasn't convinced, watching the last breaths of the guard, who killed the sentinel, who killed the captain, who killed the assailant. Blood was still sputtering from his lips, and his chest was convulsing. Hideo stared through the keyhole. He could swear that grin was still sliced across his face until his life had withdrawn from him.

Hideo turned slowly. The guard, without a spear, entered Hideo's peripheral vision just in time to watch him trip his friend to the floor. The downed soldier tried to lift his spear at Jun-ho, but he was powerless to stop him as he yanked it from Dae-sun's fists. Jun-ho spun the spear in his hand and, in one fluid motion, drove it into his friend's skull.

He pulled it out before looking at Hideo. It wasn't the murder that scared Hideo the most. It wasn't the blood dripping from his spear or the splattering of red littering his armour. What scared Hideo the most was the long, thin grin that ran along his face.

Hideo finally drew the sword at his hip, pointing it out as he adopted a solid stance. The guard chuckled, and Hideo could swear he saw tears forming in his eyes.

"Finally," the guard whimpered, running his hand through his hair. "I've been thinking about this moment for a long time."

Hideo remained silent, holding out his sword as the sound of the metronome emanated from his desk.

"What's wrong?" shrugged the guard. "Not gonna strike me down? I'm wide open, and you're standing too close for me to get my spear up in time. Why don't you kill me?"

Hideo chewed that question around in his head. "I understand what has happened here. If you kill me, I die. If I kill you, I die. I can't even call for reinforcements because if they come in and kill you…"

"They die." The guard finished through his grin.

Hideo's breathing was laboured and jagged as he tried to calm his muscles and nerves. "Did Seradok send you?"

"Seradok!" bellowed the man, casually spinning the spear around in his hand. "Well, in a way, yes. But I would have come for you regardless. Of course, I wouldn't have been able to kill your son, destroy his army, and get here without much of a challenge."

Hideo's eyes welled at the mention of Koji. "You killed my son?"

"YOU KILLED MY DAUGHTER FIRST!" the guard bellowed. "And my brother."

He stepped closer, causing Hideo to drop his sword and smack his back against the thick doors. The guard continued. "At least I had the decency to kill your son with my own hands."

Hideo could taste the salt water on his lips. "Who are you?" he whimpered.

The guard moved his hand up his spear until it was close to the tip, the pole of the spear brushing the carpet. "I'm some goutuizi piece of shit, judging by the armour."

Hideo squinted, tossing more tears loose. "Goutuizi? You're a Northman?"

The guard's grin got wider. "I'm not just any Northman. We've met before. The last time I saw you was outside the gates of Wu Wei. I was with my brothers, ready to negotiate peace terms with your Emperor. We came for peace. Then you killed Doran, you raised a mountain and buried my daughter, and you even had me executed by your shadow archers."

It took Hideo a moment before he put all the pieces together. With a sharp intake of breath and eyes as wide as blood diamonds, the face of the man he was speaking to finally shot into his head. "Akkael Torne?"

Akkael threw the spear to the ground with such force Hideo jumped out of his skin. He began clapping like thunder and cheering as if there was something to celebrate. "Congratulations! You win!" The clapping slowed as Akkael gave a cathartic breath. "If there were gods, I would thank them. I'm going to enjoy killing you."

The metronome's ticking echoed in the near-silent chamber as Akkael walked towards him. Hideo knew there was no way to win a fight with Akkael, and it would be futile even if he did. The only way to beat the phantom Northman would be to use Seradok's gift, and the only obstacle was the man determined to kill him standing between him and his desk.

Hideo wasted no more time. He tried to retrieve his key from his pouch again, turning towards the door. Akkael was on him quickly, clasping one hand around Hideo's pauldron as he pried the key from his fingers. Akkael threw the key into the corner of the room. Then, Hideo swung his iron hand into the side of Akkael's head, discombobulating the Northman and causing him to stumble backwards.

Hideo turned into the room, stepping onto the table in the centre and vaulting over his sofa. He was nearly at the desk, arm already outstretched towards the metronome.

But before he reached it, Akkael grabbed him, tackling Hideo to the ground. Hideo smacked his head against the desk, blood trickling from his temple.

Akkael kicked his side, flinging him on his back, before pressing his foot into Hideo's chest. "What were you even trying to do?"

The metronome was on the edge of the desk facing them. It was as if it were watching, mocking him. Its hand reliably moved back and forth with the cadence of a laugh.

Hideo didn't notice Akkael follow his line of sight to the black, ticking device until he saw his hand pluck it from the desk like a weed. His stomach sank as Akkael held the metronome in his hand, squinting down at it.

"This?" said Akkael, holding it out towards Hideo. "Why?"

Hideo remained silent, eyes following the tip of the rod.

Turning it back towards him, Akkael shook his head as he considered the box. "Well, it's annoying." He moved his free hand towards the stick of the metronome to stop its pacing.

"Wait!" Hideo bellowed. "Don't touch it!"

Akkael recoiled, turning back to Hideo. "Excuse me?"

Hideo sighed, the back of his head finding the carpet below him. "Please. Kill me, but don't touch that metronome."

Akkael looked between Hideo and the metronome, eyes widening as realisation flooded his face. "Is this how you did it?" he asked, voice almost a whisper. "The mountains. Koseki. This thing caused all of that?"

Hideo's silence spoke volumes that he wished it didn't. He just stared up at the ceiling as if he could see through it. The Emperor's floor was just above him, where he had been imprisoned along with Doran Torne.

Hideo's eyelid's clamped shut, a tear pushing through as he considered his loss. Everything he did - his many treasons, betrayals, and murders – were excusable at the moment because they would all be justified in the end. No one would remember the bad once the terror of the Northmen was gone. He may have destroyed his entire army, broken the world, and sent his son to his death. But indeed, that was a small price to pay.

However, with the enemy flooding the city and his death imminent, he didn't think about everything he wanted to achieve. He didn't think about the death of every Northman or shores free from their boats. He thought about his son, his friends, his country, his Emperor, his honour, and his legacy. He thought of everything he had lost or destroyed.

The tear hit the carpet, Leaving a wet dot in the Edokand'i red of the dyed fur. "I'm sorry," he whispered. Hideo wasn't speaking to Akkael or anyone who could hear him. He didn't really know who he was saying it to. He just thought it was something he needed to say.

"What?" Hideo's eyes shot open at the sound of Akkael's voice just before he drove down on Hideo's chest. "How dare you?" Akkael repeatedly stomped on Hideo's torso so hard he swore he felt some of his ribs splinter. "Don't you dare fucking apologise to me!"

As Akkael was beating down on Hideo, something erupted from outside, followed by an impact that shook the palace. Akkael's foot slipped as the floor rocked. He put his free hand against the desk, still holding the metronome. Hideo was too pained to stand, lying still as he felt the vibrations under him.

Eventually, the tremors died, and Akkael and Hideo remained still, almost in anticipation. After moments of tense silence, Akkael said something sharp-tongued in Solstic that Hideo didn't understand.

Then they heard another explosion. Hideo and Akkael braced for the impact, Akkael keeping his hand on the desk while Hideo folded his arms to his chest. The palace shook more ferociously than before like something hit the floor above them. Both men looked up as cracks began to form in the ceiling, debris floating around them.

Hideo raised his iron hand to his face, folding into a ball as the palace creaked and groaned, the gaps widening.

"Oh fuck," Akkael breathed as the ceiling collapsed on top of them.

[CHAPTER 55] — EARLIER

Wu Wei was beautiful. Stone sculptures of forgotten gods lined the street like in Takakawa, and red bunting hung from the rooftops. Window shutters were folded closed, hiding the families inside, though some homes and shops had clearly been broken into. Paper windows were torn, and doors smeared with bloodied hand marks hung off the hinges. A woman in a dirty frock lay cold in her doorframe, and further up, a man was impaled by a spear. Skane looked at every symbol of war with no expression on his face.

He saw the first Sekandan dead, blue armour marked with their own lifeblood. Three women died together. One had a spear in her chest. The second's helmet had caved into her skull. The last Sekandan had blood pouring down her breastplate from a slash in her neck.

"No Sekandan deserves to die so far from home," said Moon, slowing down to stare at her dead countrywomen.

Skane spat beside her, stepping to the side of a pile of half a dozen dead Solstic and twice as many Edokand'i.

He calmed himself. Today was not the day to cast judgments or sly side glances. Skane knew the price of war and the hypocrisy of those involved. This was his last day of the war. Win or lose, everything would be decided here. He put on a stiff upper lip and walked on. All he had to do was anything and everything necessary. Then it would be over.

The buildings turned red, the streets became more expansive, and Skane knew he was getting close to the top. More plundering took place here than in the poor section of Wu Wei. Fewer corpses were in the way, which was pleasant, but the carnage was different. Windows were smashed in nearly every establishment, and gold littered the street from overzealous looters who couldn't fit enough money in their pouches.

Echoes of voices and footsteps emanated from further up the volcano. "We're getting close," stated Moon.

Skane nodded just as a pink paper lantern rolled in front of him. He looked toward where it had come from and saw a large grassy space. A thin path sliced the field in half and led to a small red temple. Shattered pots lay on the steps; many of its doors had been bashed in. In the centre of the field, multi-coloured lanterns hung from a collapsed wooden frame. Some had been released and rolled down the green, others left smouldering patches in the grass.

They had walked past similar carnage with a look of disdain. But this time, Skane stopped in his tracks. He wasn't looking at the temple or the lanterns. Leaning against the broken frame was the body of a man. He wore the purple robes of a sage, which was all Skane could discern from his appearance. This was because the man's head, severed from his body, was lying face down in his lap.

Two Solstic warriors, a man and a woman, left the derelict temple. They were young, each with blue spirals tattooed on their bare shoulders. Their weapons hung in their belts, and a shield suspended from the woman's back. Dirt and blood clung to their skin, and the scars across their bodies suggested it wasn't the first time.

The man carried a golden effigy of some forgotten god or the likeness of a past Grand Sage. The woman held a small chest filled with gold. They were facing each other, smiling. The male warrior pushed her against the door frame, his free hand gripping her upper arm. He kissed her, the blood on her lips reddening his own as the young lovers embraced the moment of passion amongst the carnage they had caused.

Skane could feel his blood boil. His ear's burned, and his teeth pressed together so tightly they might have cracked. "You!" he barked. "What the fuck do you think you're doing?"

The woman pushed her lover away, recognising almost immediately who was speaking. "King Skane?"

The man's eyes widened when he heard Skane's name.

"This is your battle glory, is it?" Skane hadn't realised his axe was out of his belt and in his fist. "Killing a sage and destroying his home."

The man stuttered a moment before speaking. "He's the enemy."

"He's unarmed!" Skane stepped closer to the young couple, the axe handle pressing dents into his palm.

The man moved in front of the shield maiden but didn't draw his weapon. Skane thought that foolish.

"Skane." Moon moved into his peripheral vision as she spoke, stopping him. "We need to keep going."

As if to emphasise Moon's statement, cannon fire filled the air. Skane looked back at the couple one last time, scowling at them. He spat on the ground and returned to Moon's side at the head of the group. He gave one last apologetic look to the dead sage before continuing up the hill.

Everywhere Skane looked, there were more reasons to despise the life he had once languished in. The stench of death permeated the streets, and the crows began to get impatient, squawking overhead. Skane passed various groups of marauders on his way up the hill. Most were Solstic, carrying smiles and gold as they looked for more to loot.

Some Sekandans joined them. One woman in blue armour laughed at the blurb of a book she'd always wanted to read, the library burning behind her. Some were remarking on the slight differences between Edokand'i and Sekandan money as the bank teller lay dead over his counter. They were left behind to secure each district of the city. Some might say they did their jobs well.

The further Skane got towards the caldera, the louder the voices. As were the musket shots. They were happening in quicker intervals, making Skane wonder what awaited him at the top of the volcano. Then, as he turned the corner of a winding street, he saw something that distracted him from his ascent.

The stone buildings around them had all but crumbled. Some were lucky, with a dent in the bricks or a lone hole in the wall. Others were less so. The first building was a school. It had been reduced to rubble, pebbles, and dust. The roof and bamboo guttering lay like a jigsaw of the dilapidated structure. Skane had seen many battles and witnessed carnage like the temple. But something about this felt stranger.

"Cannons." Skane turned to see Moon pointing down a short alley to their right. A heap of bricks and wood from an apartment building that used to darken the path blocked the way. Sat on top of the debris was a lone steel cannonball.

"Did we bring any cannons into the city?" asked Moon.

"No," answered Skane. "All three of ours are outside the walls. The Edokand'i are destroying their own city."

Moon breathed out slowly, looking around at the rest of the damage. "Why?"

Skane shrugged. "If we lose this battle, history books will remember the bloodshed and destruction we brought to Wu Wei. It won't remember anything else. That's what Hideo cares about."

More musket shots echoed across the city. They peeled away from the broken alley and the carnage caused by the Edokand'i. There was a numbness inside Skane as he walked deeper into Wu Wei.

The walk was short compared to the marches they had done over the last few weeks. But the more he walked through Wu Wei, the more tired he felt. His breaths were laboured, his legs were heavy, and he tried not to look at anything else around him.

As Skane approached the top, he noticed the crowd waiting outside the palace walls. A sea of blue breastplates blocked the streets, and Skane couldn't help but note that the Sekandans were at the rear. Skane, Moon, and the forty warriors at their tail pushed towards the front of the army.

As Skane made it through the throng, the Sekandans thinned quickly, and he was welcomed by his Solstic kin.

"King Skane!" someone cheered, adding to a chorus of other tributes.

A smile was on his face until he found an opening in their forces. It was close to the gates of the palace. As Skane approached, he saw a figure resting against the wall of a livery. They had one hand resting against a stall as they gripped their chest with the other. Skane's face sank when he recognised the person in front of him.

"Astrid!" he exclaimed.

She looked up at the sound of her name. Her face was pale and caked red. Black eyelids surrounded her green eyes, and the marks on her teeth had crusts of blood in them. "Skane," she said weakly.

Skane was still shocked by her appearance. "You look awful."

Astrid breathed a laugh. "I feel awful."

Moon snapped her fingers behind them and beckoned forward five shield maidens. "You women. Take Astrid back down the city to the sages. She needs attention."

"I'm fine," protested Astrid before her arm gave in, and she collapsed onto the wall of the livery.

"Now!" Moon demanded, punctuated by the musket fire. It was so close Skane could swear he heard one of the shots ricochet off the stone of the stable house.

Skane waited until Astrid was reluctantly in the care of the shield maidens before pushing deeper towards the palace gates. When he got there, he noticed the barred gate to the palace had been pulled down. He stepped over it on his way to the front and peered through the aperture of the entrance, staring into the deep bowl of the caldera. The walls were erected to look flush with the natural rock formation, the teeth of the volcano blending with the bricks.

The pagoda sat in the centre of the bowl like a tongue. The five levels were defined by a turquoise, tile, outcropped roof, which clashed with the red wood of the building. Each side of the ground floor had an entrance and stone steps leading to the raised platform on which the pagoda sat. A network of terraces also spanned the caldera, in keeping with the turquoise and red colouring that spread across Wu Wei.

Skane didn't know why, but he expected to be more enamoured with the palace when he saw it. Corpses hung from the blood-stained tower, but that was a minor distraction. The gardens were still beautiful, the architecture was baffling, and the volcano was awe-inspiring. Still, it all fell flat for Skane. Despite it being objectively impressive, all Skane saw was an obstacle. It was another thing on which to inflict the instant decay of war.

On every side of the pagoda's third floor were balconies that leapt from the palace like petals. The stone railings were visible, but the rest of the platforms were coated in red steel from the goutuizi armour. Five-hundred sentinels, spread across the three balconies, stood like a pool of iridescent magma due to the sunlight. The tips of their muskets caught the sun, almost blinding Skane before they fired.

It was like the volcano below them had erupted. The sound was excruciating as it reverberated in the caldera. Skane ducked in the aperture of the fallen gate, gripping his ears to block out the deep and guttural explosion. Suddenly he felt two hand press onto his shoulder and yank him out of view. Musket balls flicked the rock of the mountain and the stone of the walls like hail hitting a window.

When the sound dissipated, Skane turned to see Heiyang and the other two shadow archers behind him. He thanked them for saving him, waiting for his ears to pop and the ringing to die.

Moon caught up to them after the barrage. Heiyang turned to face her and began to sigh.

"This is the only entrance into the palace," she translated. "It's impossible to storm without massive casualties."

Skane peeked back through the entranceway at the palace below him before turning back to Heiyang and Moon. "Any ideas?" he asked.

Heiyang shrugged before signing.

"We could wait for them to fire and hope the reload time gives us enough opportunity," repeated Moon. "But he doesn't think we have the numbers left for that."

One look at the army behind him showed Skane that Heiyang's concerns were accurate. He wondered how many Solstic were left, maybe half of those who left Chuton, if he wanted to be optimistic. He sighed and rubbed his forehead, trying to free himself from that thought.

Suddenly, something occurred to Skane. "How do we get up onto the parapets?"

"There is a staircase on the other side of the wall to our left," said Moon, watching the shadow archer. "But it's thinner than the gateway. Also, we'll be open until we get to the parapet."

Skane looked down at his boots. He knew he wasn't better than those who trashed temples and looted corpses. It was that realisation that drew out his rage. He'd killed in war. He'd dismantled, dismembered, destroyed. He might hate war, but he knew what was necessary when the time came. He knew it took bloodshed and devastation to win.

Skane looked back to the shadow archers. "Here's the plan," he started. "You three teleport onto the balconies and distract the muskets. Moon and I will lead the women we arrived with onto the wall."

"Why?" asked Moon. "It's not like Chuton. There are no bridges from the ramparts to the palace."

Skane's eyes were like stone. "We don't need bridges. What destroyed the alley we walked past?"

"Cannons..." Moon shrugged right before realisation hit, and her face changed. "Cannons." She repeated.

Heiyang signed something to Moon, probably confirming Skane's plan, and everyone got ready. Skane walked back into view of the palace watching the sentinels with a stone-cold expression.

This was his last war. He and Magar had already agreed. He was going to do anything he needed to ensure that was true. He wasn't a sage. He hadn't opened his chakras. He wasn't Rigpa. Skane Torne was a Solstic warrior and would play that role for one more day if it meant he could spend the rest of his life pretending he was something different.

Heiyang and the shades teleported onto the balconies, one on each. Almost as soon as they had gone, Skane, Moon, and the forty women entered the caldera. Skane struggled to gain footing as he stumbled onto the decline of the bowl. His axe rattled against his leg as he barely stayed on his feet. He spun his body left and saw the staircase up the wall. There was scarcely enough space for one person to walk up at a time, and the steps were shallow.

Some stray muskets hit around the group as they made their way single-file up the steps. Skane was first to the top and saw a smattering of sentinels still on the wall that hadn't managed to fall back to the palace. They looked petrified, huddled together as if they were on a raft surrounded by sharks. The wall was already littered with corpses made by the shades, who had culled the Edokand'i archers.

Skane drew his axe and launched into the skull of the closest sentinel as the Sekandans and shield maidens flooded around him to join the fight.

Skane ducked behind the crenellated wall, waiting for Moon, who was at the rear of the company, to climb the steps. The warriors did short work of the remaining goutuizi, and Skane looked around for the cannons.

There were three. They were close together, all facing Wu Wei. The cannons had been made redundant as soon as the arm reached the wall, as the Solstic and Sekandans were too close for the artillery to aim at them. Skane looked over the wall and saw the streaks of destruction the cannons had caused. They looked like scars or claw marks.

Skane faced Moon and nodded. As they both stood up to make their way towards the cannons, Skane looked over the parapet at the palace as cheering bellowed from the closest balcony. He paused to see what the commotion was about and watched as the crowd of sentinels tossed the corpse of a shadow archer from the railings. Skane bit against his teeth but didn't have much time to take it in before another barrage of bullets blasted across the bowl.

Skane ducked behind the crenellation. Sparks and chips of rock rained down on him from where the projectiles found the stone. Some Sekandans and shield maidens died, but Skane had no time to count. He continued towards the cannons.

Skane took the furthest weapon, Moon the middle, and Sekandan took the last. It took a few people on each cannon to rotate and set them in place. Boxes of tools lay within reach of each weapon, and a few sacks of powder sat in a crate next to a barrel of cannonballs. Moon was closest to the containers and tossed a sack to either side of her. Skane caught the powder, leaning over and throwing it into the cannon's mouth.

Another sputtering of musket shots was fired before Moon could reach the cannonballs. She rolled them along the parapet towards Skane and the Sekandan. He dropped his into the barrel of the weapon before rummaging in his toolbox for everything he needed. He pierced the bag of powder through the thin hole before feeding the fuse. Then he took the flint and steel and lit the end of a torch.

Turning to his right, he saw the other two were ready to launch. After a few final touches with the aim and a moment of patience before Heiyang and the other remaining shade cleared the firing line, Skane placed his torch against the fuse and moved out of the way.

The cannonball hit the balcony, sending sentinels down with the splinters. Muskets flew into the air as their wielders threw their hands up in terror just before the platform fell under them. It crumbled, slipping down the pagoda like a landslide. Goutuizi made noises Skane had never heard a person make, as their bodies broke against the stone steps below, dropping with the debris like torrential rain on a puddle.

The steel ball continued to slice through the palace. The outer wall facing him shattered, revealing the floors inside, like hacking off flesh to reveal a ribcage. The ball crunched through the interior, smashing, breaking, and snapping anything on its descent.

When all went still, Skane removed his hand from the tufts of his hair. He was horror-struck, his mouth wide as the muscles in his face contorted like waves in a storm. No part of him was relaxed, but his breathing was slow, as if he were trying not to cause further damage to the pagoda by moving too suddenly.

"Oh shit," Moon exclaimed. Her loud voice made Skane's heart leap into his throat.

Moon stared wide-eyed at the cannon before her, the fuse racing towards the barrel. Almost as soon as she yelled, the weapon fired. She moved out of the way as it recoiled back, rolling off the other side of the wall. Behind her, Skane saw the tensed Sekandan on the other cannon just before a third blast rang in the caldera.

Moon's shot smashed into the second balcony. Goutuizi fell and screamed as the walls cracked above them. The tiles of each overhang on the pagoda began to slide off just as the third cannonball hit, missing the balconies completely and crashing into the pagoda's top floor. Moon slapped her hand across her jaw as the cracks from the first two shots began to reach around the palace. Then, like an avalanche, each floor in the segmented pagoda collapsed.

The top fell through first. The ornate roof peeled from the structure and slid into one of the other palace buildings. One by one the sections of the pagoda caved in, the overhanging roofs snapping away and creating a ring of smashed tile.

Skane lowered his head, listening to the thuds of each floor crumbling into the one below. Screams from in and outside the collapsing structure bounce across the bowl of the caldera. The Solstic crowd behind the wall rejoiced, their cheers drowning out the last of the devastation as they charged down the caldera towards the crumbling palace.

Skane pinched the bridge of his nose and shook his head. He witnessed the horrors of war enough to know the intent was irrelevant. He may have wanted to come to Wu Wei in pursuit of peace. Still, he was one man with one agenda who just contributed to demolishing the Emperor's palace. Regardless of whether Doran and the Emperor were still alive in there, a fair peace would not be possible.

Why would it be? They had won the war.

[CHAPTER 56] — KING DORAN AND THE EMPEROR

The closer Doran Torne got to the Emperor's chambers, the more nervous he felt. It was a strange feeling. Everything that had led to this meeting had been perfectly calculated. Over the last four years, he had overseen the forging of a new settlement without displacing the natives that lived inside his conquered lands. He had assessed the right level of carnage to keep the warmongers of his forces sated, while also ensuring he didn't hinder the possibility of negotiations. He had evaluated the deaths, annexations, and humiliations while plotting every step that led him and his brothers to Wu Wei. Everything had been laid out like schematics in his head. But, like any architect, his plans could go awry with the simplest rock in the soil.

Doran's eyes faced the floor as he played with his father's necklace, a triangular spiral with a line through the centre of each loop. He followed his escorts down the palace corridors, ignoring the stunning architecture, paintings, and statues that would have caught his eye any other day. All the hard work he had done over the four-year campaign was at the mercy and the whims of a man he had never met. The Emperor of Edokand.

The sentinels escorting him stopped at the top of a flight of stairs so suddenly that Doran almost walked into them. They moved to either side of a large ornate door. The red inlay of the symmetrical, ridged pattern was more like a shining ruby than the other reds Doran had seen in the palace. The design was like someone dropped a stone in a pond, the ripples leaving waves across the door. It was taller than three men standing on top of each other.

"These are the Emperor's chambers," announced one of the sentinels.

Doran squinted. "But we just got to the top of the steps. He has a whole floor of the pagoda dedicated to where he sleeps?"

The goutuizi were still. Doran raised his eyebrows, the decadence of Edokand still not lost on him after so many years.

The other sentinel lifted one of the enormous brass knockers and slammed it against the door. Then he spoke. "There is a red line on the floor. Do not cross it."

"Or what?" asked Doran.

"You die."

After a moment, Doran heard a little bell chime from inside. The sentinels took it as a signal to open the great doors and usher Doran inside. The first thing Doran did as he entered the Emperor's chambers was scan the floor. The floorboards stained a burnt black creaked underfoot as Doran approached the long red line that was his boundary for the meeting.

As his eyes rose, he took in the thin room. It was almost like a foyer, with two doors on either side of the opposite wall suggesting the scale of the pagoda's top floor. Light from two windows on either side of the room shone equally as bright in the noon sun. Plants that Doran couldn't name sat proudly in ornate pots, painted with red floral patterns that almost hid behind the thin gold streaks were stark on the ceramic. The entrance to the chambers was symmetrical. Each ornament, painting, or structure had a counterpart on the opposite side of the room.

After gliding to the left and the right, Doran's eyes fixed on the centrepiece of the foyer. A raised dais sat against the far wall. Atop it was a folded screen with a beautiful pastel painting spread across all five panels. It was of a red sun over a pink mountain range. In front of the screen was a large pillow with a small bell on the ground in front of it. Kneeling on the cushion was the Emperor.

Doran's eyes shot open like discs after seeing the Emperor of Edokand for the first time. He was a boy, no older than fourteen. His hazel eyes were almost the colour of a tiger's, and his cheeks were blushed with make-up. He wore a cloth hat that was bigger than his head. It was blue with knitted flowers dangling and shaped like a bee's hive turned upside down. He wore a red robe that reminded Doran of a sage's outfit as he sat with his hands tucked in the sleeves.

He didn't know what to expect before meeting the Emperor. He'd heard almost nothing about him in the years the Solstic had been in Edokand. But a child was not what he had in mind.

Speechlessly, the sentinels that had escorted Doran inside bowed and exited the room, shutting the door behind them and leaving Doran in the place he'd dreamt of being in many times. The silence between them lingered too long for Doran to bear. Eventually, he spoke.

"Interesting you decided to be alone with me," he said, still finding it difficult to think of the child as the most powerful person in the country. "One might think that you were naïve."

"I find it interesting that you think that," said the Emperor, his voice higher than Doran expected but with a certain gravitas that only comes with power.

"That I think you're naïve?"

"That you think we're alone."

Doran couldn't help but smile, but the Emperor's face remained as stiff as a portrait. "Very good," he said. "So, what do I call you?"

"My name is Kanmu," answered the Emperor.

Doran pictured the name phonetically in his head and thought it was a good fit for the boy Emperor. "Well, hello Kanmu," said Doran. "You're younger than I thought you'd be."

Kanmu spoke without a pause. "And you're leaner. I thought you Northmen were meant to be these burly brutes."

Doran scoffed. "I should have brought my brother with me. Magar fits that description perfectly."

The Emperor's expression didn't so much as waver, and after a brief lull in the conversation, Doran spoke again. "I am curious, though. How did someone so young become the ruler of this great country?"

Doran watched the Emperor's eyes widen as he glared at his feet. He looked down and saw he had stepped dangerously close to the edge of the red line. Stepping back, he offered a look that conveyed an apology.

Kanmu took a deep breath before deciding to answer Doran's question. "I was crowned Emperor before I was born."

Doran's jaw opened as he waited for Kanmu to continue.

"My father died of sickness when my mother was pregnant," he said. "My mother died in childbirth. After that, there was a great war to determine who should inherit the throne. My uncle tried to usurp me. By the time I was teething, those loyal to the true line of succession had won. If it weren't for Hideo Kazar, I would have died before I had a concept of death."

Doran took a deep breath when the Emperor had finished talking. "I never knew this."

"You're ignorant to many things about our history," said the Emperor, the hints of a scowl on his stoic face. "Over a decade after that war was won, we were embroiled in another war. The war against you. So, King, you have gone to great lengths to ensure our meeting. You embarrassed Lord Hideo at Utajima."

Doran squinted and smiled. "He embarrassed himself."

"You usurp my people from their homes in Takakawa."

"No, that is not my goal," interrupted Doran, stepping too close to the line. "I wish Takakawa to be a city for both our peoples."

"What do you want with Edokand?" asked Kanmu.

"Exactly what I said," Doran shrugged. "I want our peoples to live together. Farm together. Drink together. Laugh, sing, and fall in love. That's all I want. Unity."

"No one invades a country for the sake of unity."

"I do."

For the first time in their short meeting, Kanmu stood up from his pillow. The long robe hid his shoes and made it look like he was gliding down the steps of the dais. He didn't get too close to Doran, but it was close enough for Doran to get a better look at his face. His youth and stature took nothing away from the stoicism in his appearance. He had made his statement, and he wasn't afraid.

"And who will oversee this unification?" asked Kanmu, tucking his hands back in his sleeves.

Doran looked around the room before planting his hand against his chest. "I will."

"Exactly," scoffed the Emperor, smiling for the first time. "You're not an altruist; you're not selfless. Your invasion was a land grab. As if the province of

Urkanza your father annexed wasn't enough, or the lands your people stole in Rhayne."

"I have no power in Urkanza," Doran corrected. "My father gave that away almost as soon as he had it."

"So that's it then," said Kanmu. "You feel slighted and desire dominion over a new kingdom."

"No. I never wanted to be King."

"Isn't that what everyone says?"

"It's true," spat Doran, visibly irate at the boy's accusations. "It might be hard to believe for a child who has known nothing but power, but the name *King Doran* never interested me."

Doran chewed that name around in his mouth, flinching at the taste.

"King Doran," he repeated. "Did you know Doran isn't a Solstic name? it's from Rhayne. My great-great-grandfather named my great-grandfather Doran after an old Rhaynese friend of his. My grandfather was named Magar after some relative, then my father was named Doran again, and that's how I got my name."

"What about your other brother, Akkael?" Kanmu asked, humouring the tangent. "Where does his name originate?"

"He was named after my uncle," said Doran. "As for who my uncle was named after, I don't know."

The Emperor shrugged. "Maybe he wasn't named after anyone."

"No, it's tradition. Everyone is a namesake."

"But the names had to originate somewhere."

The Solstic King nodded to himself. "Most of them come from our old gods. It's strange; all the world religions are dead, but we still cling to their customs."

Doran looked up just in time to watch Kanmu squint. "How do you mean?"

"My culture stems from a warrior religion," he said, pacing along the line on the floor. "We wanted to sail the world, conquer new lands, and war. Centuries after we stopped believing in gods, we still do the same thing."

Kanmu stepped closer to Doran's boundaries. "Most of our religious traditions are echoes of the past. No one can really remember what they were for."

"Same with us. And the Rhaynese, the Urkanzans, and the peoples of every land I've been to." Doran stopped pacing suddenly and snapped his head toward the Emperor. Kanmu recoiled at his sudden movement. "Don't you find that strange?"

"Strange?" said Kanmu, tilting his head.

Doran became more animated as he started talking with his hands. "Every culture around the world abandoned their religions simultaneously; collectively."

Kanmu was coming to the extent of how long he could humour this digression. "Lord Hideo always said we were foolish to believe in such things as gods."

"That's what I believed too," nodded Doran. "That's what everyone in the world thinks. That's what's strange. People can't agree on anything. We have our own ways of farming, of fighting, of living. But, suddenly, every person in the world shared the same thought. Gods don't exist."

Emperor Kanmu rolled his eyes. "I doubt you've come all the way from your tundra to talk about religious theory."

"On the contrary. That's exactly why I've come here." Doran lifted the necklace around his neck from his chest and pointed it towards the Emperor. "This necklace was my father's. The symbol is also Rhaynese. When Rhayne had its religions, this symbol was used to shame those questioning their gods' existence."

Kanmu leant in to get a better look. "It's pretty, but I don't see its relevance."

The necklace made a soft thud against his chest when Doran dropped it. "Just like now, the opinion on gods was static and unwavering. We believe gods can't possibly exist with the same stubbornness as those in the past who believed they did. And those who question are the odd ones. Do you know what agnostic means?"

"No," said Kanmu, shocked by the sudden question and increasingly perturbed by the aside.

"Nor do I really," said Doran, looking back to the symbol around his neck and shrugging. "But that's what this is, the mark of the agnostic. My father gave it to me before he died, and on his deathbed, he expressed one wish."

"What was it?"

"To integrate." Doran backed away from the line on the floor and stood facing the Emperor, not allowing himself to fidget. "Some of my people want the land to farm. Some want to live a winter without the fear of waking up to a giant bear standing over them. They want good lives for their families. All noble pursuits. But what I want is to live side by side with your people. I want to learn, to piece together the disparate parts of your dead religions and understand the puzzle that has haunted my family for generations. Why don't we believe in gods?"

One of Kanmu's eyebrows was raised above the other. "That's the plan of the great Doran Torne. To invade every land in the world so he can talk about archaic concepts with whoever survives his marauders."

Doran paused for a moment, then shrugged. "If that's what it takes."

A silence fell over the two of them, only broken by the Emperor's steps as he walked closer to the northern King. "I don't care about gods," he declared. "What I care about is my country and my people. You have taken swathes of my land; this I cannot abide. I also cannot allow this war to continue. So, we need to come to an arrangement."

Doran folded his arms. "What arrangements?"

"First, I want to discuss Utajima." As Kanmu spoke, Doran couldn't get over how mature the young boy sounded. The Emperor continued. "I believe you call that island Skaldgard, which has come as a great insult to my people. But I am a realist. That island was not well populated and offered little imports we could not make up for elsewhere. With this in mind, I can gift you the island free of challenge."

Doran smiled. "It's already free of challenge."

"Also," continued Kanmu, ignoring Doran's comment, "we will allow some of the lands in Tsul to remain in your control under the conditions that those

Edokand'i who live there will be able to stay there and contribute their taxes and produce to the crown, country, and culture they belong to."

"I would expect nothing less," said Doran, bowing. "We can draw up the specifics later."

"Lastly is the matter of Takakawa." Kanmu broadened his shoulders and widened his stance. "I want the city to be returned to Edokand immediately."

"I'm afraid not," said Doran.

The Emperor was close enough now for Doran to see his jaw clench. "Takakawa is an important linchpin in the stability of its trade routes to all islands in Edokand and our relationship with Sekando. The Sekandans are reliant on fish, seaweed, pearls, and other important exports, as well as traded goods. This is non-negotiable."

"Takakawa will be important to the stability of our relationship, too," Doran replied. "I have made every effort to turn Takakawa into a haven for Edokand'i and Solstic. I will continue to do so while I remain in control of it."

"King Doran. You misunderstand." The Emperor was tensing under his robes. "I know you're new to our language, but non-negotiable means I won't negotiate. You either concede or prepare for an even longer war."

Doran smiled, bending over the red line to be at eye level with the child in front of him. "Are you sure you're prepared for a long war?"

"Your exploits in Tsul may have been fruitful," the Emperor conceded. "But your people will not find the same victory in Trim. If you choose the path of war, I assure you, you will forever be the last Northman to set foot in Wu Wei."

The two stared at each other, one with a contempt he tried to hide, the other with a stubbornness that would not allow him to relent. They were transfixed with the tension of the moment they didn't notice the light pulsating through the window the first few times it occurred.

The room, lighted by the noon sun, began to darken as if it were a windowless room. The darkness held for a few seconds before the light started again. But it wasn't the same as before. The room was illuminated from the eastern window first. Shadows paced along the floor until the light source switched to the western window. Then they would be submerged in darkness once again.

Ignoring the red line, Doran walked to the window on his left. Kanmu didn't seem to mind, as he was also transfixed by the unreliable light. The Northman peered out, noticing the sky's hue turning like the ebb and flow of the tides. When the sky began to lighten again, Doran saw the sun. He followed it with his eyes as it raced over the top of the pagoda. After a while, the sky would turn black again, with stars gleaming with the moon. They would disappear, and Doran once again followed the ascent of the rapid sun.

"What's happening?" asked the Emperor, a childlike fear in his tone.

Doran tried to find the right words. "It's the sun," he said. "It's moving quicker."

Kanmu bolted towards the door of his chambers. "It's locked," he announced. The Emperor knocked, but the sentinels standing guard outside didn't answer.

"Do you have a key?" asked Doran, once again watching the stars fade away, and the sky turn pink.

"In my bedroom." Kanmu raced to the door furthest away from Doran. But, by the time he reached it, the sky had stopped changing. It was the same noon sun as before, light leaking in from both windows equally. They turned to face each other simultaneously, looking as lost and confused as the other.

Then a sound like a thunderclap burst around them. They only had a brief chance to raise their hands to their ears before the floor gave way under their feet. The last thing Doran saw was the palace breaking apart as he fell.

[CHAPTER 57] — THE PALACE RUINS

"Doran..." The light through his eyelids was crimson and hot. "Doran."

He blocked the blinding brightness with his arm as he let his eyes flutter open. He couldn't entirely focus on anything yet, and his head felt heavy. When his hand dipped onto his forehead, a sharp stinging sensation made him recoil and wince, a spot of blood left behind on his knuckle.

The glow slowly got more bearable, like a dying flame. The sun peered through a hole in the roof. Or was it the wall? The palace was so derelict it was hard to tell. The remaining structure was patchy and erratic. Only luck kept certain planks and pillars standing. It looked like fractals of ice, jagged and rough patterns slicing through the cloudless sky.

"Doran!"

He remained dilatory, dazed, and distant, but something in the name sparked a light curiosity. He tried to remember what it meant.

A man jumped into his vision, sending a pulse of adrenaline through him that nearly woke him up. It took a moment for his eyes to adjust enough to see the stranger. It was a sentinel, the red of the armour blurring into the silver trimmings. The face was still dark and indistinct, and his voice sounded familiar.

"Doran, can you stand?" the sentinel asked.

Recognition and realisations piled into Doran's head like a flood, and he started to remember everything. The sun rushed along the sky, the explosion like the dormant volcano underneath them had erupted, the fall. It all rushed to him with a sharp intake of breath. His eyes bulged like the memories and concerns were filling his head to capacity.

"Kanmu," said Doran, through a sharp pain in his side. He reached for the silver helix necklace around his neck to check if it was still there. It was, which was a small relief.

Doran could see enough of the sentinel now to watch his eyebrow rise over one dark eye. "Who's Kanmu?"

"The Emperor," said Doran. "Where is he?"

The sentinel shrugged. He sat up a little more and scanned the excuse for a room. It wasn't the same room Doran had fallen from. The smashed dining table and statues peering through the detritus gave that away. Torn red flags dangled from the rafters in threads and tatters, so he knew he was still in the palace. But the painting in the broken, gilded frame was not one he had seen on his way to the Emperor's chambers.

After surveying the room, the sentinel pointed to a young figure under a pile of rubble on the other side of the table. "Is that him?"

Doran was lucid enough to find the lack of concern or deference in the goutuizi strange. He didn't know the Emperor's name, didn't know what he looked like, didn't show an iota of alarm. Doran stumbled to his feet, dawdling towards Kanmu. Dust descended on him as he looked up into the wounds on the palace, wondering how far he had fallen.

"Kanmu," said Doran, collapsing to his knees into a pile of splinters and paper doors beside the Emperor. Kanmu stirred, and his eyelids trembled open. Doran smiled, breathing a sigh of relief.

The sentinel strutted over to their side. "I don't understand," he said. Doran couldn't put his finger on why the voice was so familiar. "How are you two alive? It's been so long."

Doran's attention was taken away from rousing the Emperor. He looked at the sentinel through the corner of his eye. "What do you mean? How long have we been out?"

The goutuizi made no effort to answer. Doran didn't understand why, but the sentinel raised his hand before his face, looking exasperated. He flung his hands to his side and stared off into the distance, eyes flicking back and forth as if he were thinking.

"Soldier," barked Doran, regaining the sentinel's attention. "Answer me. I don't know what's happening here, but you must stay with me, okay?"

The Edokand'i breathed a laugh. "Doran, I know you think you don't know me, but you can trust me. What do you remember?"

"Nothing," Doran shrugged, ignoring the confusion he felt from the sentinel's words. "I was negotiating with Kanmu, and then the building collapsed."

Doran scrunched his face, trying to think harder about what he saw.

"The sun was acting strange."

"Strange?" The sentinel stepped forward, still standing as Doran crouched at Kanmu's semi-unconscious side. "How do you mean strange?"

Doran thought of how best to describe what had happened without sounding insane. He described how the sun raced across the sky, the moon changed shape in seconds, and the stars blinked on and off as the sky fluctuated between dark and light. "It was like the days were a second long."

The sentinel stood frozen as Doran spoke. When he'd finished, he turned around, sliding his gauntleted palms down his face and groaning. Then, he spun back around sharply and glowered at Doran and the Emperor.

"Let me get this straight," he said. "You still think it's the same day? The day you left for Wu Wei?"

Doran didn't know how to answer the question. He stood up, shoulders square, in front of the strange Edokand'i soldier. He had started to realise how casually the goutuizi spoke, much more relaxed in the presence of his Emperor and an enemy king than he would expect of the regimented, disciplined sentinels.

"I don't know your game here, soldier," Doran exclaimed. "But your Emperor is injured, and the palace is in ruins. If you had something to do with this or know who did, spit it out."

"What did you say?" the Emperor croaked beneath them.

Doran's neck snapped towards the Emperor before his words registered. But when they did, they hit like storm waves against the rocks. Kanmu didn't understand what they said. Why would he? Doran didn't know why it had taken him so long to realise. The whole conversation, every single line the sentinel uttered, had been spoken in Solstic.

Doran turned back slowly to the sentinel, ignoring the desperate flailing of Kanmu as he attempted to sit up.

"You speak my language," said Doran quietly. "How?"

The sentinel turned to stone, breathing slowly through his nostrils.

"How do you know my language?" Doran repeated, moving closer to him.

Suddenly, a loud slam came from the floor below as if to break the tension. Both Doran and the sentinel reached for their weapons in tandem. However, Doran's axe was confiscated before he met with Kanmu, and the soldier was also unarmed. A chorus of stamps and stomps shook the building. It sounded like hundreds of footsteps were climbing the stairs of the palace ruins.

The sentinel grabbed Doran by the shoulders and turned him to face each other. "Look, Doran, you need to trust me," started the goutuizi, still speaking Solstic. "You've been frozen in this palace for months. I know that sounds ridiculous, but you haven't heard the half of it. This may be hard to believe, but…"

"Sentinel!" Both Doran and the soldier's gaze followed the voice. A man stood in the doorway under a hole in the ceiling. Doran squinted to get a better look at the man. He thought he must be concussed or hallucinating because the large figure in front of him looked familiar.

"Skane!" The sentinel vocalised Doran's thoughts. Doran snapped back towards the soldier, wondering how he knew who Skane was.

"Back away, soldier," said Skane, axe in one hand while the other was outstretched. "The battle is over. Back away from Doran and the Emperor."

The sentinel strode towards Skane. "Skane, it's okay," he said, speaking Solstic. "It's Akkael."

Doran felt his lungs deflate and his ears heat up. It was an obvious lie, a ridiculous ploy for some strange game. However, once the sentinel claimed he was Doran's younger brother, those in the doorway turned ridged. Skane's hand dropped as three others peeled away from the crowd of shield maidens standing in the doorframe.

A Sekandan woman Doran didn't know entered with Queen Kya, wearing a blue dress that failed to conceal the armour plating underneath. The third woman used the wall as a prop as she swung into the hall, clutching her chest and panting hard. It was Astrid.

"Astrid, what happened to you?" There was a look of genuine concern on the sentinel's face that boiled Doran's blood.

Astrid ignored the question; instead, with one palm resting against the dilapidated wood, she stretched herself as far as she could across the room and pointed at the lying goutuizi.

"Prove it," was all she said. "Prove you're Akkael."

"Okay, hold on." Doran had reached his limit. He was getting more light-headed, angrier, and louder, but he didn't care. He needed answers. "Am I the only one who remembers what my brother looks like? Astrid, why are you entertaining this man's lies? And Skane, you lead a band of my soldiers into the palace of Wu Wei. What is going on here?"

"Rigpa?" A voice behind Skane interrupted his train of thought. He turned to see Emperor Kanmu leaning against a pile of rubble, peering over the collapsed dining table between him and the doorway. Skane turned back to see the purple-robed Grand Sage dawdle into the room. Her robes were dirty and torn, starkly contrasting the pristinely dressed old woman he had met only a few hours ago.

The sage had a large arm clasped around her shoulder. When she faced Doran, he realised the arm belonged to Magar. His youngest brother looked as bad as Astrid. Bandages swirled up his body, and he was leaning on a thick wooden crutch, as well as the old woman's shoulders. When Magar's bloodshot and tired eyes fell on Doran, he gave a weak smile.

Skane turned to the doorframe and addressed the soldiers on the other side. "Fill the room as much as you can. Leave a large space in the middle for us to talk. The rest of you search further up the palace. If you see anyone and they surrender, don't kill them. Bring me Hideo Kazar, dead or alive."

The band did as Skane told them, with almost a hundred Sekandan and Solstic soldiers filling the derelict room and the rest pounding up the stairs to the higher floors that Doran had fallen through.

"Hideo!" the sentinel exclaimed. He then began searching the rubble.

After a moment of stomping through the wood and debris, digging through piles and brushing large planks aside, Skane spoke. "Akkael, what are you looking for?"

"He's not Akkael!" Doran's head was pounding, and his breaths became too quick and sharp to control.

No one seemed to notice; everyone's eyes fixed on the fake Akkael as he scoured the ground. "There's a metronome. It's small and black. Does anyone see it?"

Skane tilted his head. "Hideo's metronome?"

"What's going on?" The Emperor's responses were slow, and it looked like he was about to pass out again. Rigpa left Magar to stand alone, and she rushed to Kanmu's side, kneeling in the splintered timbers as she assessed him.

The sentinel pretending to be Akkael paid the Emperor no mind, still looking at the floor beneath his feet while answering Skane's question. "The metronome is magic. It might be how Hideo did everything he did."

"We know," said Skane.

"What did Hideo do?" said Doran with a breathless voice.

Skane looked at Doran with pity, making him more furious and frightened. Then he turned to the Sekandan that Doran didn't know. "Moon, help Akkael find the metronome," said Skane before striding across the room.

He planted both hands on Doran's shoulders, which sent a small, soothing wave through him, Skane's blue eyes darting between his own.

"Doran," said his brother-in-law and brother-in-arms. Doran had trusted Skane with his life many times. "This will sound strange, but you've been trapped in this place for months. I know that's hard to understand. I don't fully understand it myself if I'm honest. But you need to trust me."

393

Doran squinted as Skane said the same thing as the sentinel. He needed to trust. It was the only thing that had any substance, any tangible link to a sort of reality. He'd been in Wu Wei for a couple of hours. How could months have gone by?

So many questions were swimming around in his head like a shoal of bream. He tried to hang on to one, like thrusting a spear into the water and hoping that something was flopping on the other end. He pointed at the man in the red armour. "Why is he pretending to be my brother? Why isn't Akkael here? I want to see him."

Skane paused, a croaking from the back of his throat filling the silence. "I will tell you everything," said Skane, eventually. "You've had a rough time. We all need to establish some calm, and then we'll all talk, okay?"

"Fuck!" said the sentinel, as if on cue. "Where is the metronome?"

"Where's Hideo?"

Doran wasn't sure who spoke, but the fear that clasped onto everyone's face meant it was a concern at the back of their minds. They looked around, but there were no other bodies in the room. They knew the floor beneath their feet was almost completely intact, with only a sparse smattering of boards snapped or broken, so there was no way he could have fallen below them. Doran looked up at the ceiling. Half of it had become the piles of debris they had all been wading through, but the other half was still hanging precariously above them.

Doran still didn't understand what was happening but felt calm enough to contribute. The sooner everything was accounted for, the sooner he would get his answers.

"Maybe he landed upstairs," suggested Doran.

Then, just as he finished, something began to hinder his vision. A fine powder seeped through the floorboards and over the ceiling's ridge, blurring his sight of the floors above. As the sandy substance rained down on top of them, Doran noticed a small tapping sound descending like hail. He tried to follow the noise as he brushed the ash from his blond hair.

"What is this?" Moon asked, holding a small, white fragment of something pinched between her fingers.

A second piece fell next to Skane's foot, who picked it up to inspect it as Rigpa got up from the young Emperor's side.

The Grand Sage had a harrowing expression on her face, her eyes pacing back and forth in her head. "Your warriors upstairs," she said with a wobble. "They're gone."

"What do you mean gone?" asked Kya. Doran hadn't noticed the Queen much since they walked through the door. He didn't even notice the other Sekandan standing in front of them. She wore gilded blue armour and stood with a straight back, so Doran assumed she was some sort of general.

Skane cleared his throat, gaining the attention of everyone in the room. He held the white fragment up for everyone to see. "This is bone."

Doran's heart leapt into his mouth. He pinched some of the dust off his shoulder and considered it as it fell with the bones. The texture felt more like ash as he rubbed it together in his fingers. He wiped it on his trousers when he realised what it was: people.

"What is going on here?" he said, feeling nauseous again. "How is this possible?"

"I'm going to look upstairs," announced the sentinel pretending to be Akkael. He made his way for the entrance with the same tensed jaw and stoicism as everyone else in the room.

However, before Akkael, or whoever he was, managed to get halfway to the empty doorway, a new figure threw himself into the frame.

"Don't move!" It was Hideo. Blood was streaming from his forehead, and his white hair was down. One arm was limp at his side, but a twinge around the eye every time it swung suggested the arm was broken. His armour was hanging loose, and he was missing a pauldron and both armoured sleeves. In his metal hand, he was holding a small black box. Doran couldn't make it out due to the distance, but there was a soft ticking.

Sekandan swords sang as they left their sheaths, drowning out the softer sounds of axes being removed from Solstic belts. Every soldier left in the room had their weapons out, already pointed at Hideo.

"Wait!" yelled Skane, holding out his hand to every soldier around him.

Hideo lifted his broken arm with much labour towards the device in his other hand. He grinned, the blood in his teeth making him look more intimidating. Astrid bared her marked teeth as Magar wiggled the large sword on his back out of its scabbard, nearly falling over as the tip arched toward the floor.

Skane opened his mouth when everything had gone still, and no weapons were left to be drawn. "Hideo, it's over. Put down the metronome."

Hideo chortled, blowing the hair out of his eyes. "Yes, it is over."

For the first time since the chaos had begun, Emperor Kanmu got to his feet. Doran hadn't noticed before, but his red robe was now stained with blood. He squinted at Hideo before speaking, his voice still fainted. "Lord Kazar, what is the meaning of this? What have you done?"

"I've won the war." The words tumbled out of his mouth so casually it was almost as if Hideo believed them. He shrugged with a coy grin streaking across his face. "Look around. Doran Torne. Magar Torne, Skane Torne, Astrid Torne."

He pointed at everyone in turn before his finger landed on the sentinel. He briefly paused, looking his red armoured ally up and down. Then he spoke with a growl underlying the last name on his list. "Akkael Torne."

Doran was incensed. He couldn't understand why his brother wasn't there and why everyone was content calling the Edokand'i by his name. Even Hideo, who had just walked in. Why?

"Brother, stop!" It was Kya. They stepped forward as if Hideo were on an all-round stage.

"Ahh," breathed Hideo. "My traitorous sister."

Kya scoffed. "We are no traitor. We were always loyal to Sekando."

"I'm not talking about Sekando; I'm talking about me!" Hideo clenched the metronome so tight Doran thought it would shatter.

Kya and Hideo were fixed on each other. It was as if their breathing matched tempo; their heartbeat raced to the same ferocity. Everyone in the room felt the lull, encapsulated by their brief caesura.

Eventually, Hideo spoke. "You betrayed me. You watched my son die. He was your nephew, your blood! You left him to die."

We're sorry, Hideo." Kya sounded sincere as they looked down at their shoes. "There was nothing we could do. He-"

"Liar!" Hideo's voice echoed in the ruined hall, causing the Queen to jump slightly. "You're pretending you're so sorrowful. You were meant to keep him safe. To secure his victory. Instead, he died, and you didn't even wait until his body was cold before you sided with the people who killed him."

"Akkael killed Koji," said Kya calmly. " No one else."

"They are all the same!" Hideo spat, gesturing to every Northman in the room.

Then, he paused. Doran noticed Hideo's jaw clench as he let his eyes briefly drop to the rubble-covered floor. He was familiar with nationalist rhetoric and used it himself to spur on the Solstic. Doran also knew how it felt when it turned sour in the mouth.

Hideo took a sharp breath, turning away from his sister. He stepped further into the derelict dining hall, gesturing to the palace ruins around them and returning his attention to the Emperor.

"Look at this place. Did you really think inviting these savages into our city would have any other outcome? They were born to destroy, and they'll keep doing it until our very way of life vanishes."

The Emperor shook his head. "We were discussing peace."

"And why should we make peace with those who have ripped our people from their homes and invaded our islands?" yelled Hideo. He took a deep breath before speaking softer, holding out the metronome for the room to see. "Do you see this device? With it, I could wipe them all out. I could destroy the Northmen and reduce them to dust, along with the Sekandans who aided them in destroying your city and your home."

The warriors around the room began to shuffle restlessly. This time Skane didn't tell them to resist. His grip tightened around his axe, and he clenched his jaw. "Hideo, last warning. Put it down."

Before Skane could finish speaking, the lone sentinel began charging across the room. He didn't yell, just sprinted, dodging the litany of hurdles that layered the ground beneath his feet. Doran watched as Hideo's fingers moved closer to the hand of the metronome, ticking in a reliable rhythm as it rocked in his palm.

The sentinel was closing the gap fast, just an arm's width from Hideo, before something knocked him to the ground. Doran didn't see what caused him to tumble backwards, but he hit the ground hard, moving the debris aside as he slid across the floor.

Hideo was still moving towards the flicking rod of the metronome as Akkael came to a stop. Then, suddenly, his arm shot up. He let out a visceral scream as his broken arm was stretched over his head. Doran didn't understand what was happening until he noticed a thick black rope tied around Hideo's wrist.

"That's enough from you." Doran couldn't find the source of the voice. It sounded like steel running slowly along the stone. But it was loud and ethereal, appearing to derive from every direction. Those around Doran craned their necks to the ceiling to find the source of the voice, but Doran kept his eyes fixed on the black rope around Hideo's wrist as it pulsed and slithered further down his arm.

Hideo's eyes twitched as he squealed involuntarily. Then, as if growing from the moving bind, a large shadow was cast above him. More ropes descended, almost touching the ground. They wriggled under a cloud of smoke, emitting a green hue that cast the room in a diseased light. Doran started to see that they weren't ropes at all. They were tentacles. He looked up at the forming cloud as large eyes blinked onto the lime smoke, floating across it like bubbles in a bog. The last thing Doran saw manifest was a large, malicious grin hanging in the green fog.

Doran was speechless. Everyone was. It seemed like, for the first time, everyone in the room was on the same page. They were horrified, scared, and confused all at the same time. There was little solace in that thought, standing in the disgusting glow of the creature before him. He just watched as one question remained the only thought he could muster. *Was this a god?*

Deference and veneration were far from the reaction of the warriors in the room, as fear led them to charge at the beast, yelling their battle cries. All Doran could do was watch as it thrust its free tentacles into the ground. When they emerged, they impaled the Sekandans and Solstic, who approached it. The tentacles killed them instantly before sinking back into the floor only to breach again, thrusting into others. It even let Hideo's arm go, using the tentacle to kill the oncoming warriors quicker.

"Stop! Stop!!!" screamed Skane as the monster finished off those who failed to listen.

Out of nowhere, two shadow archers appeared in the room, probably concerned by the sounds from the palace. They looked at the beast, and their eyes shot wide like dinner plates. They had crossbows and reached the bottom of their weapons to remove a bolt from its clip.

"Don't!" said Moon, holding her hands up to the archers.

The sentinel retrieved one of the dead Sekandan's swords and held it to the beast. There was something different about the fear on his face. It was less wide-eyed, open-mouthed, and ignorant. The tenseness of it made Doran think this man had seen the monster before. It was the same determined, teeth-grinding fright that Hideo also wore.

"Seradok!" The room went silent as the monster turned its attention, from the countless men and women it had butchered, to Hideo. His hand shook as all the countless moving eyes watched the rod of the metronome dance between his fingers. It wasn't just Seradok either; everyone had peeled their eyes off the abomination in front of them and watched the Edokand'i lord toy with the device in his palm.

The ticking clashed with a guttural clicking from Seradok as its laugh began to build. Before long, his chuckle was loud enough to shake the ceiling, sending more dust floating above them. Hideo attempted to look unfazed, and it worked for the most part. There was the slightest quivering, but his jaw was tight, and his stance was firm. Doran didn't understand the implications, but he knew it was a threat and, judging by everyone else's expressions in the room, it was an effective one. Hideo looked almost stoic, standing face-to-face with the nightmare in front of him.

That was until one of Seradok's tentacles burst through Hideo's stomach. It came from behind, lunging straight through him. Seradok faded away only to reappear, joining with the appendage in Hideo's back. He went limp, the metronome slipping through his fingers and landing in ash and splinters.

The metronome was still ticking under him, lit by a hole in the roof as its hand waved to the sky.

[CHAPTER 58] — DOK OF THE SERA FAMILY

Akkael stood as stunned as everyone else in the ruin of the palace, watching Hideo cough blood onto Seradok's tentacle as it protruded from his stomach. He felt his sword fall to his side as he watched. Though weapons were drawn, those encircling Seradok were cowed into complacency by the corpses that littered the sunlit room.

After a moment, Seradok removed the tentacle from Hideo. He clasped his iron hand over his belly, struggling to stay on his feet. Akkael looked down to see no wound in his body. Seradok then floated around to face Hideo. Those looking on recoiled as the nightmare flew too close. When it faced Hideo, it drove the tentacle into his body again. His face contorted as he whimpered in pain.

"Lord Kazar Hideo," said the monster in the grating voice Akkael remembered well. "The Sekandan prince turned armoured cripple. What a tragedy your life was."

Seradok twisted the ligament in Hideo's gut, causing him to moan as tears mingled with the blood on his cheek. "Do you even remember your defeat at Utajima? That was your moment," Seradok continued. "An opportunity to cast Doran's marauders into the sea. Your loss gave these invaders a home for four years. It made this day inevitable if you think about it."

Akkael was sure Hideo couldn't hear the monster's speech over the excruciating torture he was going through. To make it worse, Seradok lifted Hideo into the air, high pitch groans bursting out of Wu Wei's protector.

"Of course, it doesn't stop there. You raised the mountains and perpetuated this war. You imprisoned your Emperor while he was in the middle of peace talks. You destroyed the shades, killed some Northman, betrayed the Sekandans, and caused the survivors to seek revenge. You sent your son and the bulk of your army to their deaths before erupting a volcano on the rest."

For the first time since Seradok thrust its appendage into Hideo's chest, Akkael could see a glimmer of recognition in his bloodshot eyes. He went silent, no

401

longer reacting to the overwhelming pain he must be experiencing. He just stared into Seradok's closest eye and listened.

"I wish this was a story where the odds were fair. But every facet of this defeat was your fault. You wanted to be the hero of Edokand, but you are your country's greatest disgrace." Seradok grinned before finishing its speech. "Ultimately, they will all thank me for killing you."

Hideo tried to grimace. He tried to have a last moment of defiance before his death. But something changed in his face. His shoulders slumped, and his head bowed. Akkael felt the corner of his mouth curl up as he watched Hideo die, the shame and failings he had accrued circling his mind. A tear fell from his cheek just as Seradok dropped his corpse to the floor, and Akkael wondered which hit the ground first.

Akkael pulled his eyes away from Hideo's body long enough to watch the slack-jawed expressions of those around the room. Queen Kya hid behind Moon and Kwan, shielding their eyes from the gore of their brother's death. Astrid leant against a broken pillar, axe in hand, scowling like a wolf. Propped by his crutch, Magar stood beside Skane, with the Grand Sage, Rigpa, close by them. Then the shadow archers, a smattering of surviving warriors, Doran, and the Emperor. All had the same horror on their faces. The same dread.

"Well," said Seradok, its fume-cloud body spinning around to look at everyone. "Now that mule is gone, it's time to deal with the rest of you."

They all remained quiet, petrified by the disconnected eyes floating in the green hue. Then, Akkael's head spun to the side as he heard Doran's voice break the silence.

"What are you?" he said, voice wavering.

Seradok glided up to Doran, who repelled as every one of its eyes bent towards his. The smile it gave was harrowing like it got some satisfaction from Doran's cluelessness.

"Why don't you ask Akkael?" said the monster, dangling above Doran. "He knows me well enough."

All heads turned to Akkael, even Doran and the Emperor, though their gaze was marred by confusion at the visage of the sentinel he hid behind.

Akkael's attention was still half on Hideo's corpse as he searched for something to say. "This is Seradok, the thing that gave me this curse."

"Curse?" Seradok bellowed, causing everyone's hearts to jump into their throats. "You were practically begging for this. If you weren't already on the ground, you would have fallen to your knees before me."

Akkael stared at the creature for as long as he could before his head dropped, wondering if Seradok's words had any truth.

"Seradok." Akkael's eyes shot up as he began searching for the speaker. It was Rigpa. "The brother of the Seraphim," she said, stepping in front of Skane.

Seradok spun around and grinned at the sight of Rigpa. "Ahh, now the old woman speaks. Pity Phim's spirit is still tied to such a decrepit shell."

The Grand Sage ignored the insult and remained composed as the monster sped towards her. She took a deep breath.

"I don't know you," she said. "But a lifetime of being attached to your brother's spirit has given me a little insight into your world, if only subconsciously. Your brother has a kind soul. I know it because I feel it inside me. I can't imagine that you are so dissimilar."

Seradok's tentacles slumped to the floor. "Is that so?"

"You were a human, just like us." Rigpa was the only one in the room who showed no signs of fear. Akkael stared in awe as the Third Pillar of Edokand, an old, frail woman, never wavered as she addressed the unimaginable horror in front of her.

She reached a hand toward Seradok and continued. "Every human deserves understanding. I know there is a great pain inside you, and I can help you on the path to easing it. I know it must seem like the world has been taken away from you. If you let me, I can try and soothe your suffering."

"Enough!" yelled Seradok, tentacles slamming against the floorboards. "You're not important here. I'll see you in your next life, brother."

It raised one of its appendages in the air as Rigpa clamped her eyelids shut. The rest of her face was relaxed. Still no fear, still no dread. She stood, eyes closed, as Seradok brought its tentacle down. It sliced through Rigpa's body, and she followed the tentacle's descent until she was rolling across the floorboards. The tentacle left no wound, but there was no mistaking that the sage was dead.

"Rigpa!" shouted Skane. He stepped forward, clenching the axe as he scowled at the creature.

"What are you going to do, Skane Brick-Chest?" bellowed Seradok, hovering over Rigpa's body. Skane paused when it spoke, but he took one more look at the Grand Sage's corpse and stepped forward again. It was hard to read the expressions on Seradok's excuse for a face, but Akkael knew it was annoyed. It waved its tentacle and knocked the axe out of Skane's hand.

"Really?" said Seradok, exasperated. "Stand back in line, or you'll be next."

Skane looked back and forth from Rigpa to Seradok. Eventually, he shut his eyes, turned away, and retreated to Magar's side.

Seradok thumped its tentacles against the floorboards so hard the room shook. "I have given you every tool you need to protect yourself, and what do I get? This pathetic scene."

"You think you did this for us?" scoffed Astrid, her voice shallow as she spoke through her pain. "You did it for your own sick satisfaction."

Seradok slowly spun to face her, grinning sadistically. "Can't it be both?"

Akkael went rigid as he watched the monster approach his wife. It was a quick moment before he opened his mouth.

"Oh, come on," said Akkael, distracting Seradok from moving closer to Astrid. "You did it to play some game with the mortals you forgot how to be like. You're just as bitter and vengeful as me."

Seradok moved so fast Akkael felt the still air rush past him as his jaw clenched. It raised one tentacle so close to Akkael's face that he went cock-eyed.

"No, you see, that's where you're wrong," said Seradok. "I thought I was."

Floating away, Seradok's eyes drifted as they darted across its reverie. "I hated that woman for turning me into what I am. I remember drinking with friends, laughing, flirting. And with the snap of her fingers, that was all taken away from me."

Akkael remembered the dragon's vision, the woman Seravex had told him about, and how she had altered all three of the Sera brothers.

Seradok continued. "But then I realised. All those friends; Those speeches I made about the men and women of Sekando finally working together; It was all meaningless. Futile. Redundant. Alawa showed me there was something beyond us, and even though I didn't understand it, I was in the fortunate position to protect the whole world from it."

"You call this protecting the world?" Akkael looked around and saw it was Queen Kya who spoke.

The creature turned to face them, giving what constituted a shrug. "This is your mess. My hands are clean."

"You were the one who manifested it," they continued, their stoic voice hiding hints of fear. Their eyes danced across Hideo's lifeless figure before staring back at the creature. "None of this would be possible if it weren't for you."

It sped towards Kya, Kwan and Moon, who pushed the Queen further behind them. "Exactly!" it screamed. "That's what I'm saying."

Seradok floated away slowly. When it spoke again, Akkael noticed the change in its voice. He tilted his head, listening. "I wanted to build an army, something I could use to fight other invaders of our world, like Alawa. I designed the perfect afterlife to prepare the dead to fight when the time was right."

It sounded like the naïve plans of a young man. For the first time, the horrifying visage of Seradok peeled away, and Akkael saw hints of the young Sekandan activist it used to be.

Dok continued. "But people died faster than I thought. All over the world, wars, famines, and diseases filled my heaven to capacity. Worse than that, the monsters inside were committing the same disgusting crimes. Rapists, child molesters, anything you can conceive. Eventually, I had no choice. I turned my utopia into a prison."

Akkael's eyes shot wide as he remembered his first meeting with Seradok. After the shadow archer killed him, he woke up in a dungeon. He saw the tortured Urkanzan reeling behind the bars of his cage. The vision of the young radical faded away, and all Akkael could see was the monster once again.

"I knew an army of prisoners wasn't enough," said Seradok. "I had to think more down to earth."

In the corner of Akkael's eye, he caught the lead shadow archer stepping forward from the corner of the room. His mouth was still covered, but his eyes were like dinner plates as he aggressively ran his hand horizontally in front of himself. Akkael didn't know what that meant. The shade was looking towards Seradok but not really at it. Akkael followed his line of sight.

The smoke of an appearing shade blended with the haze of Seradok's body. It wasn't until the second shadow archer emerged behind the monster did Akkael know what was happening. The shade had a sword in his fist. He swung into Seradok's cloud, the weight of the swing carrying him through the monster's body, stumbling to the other side.

The air was still, everyone as mute as a shade. Heiyang's eyes went glassy as he stared at his friend. Slowly, the shade with the sword turned around, neck cranking up as he saw Seradok hovering above him, its grin so close to the archer's face it must have expanded past his peripheral vision.

Merciful wasn't the right word, but Seradok made it quick. It raised an appendage and decapitated the shadow archer in one motion. The head rolled on the floor, but no blood poured out of him. In fact, if Akkael hadn't just witnessed his execution, he would have believed the death happened hours ago. Akkael watched the black and dry stub of a neck roll on the floor. The only person in the room not looking at the third fresh corpse was the last shadow archer, his eyes clamped shut as he faced a hole in the ceiling.

Eventually, Seradok's cackling drew Akkael's attention from the dead shadow archer. "I suppose I should mention these mutes next," it said. It raised the shade's head by his hair, jiggling it back and forth as it spoke. "When I created the shades, I had a new approach in mind."

"You created the shadow archers?" Moon whimpered.

Seradok's sadistically jovial tone faded as he dropped the shadow archer's head with a thud. Its ligaments began to tense and quiver as its eyes shivered towards the ground.

"Are any of you listening?" Seradok seethed in a vicious rage.

It began to shake more violently. In a heartbeat, Seradok launched its tentacle at Moon and smashed her into the ground. Her head hit the floorboards, breaking them under the force. Blood poured out of the crack in her skull.

Astrid immediately peeled herself from the wall she had been leaning against. Kya stepped back, covering their mouth so a gasp couldn't escape. Kwan also readied herself to retaliate.

"Don't move!" screeched Seradok. The silence allowed the room time to hear Moon's whimpers. She was still alive, but she needed a sage's attention.

A sigh emanated from Seradok's maw. "I don't like being interrupted," it said, exasperated. "Yes, I created the shades."

Seradok moved away from Moon as she began to quiver. The monster started another monologue, now with four bodies lying under it, as it floated around the room. "Not immortal but deadly. Once I had another one of Alawa in my sights, I would have the perfect assassins.

Its mouth contorted into a snarl. "But I knew what people were like," it continued. "If I didn't make rules, everyone would be a shade. So, I made the ritual gratuitous, painful, and humiliating.

"But people are twisted. So many started hacking themselves to pieces I had to put a threshold on how many could exist at a time. You have no idea the number of idiots that still cut out their tongues in the hope of such a small amount of power."

Akkael saw a tear roll down the surviving shadow archer's mask. In a few months, everything that was established as fact became a lie. The shades, the sages, even the gods. Everything Akkael thought he knew and didn't know turned out to be a myth. The shadow archers aren't a cultural anomaly that made Edokand unique. They were manufactured by Seradok. The sages were created by the Seraphim. And the most harrowing thought of all; gods were real.

He stared down at the floor as he spoke. "What about me?"

Seradok arched towards Akkael so quick his hair jostled. But Akkael didn't flinch as he waited for the beast to answer.

"Think, imbecile. A man capable of switching bodies with anything that kills him. You could have literally become Alawa or anyone else like her."

Akkael squinted. In Seradok's grand plan, Akkael was meant to take over, and become, a god? If he could become another Alawa, what was stopping him from...

Akkael's eyes widened, raising his head towards the quick-tempered monstrosity before him. For the first time since Seradok appeared, Akkael could have grinned as large as him.

"So, I was just a pawn. I thought we had something special," he said, trying to subtly look around the room. The metronome was still on the floor from where Hideo had dropped it. He turned back to Seradok as soon as he saw it.

Seradok began to jitter again as it stewed in its own fury. However, instead of killing Akkael like it had everyone else who irritated it, Seradok got uncomfortably close and forced a smile. "You're funny," it whispered. "The funny little man who abandoned his wife to mourn, his brother to grieve, his people to be slaughtered, in the name of a meaningless revenge tale."

A tentacle peeled Hideo's corpse from the floor and thrust it into Akkael's face.

"Of all the people I killed today, I bet he hurt the most. I bet you would have let me kill everyone in this room if you could cause the light to fade from his eyes yourself."

It let go, and Hideo crumbled to Akkael's feet. After staring down at the corpse of the man he loathed, a question entered Akkael's head. "Why Hideo?"

Seradok scoffed. "He was nothing," it said. "Just a desperate man I could use to trial my prized invention."

"The metronome?" It caught Akkael off guard as Doran spoke. Seradok sped towards Doran, and Akkael's heart jumped into his throat, making three long, dangerous steps towards the metronome.

Once again, Seradok sighed, trying hard to calm himself. "You know what, Doran Torne, I'll give you a pass. You're clearly ignorant of what is going on here. And, after all, you were the first experiment of my little toy."

Akkael was still moving towards the ticking device lying on the ground. However, he froze as he noticed Skane looking at him with shock and fear.

He began to mouth something, which Akkael used context to decipher.

"*What are you doing?*"

He had no time to explain. "*Distract it,*" Akkael silently replied.

Akkael's heart skipped a beat when he noticed Seradok turning. Luckily, it didn't see Akkael had moved. Still, its many eyes were fixated on the black metronome Akkael was moving towards as it broke into another monologue. "A device capable of altering the tempo of time. Something I can grant to anyone I want and rip from their rigour-mortised corpse if they disappoint me. I surpassed myself with this one."

Skane was still visibly reluctant to do what Akkael had said. His face flushed, and Akkael swore he could see his brother-in-law's pulse in his neck from the other side of the room. Then, in one more glance, Akkael could see Skane realise what he was planning. His eyebrows slowly got higher, and Akkael nodded.

After a few moments, Skane's chest deflated, and he rolled his eyes.

"I don't understand?" he said, tensing up.

Seradok turned to face him and sighed, running a tentacle along the floor. "Of course, you don't," it said with an exasperated tone. "What now?"

409

Skane glanced at Akkael from the corner of his eye before continuing. He raised one hand, lifting each finger as he began to list. "A prison of dead people, some assassins, Akkael, and the metronome. What's your plan?"

Seradok was scowling. "That is my plan."

"But I don't understand how they link." Skane looked at Akkael again and saw he needed to distract the monster a little longer, despite an injured Magar fidgeting beside him. "Also, you knew by giving the metronome to Hideo, you would be starting a war. But you did it anyway? If you were doing all this for us, as you say, why cause so many deaths in the process?"

Seradok's tentacles hit the ground with a thud. "Stand there as quiet as your husband, or you'll be the next person I put in a cell."

Seradok was about to turn around when he was distracted by another voice. It was Astrid. "Wait. People are still there. In your hell."

Seradok began to convulse as Akkael leant towards what was lying on the ground. "Why are none of you listening to me?"

Once the echo of its yelling had dissipated, Akkael stood up from his kneeling position. "I've been listening," he said, grinning.

Seradok growled. "Congratulations..." The monster trailed off once it had Akkael in its sight. It glared at him with a malicious scowl.

All Akkael could do was grin. He tossed the metronome from one hand to another in time to the ticking sound it was constantly making.

"Put it down." Seradok's voice was stern, but there was a hint of fear. It was the same terror the monster had produced in those around it.

If Akkael was intimidated, he didn't show it. "This?" he asked, dangling the metronome between his thumb and index finger. "Make me."

Every one of Seradok's tentacles thumped the ground. "Put it down!"

Akkael let a malicious smile slip onto his face before moving the metronome into the palm of his hand. Then, after considering it for a moment, he sighed.

"Maybe I should," said Akkael before pointing at his wife. "Earlier, Astrid asked me to prove I was me, but, honestly, nothing would confirm my identity more than dropping this in front of everyone. I'm clumsy. I admit it. I broke a pot at our wedding. Once drunk, I collapsed into a sand sculpture Alani had made, fell asleep, and woke up to find she had rebuilt it on top of me. She didn't speak to me for three days."

Akkael saw the corners of Astrid's mouth curl, which made him do the same. Then, he continued. "Yes, I've got butter fingers. You're right not to trust me with this."

Seradok's voice had become guttural, like an axe grinding against a whetstone. "I will rip the skin from your bones."

"Oh, I'm shaking," said Akkael, rocking the metronome in his hand.

"Put it down," Seradok repeated for the third time.

Akkael took a deep breath, knowing what was going to come next. He opened his mouth, preparing to speak as he looked at everyone he loved. "Astrid, I'm sorry. You were right; we should have stayed in Urkanza. Magar, Doran. Brothers. It was my privilege to sail here with you. You too, Skane. To everyone dead now. Trygve... Alani." His hand ached again at the mention of his daughter. Though, this time, it felt purposeful, like Alani was trying to pull him away from what he was about to do.

He took one last breath before he finished speaking. "This is for you."

He lifted the metronome above his head before launching it towards the ground.

"NOOOOOOOOOOOOOOO!" Seradok bellowed. It was as if the metronome had been used, and the whole room had been slowed. A tentacle was shot from Seradok's body to catch the metronome before it fell. But it was too late. The black slate shattered the moment it made impact. Pieces of it were cast across the room as the creature's tentacle collided with the fragments of the device.

Rage was a strange emotion beyond reason. Akkael had watched Seradok lay waste to dozens of people while consumed by rage. That anger had killed Hideo,

Rigpa, the shadow archer, and many warriors. It had nearly killed Moon. Those people had done nothing compared to Akkael. He knew what was about to come and smiled.

The tentacle that was aiming to catch the metronome had changed course. It launched towards Akkael and pierced his stomach like a seppuku blade. Blood poured onto his chin. By the time Akkael had opened his eyes, there was fear in Seradok's eyes. Its maw was wide. Akkael gave a grin of red teeth.

Seradok rapidly removed the appendage from Akkael's belly, but it was too late. He stumbled on his feet briefly before collapsing to the floor. Akkael fell facing Hideo and watched as his corpse blurred. Then he gave in to death.

Akkael opened all eighteen eyes, mostly in unison. He had never bothered to count Seradok's eyes before, but now he was peering out of them, he couldn't help noticing them all at once. They weren't like human eyes, which give you one distinct picture. Seradok's eyes gave Akkael a dozen-and-a-half different perspectives of the room, each moving in different directions and speeds but equally impossible to determine. Everything was washed with a yellowish hue and his depth perception was gone. It would be nauseating if he had a stomach.

He couldn't feel anything. No pain, no limbs, no slight tension in any muscle. The tentacles dangled under him and felt like a dead arm after being slept on, only a string of pinpricks letting him know they were there. Most things he'd come to expect in existence were gone. He couldn't smell the slight stench of charred wood that permeated the derelict palace. He couldn't taste the death in the air. There was no heat or cold. These were all things Akkael had noticed in the split second he'd lived in Seradok's body.

However, he had realised something that made him grateful for all the other things that were gone. He couldn't feel his daughter's grip anymore. The phantom pain had faded away. Alani had no hand to hold on to anymore.

"Akkael?" Skane was the first to speak. Akkael felt his brother-in-law's voice reverberate like a cymbal.

The best view he had of Skane was in his centre eye. Akkael tried to focus on it, but as it moved across Akkael's smoke-cloud body, another eye took over as the better image.

Skane was staring at him, approaching apprehensively like one would a startled horse. They were all surrounding him. His brothers were just behind Skane. With one eye, he could see Astrid's face, stunned and slack-jawed. With another eye facing the floor, he saw Moon staring up at him, with blood coursing down her face from where Seradok had thrown her to the ground. General Kwan had knelt to aid her, but she was also glaring at Akkael, surrounded by the corpses Seradok had made.

Akkael only had half a view of Queen Kya. Their mouth was clenched shut, and a fist was balled.

Skane, Magar, and Doran now stretched across Akkael's vision in all eighteen images, like drawings of the same scene from different angles.

"Brother?" Doran spoke this time, his voice just as echoey. "Is that you?"

Akkael managed to raise a tentacle in front of a few eyes. It was like pulling the strings of a marionette. The yellow hue to his vision made the tentacle look even more disgusting. He dropped it and looked at the three men again.

"Can you speak?" asked Skane.

If Akkael had a heart, it would be pounding. If he had blood, it would boil. He had been so many different people. But, even with Ichika's face, or Trygve's, or just some random Edokand'i sentinel, there was always an underlying sense he'd be all right, that it didn't matter if he weren't the same, things could always go back to normal. It was a small, naïve thought, even then. But as his family looked at him with veiled horror, he knew things would never go back. Not even the metronome could reverse time.

An eye had drifted into perfect position for Akkael to get one last look at his wife. He remembered how lucky he had felt in the early years of their love and how beautiful he'd always found her. He thought he might have smiled but couldn't be sure.

Then suddenly, without hint or warning, Akkael vanished.

EPILOGUE

There is an ending to this story consumed by rage. An angry, visceral apoplexy, all-encompassing and vengeful. Or there's one riddled with confusion. Unanswered questions circling the mind with no conclusion satisfying enough to solve the mysteries posed.

Skane had witnessed those endings inside the palace. Doran and the Emperor were briefed on what had occurred since they entered Kanmu's chambers.

Doran was the rage. Spit flew as he yelled, jaw tensing while he listened to how everything he'd worked hard for had fallen apart.

Skane had known Doran long enough to calculate how long each anger would last. He was furious the Solstic had stormed Trim without his orders. However, it was an irrational fury. Deep down, Doran knew they thought he had died, so it should only last a few days.

The anger directed at Akkael and Hideo would last even less. No use in getting angry at the dead. Then there was the general exasperation at the whole situation. The kind that forced him to contemplate questions like, 'How come?', 'What for?', 'Why now?'

Though that rage was less intense, it would last a lot longer.

Emperor Kanmu just sat in stunned, vacant silence. Skane couldn't know what was through his head. But the absurdity of what he heard, the consequences that would plague his people, and the uncertainty in what it meant encapsulated his resolution to the war. It was built upon everything that wouldn't be resolved.

After informing Doran and Kanmu, Skane left the ruined pagoda, helping Magar down the steps and out to a quiet spot in the caldera. He checked his wounds before Magar lay in Skane's lap and fell asleep, snoring against his thigh. Skane couldn't sleep. He just stared at the splintered palace in an empty contemplation.

Tired soldiers sat on the decline that led to the palace, both as a display of force and a brief reprieve. Emperor Kanmu may be able to see the sheer size of the remaining force from the holes in his palace's walls, but he would struggle to make out the expressions. He wouldn't be able to see the exhaustion, the sorrow, the anguish. That's why Skane led Magar as far as he could from the pagoda; he could wear his emotions without fear of losing the posturing façade.

He had meant to count how much of his army was left, but he hadn't the heart. The bitter campaign had ended, and they had come out the victor. Pyrrhic notions and self-pity aside.

There were many things that he couldn't process. Not yet. He watched his friend take the body of an eldritch horror before disappearing into the unknown. He watched Rigpa get cut down and could not stop it or even avenge her. It may seem callous, but Skane hadn't even thought about any of that. It was like all his emotions were waiting in a neat line, waiting for their concerns to be processed by the slowest assembly.

Suddenly, as Skane stared across the exhausted faces of the army that occupied the palace grounds, a large gust of wind crashed into him. A shadow covered the volcano, and when Skane looked up, he saw a dragon fly over the city. He'd heard of Seravex, but the stories didn't do the great wyrm justice.

One wing was enough to dowse the whole caldera in shade. The long, snaking body swerved and contorted as it circled the palace, orange eyes scanning the army that slaughtered its way to the centre of the city: Skane's army.

However, it didn't seem to care about the foreign force occupying the palace. Instead, it stared through the gaps in the pagoda as if it were looking for something. The Solstic and Sekandans sat around the bowl of the volcano. They began to murmur and panic as the large, black-scaled Amphithere loomed over them. After a moment, the dragon tilted his head towards the sun. Skane couldn't be sure, but it reminded him of a human staring at a light to stop themselves from crying. Seravex stayed like that momentarily before letting out a long, high-pitched screech.

The noise reverberated in the bowl of the volcano, causing the tired, bloody warriors to grasp their ears in wincing pain. Magar awoke at the sound of the dragon's yell.

"What was that?" Skane barely made out Magar's voice despite its proximity.

Once the scream ceased, a giant swing of its wings launched Seravex further towards the clouds, the blast knocking people off their feet. Then it flew away in the direction it came, receding behind the volcano's ridge with its shadow in tow.

There is an ending to this story based on fear. An uncertainty which darkens every shadow and hides around every corner. Or there's one of guilt. Memories of lost loved ones and friends become lead grafted to the conscience.

Kya was still in the palace, probably as quiet and as heavily guarded as when Skane left. They would leave Wu Wei with the distrust and paranoia nurtured since Akkael killed Ichika. Sekando had a reputation for being isolationist and distant. That wasn't likely to change.

Then there was Astrid. She was also still in the palace and also silent. Sages tended to her wounds while she sat in deep thought on the rubble that coated the floorboards. Finally, there was nothing for her to do. No next task or easy distraction. It was just her and her mind. Thoughts of those she had lost bombarded her.

Her whole life flashed before her eyes. She didn't need to be dead for that to happen. The only people who had to die were everyone else.

Skane stared at the sky, the sound of Seravex's flight fading away until it was unrecognisable against the wind. "I saw the dragon," he said to the startled Magar. "I... I think it was sad."

He expected Magar to show a litany of different reactions. He didn't expect Magar to snuggle back onto his lap, close his eyes and say, "That makes sense."

A dragon, a creature that didn't exist a month ago, flew over the ruins of Wu Wei, screamed in agony towards the sky and flew away.

"How does that *make sense*?" asked Skane, over the chorus of the concerned Solstic and Sekandans discussing the same thing.

Magar shrugged against Skane's leg. "They were brothers, weren't they? The tentacles and the dragon. I know what it feels like to lose a brother."

Understanding motives is the sign of an empathetic character. Rigpa had said that on the way to Koseki. Skane looked down at Magar, eyes closed as he rested in his lap, and smiled.

"I suppose I'd forgotten that part," said Skane. "So much has changed. It's been hard to keep track of it all."

There was a pause as Skane wondered what was happening in Magar's mind. It wasn't hard to work out.

"We'll find Akkael, don't worry."

Magar grunted in agreement. "My brothers are alive. That's all that matters to me." He sounded convincing but couldn't hide the solemnness behind his eyes.

Skane's mind flooded instantly with everything he'd kept at bay. It wasn't Akkael's vanishing or Rigpa's death that loomed large in the darkness that encroached on his mind. Those emotions still waited neatly in the queue. The thoughts that were pushed to the front were more significant. The existential dread of a changed world. Gods were real. There was an afterlife, a prison with all his friends and loved ones held captive for the simple crime of dying. Magic existed beyond his comprehension, and creatures from the recesses of nightmares manipulated the functions of their world. But what scared Skane the most was what he didn't yet know and still had to learn.

A tear landed on Magar's forehead, dragging him from his rest again.

"What's wrong?" he asked, looking up at Skane.

When Skane was positive no more tears would fall, he answered. "Nothing, it's just… everything has changed. The world's so different now."

Magar paused. "Why?" He sounded genuinely confused.

"Are you joking?" Skane asked with a voice a little louder than predicted. "Time travel, gods, hell, dragons, Akkael. Nothing is the same."

"Doesn't change anything." Magar closed his eyes again.

"Excuse me?"

"Doran used to ruin nights in the pub talking about gods." Magar scrunched his face into an expression that suggested a protracted sibling grudge. "He thought they were real, Akkael disagreed, and they'd bicker for hours. I just drank. Life goes on whether gods exist or they aren't. Nothing changes. A blacksmith beats iron with a hammer whether there is a heaven or not."

"It's a little different to arguments in a tavern." Skane felt the muscles around his eye tensing and his forehead wrinkle. "How can you be so calm about it?"

Magar shrugged. "After everything that has happened... I thought my brothers were dead. It broke me. After that, the rest of it doesn't frighten me."

"Well," said Skane, breathing through a half smile. "I suppose you'll have no problem opening your first chakra."

"What's a chakra?"

Skane snickered, distracting him for a moment before the ensuing silence allowed his strained mind to return to his original anxiety, like bubbles in a boiling pot slowly dissipating to reveal the surface of what had been stewing. "It just seems so big."

Magar opened his eyes again, looking up at Skane with concern. "Trust me," he said softly. "Once we return to Skaldgard, everything will feel normal again."

A long groan preceded Skane collapsing backwards into the grass. "That's the last thing I need. When I was there last, Jiro and Frode wouldn't stop bickering about an orphanage. Despite everything that has happened, I doubt it'll do much to stop their trivial arguing."

"An orphanage?" Magar asked, adjusting his posture to rest his head on Skane's prone torso.

"Yeah."

"Hmm..." Then Magar said something that expelled every stress from Skane's head. It seemed more significant than the tremendous losses, the overbearing uncertainty, or even more important than the gods. What he said next prevailed over every thought, cutting to the front of the queue and warming him from the inside.

"Maybe we should adopt."

A smile shot across Skane's face. The kind of shameless smile that incorporated every muscle in his face. It beamed so bright that, if the Emperor looked from his broken palace, he would see past the ocean of maudlin soldiers, noticing first the unbridled glee in Skane's expression.

"Yeah, maybe."

There is an ending to this story rooted in love. An ending of hope and promise, implying that, no matter the anguish, loss, and unanswered questions, everything would get better.

There were so many outcomes that were impossible to know. Where was Akkael after being stuck in Seradok's body? Were the dead still trapped in Seradok's prison of an afterlife, unable to move on? Even the fate of three individual cultures now forced to live side by side was unknown, as they were drenched in an animosity that would surely worsen. There were so many conclusions that couldn't be drawn.

But, the one about love? That was Skane's ending.

Looking down at Magar, he remembered what Rigpa had said when they arrived at Skaldgard. The worst-case scenario is only one possible outcome, and he had the power to change things for the better.

Skane smiled, knowing for a brief moment everything would be okay. He'd make sure it was.

There was ample opportunity for that.

The End.

ACKNOWLEDGEMENTS

It took me a long time to write this book. The story evolved and changed over the years, and it is important for me to remember where this novel started and all the people who helped make it what it is.

First, I want to thank David Gamage of Earth Island Books. His faith in my project and the independence I was afforded gave me unparalleled autonomy and taught me so much about the publishing process. Though this book isn't their usual repertoire, his honesty and interest in my story proved I was in the right hands. Thank you for giving me the chance to follow my dream without sacrificing my vision.

Alyson and Tim, my old lecturers, deserve praise for having to read some shoddy writing during my early years at Coventry University. Thank you both for helping me find my creative voice and realise my potential.

When you tell friends and family you are writing a book, the first question they ask is, "Am I in it?" For those I mention here, the answer is yes. You may not be a character, but the advice, love, and hope you gave me over the years made this book what it is, and I couldn't have done it without any of you.

Kathryn Layne. I have sent you more drafts, more loose ideas, and more self-loathing text messages than pretty much anyone. You have been my friend through the highs and lows in the long process of writing this book and pushed me to pursue this even when it seemed illogical. Thank you.

Renato Belindro. You once said fantasy fiction is the most boring genre in the world. However, that didn't stop you from reading my book and helping me develop it into what it is. You are one of the most creatively minded people I know, and you have taught me more about chart music than I ever wanted to know. Thank you.

Tyron Evans. Our friendship is probably the reason I'm so into this genre. From kids playing Fable together, teens watching too many YouTube videos on fictional lore, to adults doing the same things. You have been my best friend since primary school, and I'm grateful you've been in my life for so long. Thank you.

Matthew Jones. For years, you have listened to me complain, moan, and other less flattering synonyms. My oldest friend, I owe you a beer for always being there for me. Actually, I owe you several beers… But let's start with the one. Thank you.

Mum and Dad. You've supported me in pursuing my dreams even when it was pretty apparent that nothing would come of it. You never pushed me towards any path and gave me the freedom to become whomever I wanted. I may not be growing anymore, but I hope I've made you both proud. Thank you, I love you.

Abbi, Alex, and Matthew. My siblings. We grew up with the same interests, and our shared memories are the basis for this story. Dressing up as Link for Christmas, playing Mario Party, watching Game of Thrones at 3 am, listening to all those nostalgic songs, or the plethora of shared experiences that made me who I am. Thank you all.

Rashpreet, Aarushi, Ellen, Rose, Nancy. My creative writing group from University. I would be remised not to mention how you shaped my writing and helped me hone my skill. Thank you all.

Lastly, I need to thank Jennifer Lee: my muse, first reader, cover artist, and love. You've taught me so much about Korean culture and helped shape the world of Edokand. Your constant encouragement and love have made me not only a better writer but a better person. Your beautiful artwork for the cover is incredible, and I'm so proud that I get to work on this project with you. Thank you for making this book what it is. Thank you for your kind feedback. Thank you for reading it. Thank you for being you.

I owe and dedicate this book to all of you. This is all I've ever wanted, and you've helped me achieve it.

Thank you!

ABOUT THE AUTHOR

J. T. Audsley is a graduate of Coventry University, achieving a Master's in Professional Creative Writing. He graduated in 2019 after four years of honing his craft and developing a keen understanding of narrative and character development.

During his studies, Audsley became fascinated by Norse mythology and Viking history. His dissertation, titled "A Literary Explanation of How Norse Mythology Has Influenced Fantasy Fiction," exemplified his dedication to understanding the profound impact of ancient tales on contemporary storytelling.

An enriching experience teaching English as a Foreign Language (TEFL) in South Korea offered him a glimpse into a vibrant culture vastly different from his own. Drawing inspiration from this journey, he expertly wove elements of Korean culture into the fabric of his fantasy world, lending it an authenticity that adds depth and intrigue to his narrative.

Heralding from a beautiful seaside town in South Wales, he is passionate for his local community, shown in various creative endeavours. He once wrote a monthly history column in his local newsletter, which initially served as a promotional tool for a Viking-themed event. He also wrote and hosted a weekly pub quiz online during the pandemic, bringing the community together during hard times. Audsley showcased his talent as a playwright by staging a short play at his local theatre, captivating audiences with his storytelling and comedic style.

Beyond novel writing, he writes poetry, short stories, and historical articles. He attended poetry events during university, immersing himself in rich artistic expression. He also attended comedy open mic nights to practice a medium he was less comfortable and familiar with, finding the experience incredibly rewarding.

As an author, J. T. Audsley aspires to transport readers to extraordinary worlds where imagination intertwines with history and myth, inviting them to experience the profound depths of emotion in "The Grief of Godless Games." With his innate ability to craft captivating stories and commitment to fostering community, Audsley stands poised to leave an indelible mark on fantasy fiction.

Me failing a ramen eating challenge in Gunsan-si, South Korea. This photo should still be on the wall of that restaurant, alongside others who have fallen to the giant portion of noodles on the table.

Milton Keynes UK
Ingram Content Group UK Ltd.
UKHW020016130923
428537UK00002B/24

9 781739 443849